Moor

THE
SEAGULL
LIBRARY OF
GERMAN
LITERATURE

Moor

GUNTHER GELTINGER

TRANSLATED BY ALEXANDER BOOTH

LONDON NEW YORK CALCUTTA

This publication was supported by a grant
from the Goethe-Institut India

Seagull Books, 2021

First published in German as *Moor* by Gunther Geltinger.
© Suhrkamp Verlag Berlin, 2013

First published in English by Seagull Books, 2017
English translation © Alexander Booth, 2017

ISBN 978 0 8574 2 833 2

British Library Cataloguing-in-Publication Data
A catalogue record for this book is available from the
British Library

Typeset by Seagull Books, Calcutta, India
Printed and bound by Printed and bound by WordsWorth India,
New Delhi, India

CONTENTS

THE FAIRY TALE OF THE DRAGONFLY
INSIDE THE RAY

Once upon a time, many years ago, at the bottom of a large expanse of water there lived a dragonfly larva and a ray. The ray was insatiable and hoped to devour the dragonfly as soon as he could. You may only eat me, it said, if you turn me into a little girl. The ray opened its mouth and swallowed the larva instead. But barely within its stomach, the larva turned into a little girl and from then on lived inside the body of the fish. Now and again the fish rose up from the mud and into the more shallow waters pierced by the sun so that soon, through its white underside, the silhouette of the little child could be seen. The little girl grew and grew and, before long, the ray could barely keep her hidden. He swam to the shore and spit his young tenant out. I shall set you free, he said, but in return you must bring me your child. If not, I shall turn you back into a dragonfly.

The lovely young woman brought a son into the world and for many years they lived happily together in a house at the water's edge. When the boy was almost a man, the mother felt herself beginning to change. She began to grow wings and grow thinner. And over and over again she was driven to the water where the ray lay in wait. One day she brought her child and, despite being afraid of the water, he swam out with her. When they were far enough away from shore, she embraced him one final time, then pushed him into the depths and down into the ray's mouth. Once he slid into the stomach of the fish, he did indeed turn into a dragonfly larva. But he was so small that he managed to swim through the fish's insides and out into the mud to hide. And it is there that he awaits the summer, the time when dragonflies hatch and fly away, away back home to mother.

ONE

Autumn

No one speaks here. There where you are listening only water, alder trees, wind pulling at the rushes. The fog too is soundless, and its shapes, which come from out of nothing, simply stare at you then go. The closest thing to words is the rain. In flowing sentences it falls, comes to a standstill in the trees, stutters consonants onto the leaves, gurgles dark vowels through the runnels, and when one drips into the other, a gust of wind suddenly spits through the foliage and raises slight ripples, rips the mist apart and bewilders the reeds, in all of this still you hear my voice.

You're crouched on top of the tree stump, umbrella in front of your face, shoulders hunched, your finger stuck into the pillow of moss along the roots, or is it the plant that's sticking to your finger, a secret caress, somehow tender. The film on the leaves feels greasy, like the drops you wiped out of your pyjama bottoms this morning. You give the feeling of the colour white. White, these mornings with Marga at the pond. Her bathrobe, the steam in the ditches, the uncertain light between the tree

trunks and her reflection on the water, which at first
brown, then clear with the rising of the sun. When you
were still a child you had to think of cola, a deep hole
where the old alder branch pokes into the water and
stubbornly pushes something down, you wondered
what it would be like to drown there in the brown,
soda-like water. But the tree never moved, nothing ever
came up, and now you are thirteen, and even when the
noontime sun stands high in the sky, the water there is
black, grim and secretive, just like the dream this morning from which Marga woke you.

You were naked and out, dangerously deep, you weren't
able to glean anything else before she took the blanket
away from you and your glance, just like every morning, fell upon the large wall clock where an egg-yolk
yellow moon used to smirk before, as a birthday gift,
she painted it over with the blood-red head of a darter
dragonfly—her first assault on your childhood. Now,
instead of a benevolent goodnight face there is a predatory insect that measures your dreams from the compound eyes of the clock-face, which at that moment
showed a little past seven, the room still dark, summer
definitively over. She pressed a sleep-smelling kiss to
your forehead and said, 'Good morning, darling, shall
we go to the pond?'

You look at your wristwatch. Almost half past seven
already. In forty minutes German class begins, and you

have to give your presentation. The topic: dragonflies. You would have happily practised it once again with your mother. She's standing in her nightgown on the bank, the damp silk showing off the curves of her body, her breasts, hipbones, the bumps of her spine as if beneath a second skin. She strips off everything, shouts 'Look at the alders!' and throws you the crumpled gown. You put your hand out, an automatic movement, uncountable mornings rehearsed in all wind and weather, you can even do it in your sleep, and do, as sleepiness comes and cripples your eyes which for just a second too long sink deep into the nest between her thighs which, when throwing, she turns to you but at the same time hides, one arm half stretched, the other bent over her lap, like two timidly unfolding wings. When a dragonfly nymph moults for the final time, you say in your presentation, its new body is still foreign to it. The moment comes to you in slow motion, like that morning when waking up you looked at the wooden clock and the second hand on the insect seemed stationary, then suddenly, it jumped to the next number.

Her nightgown smacks you cold in the face and you wake with a start. Every day she gets undressed in front of you but only now do you understand why you were always supposed to look up, towards the trees. She is moving her arms in circles, stretching her back, already standing with her feet in the water. You're shivering from the neck down, then suddenly, you feel a burst of heat upon your cheeks. The way she presents her nakedness to you. Your eyes rush to the other bank, the alders everywhere, they encircle the entire pond, it's only by the splintered branch that you pause. In the dream, you now remember, it was here that you were underwater, trapped in the bubbling darkness, and when you tried to call for help the peat sunk into your mouth. From inside you, your body began to swell against your skin and then began to split. But the branch must have jerked you back up, and you opened your eyes.

Too late, she was already holding you in her hand. You pushed her away and turned into the crevice between the wall and the mattress. Your erection felt different, harder, demanding, it wasn't as accidental as yesterday when, still asleep, you climbed up the steep peak and were awoken by the sudden feeling of pressure. Even the dragonfly on the clock seemed redder somehow, furtive, the mandibles seemingly awaiting the next jerk of the second hand to shoot out. Marga was bent over you. You could feel her weight on your neck and could smell her bath oil. Lavender, her so-called well-being scent, the one she lounges about in until midnight. You could barely breathe, air damming up about your collar, the moistness setting loose smells from deeper layers of skin, the bitter sleep-sweat, which came from her pills, the traces of perfume and cold smoke, and beneath them something sour, stagnant, something from her binge the night before or leftover from the pond. You closed your eyes again in order to make more space for yourself. You were wishing yourself back to sleep when she took your hand and pushed it to her belly button. And further below, the hair, softer than cotton grass but more bristly than the moss at the tree stump. Last night, she said, she had dreamt that she was once again pregnant with you. You imagined the gnarled umbilical scar with the grass-cleft below as the entrance to an air bladder filled with moor water that was about to pump out a mute, slippery thing, you, Dion, the pliable boy with the strange name, thanks to which you've only received mockery and laughter. *The stork it brings all little babes, all except Dion, whom the moor made,* that was how the saying went, the one that met you mornings when you stumbled into the kindergarten from the pond, past the other mothers, you, rain-soaked and with dirty shoes, past those mothers who had made sure to wrap up their sons and daughters dry and warm. 'Aren't I enough for you,' Marga answered when you once again asked about your father. In fact, you don't resemble any man in the village, you almost don't even resemble your mother. She is fair-haired, while your hair is moor-brown and tinged with red. And you have freckles around your nose which, in August, your birth month, bloom in time with the heather, there on your sallow, somewhat slack skin, which remains pale whether summer or winter, your skin which can't handle any heat at all and like the morning fog literally threatens to dissolve with any bit of sun. Marga's eyes reflect the sky in greys and cobalt blues, yours instead are always searching the dark pools for dragonflies, the ones that must rise to the light to shed.

Even your language comes from me. Gorbach, your teacher, was the first to make you aware of it, that day when your lips produced only a blubbering sound as you tried to read aloud from your book. Dumb as a dirty pool of water, he groaned and called, 'Next.' The others giggled, Benno, who sat next to you, read effortlessly, while under your tongue the saliva simply backed up, a dripping and dribbling just like in the hidden rivulets where the water rises and sinks but never flows. When reading aloud at oral exams, and when giving presentations, the words well up in your mouth, gather into long, flowing sentences that burst into the world in little bubbles of spit right into your stammering and your desire for a different and harmless language, one without any sound or sharp edges, soft and immaculate like the morning stillness at the pond. And now you only want to speak with the sounds of the moor, to break through your silence by means of my voices, a whispering in rain, a howling in storms, so if you stumble on a word the others will only hear a rushing of water down from the eaves, a soft crackling of dead-wood outside.

At some point you wriggled out of her embrace and with a little jump were in front of the wardrobe door, which only somewhat managed to hide your arousal. She stood up, went to the window, and was suddenly bathed in the white from the breaking day. 'I was familiar with your penis when it was just a larva,' she said into the dimness, into the fog that would no doubt soon turn to rain, said with a sharp and hurt sounding voice, as it always is when you've made her angry. One agonizingly long moment when you had the urge to take her arm and comfort her for something that you could not name. 'Still angry about yesterday?' she asked and came over, and it was only then that you noticed her savaged lip.

The state of her mouth has always been a measure of her moods. You can literally read her mood from the state of her lips, smooth means good, raw a terrible day, raw that she hadn't been able to paint and had chewed on her lower lip, had had a sleepless night or had done something that she regretted, it's rare that your mother's mouth and mood are free from tears and wounds. 'Ute was sick, I had to cover for her.' She lays her hand on your shoulder, you push it away but at the same time want to grab it again and press it tightly to your chest. 'There was a lot going on in the gallery,' she added, 'I didn't have any time to call'—a claim you've never believed. She said it reproachfully, as if Ute had held her back, the gallerist, the one who had once come out from Hamburg in order to make a selection of your mother's paintings and even asked you which ones were your favourites. You had pointed to the ones of the moor, birch stumps like skeletons, a storm over the pond where clouds amassed into faces. 'Nice,' Ute said, and opted instead for the nudes, self-portraits mostly, which your mother since then has hung every Wednesday, the day of the district art market and the day the gallery is supposedly full of tourists.

As soon as you're out of the house she drives off with a whole car full of nudes and comes back late at night with the very same ones. You've got used to counting the number of paintings when you help her load and unload, and up until now not a single one has ever been missing. When she gets home around midnight, she's in a lousy mood. She smokes another two cigarettes out on the porch and then gulps down wine in the kitchen. You can hear her coming and quickly hide your journal under the mattress. 'You, writing bad stuff about me again?' she grins, pulls the pen out of your hand and lays down next to you in her cold clothes. Wednesdays she smells different than usual, she smells like the city. She lies motionless for a few minutes and breathes heavily. 'What'd you do all this time?' she asks, although she already knows the answer. Like every morning you were at school, later on you did your homework, and after that you were out by the pools and ponds looking among the bracken and stems of beak-sedge for cast-off dragonfly skins for your collection. You prop your head on your hands and look at her. Sometimes her nostrils quiver, a strand of hair across her mouth will tremble with her breath, an eyelid twitch. She tries to pretend that she's asleep, but you know better, you know that she still wants something. In spite of her make-up she looks pale and worn out, the kohl around her eyes has smudged, she's already wiped away her lipstick and put on lip balm—all these layers always make your Wednesday mother a little unfamiliar to you. Wednesdays she often doesn't have any time or interest to go down to the pond, she just pulls on a pair of black hose, dabs a bit of perfume on her neck and fixes her hair, then she's in the bathroom for hours, on the way to school you pee on the fence. In the mornings she hums along with those terrible old pop songs and in the evenings curses how much of a mess the house is, a mess she herself, of course, is responsible for. At first her mouth is blood red and, after she gets back, white from the cream. You've never liked Wednesdays; they make you feel lonely and sad, and Marga herself doesn't deal with them too well. You look for a sign on her mouth as to why Wednesdays are so terrible but the cream stops you from figuring out how she feels. She turns her face to you, pouts and demands her kiss. You bend over, take the strand of hair between your lips and lay it on her temples. She says, 'Everything's all right again.'

But yesterday, Dion, wasn't Wednesday and neverthe-less she was out late. After school there was a note on the table: Have to go to the gallery, and underneath it in her sharp childlike scrawl, Don't forget to eat. Your stomach closed up, a pain began to rummage about, gnashing and tearing like a tooth-studded mouth. You lifted the lid off the pot and saw the everything-soup, so named because you can use almost everything that's in the cupboard. At least she'd prepared your favourite dish, but you refused to eat all the same. In protest. Against the lie. In the barn not a single painting was missing, all the trunk-nudes were there, your mother, posing, astraddle, dangerously bent, between her legs a black pair of prongs, no cotton grass but a deep fissure. The art market had never been open on Tuesday. The pain chewed and devoured, you sniffed the tubes of paint and cups of turpentine, the solvent tore open the wound in your stomach even wider, a red feeling, for suddenly you had to think of the sundew when you flicked the little mosquitoes off your arm onto the tentacles of the moor plants, glistening like drops of blood, those mosquitoes that immediately begin to digest their victims alive.

In your head you'd already called her terrible names and scrawled your suspicions into your notebook. The rest of the afternoon you hung around the room, looking out the window at the Heidedamm where there's never a car except for a tractor and her old Ford. Ran through your presentation over and over again just to pass the time. But the hope you'd had of being able to go over it with her at least once was now gone, swallowed up by the feeling that was even more painful than your classmates' ridicule and your fear of stuttering. With every glance the hand on the dragonfly clock seemed to move even slower, then stop, then crawl, twitch, crawl, until a little after four. You threw yourself onto your bed, laid there motionless and watched how the dragonfly tore time from out of her own body. Then all of the sudden it was five. Wednesdays at five she calls from the gallery to know whether you've eaten, you've done your homework, cleaned your room. Sometimes, when no one's listening, she asks softly if you miss her. You jumped out of bed and ran down to the telephone but, at a quarter past, the receiver was still silent and the hole in your stomach so big that it threatened to make the house, the Heidedamm, the village and the entire moor with its eternally homeless sky disappear. At some point you picked up the receiver and in the empty tone you heard my voice.

She came home late, later than usual, the dragonfly, fat and happily full at a quarter past one. You'd heard the crunch of her tires on the gravel until the Ford's motor had gone silent, then you put out the light and pretended to sleep. It was only after three cigarettes, at least, that the porch door slammed shut. In the kitchen the pop of a cork, then for a long time it was still—sleep tugged and pulled but you stubbornly held out. Scraps of dreams against your eyes, squinting, you saw her standing in the doorway. Then you felt her. The mattress quaked and you pressed yourself into the crevice. She was now so close that she blew her breath, which stunk of cigarettes and wine, into your nose. Suddenly her body began to quiver, she laid her heavy leg across you and pressed her face against your neck where, after a little while, it began to grow warm and moist. Although it itched like crazy, you never moved. She dragged your arm out from under the blanket and put it around her and as if the gesture would loosen a terrible paralysis within you, you finally pulled her towards you. The itching stopped. Nothing moved any more. Only the eyes of the dragonfly swept from your feet over your bodies to your heads and through the red night back to your feet, minutes in which you were once again that child who would feel for the strands of hair across her cheeks and wish never to have to sleep anywhere else, never to have to be anyone else, to stay with her, just like this, for ever. She turned her head, maybe shocked by the sudden closeness; instead of the strand of hair, your mouth closed upon the crust of her lips. They tasted like the pond, slightly bitter and rusty. One time only you had tried a drop, entranced by the colour, had licked it out of your own palm and disgusted by the sour, iron-like broth had spit it out. The disappointment had been similar, colourless and silent, no feeling, more like something which all of a sudden is missing.

You pushed her away and went to the light switch. She wiped tears from her eyes, sat up and said, 'Everything's okay,' but you knew that the sentence, just like the note that morning, was a lie. Even her dress seemed like an act of betrayal. It didn't belong to her Wednesday wardrobe and was red. She had messed up her good-night kiss, the child cheated by its mother. The pond had never tasted like soda but always a bit like old blood. It's going to be the time, Dion, that I tell you the whole truth. She saw your face, distrustful, turned off the light and went into the bathroom and for a long time you only heard the lapping of water in the bathtub until I pulled her down and you off to sleep.

You come out of your thoughts with a start. She's already in up to her thighs, splashing and wrapping her arms around her chest, the introduction to her 'rain pantomime', as you call this quotidian drama in your journal. You know what comes next as well as you know your presentation, which, you gather by looking at your watch, in less than half an hour must come out of your head and onto your tongue and from there out into the world. In your head you repeat the whole thing again, line by line, trying to find the places you might stutter, getting rid of consonant strings or just replacing them with other words containing fewer barbs. The whole time never letting your mother out of your sight, you even laugh in her direction, you're such a sweet lit-tle boy. She binds her hair up with a hair clip, which is pointless as it's already sticking to her neck. Soon she'll dive in and play at being the sensitive kind, though the summer water is still warmer than the air. She'll swim with her neck held out, giraffe-like, as if to protect her hair, once around then back to the side where you'll pick her up with the umbrella and hand her the bathrobe. She finds that funny, you think it's childish, but she knows that you can't refuse her anything; like today, she managed to win you over all the same.

If she had at least asked you about your presentation just once. The morning ritual annoys you now, the idea of having to go swimming when others are eating breakfast, sleeping or already at work, ridiculous. When you were still a boy, you believed the pond made your mother younger. As long as she went to the water in the mornings it would be a good day, danger only loomed when she slept through it. Often after her swim her face indeed was younger and full of smiles; on days she slept, wrinkled and cold as if made of stone. You wanted the young Marga who even wore miniskirts when cleaning the house, the stone one still scares you, she sits around in the chair until evening, nightgown clinging to her like a skin made of mould, uncombed hair like spiderwebs across her forehead and her eyes behind them like the Jesus in church the sculptor forgot to paint. Your stone mother doesn't cook any everything-soup, doesn't make you any sandwiches for lunch, she just smoulders out of the fissure that is her mouth and swallows stone-sized pills. You heave that Marga who becomes as heavy as a gravestone into bed so that she can sleep herself back to life. Place her feet on the steps and beg her to hold onto the railing so that she won't topple backwards and shatter into pieces. Even her whimper gets heavier with every step and, in the end, becomes a kind of croaking. You push and sweat and roll your mother up the stairs like Sisyphus with his boulder. On stone days she cannot make it to the pond, she'd sink, you'd need a rope, a winch and a tractor to get her back out, but by then it would already be too late and so you'd just wrap her cold body up in a blanket.

She pointed to the window and pulled on your arm, as she always does when she wants you to do something for her, cut the grass, write to the agency, massage her back for her while she's in bed on nights when she returns from her workshop in knots from staring and making her strokes. Couldn't I stay home? You wanted to ask and already choked on *couldn't*. The letters C and K have always been among your worst enemies. The latter so spikey, four edges and a sharp blade, and in its vicinity the D already, which comes out so fat and round it almost sticks in your throat.

The sounds of K and D at the beginning and end of *couldn't* turn into a hopeless slaughter in your mouth and annihilate any combat-ready vowels that follow. You just swallowed it whole and went silent before even reaching the end. When those sounds, those letters, march together, there's nothing to do but lay down your arms. Just think, for example, of when you have to pronounce your own name: Dion Katthusen, a massacre when Marga's not at home and you have to answer the telephone. You only survive those rounds of introductions at the beginning of the school year or at Confirmation class through the help of the letter *H* in the middle of your last name which allows you to get a breath of air and win a little time because it's almost invisible or, rather, soundless, soft and light as the wind through the bristly rushes.

When talking you think a moment about all the words, envelop the debris of your thoughts, which only through great effort come into rank and file, syllable and sentence, and say, *hDihon hKatt-husen* and *hCouldhn't hI hstay?* Your speech dissipates into vagueness and vapour, whatever you want dissolves, you're not even sure who you are, you wander through the world with your secret like an aimlessly wandering fog bank across the deceitful water landscape, it's no wonder, Dion, that everyone asks what it is that you've got to do with me.

Only a mother can understand her stuttering child. You didn't even need to finish. 'I'll take care of it for you,' she said with her hand pointed half to you and half out the window, a gesture embracing nothing and, at the same time, enveloping everything: you, the house, the village, the deep sky, the barn with all those useless paintings, her job in Hamburg, and yesterday, which you still didn't want to forgive her for. You walked past her embarrassedly and looked out to me, to the rain whispering at the windowpane. You've never really understood that sentence, but have always known what, after a short pause, she would add. 'Don't you love me any more?' she asked after two menacingly slow seconds, knowing the answer in advance. Your *hOf hcourse* caught in your throat again and came out too late and then with so much *H* that you yourself could barely hear it. By that point she'd already had her swimming bag in hand and, grinning contentedly, punched you to the door. She took the umbrella from out of the bucket, opened it, then pushed you into the rain.

Twenty to eight. She's still not at the other side and, to your annoyance, she's even taken the way around the opening of the ditch where the seepage water streams. She cuts a swathe through the carpet of leaves, torn catkins, sinking into the water roiled by her hands. The second hand of the clock scurries from number to number, you want to stop it and at the same time get your mother to hurry, for you still have nineteen minutes before you have to speak.

She really thinks your presentation is just an essay that you have to read. She doesn't seem to hear your stutter, or does but isn't bothered by it, day and night she sees your pain and struggles and is happy all the same to have a son who doesn't blather and complain all the time. From out of a hundred kids, she once said, and put her finger on your spastic mouth, she'd recognize you immediately. But she lied, Dion. The truth is that among a hundred children you are lost. Just having to say the name of your presentation, which Gorbach, thinking to be of help, had written on the board, 'The Lifecycle of Dragonflies', in front of the twenty others in your class leaves you speechless. A groan of annoyance emerged then from the rows, and from all the way in back David Voss piped up and called, 'Isn't it written with an *H* in the middle?'

The beginning alone is enough to get you. You would've preferred 'The Life' but *The Lifecycle* is already far too tricky. 'The Behaviour' would've been even better, you would've been able to duck behind one *H* at least, but you think of that too late. Now even your saliva has left you, your hands begin to twitch, the text begins to shift across the paper, seven pages of painstakingly formulated sentences, although Gorbach has only allowed keywords.

For days you sifted through the dictionary around the letter *H* and managed to fit a few additional words into every half-sentence so that you could safely make it over the crags. You moved nouns around and here and there slipped in a helping verb but the text was already completely enshrouded with *H*s and, at night, in bed, when you went through the sentences over and over again in your head, their bright sound, the already autumn-cool night from the open window and the hope that on Wednesday you'd be sick, slowly lulled you to sleep.

Everything has been ready since Sunday, you have copied out the presentation multiple times in order to practise and at lunchtime even laid the pages next to Marga's plate, hoping for her praise but she only moaned, when was she supposed to have to time to read it all, cleaned up and went to go and paint. For the rest of the day you sat around her workshop with the paper under your bottom while she sketched restlessly, ostensibly still lacking one portrait in her application to the Hamburg Academy of Art. She looked around, then up again and through you, yelled, 'Chest out! Face more to the right! Now, don't move!', or 'Don't look so bored!' Then suddenly dropped her charcoal, chewed on her lips and looked morosely towards the window. The thick fog had crawled up around the house and blindly looked back.

It was the moment you'd been waiting for. When she begins to stare out the window it means she's lost her train of thought, that her idea is gone, disappeared into the empty air. You pulled out the first page from under you and took a deep breath before the first sentence—a whopping six *H*s. But before you could utter even the first word her charcoal began to scratch across the untreated cloth. She said, 'Don't read now,' came over to you, took the pages away, pulled your sweater and shirt over your head, crossed your arms behind your back and, as if warning you not to move at all, pressed you to her, her mouth open. For an endless stretch of minutes you stood there half-naked, one buttock on your presentation, which managed to dig into your skin despite all the *H*s. The charcoal dug into the canvas, the fog licked at the window, tried to snatch her ideas away and help you to speak, but she didn't look back any more, either outside or towards you, she was gone. Outside, the last light was slowly snuffed out, she snapped on the lamp, your body was now reflected in the glass, in such broad outlines, it seemed stronger and older, almost grown up. Then a look to the window, a long, twinkling one, no staring into the void, more like an invocation. Now she only looked at her drawing or towards your mirror image before the night and acted as if you were no longer there. The sound of her charcoal became softer, then simply went out. Or had the fog by then managed its way into the barn, eaten up every sound and enveloped you in a cocoon? The box behind you stopped sticking into the small of your back and even your presentation stopped running through your mind. The last thing you saw was your mother happy and young behind her worktable.

When she woke you, you saw a picture of a young, naked man lying with his head stretched out over some kind of object, at first you thought it was the box but then realized it was the tree stump from the pond. One arm hung loosely to the ground, the other hand was resting on the thigh and half hid his sex, which sprung up from behind the back of his hand. Only after you had stared hard at the spot did you see, hidden in the tangle of lines, the insect. The closed fingers formed the wings, the wrists and bones, the head the male dragon-fly stretches out into the air, just like you had observed at the pond, in its courtship dance when he grabs the female by her neck with his forceps-like cerci and flies off with her in tandem, the insects entwined with one another on the leaves of the reeds often lose their grip and fly away in the form of a heart.

Shocked, you looked down at yourself, but your pants were still on. 'That's good,' she said, but her voice sounded despondent. In order to cover up the embarrassing nakedness in the picture, as if by reflex, you put your hand between your legs but discovered that she had achieved something better. What was this child with the dragonfly penis supposed to be about? The professors who'd judge her painting at the academy would consider it indecent. And anyway, she hadn't captured you well at all, as a portrait you would have failed it. To you the blurry person on the tree stump no longer appeared to be sleeping but, rather, with his scant, almost extinguished expression, he seemed to be dead. 'That's not me,' you said, the sentence lasted a terribly long time, after the second syllable she already knew what you had wanted to say, silently spoke every word along with you, as if she wanted to help you bring it across your lips and actually came close to doing so. 'Never believe a painting,' she winked and threw your sweater at you. 'And you?' you asked, and you both remained shocked, for within those two words there had been neither air nor lull. She packed up her brushes, you got dressed and walked to the house which, although only twenty metres away, you could hardly see. When you turned around on the porch to face her, she'd already been swallowed by the fog.

A quarter to eight. She is now by the alder with the trunk that has been split into three, the run-down one with the already withering leaves, the one which must have once had four limbs, like arms and legs, before lightning struck one of the boughs and it fell into the water. In a moment she'd turn on her back and swim just a little bit further until she came below the dead arms in which you've always seen the fingers of a human hand. There she'll turn again and look into the depths. Every morning you ask yourself what she's looking for in those elongated seconds under the alder claw where she stops moving and slowly begins to sink until her head goes in, and you, sitting on your stump, have to hold your breath, only when the sun comes over the horizon and the light breaks through the mirror of the pond does she come back up and are you able to breathe.

But today you hope and look once again at the clock: thirteen to eight, you think as you undo the buckles on your knapsack. She's already at the branch and today, Dion, your childhood is definitively over, the water no longer holds any images, the pond is as voiceless as your life which for far too long now hasn't received any air. There aren't any claws, no alder ghosts, there is no whispering in the rushes nor muttering in the wind, and the idea that you look like me is just plain nonsense. The colour of your hair, your freckles and your moor-brown eyes all come from your father, and your name—how could it be otherwise—you received from your mother. No one is talking when you listen to me. In reality, I am as silent as a fish but there are no fish to be found here in these ponds, only nightmares and horror stories, dead things that do not dissolve in the acidic water. Here where the dragonflies lay their eggs. So get up, take your goddamn presentation in your hand! She'll be swimming back to the bank where you're standing with the umbrella any minute and will be waiting for you to hand her the towel, it's the best chance you have to scream, not stutter, into her face all that I have been whispering to you and then even in front of the class there'll be no stopping you—'You cowards,' you'll yell in a razor-sharp voice, 'You chick-enshits, listen to me!'—and all their mouths will drop open and David Voss, your archenemy, will hide behind Thorsten Hinrich, for what you'll say will become a storm, no, a hurricane, and shall howl down and anni-hilate everything in its way.

You will only spare Tanja Deichsen. The pastor's daughter, the one who stumbles into class with the last bell and often even later, quite often even later than you, and for which Gorbach has made you both stay after school, afternoons when the schoolhouse is empty and it has grown so still that the German teacher's head sinks ever deeper over the essays resting on the lectern. She eventually nods at you, quietly gathers her things and limps to the door. In seconds, you'll have shouldered your knapsack and caught up with her in the hallway, but will still keep a metre of distance, a metre that gives room to all the unsayable feelings, it'll only be by the church that she'll turn and say, 'Bye—', in secret complicity, it seems, because Tanja, like you, is what they call handicapped, she doesn't have bones like everyone else but the ones made of glass, or, more precisely, a skeleton that is missing an important component, which is why, at the smallest strain, it could splinter apart. She is smaller and more delicate than the other girls her age and has a slightly crooked leg thanks to a poorly healed fracture, a girl who already in kindergarten stood off alone, and often in a cast. From her blurry blue eyes, which give her something secretive and exotic, she silently observes the others' jostling and is frightened when something goes wrong, when someone falls from the swings or while playing tag, but then laughs along with everyone else as soon as they get back up and start to play again. You are both kids from the playground's edge, you the speech- and she the movement-cripple, one the breath-child, the other the glass-bone-girl, connected to you in an inexplicable way. She too will look out from her row on the left to watch you scream down the schoolhouse and the entire world; she will simply stare at you, without praise, without reproach, but with that inflamed and unsettling blue look that knows.

Later, once the throng of students has left the room with ringing ears and Gorbach has silently given you a perfect mark, she will scurry away down the hall. You'll overtake her, hold open the heavy door, and the sentence you'll use to ask her to accompany you on a walk around the moor will come lightly over your lips because, unlike the others, she doesn't look away when you speak. She won't have answered it yet when in the reflection of the glass you'll see Hannes Lambert, the huge, square-headed sixteen-year-old with that blond mat of hair in front of his eyes, those eyes which are forever anxiously wandering about, like a beast of prey, followed, as always, by a clique of other older students, you'll see him strut down the hall and those who are standing around unwillingly shrink into the shadows. He'll come up to you, eyes unwavering from half a metre away like a sharp, green ray boring into your forehead. You think it must have something to do with his eyes, which are just a little too close to each other, and which, at the last minute, in fact, look past you. He smacks his chewing gum and rips the door from out of your hand. As the oldest of Farmer Lambert's children, after school he has to help out in the stalls, but unlike a farmhand he never smells of pigs, or was it that whenever he passed by you held your breath for fear that his smell might be different?

Now you can breathe him close by, but he is already past you; between your eyebrows a feeling of cold as if there were a hole where his eyes had met your skin. Tanja is standing over by the blackboard with the other girls. Hannes' gang walks through the door, the gaggle of girls chats away and makes eyes at the foxes, Tanja alone looks at the notices and, once the group is around the corner, back to you. But all of a sudden instead of her face you see David Voss. 'C-c-cack-house,' he gags, crosses his eyes, jerks his head and spits on your shoe. 'C-c-crap,' Hinrich apes and farts. Then they grab you and push you into the stink. Someone kicks your legs out from under you, and you taste the bristles of the floor mat. For a long time afterwards you hear their cackling echo through the building. But when you lift your head at some point and look to Tanja for help, no one is there.

Marga is gone too. You jump up and toss aside the umbrella which slides into the pond. 'Mom!' you yell, panic has no edges, your scream as flat and smooth as a bullet. A teal becomes frightened and flies off into the moor, from the distance you can hear its laughter. You run into the reeds, stop, begin to sink, and see nothing under the branch but the deep. The pain of having let her out of your sight, of having lost her for ever, is like a cut through your body. You tear yourself away and move from alder to alder. The trees play with your fear, they push it off and gather it again, every trunk shows you another image of the pond—at times a puddle, at times a roaring sea; first a bottomless pit, then a blazing light into which you dive and fall. As you're falling, you see the empty house below, the open porch door, the laundry hung up on the line, the ashtray on the table that she always forgets to empty until the wind blows the butts away. The barn, the puttied window, the holes in the roof, you don't know how to repair it, or, where you'll have to bring all the junk, her pictures, where, when she's dead, you'll have to order the coffin, who to call, who'll stand next to you at the grave, support you when you throw the rose, but, it occurs to you, she's always hated roses and once, together, you secretly poured turpentine on Ilse Bloch's bushes.

You run back to the stump, you hope you've only missed her, not seen her in the confusion of the bushes, that you'll see her shadow begin to rise in the water and be able to think of words of remorse and renewed loyalty, but the pond stays smooth and hard, a mirror. You fall onto your knees. The pond seeps into your shoes, a soft, almost comforting feeling. With pleading eyes you look over to the branch with the water silent below, the image I am showing you has never been as empty and truthful as it is just now.

She emerges, snorts, fingers the leaves from out of her hair. 'How long was I—,' she gasps, then laughs. The minutes she was underwater seemed like days and weeks, then all of a sudden the pain is old, the white feeling of mornings at the pond, lifeless and yellowed, it falls away from you like a dead leaf. I will devour it; you will forget it. You step back, then forward, but there's no relief, the feeling now like a weight pushing you deeper into the ground. The rain grows stronger, the wind bends the branches and sweeps the last bit of mist out of the alders. 'Don't you want to get undressed first,' she grins, not realizing how worried you really were. You begin to shiver, she too loops her arms over her chest, pushes you onto the bank and fishes the umbrella out of the water. She takes the towel out of the bag and dries you off. You fight against the pressure in your throat, but can barely calm down. You're happy about the towel on your face, she can't be allowed to see that you are crying. She thinks it's the rain, dries herself, pushes the umbrella into one of your hands and a brush into the other so that you can scrub her back, just like you always used to do as a child. On her body once there were common territories and individual ones, you dabbed at her back and throat and she the places on mothers that belong to fathers. Now you no longer know what to do with your hands. Your throat burns as if you had been screaming continuously.

'What's the matter,' she asks, shakes you and the numbness from your limbs, pulls the towel away and bows. Once upon a time the child would clap at the end of the pantomime, now you stare into the trees, wish you could go back under the umbrella with her again, into the warm towel-cover where the world would shrink back into a trusty, old feeling. There you would tell her everything you've learnt about the lifecycle of dragonflies from books and observations in the moor over the last few years. With the rhythm of the drumming and dripping rain and in long sentences that would pearl out of your mouth like the beads of water from the umbrella, you would initiate her into the secret of the insect which lives a long and boring childhood on the bottom of the pond until the strange and the most dangerous moment of its life when in the early morning hours it has climbed up a reed, shed its old skin and stands defenceless before its enemies. The act of metamorphosis can go wrong if the young dragonfly's still-awkward wings get caught in its skin or hung up on a thorn. Its first attempt at flight, the maiden flight, is clumsy, the insect a new-found snack for birds, for in this phase the adolescent dragonfly, called an *imago*, is completely concentrated on trying out its new body which is still somewhat unfamiliar to it. But the higher it rises into the air, the more confident and elegant its circles become and soon enough it is able to get around the birds' beaks and fly off into the moor from where, you say in the final line of your presentation, it comes and where it belongs.

'Everything all right again?' she asks, pulls her bathrobe out of the bag and wraps herself into the white, fluffy material. When you look over to her you notice that your glances meet on an almost horizontal line, as if time had suddenly taken over you, although in the last couple of minutes you had only got off the stump.

You close your knapsack. She takes hold of your arm and expects her kiss. 'Good luck with your presentation,' she says, 'I know you'll get a great mark, believe me,' she laughs, 'mothers have a sixth sense.' Five to eight. You pull away and take off over the Heidedamm into the village. What would a super-human maternal sense that could make you talk look like? You wonder. 'Get dressed before you go,' she calls after you, but the rain has already erased her from the scene of the pond.

The playground is empty, and the last latecomers have just left the assembly hall. You bound up the stairs, run through the courtyard, the hallway seems dark and endlessly long. You hear the chatter from the classroom, and in between Gorbach barking his commands. The bell rings for class to begin. When you're finally in front of the door, your heart is beating so loud that you barely hear the last sounds of the bell. Then all of a sudden another meter mixes in, a shuffling, irregular but familiar. In a yellow raincoat, Tanja is hurrying through the hall with bouncing satchel and dragging feet. She stands in front of you, out of breath, and says, 'Aren't you coming in with me?' You look to the ground for a long time, the bristles of the carpet, then eventually say, 'hOf hcourse.' She nods and slips through the door. You want to follow her inside but, instead the child turns, runs back into the tunnel and out into the moor, through the rain and out into the stillness to me.

She hangs the wet towel over the banister and the bathrobe on the hook, will have to remove the laundry from the line, it doesn't look like the rain will stop today. There's a pile of silverware in the kitchen, a mountain of clothes in the cellar that still need to be put into the machine. She can't forget the empties either, the lemon soda is cheaper in the supermarket in Zeeve than it is in Ilse Bloch's shop, and, furthermore, no one bothers her there, there's no whispering, no eyes in her back. She pulls a cigarette out of the pack, the matches are damp, and split, only after the third try, the splutter of a flame. The filter sticks to her lower lip and rips off the scab, with the first drag she tastes blood, then soot, the damp paper too. Recently she's been leaving her cigarettes outside on the table since, having forced herself to smoke out on the porch, she's managed to cut back to a pack a day. At least I've managed that, she thinks. Not much of a victory really, for in her studio, staring onto the cloth where her eyes draw the lines which her hand simply cannot repeat, the cigarette burns out in the ashtray while another one already between her fingers and so on, until the paint is dry on the edge of the brush. When at some point she finally risks, carefully, almost reluctantly, to touch the still, cold surface, the way one pokes at a wounded animal with a little stick to see if it's still alive, the pack is empty and her idea of the image, a beautiful and wild beast, long dead.

That is her morning, ten to twenty cigarettes, depending on the beast's tenacity. Yesterday it thrashed about for a long time, an unruly specimen, she really thought she'd had a good idea, soapsuds still covering her hands, she'd left the sink and walked over to the barn. After three hours her throat hurt, she had pierced the canvas with her stares, her lower lip already chewed raw, but the bastard bit back. One final thrust with the roughest of her brushes, at last two black slashes on far too much white, one last hole with her palette knife, then quiet.

The perpetually empty packs of cigarettes and the corpses of paintings are proof that she indeed had the desire but not the talent to convert her ideas into actions and works, in other words, into cash. Marga Katthusen, the half-dead animal growled, accept the fact that you are nothing but a dreamer and a painter only in your head, that you simply refuse to go to work like everyone else your age has done, behind a counter, in the fields, working for Nordfrost, the refrigeration company, on the assembly line or at the very least in front of the stove with two kids pulling at your skirt, a third on the way, your hungry husband at the table . . . And then she smokes the second cigarette, after all, and looks at the clothes dripping on the line, your underwear hanging next to her lacy bottoms and the black fishnet hose, the ones which always draw the village women's stares.

She knows that you'd rather be one of them, a grocer's child or a farmer's kid, have the pig breeder Karl Lambert for a father and a happy mother like Marianne, your aunt who sometimes slips an apple or even a pair of fresh eggs into your pocket with a pious air and a hello to your mother, that hypocrite, she thinks, who went around the village whispering about the shame and disgrace that her, Marga's, marriage to Karl's brother, your father, would bring to the family. She would have even sold her brother-in-law, who'd had his eyes on her house and land, the rotting walls, a long time ago if she wouldn't have then had to go away like she'd been driven off with a shopping cart full of her things—a triumph that she just would not grant him, that butcher who had her husband's death on his conscience—these were the thoughts nagging away at her while she sat at her worktable yesterday which kept her from taking the bull, as they say, by the horns. She looks at the clock, almost noon. Tuesdays you have class until the fifth hour, then you'll come home and will want to eat. She grabbed a random brush, a random colour, and once more struck blindly out at the bloodbath on the canvas where already there was nothing left alive. Then she stood up.

The line was busy twice. On the third try a grumpy male voice finally gave her the working hours of the Employment Agency in Hamburg-Eimsbüttel: Tuesdays until 4.30 p.m. She had to be able to make that. She opened the refrigerator, two bell peppers, an already opened jar of bockwurst, pickles, a few onions in the basket under the sink and some potatoes. The everything-soup would be a tiny consolation for the young boy's lonely afternoon, whipped up in twenty minutes. A lightly braised onion, a few vegetables and some slices of potato, then stock over the whole thing, salt, pepper, some paprika, thirty minutes over a low flame, time she would use to get ready, make-up, hairspray, a dash of perfume, a little bit of kohl around her eyelids to accentuate her glance should she happen to run into a man in the office. She painted the hollows of her cheeks as grimly as she had her painting. She wiped off her lipstick, which struck her as just a bit too much, but then you could see the scab—too mentally unstable, she thought, so what.

In the bedroom she rummaged through the wardrobe for the beige-coloured suit, the one she finds stuffy and had therefore relegated to the furthest corner but which seems fitting for a round with the authorities. A burning smell came up from the kitchen, she'd taken too long to choose her blouse, back to the stove, the mush was sticking to the bottom of the pot, but at least you'd be able to eat the top layer. She loosened her hair again, the bun struck her as too old-maidish. She hastily cut the bockwurst and pickles into small pieces and stirred them into the brew with a bit of sour cream. Done.

Writing the note to you took the longest. No need to tell the truth, she'd explain if necessary, and anyway, she thought, children want to be lied to by their mothers, Santa Claus, the Christ child, the stork that brings babies with its beak . . . and the story where your father lost his life shortly before your birth in a work accident in the peat bog is only a part of the truth, for the whole area was already flooded and planted with alders and the pond at the end of the Heidedamm with its faces of bark and fog spirits had always been a place of illusion and deceit. She decided to go with 'an emergency in the gallery', formed the sentence in her head, but then ruined it, as she always did under pressure, by mixing up the letters in the words, a writing disability which she became aware of in Third Grade when she scribbled her name onto the little desk plate and the new teacher from then on called her Magret, not *Magra* like she had written, and not Marga or, at the very least, Margareta, as she was called in her passport. Even to her schoolmates she was suddenly Magret who couldn't or wouldn't write properly, and Magret from then on became the name of her refusal of diligence and duty, it was even written on her graduation certificate, there in black on white above the corresponding marks which were barely enough to qualify her for an apprenticeship, let alone university, and so her aunt, her only living relative in Hamburg, immediately advised her to look for work with room and board, and anyway she, Marga, wouldn't have wanted to stay with this aunt-once-removed, Aunt Frederike, who continuously played rummy with her next-door neighbour, and smelt like cabbage rolls in the first place. And so, on the day of her release from the deaconess home, she made her way to Altona where she walked through the dark little streets and looked into the shop windows until on the glass door of a store called Siana's Fashion House she discovered a sign: Female Help Wanted.

She can perfectly remember the red- and gold-threaded carpets on the parquet and the reflection, the similarly red and gold little lamps made on the wood, which she liked, for they created a warm light and glowed off the material of the men's suits and made everything appear high-class and expensive. The perfectly folded shirts on the shelves, the trousers with their ironed pleats and the stiff lapels of the dress coats and jackets created a contrast to the ornate mirrors, the booth seating with their plush cushions, the kitsch and trinkets of the window decoration and the ruffled curtains in front of the changing rooms where the ribboned slits drew glances but didn't let them in and billowed in the draught when somewhere in the shop a door slammed and the soft sound of a woman's laughter floated in from the back rooms.

It was only then that she saw the haggard saleswoman sitting behind a large, empty mahogany desk, smoking, no register, no trays. 'What are you standing around for,' the woman bellowed with a harsh and grating accent, Russian maybe, even though Marga had never actually heard a Russian speak. The woman, most likely the boutique's owner, lifted her ringed hand and waved to follow her inside the room where—dressed in red and gold—she sat in a chair so completely at one with the colours of the fashion house that it would have been difficult to say which had come first, the shop or its owner who possessed such a perfect and artful, almost painterly, combination of austerity and ornament, extravagance and demureness, display and concealment in every detail that she now seemed to her, Marga, to be one of the multicoloured and many sided pictures that one day would come from her own hand, in her future life as an artist, that life she had often dreamt of there, between the mouldy limestone walls of the dormitory and the classrooms of the girls' home when she was younger. Once she had filled out a kind of application form under the scrutinizing eyes of her heavily perfumed and pearl-draped new boss, who just as quickly grabbed it out of her hand and looked it over, the woman flashed her rotten, smoke-yellowed teeth, laughed suddenly and then said, 'Surely your name is

Marga, not Magra.' The girl, who at that time was your mother, was certain she had come to the right place.

But, in the end, she had indeed managed to write you a note. She scribbled a giant M below the short sentences, which, no matter which way you turned it, always looked the same and had, therefore, become something like her signature; official and business matters, however, were handed over to you along with a 50 Pfennig coin. She drew a heart around the letters, a secretary's position, she thought, and flung the pencil, was out of the question. On her way to the car she went back into the barn and pulled the cloth off the rejected work. Now the black slash appealed to her, there was something violent about it, and at the same time it looked like a battered body, half-dead. Below, in the empty white, a face appeared to her, pale, bluish, trembling under the permeable brushstrokes and blurry whirls, as if deep underwater. Maybe, she thought and pinned the painting back on her work wall, something can still be done with this one.

The motor stuttered. 'Please don't give up now,' she groaned to the car, 'if I sell the painting, you'll get some oil and some spark plugs and a new transmission and everything you need,' and then in fact, the wagon grumbled and started up. She flicked her cigarette out of the window into Ilse Bloch's roses and, in front of the school building which she wanted to get past quickly, stepped on the gas. It was right before David Voss' battle cry 'School's out!' which brought about the daily kicking and fighting games on the village green, ten minutes before the end of maths class, when you suddenly heard the familiar sound and lifted your head from your algebra. A shadow had shot in through the window which, Trösch, your teacher, had opened because David had been spraying deodorant on his neighbour, Thorsten Hinrich, who supposedly stank of sweat. A blood-red darter dragonfly now sped over the crown of your head, a particularly large, shimmering specimen that must have mistakenly flown into the classroom on its flight looking for prey. Heads turned here and there and someone shouted, 'Air-raid alarm!' and threw an eraser at the insect. Trösch grabbed the register and waved it through the air. The students rolled their notebooks into gun barrels, climbed onto their desks and began to bang away. In a panic, the dragonfly zig-zagged down the middle row. Hinrich fell from his desk, Elke Niedeck stabbed the girl next to her with her ruler and David Voss shot off his poison gas. Only Tanja Deichsen remained still, the corner of her mouth quivering, at her desk. At some point she stretched an arm in the air, not aggressively, but as if she wanted to offer the insect a place to land on her hand. She looked to you and smiled, showing off her sharp, grey-stained teeth. Your eyes wandered about, found their footing at the window, on the flat horizon, with me. When the dragonfly finally found its way back outside and into the distance, you felt as if you had irretrievably lost something, something that had belonged to you alone.

The class hooted and howled, and Trösch had trouble getting everyone to settle down in their rows. At some point, however, they all were back at their algebra. You still thought you could hear the buzzing of the insect and, although you did not want to, turned to Tanja as if you might bond with her against some looming danger, but she concentrated on her fractions. Out on the street your mother's car drove by. Trösch tore your presentation out from your lap, it had been lying there since the beginning of class, 'Maths, Katthusen,' he growled, 'this is maths class, not German.' Then the bell rang, and Voss announced the midday battle.

She's off the Autobahn now, traffic is slowing down on the Elbe Bridge, cranes like wraiths jutting out of the fog. The wipers shovel water off the windshield, but hardly manage to do anything against the rain. Already a quarter to ten. The fashion house will be opening in a few minutes, and *Herr* Kaltenbronn will already be sitting in one of the booths, a kind, older gentleman in exquisite suits, a bit hard of hearing, very rich, most of the time he doesn't ask too much and shells out more than he has to. 'Good morning, Miss Mira,' he greets her, 'do please help me out of this cheap thing here and bring me something fine, would you?' What does he feel like today? 'Whatever you like,' he calls to her and waves with the first of his bills. She pulls one of the silk scarves—which always make him melt—off the shelf, and pushes the old man into one of the changing rooms. 'You, Mira, are incredible,' he sighs and snuggles into the cool fabric. The boss Siana places great importance not only on the elegance of the clients but also on the polish and manners of her employees, as well as on their pseudonyms which in both sound and style had to distinguish them from the countless Gabys, Rosis and Mizzis in the brothel windows over on the Herbertstraße.

In the middle of the bridge the traffic comes to a stop. Blue light over on the quay, sirens, an accident. She curses, stares out onto the great, grey river, cargo ships in the docks, in the distance a large, awkward cruise ship. She's going to miss her appointment, she left too late, took the laundry down but, even after using the hairdryer, the red dress she had wanted to wear again wasn't completely dry and she could feel the dampness against her neck. Yesterday she had thrown it into the washer one more time. Had the boy noticed anything? Siana, who always seems to be bathing in her perfumes, stipulated that her girls could only use decent scents so that the men's wives would not detect anything, even if Marga herself always came home with traces of aftershave. Maybe her note was not a good excuse, the alleged sickness at the gallery, that always has to stand for everything. At some point, she thinks, Ute's going to blab or tell it like it is, 'Are you feeling better?' you'll ask the gallerist the next time she visits, but Ute will reply that she hadn't been sick, your mother can already see your puzzled face, the disappointment and rage in your eyes, then the man behind her honks and she's jolted out of her thoughts.

She steps on the gas, the engine floods. She's been careless recently, she's been making mistakes, yesterday she forgot to call, bought an expensive dress, although the boy had thought she was at work; when undressing, she noticed that the American's cigar smoke still clung to the fabric, the one who had come to the fashion house for the first time and hadn't really known what he wanted, had her show him this and that until long after five. She turned the key as far as it would go and revved the engine, 'Please don't quit now, or I can forget the job completely,' the last bus back leaves at six and from Rhase, she'd have to walk, cut across the moor in the dark.

'You smell so clean again, Miss Mira,' Kaltenbronn says as she bends over him, 'Life in the country,' she laughs back. But God only knows it's not clean, all her difficulties and frustrations in Fenndorf since her husband, your father, Dion, carried her off to the sticks, that prison made of red clinker brick walls and pig stalls. Every morning she leads you to the moor like other widows lead their children to the grave, clenches her teeth, jumps into the cold water and plays at being the mourning mother. The truth is that, as she is so suscep- tible to fungal infections, her doctor recommended that she swim in the acidic water of the moors. And so, as often as possible, even if reluctantly, she climbs into the brown broth where your father lost his life. When she's swimming, she claims, she feels close to him again, for a few minutes she feels like the girl she once was, not even twenty and pregnant from a man, you're not to know, she hardly loved, but who had promised her a comfortable life, one in which she could concentrate completely on her work, her painting, and so she had envisioned all of her talents within him and had accepted his family in return, the pig-breeding clan, who she despised even then. Above all, Marianne, your aunt, who as a young woman had had your father in her sights until, as it was already settled, she married his older brother Karl; yet, she remembered, her rival had continued to skulk about the house for months, planting something in the garden here, cleaning a few things out of the barn over there or coming by in the evenings with the freshly baked bread that he, your father, supposedly, ate so readily. Surely, Marga had lit- tle experience as far as running a household was con- cerned, and she handed her the recipe while inspecting the kitchen and made recommendations on how to dec- orate those squalid bachelor-like rooms.

When she complained to her husband about her sister-in-law's meddling he'd defend her saying that she also had her good sides. 'What sides indeed,' your mother sneered and squeezed her breasts together, which he, since she'd become pregnant, thank goodness, only now rarely nuzzled. With your little body germinating in her stomach, she'd successfully kept the farmer away from her body. 'Be a little thankful,' he'd admonish her. She could have even loaned him to Marianne for a night, it occurs to her now, in order to get a break from them both. But any insinuations in that direction immediately sharpened his mistrust of her, she remembers how they'd begun to talk about her, Marga, the newcomer, in the Village Tankard pub; how they had made dirty jokes Dion's father couldn't or didn't want to respond to.

She always says and thinks of him as 'Dion's father', the expression turns him into a non-person but not inhuman, just nothing more than the progenitor of her son, a man who had believed he could make her happy with an old farmhouse and the child growing inside her stomach. She had loathed his peat business from the start because of the bookkeeping which she was supposed to take over. Writing a simple receipt had taken her a quarter of an hour to thirty minutes of struggle and doubt. She could have picked up the figures, invoices and profits, but the writing of letters, reminders and correspondence would have brought an end to the marriage in no time at all. At some point she would have had to tell him the whole truth, which she avoids talking about even today, and so his sudden death was actually rather convenient. In the village they all know the story about the accident in the peat bog, and everyone recounts it differently depending on sympathy or ill will towards the deceased and the number of schnapps they've had at the pub, which distort what's remembered in one direction or the other. In all the variations, however, in the end, your mother is always at fault, she who spurned either his love or the life he had offered her; in each and every version, just a few months after the wedding and a short phase of so-called happiness, the storm broke on the summer night he didn't come back from the pond. Those who support Karl Lambert's version claim that, together with his brother, he had wanted to tie down the tarps over the peat sods which were lying ready for removal out on the meadow. Those who have always found the influential farmer with his greed for land and money to be a thorn in their sides, say that on the contrary, the jealous pig breeder used the opportunity to take his little brother and Lothario down a notch. Both sides, however, agree that with her cold-heartedness, your mother had already worn him down. 'Leave the sod alone,' she is said to have snapped, it's just dirt anyway. 'Well, we live from such *dirt*,' he shot back, in the variation of the anti-Lamberts. To which she is said to have replied: '*You all* live from it, not me!' He pushed her away and ran to his brother's farm, and it's here in all the versions that lightning begins to shoot through the skies over the pond where your father, they say, was knocked into the water by a falling alder bough. Nonsense, the others counter, though the tree was split into two by the storm and hurled down, it was the pig farmer's hand that pushed him into the water.

Unexpectedly taken away from us, the pastor said at the funeral, thus attempting to unite the divergent sides, and a sob came from the first row where Marianne Lambert pulled the veil further across her face. As your mother handed the scoop with which she had lobbed a piece of sod into the grave to Karl Lambert his fist shook from sorrow, some say, from anger, say the others but, your mother, very pregnant and inheritor of a considerable, even if unfertile, amount of land, quickly turned away from the grave, and the next day was on the bus to Hamburg.

If anything at all, what you received from her mourning there within her abdominal cavity was only the muffled sounds of the city, the fragments of unfamiliar sounds which today you can no longer remember but sometimes think you can hear: the whisper of bus doors, whirling voices and the din of traffic in the streets through which she walked, into the boutiques where doors jingled and saleswomen purred, and you felt the sudden difference in pressure around you when the tight dress or corset pushed against her lower body and tied you deeper into the closeness of the image-less dream in which you rolled, a heavy, hopeless darkness with her voice from high above or from without, distant and gargled as if through water, and then both of you in your beds would open your eyes at almost the same time and listen to the others, from room to room into the silence of the night, and out to me.

She shuddered again remembering the dream she'd had that morning. She had almost forgotten it entirely but, here on the Elbe Bridge, in a traffic jam where time expanded, the images flashed through her mind again: she had brought you back into the city, dreaming inside her stomach, not as the unborn little child-to-be, no, but as your thirteen-year-old self, arms and legs shooting out while other parts of your body were already those of a man, and, in that dream or, rather, nightmare, in the middle of work—she was, she remembers, busy with Kaltenbronn—you began to squeeze out of her body so that she, shocked, managed to feel your wet face and press her hand against your mouth so that you wouldn't scream, now that you would suddenly see what she'd been hiding from you all your life.

At that point she'd woken up and listened to the quaking of her body, which only ever so slowly began to subside. She still feels a leftover unease and shame from the night, like a reverberation catching up with her, as if there were someone there who could secretly read her thoughts and whisper what she was feeling and thinking to you in Fenndorf, 100 kilometres away, and so she sticks her nose into the collar of her dress and manages to smell, in spite of the bubble bath she'd taken that morning, a hint of the acidic water of the pond upon her skin, the smell that made Kaltenbronn go crazy, that smell of the countryside, the moor.

On the Schultor the wall of water broke over you, a giant wave of relief, and rushed you away from the classroom and over the Dorfstraße to the Heidedamm, there where the footpath begins, the one peat cutters once used to push their carts but today, if at all, was only used by bird watchers or the confused tourist who was just crazy enough to risk walking alone along the unsecured path that cuts off behind the Lamberts' stalls, meanders for a while along a drainage ditch that reflects the stares of the stunted willows, then passes the pond and its alder grove to the left and crosses over four loose planks laid over the dark stream that trickles out of the peat ditches before losing itself for a moment in the myrtle bushes and then continues between the fields of cotton grass where there is hardly a tree, only the rough edges of reeds and one or two lone birches, before finally disappearing within the quilted terrain.

That's where you turned, half-relieved, half-scared; the village, only a couple of hundred metres away, was already sunken in rain-mist as was your glance home-ward. On all sides a white, voluminous nothing. For a moment you wondered if you really should turn around, but the sense of defiance pushed you further out across the floating bog mats. You collapsed into a furrow and looked to the sky, over to the house, the only shape that still stood out against the stormy sky. The car was parked in the driveway in front of the barn which, from where you were, had already vanished into the rushes. You still could have caught up with her by the door, but she wouldn't have any time for you, you thought, wouldn't want to know anything about the presentation you'd skipped, or, the failing mark that Gorbach would have by then entered in his book. She would only have had to call the secretary and say that you were sick, it's nothing really, and Tanja, as you had understood from her glance in front of the classroom door, would have covered for you.

But how would you have meant to tell her, there in your corner, silently watching her stumble from the kitchen to the bathroom and from the bathroom to the front door, pumps in one hand, toothbrush in the other, and if she'd had a third, she'd have pushed you angrily out of the way, 'Not now, darling, I really have to go.' Before the first sound made it to your lips, the front door was shut.

Already the night before, sleepless and anxious about the coming disgrace of your presentation, you had snuck around her bed where she, Marga, was not to be found, only her red dress and next to it a package of Lexotax which she always pulls out of her night-table when something isn't right. You picked up the dress, pressed it to your nose and imagined how she, probably in the company of some guy, had strolled through the city, danced in smoky clubs and hadn't thought about you once, was even relieved to be rid of you for a few hours. You threw the dress and the slip hidden beneath it into the corner then picked them both back up and, in spite of the sudden disgust, smelt her underwear which smelt of her bath oil. It was difficult to put all the things back on the bed in a way that she wouldn't notice. You stood around for a little while, helpless, and listened to your inner confusion tear you in different directions, the burning in your throat drove you towards the refrigerator, your sleepiness back to your bed, but then your stutter-anxiety pulled you back.

In the end you punched a tablet out of the blister pack into your hand; it seemed to be the only possible way to reach her through the emotional endgame. As you swallowed, the pressure in your body simply ceased. You looked at the window and imagined her watching you from the barn, and the distress on her face eased you. In the reflection of the glass you saw your own face in the murky glow from the table lamp, your features cast in severe cuts of shadow. The boy I showed you before the empty darkness of the lowlands was almost a child no longer.

As always, there was no parking spot in front of the gallery. A few streets on, however, she manages to manoeuvre her car into a space, the engine wheezes as if taking its final breath. I can't even take care of a car, she thinks, and squeezes herself out the door, how am I supposed to manage a child; she opens the trunk and stares helplessly inside. The painting with the faint touches of dark colours that she had finished yesterday, of the sleeping boy who turns into a dragonfly, lay on top of the stack.

She looks at her watch, just about two hours, in theory enough to convince Ute that it's the best one she'd finished in a long time. After that she has to make it straight to the fashion house where there's often more business at lunchtime than in the evenings, belonging as they do to the clients' families, favourite bars or sports clubs. At twelve o'clock Shiereisen, the sales representative from Vienna, will be there to let himself be pinned for his tailored underwear, 'Ouch, pay attention, you dim-witted girl,' he'll sigh pleasantly, 'Oh, dear, so very sorry, *Herr* Schiereisen,' then she'll look away and press the needle in deeper as by then he'll already have begun to moan. Afterwards, she'll barely have enough time to wash her hands, the heads from Hansa-Werft with Mr Nikaido, the Japanese turbine producer, who always politely bows before and after and pays in dollars and for whom Siana, therefore, offers the best the shop has to offer. She can't screw that one up too, she'd already shifted Kaltenbronn who no doubt had already

folded up his news-paper and left his booth while Siana
did her best to keep him, even recommending another
girl: 'Oh, leave it alone, Miss Siana, I'll be back,' and
the boss, who really is no miss any longer, grinds her
rotten teeth because, thanks to Marga—in the meantime, her oldest employee—she'd lost business yet
again. Siana would threaten firing her again, as she
should, she thinks, the job has become a burden, it
oppresses her and makes her sick, she hates it as much
as she needs it, is disgusted with herself on Wednesday
evenings, and yet on Tuesdays begins to feel the pressure already. The demands she has made of Siana over
the last few years have not been few either, private
health insurance for the boy, a higher percentage, the
possibility to make her own hours, but none of this can
pay off the mound of debts that continues to increase,
their run-down house that needs to be kept up, a
costly—as Siana says—hobby, painting, and a son
whose education she'll soon have to pay for if he isn't
to end up on one of the line belts at Nordfrost or with
the Lamberts' pigs. But where was she supposed to get
the money, if not at the fashion house, she, without any
presentable vocational training, as she was quite clearly
made to understand yesterday at the job agency?

The woman at the agency had been brusque. She
would have known how to deal with those pale types
in their jackets that she could see bent over their desks
through the doors as she folded the tiny piece of paper
with the number on it, she knew them well, around

forty, married, two kids, they'd show up now and again at Siana's, a bit demanding, a bit dandyish, though in their hearts stingy, their children wearing a nice find from Goodwill where the men's wives worked as volunteers, etc. From the beginning, however, she hadn't had a chance with the dragon she'd been given once, the mechanical counter on the wall finally displayed her number.

Are you looking for something in *particular*? the clerk had asked, sizing her up from head to toe. Something simple, Marga had answered and bitten her lower lip—wrong answer, she was underselling herself. A straightforward job with fixed hours, she added and crossed her legs, she was a single mother. The clerk quickly looked at her ID card, she wasn't responsible for the region of Zeeve, and she pushed the document back across the desk, case closed. Marga was ecstatic. With her use of the word *mother* she'd scored her first hit, right to the chest where no child had ever fallen asleep, she'd noticed that about the woman immediately, the woman who was also wearing beige.

'I'm looking for something in Hamburg.' Marga leant forward and saw the woman's eyes narrow behind her glasses. 'As soon as you and your son have moved,' the woman added, while pushing her chair back, in order to re-establish the appropriate distance.

The decision had come to her over the last few days when her work in the atelier had once again come to a halt. The new life she now felt ready for had suddenly appeared right before her eyes like one of those completely finished images that only afterwards became so amateurish on the paper. The apartment they would buy as soon as she left the house and the land to her brother-in-law's family and pigs would be in the Susannenstraße, among the students, artists and squatters where throughout her last year at the home on Sundays she had sat in the cafes and watched the young people who all seemed so free and hungry for life. The job—this is how the image had taken shape in her mind—which she'd found at the employment agency would give her enough time to paint and yet guarantee her an income as well as a space for the boy, and later on at the university.

She caught herself imagining how in the evenings when she came back from her workshop, you would come in and lay down next to her to tell her about your day. She would listen to your jokes about the professors while you would notice her now smooth and healthy lips. You have shoulder-length hair like all the other students. Your arms have grown muscular, toughened by playing sports, and in the hollow of your collarbone, just like your father, will sprout dark hair. In this fantasy, however—and she shuddered at the thought—she was still only a young woman of thirty-one. 'And the girls at university,' she says, opening your collar, 'do you like them?' You grin and come a bit closer, she can smell cigarettes, afternoon beer, 'Yeah,' you say and bend over her, but I like the boys even more. 'Should be okay with me,' she laughs, and turns her mouth towards you.

'How old is your son,' the clerk wanted to know. A heavy layer of foundation on her face made it look like a mask. Now it was Marga's turn to move back, disgusted by this square, this philistine, who may have intuited, so she thinks, that she herself was almost still only a child when her boy was born. 'He's thirteen,' she answers, and the other smiles sullenly. In the portrait showing you in your metamorphosis into a dragonfly she'd depicted you without any particular age, neither a child nor a man, in an in-between, diffused light in which her eyes had suddenly gone out as it began to grow dark in the window. The dust and shadows in the windowpane had wiped away any particular characteristics of your face; and now, there on the flat, only vaguely delineated surface of your body, any line of thought on her painting was possible.

It was only then she noticed that you'd fallen asleep in your corner. She stood up, went over to you and carefully began putting you into poses, and doing so was reminded of a painting she had once seen in a catalogue a long time before: Johann Heinrich Füssli's *The Nightmare*. In that painting, a sleeping woman with her thighs slightly open is offering herself to the nightmare haunting her in the form of a simian, gnome-like incubus crouching on her chest. The uncanny creature is staring at the viewer, and everyone knows just what the girl is experiencing in her dream. In her painting, which she now saw in her mind's eye, you, however, would be dreaming of a dragonfly, which, as you had more or less explained to her one summer morning at the pond as a dragonfly pair corkscrewed across the water, in the act of mating stretches out its hindquarters to its partner.

You had mumbled something in your sleep, she'd held her breath, looked at your face for some time, then softly turned back to her worktable and had only looked up from her paper when a bulging and scabrous phallus began to arise from out of your lap, half-insect skin, half-human member, with a notch at the glans or end of the penis which in a dragonfly is thick and cartilaginous around the cerci and which, in her painting, recalled a grinning mouth, the incubus' lecherous grin as it took advantage of the boy, there amid the odds and ends, and then you suddenly opened your eyes.

'I asked if you already have an address,' the clerk said and pulled out her pen. 'Susannenstraße,' Marga lied and saw the woman raise an eyebrow and frown slightly. Now, she thought, she's got hold of the scent, senses adultery and in her the adulteress escaping the countryside for a commune in Hamburg's red-light district. In which sector had she been active up until now? 'Men's fashion,' Marga answered. 'As a seamstress?' she paused a moment. 'Consulting,' she said, 'sales.' The clerk nodded and leafed through her listings. 'No,'

Marga interjected, 'Nothing like that any more!' She was looking for something totally new.

Frau Gabriele Holst, that was the name outside on the doorplate, took a deep, weary breath. The name was familiar to Marga somehow; a *Herr* Holst, Friedrich Holst, he'd been a regular customer in the fashion house for some time, a clean, always seeming a little worried man who was perennially in a hurry. But that, she thought, was only a coincidence, Holst was quite a common name in Hamburg.

The job advisor asked her about her training. Marga shrugged her shoulders. Without any formal training, the woman responded, what she would be able to offer would be rather limited, cleaning woman, nightwatch—

'I'm a painter,' Marga said.

The severe and stern agency air crumbled. House painter? Varnisher? As a woman?

Marga collapsed into her chair, fighting spirit gone. Where just a moment before there had been the desire to provoke this petty bureaucrat, now there was exhaustion and emptiness. The interview had run its course, now it would only get worse. She would be forced to explain what it was that she did all day in the barn, and would, while struggling to find words to describe what she had been struggling with for over a decade without being able to master in the least, stammeringly explain the occupation she herself found a

compulsion and an obsession, never a passion or a plea-
sure but, rather, as gruelling as a chronic illness. *Frau*
Holst would ask her about successes, grants and exhibits
and bore her pen into the gaps in her biography. Up until
now, she thinks, she'd never lost her worth with Siana,
not once in the fifteen years of employment, only excep-
tions being her first encounter with Miklos, the real
boss, and this visit to the authorities, here in the world
of German order and virtue. It was demeaning, baring.
Like a whore.

She stood up and wiped her dress flat. Don't let anything show, she thought, just carry on, smile, as she'd
learnt at Siana's, in the big mirror of the back room
where the fashion designer had pushed her. 'Have a
look at yourself,' her boss said to her with that grating
accent, the origin of which she tenaciously guarded even
today, 'take a good look at yourself, girl, and when you
like what you see, then smile'—and she, Marga, had
worriedly raised the corner of her mouth—'Not at me,
at yourself,' Siana barked and with the razor-sharp nails
of her thumb and index finger squeezed her lower jaw.
'Your smile,' she continued, 'determines everything,
when you smile'—and here she pressed her nails into
Marga's skin—'you've got the client in your pocket, just
smile,' she said, 'and it's a done deal. But the most
important thing'—and here she pushed her fingers in
deeper so that her mouth opened as if on its own—'the
biggest challenge, dear girl, is getting the guy in that

moment to excuse his own investment. If you manage that, he'll become as soft as butter and, the boss whispered, you'll only have to smear him across the bread and he'll come back every week.'

Siana abruptly let go of her cheeks, leaving two painful nicks which slowly turned red. 'The rest,' she said, and looked at her fingers as if she were looking for traces of dirt, 'is routine and training but a smile, that's something you just cannot learn, not even from me,' and she stroked her hair. 'Such a talent is a gift,' she added after a little pause and pointed to the mirror where, Marga had finally torn her eyes away from the pearl-white and ruby-red, heavily perfumed woman, and saw a good-looking—now that the corners of her mouth slowly grew into a smile—in fact, an exceptionally good-looking seventeen-year-old girl staring back at the small, shy Magret who for the first time in her life was greeting herself. 'From this moment on, you shall have a different name,' Siana said, and she: 'Mira.' The clothing designer patted her shoulder and nodded, 'Not bad.'

Her own introduction into the fashion house, however, had unfolded quite differently. These images came back to her now as the employment agent looked at her somewhat pityingly, or was it rather disdain that Marga thought she could see, as if even this woman's small, greedy eyes would delve into her past to find, hidden beneath the deepest layers of nebulous memories, maybe the darkest image of them all, the one which inspired all the oppressive blacks, greys and umbra tones in her painting, those colours that had dominated so much of her work up until now, just as in the back rooms of the fashion house there had been one dominant light that made it nearly impossible to mark off a seam or to sew a clean line with one of the sewing machines, a job or a test she thought she had to pass under the severe eyes of her superiors, when a man of uncertain age—shiny suit, silk shirt, the defined neck muscles of someone who practiced karate—Miklos, the owner of the house who Siana had called to come in, led her through the changing room into the so-called dressing room, hidden behind the mirror of the former and a door which was opened by a concealed button that led onto a windowless corridor smelling of chlorine and through another door into the sewing room and right up to the big, iron-framed bed which, the second she walked in, struck her as out of place in a tailor's workshop.

On their short way through the hallway Siana had spoken with her colleague in that harsh, consonant-full language which Marga continued to believe was Russian, and even the organ that the man wriggled out of his fly and heaved up to her seemed Soviet-like in a way with its work-willing, swelling, almost sickle-shaped curve and it caused her unimaginable and, up until that point, unknown pain, even though the ways with which he,

Miklos, the boss, was introducing her, Mira, the new girl, into the routines of the fashion house were by then no secret. And yet the way he kicked more than led her into the doggy-style position, pushed her face into the pillow, and then wedged her against the iron bed-poles and with his no less steel-hard member began to drive into her, faster and harder until her head hit the bed-frame and the bedframe smacked against the wall, at which point the clothes hangers dangling between the carefully hung suits on the garment racks began to swing back and forth, caused the pain in her abdomen, which she already knew from her first amorous adventures sneaking out of the home, to suddenly take on an entirely new dimension which from then on would always carry the smell of the dressing room: slightly dusty like the suits, a little bit musty from the smells of all the different bodies that had tried them on, and impregnated with Siana's perfume, who now lay a hand on her back, right on the tiny scar between her shoulder blades where she, Mira, could feel the cool, almost calming, metal of a ring.

The scream that had caught in her throat came out as a thin whimper with a little bubble of spit. Siana stroked her back. 'Smile,' the smoky voice ordered, then all of a sudden from much closer, much softer: 'No matter what you feel.' The words vibrated against her ear or, maybe, it was only her body rebelling through another brighter and less spasmodic sound which with her free hand Siana picked from out of her lips in an incantatory gesture as if wanting to put her into a trance. Make an effort, she ordered, pushing against her jawbones and driving her finger into her mouth. The Russian groaned. Marga felt his sweat drip onto her ass and then she bit in. 'That's right,' Siana said, and continued to stroke her back. The hangers clattered and melded into the rhythm of the rider's massive body clapping against her buttocks. 'Only lust, no howling,' she heard Siana say from above her, the hand between her teeth tug, pull her head back and forth as if trying to wrestle a bone away from a dog. And then she did actually yelp. 'More,' Siana called, and drilled her finger in deeper, as if she knew that sighs of delight were lying dormant somewhere in her new girl's body. Mira felt nauseated, which brought forth another whimper; then she tasted blood. 'Better already,' Siana said, but all of a sudden from further away, muffled, as if heard through a wall, any minute, she thought, she would lose consciousness. The next cry came softly, almost cooingly from out of the depths of her bowels where she could still feel the Russian raging. More, she heard drone in from behind the wall, the clothes hangers continuing to bang in time, but within this chaos of voices there was no sound, just the pulse her body set to vibrating, like a metronome in an empty room which, once put into motion, makes perceptible what before had been quiet and empty, had not even been there.

Marga coughed lightly. 'I'm very sorry, but I've thought it over.' In reality, she explained, she was actually quite happy with her previous job. She turned to face the coatrack where *Frau* Holst had carefully hung her rain slicker on a wooden hanger. One next to it began to sway as she took her own down. She now remembered how a few days after beginning to work in the fashion house she had taken down all the coat hangers and thrown them into the dumpster, whereby she was promptly caught by Export-Ida, the cleaning woman who had once also helped clients in and out of their clothing before falling prey to beer, Elbstern Export, which first ravaged her face then her mind, so Siana had finally moved her from the inside to the outside, that is, to the cleaning and delivery service where she now served the fashion house's clients her favourite drink in slim glasses, placing the bottles on the thin paper napkins next to them, which some johns in their hurry forget to empty but which Ida takes care of on her own out by the dumpsters in the backyard which is where she happened to notice the new girl with the unusually blonde hair attempting to toss out all the hangers, and immediately told Siana who ordered them to be brought back to the racks at once. And so it went back and forth a few times till one afternoon Siana walked into the room and let the whole bunch of hangers crash to the floor. 'I decide what comes in and out of here,' the boss shouted; behind her in the hallway Export-Ida bent triumphantly over her cleaning rag. Her little girl's pranks were now over, Siana hissed, and walked once more with the heel of her pumps into the heap so that the wood and hooks wedged into one another just like the day of her introductory exam when Miklos, the pimp, had finally emptied himself inside of her with a grunt and hurled her shaking body into the pillow, a spot of blood slowly beginning to spread from her mouth. Siana had wiped her finger on the sheets, stroked her back one final time and said: 'Good.'

She'd jumped up, rushed into the bathroom and vomited into the toilet. By the time she crept back into the room on all fours, her spine as if broken, Miklos had disappeared. Siana helped her into bed, covered her up, opened up a drawer in the nightstand and pressed out three pills from a pack. 'Soon everything will be just fine again,' she said, and opened up Marga's lips. She swallowed the tablets together with a bit of bloody spit and the rest of her vomit. Her stomach contracted and for a moment she thought she would have to vomit again, then all of the sudden it was as if everything was indeed all right. She stretched her throbbing lower back. 'You have talent,' she heard in soft, almost affectionate tones from Siana, who then bent over her and gently placed those overly done lips on her mouth. It was the first goodnight kiss Marga had ever received in her life. She closed her eyes. So that is what her work in the fashion house would consist of, she thought; then, benumbed and spared the horror of the thought thanks to the tablets, fell asleep. On the empty, unmoving image into which she was immersed in her dream—the portrait of her life that one day she would have to paint—desire did in fact manage to overtake her but, maybe, less a feeling of craving than a form of pure greed, belated and set loose from everything she had known and thought until that point like an errant, rootless and timeless echo through her body.

On the threshold of the office she turned around one final time. 'Oh, *Frau* Holst,' she said, 'would you please say hello to your husband Friedrich for me, Mira, he'll understand.' She saw the clerk's stunned face then slipped out and softly closed the door. In the hall she caught a glimpse of her shadow in a mirror, stood still for a moment and observed herself. Her skirt clung to her thighs, created unfavourable wrinkles and revealed that she had gained weight over the last few months. On top of that it made her knock-kneed, and her high-necked blouse gave her a goose-like neck; she sucked in her stomach, stretched her back straight, would have preferably torn off the whole outfit right then and there. It'd be best, she thought, not to tell her boy anything about this particular defeat. And then, craving colour and light, she ran out of the job agency and straight into the next boutique.

But it's not just her expensive addiction to clothes that increases your distrust, that scrabbling and scraping through the city's stores on the hunt for ever-newer designs and cuts, which, worn only once, were then relegated to the corner of the wardrobe, that is, if she hadn't by then already taken the new and expensive piece, cut it up and pruned it into something else, which, after hours of work, would usually just end up half-finished and unusable in the old clothes pile for Goodwill.

From out of her purse, which you went through last night, came a receipt, she'd spent one hundred fifty big ones on that red rag that had more holes than fabric but you yourself had been waiting half a year for a new bicycle. Even the six-volume *Nature Encyclopedia* that you had asked her for to help you with your plant and dragonfly research until now has remained only an empty promise. But, rather than complain, you retreat into mist and silence. The large kolk in the middle of the plain, which is hidden behind an impenetrable belt of reeds and is where most of your finds come from, has always been where you escape, where you go to hide from oral exams, and your safe haven when you can no longer endure your mother's moods.

The floating bog mat bounces under your feet, giving you an almost somnambulist-like lightness; on your excursions homeward the village has always seemed further away than it is for the spongy, water-swollen land across which you spring tricks the wanderer into feeling that he's floating above, as opposed to trudging over, the mounds until, all of a sudden, after a few kilometres, upon a sturdier piece of the path exhaustion simply stops him, most of the time where there's not a single church tower or grain silo anywhere in sight, only the stubble rows of meadow ferns and the as if gnawed dams formed by the bristling lines of dead birches rising up out of the sea of rushes, punctuated by islands of cotton grass. Off in the distance —dull green in summer, beginning in November with the colours of the high fog—the monotonous, shimmering forests which ring the plain.

There the rain penetrates to your skin. The fog makes faces in the shrubs of heather, the already bare, often splintered branches, limb-like and tendinous. You turn around yet another time in the direction of the village but there is only grass, water, deadwood, now and again a stunted, crooked pine and behind that, again, the wave-like carpet of purple moor grass and beak-sedge in which the dark streams shimmer like veins. Wherever you look I am all that is left.

Keep walking, comes the hiss from out of the gurgling rifts. There's nothing for you at home, the birch skeleton grins. And even if she were still there, you hear whisper from under your feet, she wouldn't have time for you or your troubles, in the bath waving to you with wreaths of foam as she did, 'Darling,' she coos, 'will you do my legs?' Steam floats up against you, then the stupefying lavender smell, and then her breath, stale like most mornings when the night before she'd been at work in the barn, getting drunk on the cheap wine you'd had to pick up for her right before Ilse Bloch's shop closed, where she'd intentionally turned the bottle around in her hand as if she couldn't find the price tag.

Her upper body slides further into the water, only her knees stand out from the foam, you think of the mounds of moss in winter covered by the first powder snow and how the plain looks like a sea of those little crests, mound, hollow, mound, in between the soft clinking of the frozen stalks, its body endless against the horizon. She presses the razor into your hand and says, the only thing your mother would sell today are her legs. Her skin squeaks against the enamel as she stretches her foot into the air and blows cigarette smoke into your face; but in truth it's only rain mist, the fleeting shape of her figure rising in thin threads from out of the furrow. Keep moving, Dion, let me lure you further into the fog-image. The procedure has always been horrifying to you. She dips foam onto your nose with her toe, then hangs her other leg over the edge of the bathtub and sighs, 'Beautiful legs are more important to the art market than good paintings, so try hard!' You carefully lay the razor against her skin and make the first stroke, you know how to do it already, and how delicate you need to be when your concentration or her mood is touch and go. As accustomed, you let the razor glide downward, concentrating so hard that you begin to sweat, from the heat in the bathroom or anger you are not sure, as she writhes and yawns, 'You're good at this.'

As if you were a servant! you think, and jump onto the next hump, which streams water. Like a john to a hooker! the moor snickers. You stumble, catch yourself, walk on. Think: Bite me! a fern bush whispers. Say: Do it yourself. I agree, stop being her doormat, the scapegoat for everything, for her bad mood, her terrible art; even that scrape on her leg had somehow been your fault, the razor suddenly slipping over her ankle, or did you do it on purpose, the shaving cream turning red with blood?

'Idiot!' she'd yelled and sat up in the tub. Stunned, you stared at the drops running from her breast down to her navel. Again the sound of skin on the enamel, then her voice, metallic now, 'You're just like your father, a peasant!' She got up, pushed you out of the way and snatched the towel.

Something red sprays against your leg, not blood but a leaf of sundew you've crushed under the sole of your shoe. That rarest of moor plants withered already at the edge of the pool you almost walked into as if it had been late in autumn. Its delicate tentacles colourless and dried into a crust, the leaf crumbles between your fingers like a scab. Do you remember? The day after the accident with the razor on her shin there was only a scratch which could just have easily come from a sharp blade of moor grass, not even worth talking about.

Nevertheless, she was in a bad mood as she stomped through the rain with you to the pond, you once again with your umbrella on the stump, she naked between the rushes. She didn't wave to you, and hurried mechanically through her pantomime as if it were simply an annoying duty. The way she threw you her nightgown, fiddled with her hairclip and ploughed disgustedly through the water seemed to you as if it were all done for your sake, not hers, and so that day you played the old man more for her amusement than for your own, cotton grass stuck to your upper lip and into your ears and bumbling about in front of her on the broomstick, for she was hanging around with her stone face again, and in the afternoon was still out on the porch in her bathrobe, the only sign of life the billows of smoke coming out of her mouth until at last she moved her head, joined the game and mimed the old woman who smiles tiredly at you, sucks in her lips and mumbles, 'Darling, have you seen my teeth?'

But that morning the old game wouldn't have worked. Her bitchiness as a penalty for the small wound seemed spiteful and unfair, but was that what you were really mad about? As she came out of the water and reached for the towel you swallowed your anger, breathed deeply, and forced out, 'hI'm hsorry.' But half the night you brooded about what you'd really done wrong, and the further the minute hand moved across the dragonfly clock, the more you thought that it hadn't been your clumsiness with the razor that had annoyed her. No, Dion, it resounds from all sides in the grass, the reason she is unhappy is you!

She wrapped herself into her bathrobe and looked at you morosely. 'What?' she snapped, and punched your shoulder, 'What are you sorry about?' The rain dripped coldly into your open mouth. 'That maybe?' and pointed to the pond, then in an oar-like manner to the village, the house, out into the moor and, last at you. '*I'm* sorry about all this too!' She took hold of your chin and pushed your jaws apart as if she could squeeze a reaction out of you but not a single word emerged.

A branch whips you in the face as unexpectedly and brutally as she had hit you. You swing back, kick her out of your thoughts, the wood snaps, not a single leaf left on the dead shrub, you duck underneath. Your foot gets caught in the sedge, you fall and taste the moor. You would've liked to have a hug, at least a smile, the cream-greasy kiss, something that would have comforted you: Everything's okay, again.

The earth tastes rust-like and bitter, you spit it out, stand up and run on in your lonely defiance, for her love, Dion, or whatever it is you're looking for out here, is nothing but sound and smoke, a figment of your imagination, the fondling of a fog spirit, the coddling of the thorn bushes, and an icy wind which whispers sweetly into your ear a gothic poem in which the child rushes deep into the woods about the moor until he sees only sky and is swallowed up, the earth pushing water into his tracks, here and there a naked birch tree when he's turned to the left or to the right—which, in any case, no longer makes any difference—and the horizon only shifts further back, for he's strayed off the footpath which leads over dips and embankments and boards in the mud through the meandering water grasses from Rahse to Fenndorf and which, in the rain, becomes a labyrinth to even the most knowledgeable peat cutters, in which all of my directions look the same.

On the corner of Seitenstraße where the gallery is, she remains standing in front of an office sign: Sebastian Klingohr, Voice and Speech Therapy, Office Hours by Appointment, and a telephone number. A name like a punch in the eye, she thinks, and sifts through her purse for a pen but finds only empty cigarette packs, hairclips, a pack of Lexotax, a condom. Be happy that I'm look-ing after you, stutterer, the woman coming out of the door with her child seems to want to say to him, a pale, maybe ten-year-old boy with a pinched mouth and eyes which timidly examine her, Marga.

The mother, hardly older than she was, brushed past her into the street. Marga felt the suspicious glance at her body, her dress, which suddenly seems far too short, or was it the portrait in her hand that gave her away? She quickly wedges it under her arm and hurries on, but turns back around after a few metres. Should she at least have a look at the doctor's office? The woman drags her son across the street; between the parked cars he suddenly looks back, as if wanting to warn Marga one last time about the speech therapist. She can only mess everything up, she thinks, the way she grabs you, it's always wrong.

Indeed, memories from her own school days surged up that morning when, while making the bed, she found the copies of your presentation on the desk. What she held in her hands was not the preliminary exercise to an essay but proof of a greater difficulty. She only needed to glance over the closely scribbled pages to recognize the image of anxiety concealed in the lines, the confusion. She quickly followed the contorted sentences with her eyes. Although it was difficult to decipher the words in the chaos of proofreading marks and insertions and she could barely understand the connection between individual passages —not to mention the maze of letters on the pages which seemed much more like a complicated and abstract drawing made out of ciphers and arrows—there was an eloquence to the whole which was at the same time an abyss; something bottomless, almost possessed, spoke from out of the pages, and it called forth a deep uneasiness in her, almost like an illness, and she realized that you spurn her help precisely when you need it most, as there, in that battle, which you had waged upon the paper entirely alone.

Her watch showed a little bit before eight thirty, too late, she thought, it's already his turn. She rang her finger across the lines again, they slipped away and reappeared in another place and in a dissimilarly larger mess than she herself had ever managed. After half a page she gave up. She stood for a while indecisively and watched the dragonfly clock which now showed a little past eight thirty, so that the minutes in which she stood there thinking what was to be done seemed to her like a hold in time. How long had she been there thinking? Only now did she understand that the time on the dragonfly had stood still. She could still call the secretary and have Gorbach, the German teacher, come to the telephone. Or better yet, drive over there right away and, on some pretext or other, pick him up, a forgotten doctor's appointment, a death in the family ... in which family though, she wondered, then pushed the thought away, there's nothing worse than a worried mother pulling her child out of class.

And, in any event, she would have only been postponing his classmates' ridicule, a new attack from David, that wayward offspring of Gertrude Voss' who was also a newcomer, a city person with a Hamburg license plate and a second husband, the dentist, who had given her a tiny monster wilder than the village children who hit because their parents hit and would later start boozing because their fathers had already, as they say, drowned their frustrations in schnapps. David's way of harassing others, it had become clear to her when Dion was only in primary school, on the contrary, was well thought out, it was the kind of brutality that came from a good family.

It hasn't been that long since you asked your mother whether what David had said was true, that you were a whore's son. She had arranged a meeting with the principal where Gertrude Voss energetically came to her son's defence, her little David, who, thanks to her liberal upbringing, had learnt early on how to accurately judge his peers. Expressions like 'Mother hen' and 'Mother complex' flew from one side of the room, 'A mother's duty' and 'Mother's failure' from the other like bullets. You stood silently in the corner while David sneered maliciously. Eventually the director jumped up and pushed the bickering group out of the room, a public defeat for David Voss who had to apologize to you in front of everyone. But barely out of the door he punched you in the head so that the brunette mother grabbed the blonde, and the blonde the brown-haired offender by the arm and pulled them through the corridor where the words *Bootlicker*! here, and there *Whore*! and from other end *Mama's boy*! and *hBastard*! echoed, the latter being true, as everyone in the village knew that Gertrude Voss had not had David with the dentist but had brought him with her from the city, and at the end of the argument it remained an open question as to which of the two mothers was, in fact, more disreputable; you're familiar with the word *hooker* not only from leafing through the *H*s in the dictionary where it stands among good and wholesome words like *honour* and *hooray*.

The next day David Voss scored a hit in front of the class when he told his joke about your mother standing in front of the bargain bin at a seasonal clearance sale calling out: 'The only thing cheaper is me!' Again you felt the scream stick in your chest, but, at that moment, it was not directed against your archenemy Voss or your snorting classmates but against her, Marga, a suffocating rage driving you ever deeper into that mother-mire and mother-mess, into that *mother-moor* which for years now had been pulling you into its morass of letters, for alone the nominal connection to the word *mother*—this too you discovered in the dictionary—fills up at least three rows, from *mother hen* to *mother lode* to *mother's milk*, and David Voss isn't the only one to scoff, the entire village joins in with disapproving glances and whispers so that instead of a warm mother's heart beating inside her chest Marga has merely got a lump of calcified insults your teeth can only grind when you too would have a piece of love, which David Voss was full of, as was every other child in the village whose mother took them to music and gym classes, on the weekends to visit the grandparents and every summer to the seaside or at least to camp, and if thereafter still ailing then to doctors and for cures, like Tanja, whose mother, *Frau* Deichsen, spared no expense or effort to have her daughter's glass insides hardened and strengthened in special clinics even though, as everyone in the village knew, the illness was incurable, the gradual splintering of her bones unstoppable and in a few years' time she'd probably have to be in a wheelchair which is why every Wednesday the pastor's wife took her a hundred kilometres, to Hamburg, for therapy, but your mother, Dion, had never taken you with her to the city even once, there where healers for stutterers, the so-called speech therapists, were everywhere.

Every child, Dion, the dark water gurgles, has the wrong mother, and for life. You will never be rid of her—until she dies, her love will cling to you and after that, the old resentment, for no matter what she did for you, it will always have been too little or too much, will have been either neglect or invasion; the uncaring mother sews only discord, and the mother hen hauls you to the stutter-doc but neither one ever recognizes your true needs and worries, the seething just below the surface of your silence that you yourself would have had to break, or what else, if you don't say what you mean, she should have known that your German assignment had nothing to do with a practise essay, as she still believed that morning, for which she wouldn't have been any help to you anyway, she, the one who couldn't write, the one who with one simple mistake in a letter of her own name had managed to ruin her entire life.

And so you intentionally left the copies of your presentation lying out on the desk. She was supposed to see that for days you had gone through the dictionary in order to find as many *H*s as possible to plug into your ragged text with all its sharp-edged consonants. Had she really believed all that time it was really only about an essay? If it only had to do with writing and not with speaking, you would have had it done in half an hour, from out of the *effeff*, so to speak—and you hear the wind whistle through the pines and in it the sharp sound of the letter *F* which not only looks like a talon but takes up close to seventy-eight pages in the dictionary, from *fable* to *freak* and beyond, while your essential *H* takes up close to one hundred, and the gag of a letter *M*—*Marga, Moor, Mother*—muzzles you at seventy-five, which in the catalogue of alphabetical torture instruments, however, is outdone by claw-like *K*, *K* like Katthusen, a one-hundred-and-twenty page and entire-childhood-long catastrophe, no: accident—

And yet, no matter how you wheeled and whirled about the dictionary, your topic, 'The Lifecycle of Dragonflies', consisted of twenty-one letters, almost all of which choked you, and even in a whispered, *H*-word-and-sentence-stitched world no one would hear you; one way or another your writing always leads into the silence of the moorland and groves and into the water, which looks as deceptive as it sounds, for the letter *W* only seems to be warm and velvety. In truth it is a dark whisper and vibration from deep within the earth inviting you to waltz therein through overgrown vales, and the vapour which hangs above them too seems to want to stand and watch over you without barbs or thorns . . . all nonsense, a word-washing and language-delusion, for *W* with its five spikes is the most heavily armed letter in the alphabet, even deadlier than *Z* with its prongs or sharp-edged *K*, and yet, undaunted by death, you jump over the water onto the next island of cotton grass and run on through the wind and low-lying clouds out into the distance, the desert, into the overgrown and confusing land of words, ever further out to me.

'Marga!' Ute calls and floats towards her, elegant and airy as ever, her fifty-year-old face trimmed into a permanent late-thirty by the best surgeons of the city. A sophisticated perfume wafts about her together with a plain green silk; when there is nothing going on in the gallery, Ute goes next door to Chanel. She kisses Marga left and right with pointed lips and a seemingly forced smile. She had been meaning to call for a long time, she sighs, but everything's been so up and down. She points to the canvases still in bubble wrap leaning up against the wall. A new exhibition? The gallerist waves off the question. And what was happening with her paintings?

Marga insists, the small selection of paintings that, after long discussion, Ute had herself declared ready had consistently been forgotten over the last months. Marga wandered from the wall by the display window to the centre of the room and then into the rear of the gallery. She feels Ute's hand on her back steering her to have a seat but she pulls away and observes the new pieces with their gaudy colours. 'Coffee?' Ute calls to her. Marga lifts a piece of plastic film beneath which there is a woman's portrait schematized into four separate red colour-fields, one on top of the other like pieces of a puzzle, done in some kind of print process or other.

'Daniel Röcker,' Ute gushes, and is suddenly standing behind her with two cups in her hand. 'Difficult colours,' Marga replies. 'Red's in,' the gallerist says, takes a sip from her cup and points to Marga's new dress. 'Röcker was a master's student of Professor Wiepersfürth's,' she adds, she had allowed herself to be talked into presenting his graduation exhibition. Talked into, Marga thinks, the fact that she herself had been working at Ute—that cold-hearted wench—for years and still hadn't managed to get anywhere close to Wiepersfürth . . . a call would have been enough and she'd have been in, in the master's class, in a conversation, in life. She looks into Ute's face to determine what her relationship to this painter was, the name she thought she recognized. Ute gave a tight-lipped smile, her eyes guarded behind the polished glasses, any potential emotion hidden. The wounds which also ran jaggedly through her life, Ute's, were almost impossible to recognize any longer in the masterpiece that was her face, the worry lines and borders of sadness from the time when, as an aspiring art-critic, she had decided to go against her own dream to be a successful painter, had decided to go against becoming a mother too, expertly removed and painted over.

And Marga knows the sentimental longing she causes in the gallerist as a single mother, which is also quite possibly the reason why, in spite of the lack of sales, her work still hangs in the furthermost corner of the room. Ready for battle, she pulls the portrait of the dragonfly-boy out of its wrapping. Ute looks at it in surprise. Marga turns away, walks a few steps, looks at the new Pop-coloured exhibit and out of the corners of her eyes observes the gallerist who, with a face revealing nothing at all, is standing under one of the overhead bulbs which bathes the room in a soft, diffused light that made everything look a little bit better and a little bit more expensive than it really was. 'But that's Dion,' Ute says after a little while, and Marga feels a bitter triumph. 'Four thousand marks minimum,' she answers, 'and you show it to Wiepersfürth.' This time, she thinks grimly, it won't just be an honourable mention like three years ago when the art foundation of that Hamburger bank gave her that third-class award without any prize money or noticeable career effects whatsoever.

You stop yourself just in time in front of the suddenly gaping moor-eye in the grass and look down into the still, rain-swollen water. Remember that evening, Dion! the dark deeps seem to want to call to you, and therein lies the fleeting image you dive back into: how most of the night in the foyer of the foundation's headquarters your mother had leant on the wall by her painting, like someone waiting on a street corner for a blind date, and through her cigarette smoke had observed the guests strolling back and forth chatting and only occasionally casting a glance at the award-winning piece. They nodded to her and faded into the throng which had emerged around the winners. Marga energetically exhaled the smoke through her nostrils and grinned at you. 'You look good,' she said, but you had felt her hand tremble as she pulled the back of your suit straight, the suit that she, as she never tired of reminding you, had sewn just for the occasion.

You bend over the water. On the dully shimmering, slightly oily surface you see the pale shadows of your face. You'd looked like a window mannequin in that suit and tie, and it pinched your throat. You were hungry and weren't in the mood to play the mascot any longer. Your feet hurt from your hard leather shoes, the ones you always tried to avoid wearing, and the smile that she had practised with you in front of the wardrobe mirror the night before had frozen into a grimace. 'That's how we'll butter them up,' she had said, and with her fingernails pushed your cheeks together, and you opened your mouth and bared your teeth. 'Smile, don't threaten anyone,' she laughed, and growlingly bit your lip.

And yet she had long since become irritable. As you forced her to the buffet, she pulled the knot of your tie tighter and with her eyes indicated a woman who was hurrying over to the winner, a young, somewhat too-stridently dressed man with a dark head of hair, a fuzzy beard and white cowboy boots. She bent down to you and whispered, 'The old one is the gallerist Ute Hassforther. She's the one we've got to get.' And at that very moment the man turned around and looked over.

The door bursts open and startles her. She stares at the man who's suddenly standing in front of her in a bright blue shirt, two buttons open at his neck. 'Daniel!' Ute cries in surprise. Marga feels his eyes assessing her body from her feet to her neckline, where he pauses just a second too long. 'And so we see each other again,' he grins, she nods curtly, then a flutter of kisses on the cheek, Röcker winks at her over Ute's shoulder conspiratorially. Already at the vernissage, she remembers, he had winked at her swaggeringly, and even you, Dion, had noticed that something, as they say, was afoot.

From somewhere above you a light goes out. You turn around and see the sky torn open above the plain, behind the shreds of clouds a waxen, washed-out sun. Your limbs hurt from running and stumbling, they throb within your wet clothes which suddenly seem too tight as if your body had expanded during your flight and was now rebelling against its own skin, a feeling just like that evening you'd have so happily torn the boys' suit off your back. How you cursed her at that moment! You rip off your rain-soaked scarf and throw your knapsack into the grass. Yeah, you show her! you hear from the ground. She had simply left you for that guy after glancing at him all night as he strutted from one group to another, surrounded by journalists and cultural functionaries, while she just stood, for the most part alone, next to you by the wall.

Her head, she now remembers as she observes Röcker, had hurt from all the chain-smoking and the three Lexotax she'd taken, which had hardly helped to numb her dislike of the event at all. And her stomach had hurt from all the Sekt, she felt haggard and at the same time overfed by all the feigned compliments, she wanted to continue to devour the others' accolades and vomit them back; then she saw the prize-stud step out of the crowd and with a swing of his hips and a final glance in her direction disappear into the hallway to the toilets. 'Wait for me here,' she said, pushed her glass into your hand and pushed herself off of the wall.

Röcker uncovers his latest work. Beneath the film she recognizes the puzzle-woman, now in yellow. Ute takes the portrait out of its wrapping, praises the shifts in colour and the composition, and at the same time pushes the dragonfly-boy back into Marga's hand. She hides the painting behind her back, Röcker looks at her ass—the best of the night, first prize, he'd said while grabbing her in the bathroom stall. But now he whistles through his teeth, pushes a wet strand of hair off of his forehead and looks at Marga challengingly, 'No son today?' Ute looks from one to the other, astounded, 'You two know each other?' 'The bank,' Röcker nods. 'God! Of course!' Ute says somewhat too loudly, in her face at last a trace of tension. She tilts the canvas into the light, 'Really good!' she repeats, almost like an order. Marga feels forced into saying something, mumbles, 'I don't like yellow,' which is not a lie, as yellow stands right next to red on her list of colours to avoid, colours that touch the primitive instincts, in her colour-world yellow was children's rooms, the sun, the moon, the Star of David, roses on hospital tables, pus and death.

'I'll bring it in back,' Röcker turns and touches his curly-hair framed forehead with his index finger. 'But my stuff's hanging there,' Marga protests. One of the gallerist's eyebrows twitches. 'You clear the whole gallery for this shit?' Ute's features fall. Her gallery is neither a shop, she snaps, nor is the painting shit.

Your mother laughs, short and shrill, the same sound—half-doubt, half-attack—which had come that night from out of the stall. When after five minutes she still hadn't returned, you'd given up your post by her painting and walked up and down the buffet a number of times where it was so crowded that you were unable to snatch a single meat patty from in between all those bodies in their suits and evening dresses. You were unable to find a seat at the bar either, but did at least manage to nibble a few pretzel sticks. On a stool you saw the man from the foundation who at the beginning of the evening had welcomed you so arrogantly. Now he was raising his glass and toasting you. If you had lost your mother, he called over to you, heavy-tongued. 'His mother?' the man next to him had laughed, he had thought the little twerp was her bodyguard. The men guffawed and turned away. You had felt the pressure behind your eyes, the burning in your throat that grew from your stomach up to the knot in your tie which after a few tugs you managed to toss to the floor, and as you thought that any minute you would have to be sick, you ran into the corridor to the bathroom and, in front of the second stall, in the crack between the floor and the door, you saw the pointed, white cowboy boots between her stiletto heels.

At the sound of your hands on the door she started; first a timid knocking, then punches. Röcker froze, she took his hand and pushed it under her dress again but he pulled it back out and hissed, 'Shit, who is it?' She felt a great weariness, the certainty that she was finally done for when from outside she heard your voice, 'hMama?' At first a frightened child's question in the dark, then, after a short pause, hard and uninterrupted, the furious yell of an adult unable to be disappointed any further.

The man grunted, annoyed, pushed her away. She quickly turned and pulled his penis out of his pants, slid to her knees and began to suck, the smell of her own spittle clinging to his shaft, however, began to make her feel sick. Your fist again against the door, Röcker's curses, 'That's not going to solve anything now!', a fart from the stall next to theirs followed by a deep sigh, then the sound of water, the sound of the crowd in the foyer sloshing in between, everything muffled, clipped, as if your ears were suddenly stuffed; the effect of the pills caught up with her from one second to the next and levelled her with a feeling like falling. She buckled, then felt the desire, the antagonistic greed which had just shuddered through her, outside her body, tight, unyielding, like a tank threatening to crush her. Next to them the toilet flushed again, a lock snapped open, then your strange voice 'hCome hout hof hthere.' Röcker no longer hard, she pushed him away. A laugh erupted from her as he tumbled into the partition then broke off as quickly as it had come.

And yet it wasn't the faint, slightly drawn-out laugh that eventually dragged her out of her torpor—as you rub her face with your cotton-grass lips in the old-man-game—but a cold, splintering one. It echoes from the plain as you pull your jacket off and toss it into the grass. You look up, shocked, but realize it is only a creaking of deadwood in the wind that has deceived you, the hollow sound out of the silence into which you hurl your sweater, shirt and, in the end, even your pants.

Your jeans slowly sink into the black, under the ever-
stronger mist, shoreless-seeming lake, to which, on previous expeditions, you had never penetrated, no human
ear had ever heard the whispering of the distance, a
sound like the most delicate beating of wings over the
unmoving water, so dead and acidic that the birches
arising from it—which have barely made it into
crooked trunks and deformed branches—die, are split
in two by the wind, and their skeletal hands grasping
emptily into the sky remind you of a stunted and hopeless childhood; remind you of the large kolk which is
the end of all paths and where footprints simply lead
into the marsh but never back out again, that sluggishly
pumping heart of the high moor locked away by the
rushes, by the twisted, barbed-wire like undergrowth
and the unrelenting fog, the heart from which the
ditches and streams pull the water that secretly winds
for kilometres through the peat layers and only meets
the little river of the Jumme after hesitating through the
forests and bog myrtle, that river which meanders along
the edge of the village and then northward to the Elbe
but here arises under your feet from out of innumerable
veins deep in the earth at the highest point of the plain,
in the middle of the raised mounds and their rough,
filigree-like roofs of moss, like red shingled domes
growing ever-further out into the surrounding areas, less
than a millimetre a year and so silently that the first
and last sound a person would encounter over the not
cola- but amber-coloured water would be the flight of a

dragonfly as it buzzed alone through the desert, not so much a noise as a felt, as opposed to heard, sound of abandonment, which, as you walk into the water, breath held, tears apart like a membrane beneath your feet. And, as step by step and with ever-darkening skin you sink slowly down into me, for one moment everything around you and within you becomes completely still.

She remembers the scene exactly—how Röcker had tried to push his way past her out of the stall but she had blocked his way. 'Are you kidding?' he'd hissed, 'Let me out of here!' She turned her face away and leant into the corner where she could smell the cigarettes on her breath wafting against the wall, his aftershave on her upper lip, and was disgusted by both. For a while she listened to her pulse waver in her ears, quick, overlapping beats, before the chaos of voices from the foyer streamed in. From somewhere the sound of a faucet dripping, a hand dryer, then, suddenly, very close, a sound like the ripping of cloth. Röcker opened the door and stumbled away. She quickly closed it back up and locked it.

'What's wrong, Dion?' she asked quietly, 'can't you even leave your mother alone while she's taking a crap?' Again the ripping sound followed by a scraping and a kicking, then a black trouser-leg slid under the door. 'Why aren't you by the painting?' Her exhaustion distorted the sentence, and it sounded mechanical. 'hIh hate hyour hpainting,' she heard stuttered from outside the stall, more painstaking and tortured than she'd ever heard it before. She closed the toilet lid, leant against the tank and closed her eyes, felt the overwhelming desire to sleep, to withdraw from everything. The anti-anxiety effect of the pills had lulled her into a forced apathy which, nevertheless, was liberating, even intox-icating. Soon her thoughts would be louder than the voices from the lobby. He must hate it, she thought leadenly. Maybe she had finished this painting—which she had begun ten years ago but after a short phase of almost obsessive work had once again abandoned—for the contest only so that you, Dion, would be able to hate her, your mother. Wasn't that the end goal of all of her struggles? Even if she herself had disappointed you and lied to you for over a decade, in her painting she told the truth, more genuinely and brutally than she ever would have been able to put in words.

It wasn't her talent or her technique that the jury had found particularly interesting, but her weariness, a cyn-icism that filled them with bitter satisfaction. Further-more, the event that had inspired the idea was a decisive point in her life: just a few months after moving to Fenndorf and seven-months pregnant, the peat workers working in the ditches with the excavator uncovered a body. She herself never saw the corpse and paid little attention to the whole affair but found herself unsettled and disgusted by the villagers' delight in such horror stories. For days, she now remembers, Dion's father couldn't stop talking about it. The dead body had looked him in the eye as if it were still alive, he stammered at the dinner table the day of the find, fork shaking in his hand. Nights when he awoke he pressed against her from behind, moaning about hearing the dead body whimper from the pain; during the body's excavation the bucket had torn off a hand, which, however, the archaeologists managed to salvage, completely intact, they said, with a verifiably broken bone at the second knuckle of the index finger which stoked speculations of a violent death, the body there in its damp, but abacterial grave, protected from any inflow of oxygen.

The local paper talked about the sensation non-stop and even printed a dark picture of the moor cadaver, its mouth—even the contour of its lips, she thinks, were noticeable—half open, as if in the middle of a scream or solidifying precisely at the moment of death. From the village gossip and the newspaper, a living body began to take shape in her mind in an unsettling and exciting fashion, the image of an emaciated child, skin tanned and charred from the humic acid, likely to be more than a thousand years old, the article stated, and in the next few days and weeks they would show the withered tendons and muscle fibres on the bony limbs, the leathery face with its petrified fear of death and even the boy's shrivelled genitalia which led the specialists to estimate his age at the time of death to have been between twelve and fourteen.

The coroners who examined the mummified body found additional signs of violence, strangling and cut marks on the throat and a dislocated shoulder; in addition, in the area surrounding the pit they found the threads of a cord, which, according to the examiners, could have been used to drag the deceased by the neck before it was severed by the excavator. Even his last meal could be reconstructed through examination: from the stomach of the drowned—or otherwise executed—young boy they retrieved three apple seeds, which led the scientists to conclude that he must have died in either autumn or winter. Which in turn led to the fact that in the village grocery where Ilse Bloch enjoyed undisputed first rights to all the day's news the rumour that a cold-blooded child murderer had lived among the ancestors of the present-day Fenndorfers soon began to make the rounds.

The image of the sunken boy began to follow Marga everywhere. She saw his face and toothless mouth staring up at her from the dark dishwater, in the sad office where she sat with the bills, his brittle and leathery skin wrinkling in her hands instead of the paper, and one night, in a turbulent dream, the peat cutter whom she had just married lobbed a dark infant into her lap with a shovel. She opened her eyes, listened to her body and laid her hands on her stomach which had begun to bulge out into a kind of dome, silent and motionlessness as within a coffin.

Her body became heavy and hot. She felt the damp sheet coil around her thighs and pull her down into the mattress, away from the man snoring next to her, and into a soft, lubricious dark. She kicked away the cover, stood up and went into the bathroom. Once there she stood before the mirror and observed her body which with every passing day grew more out of shape; after the birth of her child her life too, she thought, would become deformed, it would jam and swell into a monotonous and endless routine between kitchen, office and the child's room, not to mention her husband's beer-bitter kisses which she only tolerated so that, once the brief surge of his passion had ebbed, she could indulge in her thoughts, most often nights in the work corner she had set up for herself in the barn with all the tools, next to the old wood-burning stove across from the dust-covered window that had once been a door but now, even with sunshine, cast an even light onto her work wall that was perfect for painting.

She stretched herself in front of the mirror but her once-so-slender thighs, where just a few months ago everything had still been in order, remained an unsightly bulge. She touched her tight, pointy breasts which, she imagined, would soon become swollen teats, then squeezed her stomach which would not let itself be pushed away and instead protruded out between her hands. At a fork in the old rural road between Fenndorf and Rahse lived old Pettersen; she had once been a nurse and now and then earned some extra money by working out of her kitchen or, if you like, office, that, people said, consisted of only a pallet and some out-dated medical instruments with which she freed young girls, secretly brought to her by their mothers, from the results of their trips to the peat diggers' cabins.

If only a few months ago, she continued to imag-ined, she, Marga, had gone along the road one night or the path through the moor, through the dark, and over to her, that by-now-ancient old woman who even today would have accepted the bundle of bills and in return pumped in a solution of lye which without any further ado would have got rid of the problem and fixed the irreversible mistake she had made when already on her third date with him, Dion's father, she'd let herself be conned into an engagement . . . she pulled at her wed-ding ring but it wouldn't slide back over her swollen knuckle. Even her own hands, she thought, and pun-ished her reflection with a disparaging glance, were no longer the magical tools of a painter nor, as Siana in a rare display of sentimentalism sometimes called her girls, Messalina, but the paws of a mother animal.

She could have also taken a knitting needle. Simply poked out the steadily growing and oddly shaped body which only a few months ago had still been an easy-to-remove bundle of cells, barely human, probably insen-tient, and which, once pricked, at some point would simply have bled out of her, as it would even now at this rather advanced stage, she thought, everything would most probably just drain out of her belly, even if, of course, not without a little pain, maybe a bit of fever, some serious inflammation . . . there it would be with eyes already or the beginnings of eye-sockets, a white membrane looking up at her out of the waste basket, blind, but at that point—long before its first experience of light—banned for ever to the dark, maybe even an arm or two rising out of the muck, a little foot, a clump of cells in the form of a head, the sight of which would doubtless cause her to fall unconscious, either from pain or loss of blood, just like the girl from the fashion house last year, Nadina, who had come from Argentina hidden below the deck of a cargo ship behind mounds of unripe fruit and who Siana had christened Naranja after feeling her breasts, firm and fleshy like two oranges. 'The best tits in the whole neighbourhood,' she'd said and here Marga had had to agree with her boss as the girl was truly a prodigiously endowed beauty, the reason why already just a few months after her start in the fashion house Naranja or Nadina got pregnant from a client or one of her string of lovers who sometimes waited for her in front of the shop smoking, a dilemma that did not escape Siana's vigilant eyes, there was no other way she, Marga, could explain why the Argentinian did not allow herself—though it probably had to do with the fear of being thrown out or maybe simply a lack of money—to seek out a professional like old Pettersen, but instead, grabbed the knitting needle herself, alone at home and numbed by one of the strong joints that, even at work, she incessantly smoked.

Freed by the drug from the pangs of conscience and doubt, she had boiled the needle in hot water, as she told her, Marga, in a bar a few weeks after having been fired, incidentally, as if passing the tip on to someone who was carefully preparing her own tool to introduce into herself, straddling a chair, Naranja continued, feet wedged into two chair-backs and tied down with belts so that you don't close your legs as a reflex, then you slowly probe, you'll feel it when you're there, Naranja said in her heavy, almost incomprehensible accent, greedily inhaling the resinous smelling smoke. 'But do it right or she'll throw you out, too, the old witch,' she said, meaning Siana who had also had to bleed in order to cover her illegal employee's two-week-long hospital stay, and in cash, too. Marga ordered another round of whisky-colas from the waiter—who kept grinning at them—and after that woman-to-woman talk never saw Naranja, the beautiful, black-haired Latina with the orange-breasts, ever again.

Disturbed by these memories that night your mother went closer to the mirror, sucked in her abdomen, then abruptly pressed it out again and tightened her pelvis in a jerky staccato until her diaphragm began to burn. But what was in her stomach would not let itself be pumped away. For a while she stood there motionless and just observed the white surface of her skin, then she turned the lamp above the mirror against the wall so that in the half-shadow the curvature of her body seemed to smooth out. She took your father's razor, fished the blade out with a pair of scissors, cleaned it with a few sprays of his aftershave then put it back into place. In a vertical then horizontal line, which crossed at her navel, carefully and with utmost concentration, like applying a delicate colour which can either complete or destroy a close-to-finished canvas, and breathing deep into the pain, she cut her skin into the shape of a star in the way one cuts an orange at the stem in order to peel it better.

The sticky blood immediately transformed the simple red cross on its white background into a complicated shape which then branched out into the most delicate strands all the way down to her pubic hair where she could feel its warmth and stickiness begin to tickle and itch, an urge she at first withstood but then, as the stimulation turned to arousal, gave in to, initially with hesitant, apprehensive touches until the blood mixed with the dampness of her vagina on her fingertips and she pushed her finger in deeper, then pulled it back out, then inserted a second, and then third while staring at the wound in the mirror, which began to swell slightly with her movements and seemed to open and close as if the silent whisper of a mouth salivating in tiny drops. She bit back any sound. She heard the bed creak, followed by your father's soft snores.

She continued to watch herself for some time, holding her breath, the still, dark, trickling painting of her mutilated stomach, then she wiped everything away with a piece of toilet tissue, washed her hands, stuck a plaster across the cut and tiptoed into the kitchen where she poured herself some wine and smoked at the open window although her doctor had advised her against doing both. She pulled on her oil-smeared work jeans, a jacket, turned out the light and stole across the yard into the barn, disgusted and at the same time attracted by the idea that the boy in the moor had been dead for one thousand years while his body, however, had remained in the same tight skin of childhood from which there was no escape, all those nameless desires unredeemed and all the questions his mouth at the moment he sunk down into the marsh had formed in a scream, which would never disappear, unanswered.

She made room in her work corner between the equipment, nailed a canvas up on the wall, mixed a narrow spectrum of red, brown and black colours in some small plastic cups and arranged the light to shine onto the dully shimmering white. For a long time she didn't move, she simply sat there and stared out into the night where already a bright line had begun to glow in the sky. Then she began to paint. Layer after layer of dark and muddy colours, the smoothed edges of which did not seem to thrill any of the art and experts of the jury who had chosen her painting, until over there on the pond the sun came over the alder grove, and in the breaking morning, with a hurried hand, pinched eyes and, as if caught in a scream, half-open mouth she painted the departure of her child in the moor.

You immediately begin to sink. Below yourself you feel the sluggish weight of the metre-thick peat moss, the heavy, fat skin that embraces you. I enclose you in water, earth or a mixture of both: damp topsoil, soft tree roots, bifurcated arteries above half-rotten branches like bone, and further down the heart of the deep: pulpy, cold and pulsing. Only two hundred years ago the residents of Fenndorf feared me, me, a black, slimy beast that lived beneath their houses and devoured their children. A thousand years ago their ancestors would place clay bowls full of food into the wet graves of the dead in order to appease my hunger. In me others saw a meat-eating plant whose shoots they had to hack off, those shoots that would grab their possessions, their bodies and their souls. Today the blades of the peat machines, the same ones your father used to run, dig up to one metre down into my innards and then dismember, dry and stack them in gloomy pyramids like pagan tombs which tower for an entire summer in the plain, in no time plundered and sold off, at one time, to farmers as fuel for their damp houses, and today to weekend gardeners for their rose bushes.

Drained, punctured and ploughed I lie like a black cadaver in the landscape, covered by festering craters and manges of heather, with a boardwalk for an artificial spine above my pacemakered heart, flooded with water from which they filter out the manure that seeps over from the fields with dams and hedges as if I were on dialysis. They close up the drainage ditches, remove the birches from the peat moss plains and put the moor frog back into the grasses, which soon die off again in the faeces of the ducks for which the village ponds have become too small. They drive the moorland sheep across my face, those sheep that are supposed to lick my wounds, eat up what should not grow: boils from the surrounding woods and meadows, beech shoots, daisies, the couch grass everywhere . . . they even had to fell a stunted little apple tree which had been sown by the wind, by hikers' picnic binges or by the deer which, where once the poisonous sundew glowed, now pull up the fields of clover. Biologists, ecologists, zoologists and botanists gather round my deathbed like an army of doctors sent to resuscitate me with complicated machines to measure the acidity of my body fluids, the pH balance of my skin and the temperature of my insides; and still, in spite of all of their bandages, the tubes, pumps and feeders from their laboratories, I collapse into a fever, bleed, lose weight, and move on to death with a rattle.

And yet my pain is as old as their fear of my voraciousness. Too dry to navigate, too wet to walk, even two hundred and fifty years ago scholars believed in my hermaphroditic nature: neither water nor land, neither alive nor completely dead, desolate and yet in constant transformation, barren yet full of valuable testimony to past; and so they measured and traced my body with its water-soaked fossils and in their books described me as an 'emission from the sea'. Earlier I was the indomitable monster before their doors, today I am their costly museum—there is a pay meter in the parking lot for the upkeep of the paths and the support of the nature conservation association, the information sheet is free.

You flail, try to escape, fight against the being taken in, as angry as you were that evening of the artists' award ceremony with Marga when you'd torn off your suit, there you wanted to get rid of your mother, here you want to shake off the ghost of the moor, the horror story of sinking and drowning within which you had got hopelessly lost, still Marga had not come out from the toilet, left you half-naked and standing in front of the stall together with the pitying glances of the peeing men. There's no escaping this nightmare, Dion, so keep still, stop your howling, you are deep below with me now, your body almost forgotten, soon it will only be a malleable memory of dark colours, old fears and half-conscious thoughts like in that praised painting of your mother's, that gloomy depiction of an abortion or still-birth which, that time in Fenndorf, she remembered as she heard your fists against the stall door once again, she had almost sold while here at the foundation where the collectors and gallerists of the city had gathered no one seemed interested at all.

A Dutchman, a tourist of all things, one of those who in the weeks after the finding of the cadaver had come sneaking about the house on the Heidedamm and, throwing curious looks into the atelier, had offered her a hefty sum. The curious came from near and far and even with buses across the border. They made a pilgrimage to the overgrown track where the peat wagons had once been, to the ditches, looked a few seconds long into the pit which had long been battered by the peat workers' excavators, and then wandered aimlessly through the village and directly into the clutches of Ilse Bloch who in those days had not only turned the moor corpse into a business but also the high point of her life, really giving the story her all, suddenly teeming with moor victims and the visitors stood hanging on her every word while she pushed overpriced drinks and bags of provisions over the counter together with a map of the surrounding area which she of course had marked with the places she believed the villagers' forebears to have sunken and drowned.

Even the Dutchman had been one of the ones that couldn't get enough of the horror of the moor. All of a sudden he was there in the barn and looking at the painting she had been working on for days, mostly at night or as soon as she knew her husband was in the peat-pit, with greedy eyes. The tourist—a lanky type in hiking shoes and a raincoat—had haggled for the picture in English and in the end had laid a bundle of bills on the table, when suddenly your father came through the door. What was she up to? he asked her and looked at the stranger. 'I'm working,' your mother answered. 'I earn the money for us,' he yelled, swept the money off the table and trampled it into the dirt. His child, he added and pointed to her stomach, would live from *clean* money. Dirty money, he snapped at the Dutchman. The latter bent down, scraped up the bills, handed them to your father and stammered: 'No, no, it's not fake. It's from the exchange office.' She turned and began to dab away again at her picture. From out of the corners of her eyes she saw how her husband's well-proportioned features, which she had once found desirable, before she could see the bleakness behind them, distort. He grabbed her arm and tore her off the stool. 'And what that was supposed to be?' he growled and pointed to the painting. Then he spun her around and pushed her to the door. 'You monster!' he thundered, he had planted his child in a monster, she remembered how even when he was angry, Dion's father, he spoke of plants and seeds, the farmer. The Dutchman stared, unfolded his map and said: 'Yes, monster!' Show me where! Your father roared and kicked both the monster and the monster-hunter out of the door which in the days to come was soon blocked by a heavy padlock.

One night she had broken a windowpane with a towel wrapped over her fist and opened the door. The portrait hung untouched on her work-wall in the dim light of a crescent moon in which, as she looked upward as if through a black, half-transparent skin, she could recognize the hidden side which was only revealed to those on earth who stared too long into the abyss of their dreams.

She taped cardboard in front of the window and stirred new colours in the crusty cups. After just a few brushstrokes she noticed that the dark excitement that had earlier spurred her on and sharpened her senses had suddenly changed into indifference. The subject now made her sick, she found it pathetic and its extremity shameless, she was angry she hadn't foisted it on the Dutchman who had offered her a decent amount of money. She tore the canvas off the wall and threw it into the corner where the portrait of the moor-child corpse soon disappeared and was forgotten under other sketches and unfinished paintings.

Only ten years later—due to a lack of ideas when sifting through the mountain of trash in her atelier looking for something to use for the Hamburg Foundation contest—did it find its way back into her hands. In just a few days she had it ready, indeed more skilfully than before, but more out of a sense of duty to her overdue success and, outside of Dion's father, the Dutchman and maybe Ute Hassforther, so she thought as she lifted herself off the toilet seat, only the boy seemed to have understood what was concealed in the mixture of colours: your child's body pierced by sharp-edged beams or boughs and covered with roots or a network of veins and coiled up into a creeper like an umbilical cord, eyeless, without hands, and with an abstract, not quite formed or already wiped out, face, an expression between sleep, forgetting and a thinly brushed longing for shape and for world, still becoming or already gone out, almost, but not quite dead before you had even begun to live.

'I don't want you to be my mother any more,' she heard your voice say from outside the bathroom stall door, frighteningly clear and without any stutter at all. When she finally unlocked the door she found you standing in your underwear and staring at her wide-eyed out of eyes swimming with rage and tears. She fell down to you, leave me alone! you pushed her away. In your voice a hard and distant tone. She pulled the trampled trousers from out of the crack under the door, pulled your jacket back into shape and tried to put you back into your suit. You held onto her and bit her hand. Her slap echoed through the coldly white-tiled room. She immediately regretted her slip-up. 'My poor darling,' she whispered and bent down to kiss away the red welts from your cheeks, but you turned away and bared your teeth so that she thought she could already hear the cry for help which in the next moment would break out of you and draw people in droves. She had almost put her hand across your mouth until she understood that you were not screaming, but smiling, tortured all the same just like she herself had once smiled in front of the giant mirror in the fashion house when Siana had shown her how to welcome life.

She followed your eyes and saw Ute Hassforther standing in the doorway. 'A little bit of a mishap,' Marga said and pointed to the toilet, 'Too high!' The woman locked at her and nodded. 'We often forget children's perspective,' she said, and for a moment her face seemed clear and soft. Then, as if remembering her role, which allowed for no sentimentality, her features froze again, she wiped away a piece of lint from her skirt and left.

Marga stuffed you back into your suit. 'Now you've really screwed up,' she hissed and closed the upper collar button. Then she pushed you to the door.

When you both came back into the foyer, the gallerist was standing in front of your mother's painting. She quickly let go of you, slowed her pace and straightened her dress which had been wrinkled in the scuffle. Then she wandered over to Ute Hassforther as if by chance, lit a cigarette and acted as if she were looking at her own work. From the corner of her eye she saw how an eyebrow twitched in the woman's face but otherwise showed no judgement at all. She could feel your eyes in her back, or was it Röcker's contemptuous glance, leaning as he was now with another young woman against the bar, she thought all the eyes in the room were on her as the gallerist bent down in order to more carefully observe one of the smoothed points and finally said, 'Not bad.'

From the other side she felt your look, angry, appalled, almost mocking, the same expression as the day she was putting the finishing touches on her painting and suddenly you were standing behind her, eyes like slits, the corners of your mouth drawn. 'What do you see in it?' she had asked you defensively, already awaiting a hurtful response. You shrugged your shoulders although in the canvas you had recognized a lot, indeed much more than you had liked. The bloodygrimy mixture made your chest constrict, your heart beat faster and caused a wave of heat to grow through you like a fever. You gave the feeling the colour brown, a moor- or cola-brown, which among all the dirty umbra tones was the one colour in the picture through which a kind of light flowed, like in the pools when a ray of sunlight pushed into the deep and stained the water amber so that there, where the layers had been scratched away or abraded with a wire sponge, you discovered a delicate, parchment-like, at points almost see-through-like structure that reminded you of your collection of dried dragonfly skins standing in rows in the glass preserve jars on your shelf. You had turned around, walked back to the house, and holed up in your room. When she called you down for dinner, you had laid the exuvia of a green hawker on her plate, the most beautiful and largest specimen from your collection, and looked at it pleadingly as if that awkward moment in the life of the dragonfly could take place again, that moment when the internal pressure increases upon the larva, the skin splits open and the insect is forced out into freedom from all the dark years underwater and into its one and only summer over the moor.

'Yummy,' Marga grinned, and blew the shell off her plate, but then scooped it up with her spoon and held it up to the lamplight. Every detail of the grown insect was visible already, the segments of the rod-shaped abdomen, six long, three-legged limbs, the beginning of four wings, even the mandibles. On the head two transparent bubbles had formed the hollow of the eyes, and behind them, on the back, its shell was slit and the air was caught in a tiny opening; the little legs began to quiver as if at any moment the empty dragonfly would lift into the air. 'Like a little palace,' Marga whispered, suddenly fascinated, and you nodded triumphantly. Then, holding your breath, you had both bent over the artwork, sought each other's eyes and at that very moment thought the same thing. All of a sudden the exuvia fell off the spoon, maybe because of her breath, and broke into two pieces on the edge of the plate. When you tried to shake the skin carefully into your hand, it broke apart. 'hYou hbreak heveryhting!' you yelled, threw your head back and stamped the ground a number of times as if in so doing you could hurl the words out of your throat. She pulled you to her but the brown feeling turned into red and with balled fists you ran away from her and up the stairs. 'But you have a hundred of them!' you heard her yell from the kitchen, hurt, then you slammed the door and pushed the bed against the wall so that in the crevice where you had wanted to escape there was no longer room for even a finger.

It's called 'Moor'? Ute Hassforther had asked doubtfully and tilted her head to the side as she looked at the
little sign with the painting's title and related information. Marga saw you standing close to the gallerist, your
face now narrow and hard, everything childlike gone.
On the evening she had broken the shell, you had suddenly appeared so foreign to her, almost an adult, that
she was afraid. It was, she remembers now, the first time
that you had ever locked yourself in your room; until
then she hadn't even known that there was even a key
for the door. She had come to it multiple times and
knocked softly, but even when she rattled the door handle the room remained worryingly still.

She went into the bathroom, swallowed two Lexotax,
warmed up the rest of the everything-soup in the kitchen
and put a plate in front of your door. Then she went over
to the barn in order to improve a few spots of her painting, which had just occurred to her. When she came back
to the house around midnight the door was still closed
and the plate full. 'Goddamn stubborn!' she yelled, a bit
confusedly, tongue furry from the cigarettes and wine
and sticking to the roof of her mouth. She picked up the
plate, staggered through the dark hallway and bumped
her head against a corner. A whole bottle of wine had
been a bit too much of a good thing; however, the alcohol
together with the Lexotax had indeed made her more
courageous with her final touches and she was happy
with the results. But now her skin felt numb, her steps
unsteady and her movements as if remote-controlled.

And as she came into the glaring light of the kitchen in the plate she saw a mealy, rotten mass. Her hand began to shake and the mixture fell over the edge of the plate, tiny legs swarmed about her joints, broken wings flickered, torn tails, beady eyes stared from out of the pulp of crushed shells. The plate smashed on the floor, shards and skins shooting out. Moaning she lunged up the stairs, which suddenly felt as steep and wobbly as a ladder. She rattled the door. 'Who the hell do you think you are?' she screamed and pounded her fist against the wood. Only after a few seconds did she realize she was standing in front of the entrance to the attic. She turned around, stumbled down the steps and at the end of the hallway threw herself with all her might against the door of your room, which burst open so easily and willingly as if it had never been locked, your empire behind it open to her for the entire night, as welcoming as ever. She slid over the rolling preserve jars, was caught by the bookcase and stared onto the empty bed. Her boy had hidden himself in the crevice between the mattress and wall, arms at his side and head retracted, a long, thin bundle like a rolled-up blanket. 'Who the hell do you think you are?' she shook you, 'What did I do to make you like this?'

How broken he suddenly felt. Almost bodyless, she remembered, he had simply hung there limp in her hands—and she looked from you to the gallerist and then to her painting, then finally back to you, alarmed and cringing, for once she had imagined the skin of the child's corpse to be just as brittle and rotten, he whose skeleton had long since decomposed in the acidic peat, whereas the moor water had preserved the skin and tissue, even the fingernails, so well that a team of specialists speculated that it could have been the victim of a ritual murder, as Dion's father had read aloud from the paper one morning where they had dedicated an entire page to the find. Thanks to carbon dating, a measurement of the carbon remaining in the cadaver, they had been able to backdate the time of death of the boy's body—in the meantime floating in formaldehyde in the Institute of Pathology—to around the second century before Christ, the Ice Age, where he had most likely been strangled and then thrown into a pit, a method which, the author surmised, suggested child sacrifice, a rather gruesome but at that time not-unheard-of rite to the honour or pacification of the gods, whereas the archaeologists and doctors did not want to decide whether the wounds which could be found in the genital area, the tears in the tissue and abrasions, had been caused by the improper process of recovery, by the pressure exerted from the earth during the body's long storage at a depth of three metres or by sexual abuse during or before the sacrificial ceremony, the more so as among various Ice Age Germanic peoples, moor executions were a common retribution for sexual crimes or the refusal of military service, as well as for sodomy, which spoke precisely for the so-called retribution thesis; in other words, the scientists supported the hypothesis that such pre-Christian sacrifices could have had important social and juridical meanings, for, as the Roman historian Tacitus helpfully noted in his *Germania*, cowards and the battle-shy as well as the physically defiled, and so the article concluded, were thrown into the swamp, and especially the morass, which, furthermore, was then covered with wattles.

She remembered how with that sentence Dion's father had angrily folded up the paper and snorted, 'Just what is such idle talk supposed to mean?' She had laid her hands across her stomach through which, as so often lately, a little quake had passed and looked over to the pond where evening slid across the plain like a black wall. 'They fucked him beforehand,' she said, turned off the gas flame under the pot with the soup and placed a bowl on the table. Once back in the barn she had stretched herself out on the discarded sofa with the chirping metal springs, let her head fall to the side and stared for a long time at the oil painting she had just recently begun to make inroads with, upon a background of far-too-much white a pair of brown strokes crossing, awkward and aimless; Ute Hassforther alone must have recognized some kind of special talent there. Eventually she turned to your mother, looked her up from head to toe and asked: 'Where, Marga, did you study?'

She winced. Her answer, she thought, would spoil everything, she would lose the chance she had been waiting for the whole night, as she wouldn't be able to name any academy or school, couldn't show off with any theories or formulate any hypotheses about contemporary art. She hadn't read any books and hadn't immersed herself in the lives and passions of any of her models in all those years, with the exception of Füssli's *Nightmare* hadn't even *had* any models, only the stillness, the dust and the rust of memories in a barn where the rainwater slowly dripped down her work wall.

'hSimphly hin hthe hmoor,' she suddenly heard the familiar breath behind her, turned and saw you quite close. 'Then we'll soon be in business, young man,' Ute Hassforther said, shook first your, then your mother's hand and handed her a business card. 'You should call—I can use Marga, no?' she smiled and then swished off. Marga waited until the gallerist had disappeared into the crowd of guests being pushed through the revolving door and out into the night before snapping 'Cunt!' behind her with bared teeth, then she bent down and undid the top button of your shirt. 'Clothes make the man,' she grinned, but her lips were tight and seemed bitten through.

'Leave the painting alone!' Ute grabbed her hand, 'I'll see what I can do with it.'

'No!'

Her voice like a cut ripping through everything, the ever-painful point of her spine between her shoulder blades the last thread tying her to her gallerist, in Ute's do-gooder face the mask of empathy, which really was always just pity, then finally so decisive and powerful a movement that she stumbles back and for a moment long saw unadorned contempt—or was it jealousy?—staring back at her from Ute's eyes. 'You should stop painting Dion over and over again,' she says, clears her throat, an eyebrow twitches, then her mouth, then everything goes back to its right place. 'You have been stagnating for years,' she added, 'and it hurts the boy too.' 'The art's still hanging in back,' Daniel grumbles, who is suddenly standing next to her again. 'On Monday someone from the press is coming,' and he glances annoyedly around, 'and everything's got to be ready by then at the latest.' Marga turns on her heel; with an overwhelming clarity in her inner eye she sees the picture of how she leaves everything behind, painting, the fashion house, Fenndorf and, finally, the mother within her who manages to just barely hold everything together.

I break open your casing, work through your skin with my iron-yellow and acidic water. From out of your throat a final surge of air, far above you a bubble bursts. A childlike and slightly buttery smell streams out of you and you are ashamed for not having washed yourself that morning but I unhesitatingly take you into my mouth all the same. There you finally relax your muscles, let me in, remember sinking downward from out of a time without any images, led into an unconscious darkness, free from fear. Only those traces of language on your tongue that never found the right sound still taste bitter, then you forget your stutter, all the insults it has caused you until now, lose the names of all those feelings you have never uttered. I put them in order, gather all the shreds of your sentences, pull one after the other out of you to lay them around your body, a skin made of words, as many-paged and silent as a book.

The way outside seems dark, the pavement in front of the door slimy like the Heidedamm in spring, sodden after a long frost. It's still raining. Röcker catches up with her at the corner. Her paintings weren't really so bad, she hears panted behind her. She had already heard the clacking of his cowboy boots before a second stab reached her spine, had already felt the man before his aftershave had caused her nose to itch. Now she feels his hand between her shoulder blades, a gesture which doesn't cause her to stop but only to walk even more determinedly upon her way, her back pain the result of an ever-missing caress. And so she keeps on walking, warlike and goose-stepping into the final picture. It's almost finished already and done with the purest colours and in the most radical form. And she would carry it out, stroke for stroke, layer upon layer, she had never been as sure of anything before in her life.

'Where you off to in such a hurry?' Röcker rushes forward, falls back behind, the ground beneath her feet like a rolling belt which would finally make up for life, for all the wasted time. 'Home,' she says, 'to my *son*,' she almost spits her boy's name, Dion, whom Röcker already knew.

'No father taking care of him?'

'No.'

'Not any more?'

'Not ever.'

Where did she know Ute from? Did she have time for a drink? The questions thrown at her from behind like arresting hooks. She suddenly came to a stop so abruptly in front of her car that he ran into her. He pulled her unwillingly into his arms; sadly he'd forgotten her name. 'Mira,' she says, rips open the boot lid and throws the portrait inside. Daniel glances at the stack of canvases, all the alibis of her life. 'Mira?' he grinned, 'is that your artist's name?'

She emits a laugh at this little kid, rebellious and raw, his jokes, at the paltriness of her own lies and at how quickly, having finally reached the reality behind her paintings, the truth arrives. For, in fact, Mira was not only her name in the fashion house. As a child in the girls' home, it was already a synonym for a brighter future, the title of a still-white and empty canvas that begged to be filled in with colours, with bodies and magical symbols. *Mira* had also been the name of the big city outside, the Saturday night into which she escaped almost every weekend together with her classmate Ingrid—and here she feels an almost painful longing at the thought of her former and perhaps only true friend she'd ever had—whose lingerie and miniskirts had fit her, Marga, as if cut for her alone, the shortest and the scantiest, scrunching through the laundry-room window out into the garden and into the glittering streets. At the next corner already they would begin to sing softly and sway like two dance figures, for Saturday nights were full of secret movements and promised to be different than all the Saturday nights of the years before, not the intolerable desert-like weekends of little girls' games like skipping rope and rounds of Nine Men's Morris, but a bigger and truly enchanted forest that would instead offer the right girls the right games while providing them with pseudonyms which would not give away their true origins, there in the caverns, cabarets and dance clubs with alluring names like Bikini, Kaiserkeller or Club Fatal whose doormen, instead of the obligatory 50 pfennig coin, would usher in underage girls, when their lips were red and their heels were high enough, over the stairs and through hallways into the sweating crowds where no one could ever be young enough and no one was ever really named what they said, no one was what they said they were, and which was why the two, Marga and Ingrid, on Saturday evenings at ten o'clock became Mira and Gila, the twin sisters from Harvestehude where the houses looked like palaces and the doctors, professors and actors who lived there were fathers who could refuse their daughters nothing and the famous theatre director they had chosen to be theirs had driven them to Millerntorplatz in his black Jaguar on the way to his evening performance and with a slightly concerned but trustful wave had dropped them off into life, his glorious daughters, Mira, the blonde, and Gila, the black-haired one with the untameable curls, the two who didn't really look like each other at all but who, in the Saturday night, complemented each other like the light and dark side of the moon, the magical clip which bound them and, of all things, a clothes hanger, which is just as curved as the waxing or waning celestial body and then later too the pimp Miklos' penis, which would remind her of all the wasted promises of those nights, a sickle-shaped hanger or club had come between the two of them, Mira and Gila, her beloved friend, right at the height of their history as twins so that the image that seemed to be almost whole in the colours and connections of the long ago night from one moment to the other had again turned white and became emptied of all its secrets, a void, and without the moon's wonder, and had remained so until today.

She slams the boot door, in the process almost catching Röcker's fingers as he dug about attempting to assay her talent or was it her failure? He jumps back, grabs her hand and puts it on his collarbone, into the hollow below his Adam's apple, that place on a man that, when a drop of sweat or semen collects, turns her on. Everything else just tricks and routine, the usual business: she'd jerk the guys off to half-mast and almost make them cum with her tongue while fondling their testicles. When she noticed it got them off, she'd work up to the perineum below which was the prostate, push gently on their sphincters, then slowly work in a finger until the pre-cum began to drip. They'd always beg her to finish; she knows their wives or girlfriends hardly have any time to spend on that so-often overlooked backside. If she can wipe it out of the hollow of their collarbones afterwards, she knows she's done a good job and that they'll be back.

For some time now there's been a TV in the dressing room; she turns it on whenever she's with a john who feels disgusted. They rarely complain about the noise, maybe there was something comforting about the sound of a running TV, like being at home in the living room. Once, she remembers, the thriller had been so exciting that they gave up in the middle of the session and watched the movie to the end. He was a younger client who knew what he wanted and even asked her what she liked, not bad. She lay there with her temples on his shoulder and smoked. He had paid all the same, even the overtime, until the murder was solved. For a while she had hoped to see him again; first they would fuck, then watch a movie, or the other way around, and for a special rate. But he was one of those who needed a different girl every time and therefore never became a regular in the fashion house, which she was sorry about; most of the time the chronic return guests were also those who had the TV turned up the loudest.

Now, however, she would rather swallow a Lexotax which she kept in her handbag precisely for such moments. She could manage to take the pill between her thumb and index finger together with a cigarette and, with the filter, stuff it into her mouth unnoticed, just as she did in the fashion house sometimes. But she didn't move. Röcker pushed her fingers onto his collarbone and hissed between his teeth. And she had to think of Dion's father who, there where now her hand was lying, had not had a hollow, not even a groove, nowhere for the drops of sweat to gather when she brought him to climax. Maybe that had already been the end of the affair, or his attractiveness, when, undoing his shirt for the first time, she'd noticed that below his Adam's apple everything was flat and without any promise at all.

And now? She turned away, tore open the driver's side door, with energy, for otherwise it stuck. Then fell into the seat, deathly tired, the pain poking her in the back. In this condition, she thinks, the trip home would be hell. 'What are you waiting for?' she called and Röcker hopped in. She could tear open his shirt so that the buttons would pop off and over the seats, just like she'd seen in an American film recently. 'So are we going to yours?' Röcker asks and wipes the rain off his forehead. She grabs him by the mop of his hair and turns his face to hers; for a moment his paleness makes him seem small and frightened, then he collects himself and makes a move for her mouth. 'Doing it in the car is too American for me,' she says, and pushes him back into his seat.

'Would you prefer it French?' He knew a by-the-hour hotel on the Steindamm. His grin froze. 'It won't work at my house,' he quickly added, she says: 'That's clear,' and sticks the key into the ignition. The idea of bringing him to Fenndorf takes hold of her. She'd take him to Ilse Bloch's to buy wine and cigarettes and she'd dig the change out of his jean's pocket. Half an hour later the news would have already made it through the village, not an issue of slander this time, no, but the naked truth. In the kitchen a few minutes later with a feeling of triumph—or would it be, after all the secrecy, one of relief?—she would rip open Röcker's shirt just like she'd seen in that film, and watch the buttons roll across the floor and nod to Dion, who would be standing in the door and watching her quizzically. She'd pull her new lover's pants down to his thighs, turn him to the boy and ask: 'Do you like this ass?'

The next day, she thinks, he'd have already got over it, would be back to gathering dragonfly larvae and at the same time would've learnt something about life, about his mother and his father, who had also been a client, dragged to the fashion house by another regular, a shady exporter from Hamburg, she thinks his name was Rasmussen, who had closed a deal with him, Dion's father, and in order to celebrate had sprung for three girls and two bottles of champagne at one hundred and fifty marks a piece, the drink, not the whores, who cost twice as much, which had once again caused trouble between Siana and the businessman who kept trying to haggle about the price so that Siana, who often paid more attention to her clients' interest in drink than in women, on the condition that he would order at least another bottle, had offered him Mira as a bonus and Rasmussen had let the corks fly and slapped his new partner on the shoulder, he who would deliver peat sod to Rasmussen who in turn would ship it to Spain, just imagine farmers using soil from Fenndorf to salt their leached tomato fields, indeed, salt, she could still remember his words, 'We'll salt the Spaniards' tomatoes and all of your pussies,' he'd hooted, and pushed her into the arms of Dion's father who had been standing shyly in a corner. The deal, however, had gone sour on account of customs regulations, for Rasmussen had been operating with illegal export papers but by that point she'd already been on the way to Fenndorf with her client-tuned-fiancé.

They had wanted, like typical new lovers, to make a side trip to the coast, but had only made it as far as Marsch because far from any gas station the brand new car had run out of gas, as would their love affair which, like the Spanish peat contact, was in truth just an instance of horse-trading, but not before having a child planted in her belly and his begetter's capital planted into life: a decaying house in the moor together with a young mother's dream of happiness.

Ilse Bloch, at that point herself still, or yet again, pregnant, had fumbled around for the price on the package of dry milk which Marga had purchased or had had to buy in her shop even though the sell-by date was already well since past as no mother in the village would have ever sought it out in the general store under the owner's gaze where dry-milk-mothers were those women for whom curves were more important than the growth and well-being of their children, the newcomer to the village, barely a widow and already needing men's eyes on her breasts from which her child did not feed, but some kind of milk formula or other, something or other like that is what the grocer probably thought. But, in the first weeks, Marga still remembers with painful exactitude, from dawn to dusk—and nights too—she had sat pumping milk and, bent over, could barely find the strength to pump anything else out of her body and into the weak and ever-weaker little child who didn't want to suckle, to then pump it back in with pacifiers from the bottles towering on the tabletop as she constantly applied the suction valves and then took them back off, as if her kitchen were a cowshed and the pump equipment a milking machine that had to feed and fill an entire village or, more precisely, *the* village, Ilsa Bloch's gossip-hungry clients who regarded her, Marga's, business with the pump as proof of her sloppiness and that the child of the dry-milk-mother would already be emotionally crippled and unfit for life. And, in fact, it all looms again right there before her eyes: her child lying there motionless *in front of*, never between, her dripping, almost intolerably painful breasts suppurating their nourishing drops; for you, Dion, I must now remind you, would turn your head away and press your lips together as if the warm and fat milk were responsible for the erosion and corrosion of words in your mouth before you had even emitted a single sound, an early rejection, or act of defiance perhaps, which you no longer know anything about nor would you ever learn were I not at this point to bring your mother's torment to your attention—thanks to my love of the truth—before all knowledge unequivocally dims for your body, tanned now by the acidic water and soon to become leathery here in the depths between peat and mud while the scraps and excretions of your extinguished life, the legends, conjectures, and so-called village chit-chat remain behind, and year after year the by-now-unsolvable riddle will accumulate and condense in strata of earth, dead cotton grass, water and once again earth with the mummy of your body at its core in a grave of half-rotten and long-forgotten facts, for the whole predicament, that you, the present thirteen-year-old, should at the very least accept some responsibility for; because the fact is that you, though at that point an infant and still innocent of insult, resentment or vindictiveness, literally left Marga hanging in her struggles and troubles to bring colour and strength to your pale and tiny body, she with her heavy load of spurned mother's love and a milk that trickled past your little mouth no matter how much she tried to tickle and coo, in her memory there's hardly a single moment she was given the joy that so many women swoon over, the first time in her life she had ever had a child at her breast, Dion, namely, and once again she sees her boy lying there with his big, somewhat empty eyes and, after endless means of trying to entice him, just putting his feeble mouth on the nipple, sucking a little bit then turning away. He never cried once, he simply rebuffed her and stared somewhere off into space.

And so she pumped and continued to hope for a miracle. At some point she wrapped the half-starved little bundle into a coat that Marianne had given her together with a few other used romper suits and sleeping bags, got onto the bus in front of Ilse Bloch's shop and went to Zeeve to go to the doctor who diagnosed her child with a rather advanced inflammation of the glands and a diminished sucking reflex, a problem in the functioning of the mouth muscles, which, he reassured her, sometimes occurred in infants, but that the child would soon grow out of and without any effect on the speech apparatus. He advised her to stop nursing immediately. She left the office feeling better and picked up the right medicine in the next pharmacy and then she was finally calm.

In spite of all the gloomy predictions from the village shop she had, in fact, managed to do it all even without a man by her side, managed to bring the boy through it all without a father's strength and a mother's milk, and over the years even managed to establish a sort of happiness, threatened with sinking into lies just like the whole house into the swampy ground as it was but which compensated her however occasionally for the giant failure with his father.

She still remembers how she swore she'd never bring another man into that house again. Now she was observing Röcker in the passenger seat. The boy would be distrustful, maybe even a little bit jealous. She'd have to prepare a dinner, no everything-soup but French fries and steak the two men would have to grill together. Then they would play Klabberjass, Dion's favourite card game, which often ended in a fight, even with the slamming of doors, for, thanks to her years in the girls' home, she knew all the tricks and therefore won almost every time.

Tonight, however—that's how the image of the new family takes shape before her eyes—she would play dumb, the woman among men, and grins to herself. First the boy, then Röcker would win so that the two would bond and she would sit in her chair and pout and then Dion at some point would lightly touch her with his foot and pull a face, perhaps from out of his Old-Man-Game's repertoire, sucking in his lips, a sign of reconciliation that would make her laugh again and would lighten the mood so much that the boy, who up until then had sat there speechlessly, would get his mouth open and Röcker would wait for him to finish and wouldn't look away embarrassedly when in explaining the complicated sequences Dion wouldn't get the crucial word out, that's how much she could expect from him, the new man in the house and the boy's stepfather. By the end of the night Röcker and she will have had too much wine, but you, Dion, just to round out her vision from your perspective, will have had two bottles of lemon soda and shortly after falling asleep will wake up having to pee.

A beam of light falls out of the open bedroom door. Shadows bend over the floor and doorframe with a slight moan. You push yourself along the wall, before the bright spot you see your body as a thin pillar protruding out of the labyrinth of the others. Full bladder now a burning pain. Thinking you can't hold it any longer, you bend over and peek around the corner. You'd seen Hannes and Daniela, the Bloch's daughter who was in your class, in the same position, on her back, he above her in a kind of press-up, down at the pond some time in early summer when with a marmalade glass full of fresh dragonfly skins you were making your way home. Hannes had also had his underwear down around his ankles, and had also emitted those half-swallowed, hardly sensual but, rather, mournful and distorted sounds out from between grinding teeth. You had carefully poked your head out of the grove of alders at the same moment that Daniela turned her face to the side in the grass and put her hand onto his back, down to his tailbone, where now Marga's hand was in order to direct the man's movements, the one who had moved into your house today. You had quickly ducked back into the undergrowth but Daniela had seen you, and she let out a quick cry and pushed Hannes off her who sprang back, his angular-looking penis coming out of the girl and flicking against his stomach in the same way you had recoiled and jumped up, spring-like, out of the undergrowth and out through the rushes and into the meadow whereas Daniela had already pulled up her jeans and snapped 'You peeping Tom!' but you were already far away, in a zigzag, pierced and pricked by yellow and dangerous-seeming feelings, running as if through a storm while from over there Daniela let fly the worst insults, and with bolts of lightning in your stomach and thunder in your head you ploughed homeward, right past Marga and into your room and immediately into the crevice.

Had it only been an acoustic trick, your blood beating in your ears, or could it perhaps have been a thought spoken aloud? Between the girl's droning for a moment it was as if you had heard Hannes' deep, calm voice saying something to Daniela which caused you to waver for a fraction of a second before jumping over the ditch that separated the solid from un-solid ground where for a little bit longer the echo of the sentence shivered and bound you in a sinister, almost unsettling way to Hannes and you slowly push yourself out of the dark behind the half-open door, forget about him, he won't say anything, those had been, you are now sure of it, his words, and, with the sudden knowledge that you had seen something which was meant for you alone, you step over the threshold into the light.

She grabs Röcker by the hips, flips him over and straddles him; when she moves her pelvis in circles, she can dictate distance, tempo and depth. She lays a hand under his throat where the sweat runs into the hollow, throws her head back and exhales a long, dark sigh over towards the hallway. Her boy is standing in the hole of the door, dark, almost unrecognizable, moulded into the shadows. Only his eyes, or a light within them, burst forth and into her, into her chest, stomach and abdomen, and she forces his eyes to move up to her face.

You unwillingly look up. She smiles at you in the way she winks over at you in mornings when she swims under the split bough after staring for a long time into the water; she likes that part of the pond where the reflections of the alders walk away from the banks and, depending on the colour of the sky and the cloud cover, cast varying images across the face of the water.

She turns Röcker's face into the pillow and away from you, then begins to moan, louder, in the end almost screaming, the entire time fixing you with her eyes like one of those invisible but in her thoughts already perfect figures on the blank paper until she can see her boy almost white before the black hallway, like a kind of X-ray that peels what had been hidden and protected by flesh out of the inside. Only down here with me in the depths of the moor where your body is dissolving in an opposite direction, not out from the skin but from the heart, you suddenly find a voice for the unsayable which had been stuck in your throat. At the climax of her screams you stumble into the bathroom and in front of the toilet; and yet no matter how much you push and squeeze, the stream of urine sprays upwards against the tank.

The next morning—this is how the image of the family could look in the daylight—you are all sitting around eating your breakfast like any other parents and kids and kitchen; Marga in her bathrobe and smoking in her chair, you, as always, next to her with your bowl of cornflakes and, on the chair across from you, which, as opposed to the usual overflowing state of newspapers and odds and ends of the others, was always empty as if she had kept it clean it for a guest who never came, sat Daniel Röcker in shorts and bare chested, gobbling down his bread. He reaches for the butter dish but you push it away. He reaches again, you push it away again. 'Why don't you put a little butter on the bread for me?' he says and grins. You shrug your shoulders and look to Marga. She takes her knife, cuts a thick piece and places it on her tongue. Her cheeks swell and you say: 'hYhuck' as she fishes the bread off of Daniel's plate and then spits the butter back out. Daniel looks disgusted. Marga moves closer to you. 'My house, my child, my butter,' she says, and you nod and stick a spoonful of cornflakes first into her, then into your own mouth.

Daniel simply stares, at first appalled, then clearly intimidated, and, finally, bold once again, ever the winner. He takes the bread, licks up the butter and swallows. Under the table you feel her toe, then her calves against your leg and in between Daniel's naked foot. It wanders up and goes astray in your crotch. You look around yourself and see the toes smirking like dwarves with triangular mouths and sparse black tufts of hair. Hadn't you already seen these five before, some time ago, when you were young? A foot rising high and wide above you, from the frog's eye view the row of toes gradually growing up to the big toe, singular hairs sprouting on the bones. You had climbed—or had you crawled?—up them, now you can't remember what kind of movement it was, only its goal: this foot you played with, when you finally arrived, for a long time. The toes were little, wriggling and bearded men that would not allow themselves to be caught, the instep the house from which they peeped out, the cracked sole, the garden and the ankle a mountain behind which the world began. Then someone picked you up and you think you started to cry. You never saw it again, but are sure it was your father's foot in spite of Marga's claim that he died before your birth. Or did you invent the toe-men so that your father, if not a face, than at least had feet? Real father-feet with uncut nails, lint between the toes and dotted with little black hairs, feet like Daniel Röcker's. Having Daniel for a father wouldn't be all that bad. He could play cards pretty well, rides, he says, a motorcycle instead of driving a car and is younger than all the other fathers in the village. You bend down and sniff about the big toe and think you can even remember how your father's foot had also smelled like old cleaning rags.

Marga snorts with laughter. 'You're kidding, right?' Röcker sputters, tosses down the slice of bread and jumps up. On top of it, he had to get going; he climbs into his jeans, which were standing inside out on the kitchen floor like some kind of mysterious sculpture. Asks if he can borrow the car. Marga grabs the half-eaten sandwich, takes a bite and munches a no. She looks to the clock, 'The bus leaves in ten minutes.' 'Bitch,' he grunts then is out the door.

'Should he come back?' she asks you through the cloud of cigarette smoke as you both stand outside on the porch. Daniel, whom you had almost begun to like, not because of his feet but because of his motorcycle, his promise to take you to the seaside and because, unlike Marga, he doesn't call you *my boy* but simply *pal*, by now the man who could have been your new father, is only a blurry point at the end of the Heidedamm and soon disappears between the long shadows of the houses on the Dorfstraße. The sun stands high in the sky, butter-yellow over the dew-glistening plain. It had stopped raining during the night, the sky now cloudless, the moor vaulted by an immense, pastel-blue tent of transparent air and the wet smell of earth and leaves. And yet the light is different than it had been over the last few days, it has lost some of its power as if the rain had washed away all the colours which now seem as if they have been infested by a grey or brown hue, and even in the glowing red apples—which you should have picked by now—over in the tree, autumn has already appeared with this form of weariness or lifelessness, an ever-present shadow that, starting in September, begins to eat its way out of the woods, the meadows, the fruit and last flowers, from out of the middle of summer.

'hDo hyou hwant him hto hcome hback?' you whisper and Marga looks at you for a long time. The boy's got a nice face, she thinks, small like his father's but with much finer features and without that touch of the farmer, which proved his handsomeness to really be plainness whenever they fought passionately or made love; for in that surge of emotion, his balanced face would suddenly appear distorted, and both were moments she felt she didn't love that man with whom she had just fought or slept as, up close, she couldn't handle his ugliness.

'For all I care he can take off to where the pepper grows,' she says, and you ask yourself just where that's supposed to be, a dusty, parched or even burning place beneath a raging sun, a place most probably where people were sent by those who don't want them around any more. She wraps the belt of her bathrobe tighter around her finger, then undoes the knot. 'All the same, he was good at Klabberjass,' she says, and walks back into the hall. 'hYou hare hbetter,' you say, the phrase growing longer and longer, it hangs in the middle at the sound of *K*, but she missed the point; when you turn around, she is standing on the second stair with her robe open and looking over you out onto the plain, towards the pond, from where, for a moment, it seems as if something was winking at her. Then, as she usually does on the bank of the pond right before getting into the water, she lets the material slide off her shoulders, extends her hand to you and says: 'Are you coming?'

But, in fact, she hadn't even begun the picture yet; here, in Hamburg, with her hand on the keychain, the painter in tow, it is even less than an idea. On the third try the motor still doesn't make a sound. 'What the hell is this kind of machine supposed to be?' Röcker asks and looks around the car. She wrenches the key out of the ignition. 'You good with cars?' He shrugs his shoulders. His father had been a master mechanic, as a child he'd hated cars, that's why he rode motorcycles. 'I had to play between the old pieces of junk,' he begins to blabber, 'cause there wasn't a garden around his parents' house, not even a courtyard, and she has to bite back her anger, this childhood story is really not what she needs from him right now. 'I would've liked to have had a father to show me how to repair cars,' she cuts him off, and, cursing, punches the steering wheel but Röcker just sinks deeper into the seat and into his past as if to ensnare her with his wounds. Even today the smell of gas and burnt cables makes him sick, but, most of all, the memory of his father who had forced him, just ten years old, to scoop up the waste oil from a bucket he had spilt while playing with his hand and put it back, with these hands, and he meaningfully lowers his voice and shows her his graceful fingers which already at the award ceremony had struck her as the hands of a person who didn't have to get his hands dirty but sculpt. She slides against the door panel, closes her eyes. 'How I cried,' she hears him whisper close to her ear, but his father had threatened the young boy once again with the home if he found even a single drop of oil left on the floor. 'Do you have any idea what a home is?' she interrupts him wearily, her mother had dropped her, Marga, off at the front door of an orphanage with a 5-mark piece stuck into her fist. She opens her eyes and the look in Röcker's face is as if she had just spoken Chinese. 'Boarding school,' he corrects himself, 'I was going to be sent to boarding school.' The waste oil that he, Röcker, had to scrape off the floor in front of his father simply could not be scraped away, it was more liquid-like than sand but more viscous than water, and it caused, and here he sighs, 'Blisters and holes between my fingers,' and he looks at her like a little scolded boy, but then, all of a sudden, he had seen, he begins again after a pregnant pause, a face within the puddles of oil on the garage floor, the face of a woman, and one month later he was in a home. 'Boarding school,' she corrects him, 'Yeah, an artistic one,' he nods, 'that was what saved me,' and the reason, she thinks, why now he smears this woman's face from the motor oil of his father's car repair shop in all colours and tones on canvas. 'And so?' she asks.

Or maybe she *should* just tear off his shirt, here, in the car, in front of all the people passing by? The buttonhole could be repaired, she thinks, his girlfriend would sew it, or his mother, if he still had one, for they had stitched her back up, too, she, Marga, the mothers and teachers from her childhood or, rather, Doctor Mellrich, the doctor of the deaconess home who was responsible for everything that had to heal quickly with the girls, for measles and mumps, then tonsillitis, and, later still, menstruation troubles; she had, she remembers, begun to bleed at eleven, in the middle of maths class which had terribly embarrassed her teacher. Then again at the age of sixteen, at some point in the backroom of Club Fatal, but Gila had helped her. A half a year later once again under the eyes and hands of the night nurse, Marita, and with the strong hope that Gila would help her, but she had been away and the clothes hanger had caught her between her shoulder blades, not the actual hanger but the hook it was attached to, it was no accident that the clothes hangers in the deaconess home were without exception made of wood. Wire would simply have bent, plastic might have broken; furthermore, wire and plastic hangers would have, when pushed together, only made a slight noise and not resounded like the wooden ones hanging on the racks which were set up everywhere in the hallways of the home even though there was rarely anything on them, a forgotten hat maybe or the jacket of an aunt who had come for a visit. Most of the time the hangers just hung there naked and motionless upon their hooks, but with the draught from an opened door or the vibrations of footsteps on the old wooden floors they would begin to clatter, unmistakable even in the back rooms of the Christian children's home which presented itself to the outside world, to the city, as open and fenceless but which was outfitted within with a finely tuned alarm system that, on certain occasions, was called into battle by the deaconesses, the *hornets* as the girls called them, when nights—and she and Gila had doubled over in laughter at the thought—they buzzed about the refectory straightening the clothes hangers, their model the real stinging insects which built their labyrinthine, palace-like nests with wood they'd chewed into a kind of papier mâché, and they'd still be giggling about the nuns when, high heels in hand, they'd sneak past the dining hall behind which, as the girls in the home said, the deaconesses sat at the tables they used during the daytime to ladle out mashed potatoes mumbling over the divine fire to the clothes hangers into which Doctor Mellrich, in the final step of the process, would place the hooks before placing the now-finished guards to dry out on the clothing racks. That Saturday night, however, it had been unusually quiet, for they, Marga and Ingrid, in their everyday clothes—ever the inconspicuous girls of the home—had thought ahead and had placed here a shawl, there a cap, in order to dampen the rattling so that it wouldn't reach the office where Night Nurse Maria would be sitting with her book of crossword puzzles or personnel files.

But as often happens with such stories, they had forgotten to set-up the laundry room properly. On washdays the deaconess' blouses were hung up to dry on innumerable hangers but on Saturdays, when there were no chores, there was only the occasional sound of a lone, forgotten hanger or a uniform leftover from the seamstress dangling in the draught created by opening the cellar window high up in the wall. She can still perfectly remember the ticking as if from an ever-more-quickly revolving clock, a sound which today still shudders through her when, as now, she believes herself to be on the threshold between a tattered idea and the possible form of its realization, on the way from here to there, out of muddled and hard-to-be-seen-through reality and into the carefully considered, if no less chaotic, arrangement of a painting, or vice versa, from one kind of bewilderment into the other. It is the moment she leaves something vague and unyielding behind, unfolds herself out of a nearly boundless state of apathy and into a sharply delineated body covered with feverish nerves; and this desire for stimulation and contact, this hunger for the Saturday night outside, its lights and its bodies, was the reason why, she thinks today, in all her haste and euphoria she'd forgotten all about the hangers there on the tightly stretched lines in the laundry, which she otherwise had always managed to arrange in just such a way that even were a storm to burst in through the window, not a single piece of wood would touch another.

As one after the other they crawled their way through the narrow chute into the open, from behind her she heard the soft tack-tack and she, Marga, almost Mira already, turned around and saw the nodding and grinning watchman, but she was already out and had no intention of going back. Her plan for the final escape from the home had been almost perfect. In the meantime, the doormen from Club Fatal would wave her to the front of the line because Gila was going out with one of them. She was going out with the other one, too, but only she, Mira, her twin sister, knew that. They had sworn to each other not to take a single step more in life without the other, and they realized the oath every minute of Saturday night. In the backroom the doorman first slept with Gila, then turned onto the other side of the plank bed and slept with her. They just barely made it through the laundry-room window in time for Communion; Gila threw on a blouse and quickly buttoned it up all the way, on her breast a love bite. During Communion they couldn't keep from giggling, the punishment: two weekends house arrest. But it didn't matter; there was always the laundry-room window. The doorman had promised to get them a place behind the bar, or dancing on the stage, and they were good. A crowd always formed around them and it wasn't only the men who'd hoot and clap when they mimed the dead rock 'n' roll woman along with *I Love You, Baby* or kissed each other during Freddy's *Heimweh*. On their last Saturday night, she remembers, the owner, a guy around forty who didn't let himself be affected by anything but who, as the waitresses said, wasn't bad at all, invited them to a bottle of champagne. He messed about with her, Mira, at the bar, then disappeared for the rest of the night with Gila who, before following him into the office, turned around once last time and stuck her thumbs up into the air. She'd been jealous, not of Gila but of the owner.

A guy at the bar bought her more whisky-colas. Before leaving with him, she stuck out her hand. He looked at her aghast, then lay down a 10-mark bill. She didn't take her hand back; he grudgingly gave her another. It was dawn before she came back, Gila sitting at the bar, drunk. She slid off the stool, grabbed Marga's shoulder and shook her. What was all that supposed to mean, they'd promised to do everything together! She couldn't get the consonants out any longer, the kohl around her eyes smeared. Had she been crying? Grinning Marga showed Gila the money, but she knocked it out of her hand. 'We should at least come to the dance audition!' she hissed and ran off into the street. It was their first fight, daylight's first rip in the fabric of night's wonder.

The second one came just a few minutes later in the laundry- room window. Outside it was already light. The moon like a pale egg in the sky, blotchy, wrinkled. Marga jumped out of the chute in the cellar and right in front of Sister Marita's feet. 'God sees everything,' she shouted and quickly pulled a hanger down off the line; behind it hundreds of others began to swing and clap just as a few hours before the dancing crowd had done after they'd finished doing the twist. 'If you scream, you'll get it twice as bad,' the deaconess said, and Magret bent over and bit into the backrest of the chair while Gila, who had been keeping watch outside, jumped over the little wall one final time and back out into the street where God's glance ended and life began, however noisily the clothes hangers at that moment rang out for her return.

Most of the time Doctor Mellrich stitched without anaesthesia; wounds from playtime in the courtyard and the Tartan track, knife cuts on the fingers of clumsy girls on kitchen duty, the stigmata of miracles. She screamed so loud that the nurse pressed her hand over her mouth. Magret bit her. The deaconess grabbed her by the hair, pushed her onto the couch and held her arms and feet tight while Doctor Mellrich pulled her panties down to her thighs. His finger felt like a piece of metal. 'Your assumption is correct,' he said to the nurse and pulled his hand back out, 'the hymen is unde-tectable.' She stood up and spit in the doctor's face.

The Saturday nights of her final year in the home were spent in the laundry room where she had to iron the order's blouses, quite often fifty at a time. The clothes hangers remained still. Bars had been placed over the chute. From there you could no longer see the moon. On long summer evenings the light of the setting sun came in through the cellar window and threw the shadows of the iron bars across the white tiles, the linens and crucifixes that crawled, slowly bent and, together with the joint grid, formed complicated shapes until the pattern was extinguished in the lack of light, and it was only thanks to the fact that at some point during her pauses she had begun to sketch the peregri-nations of the shadow images, so she believes today, that, on all those deaf and dumb Saturday evenings, she didn't completely lose her faith in the future.

One year later, after her release, she had gone back to Club Fatal. The doorman who she had slept with back then was standing at the entrance waving the pret-tiest girls inside, herself included. He was, she recalls, one of those guys with a rather pronounced collarbone; she'd laid her head on top of it, Gila had come from the other side and the tips of their noses met. They had grinned at each other while their faces rose and sank on top of his hairy chest. Now he no longer recognized her. She introduced herself as Mira and asked about Gila but neither name meant anything to him.

She leads the way, starts off in one direction but doesn't have any goal, only the feeling she has to keep walking to keep her back pain at bay. 'And the car?' Röcker asks her from behind. 'We'll bring it to your father afterwards.' 'Ha,' he says, catching up to her, 'he's been dead for years,' keeled over the hood of a Benz. She can feel the exhaustion, the weariness or vulnerability of her body that wants to lean against his, needs to be touched in ways that won't go wrong, won't surprise her by coming up cold from behind. 'Let's get something to drink,' he says and points to a bar they're passing, or is she the one passing over the possibility of contemplation and change? The image rushing towards her dissolves before her eyes when she shifts her glance just the slightest bit from the vanishing point to the edges, like the object at the edge of the field of view in a magnifying glass—almost, she thinks and says, 'Let's skip the drink,' she would take the chance to stop this time, to do it differently, maybe even to like him or, if he disappointed her again, at least tolerate him. The image would pass by, change into another one, she could see it, and, in the end, laugh at its imperfection. She walks on through the rain over pavements and rubbish and ever further into the grey mist that was thickening into an early evening between the rows of buildings. She had a plan. She would transform him, push him to perfection but, should he not bend to her will, destroy him with exactly the same force. Even Röcker's Roman-cut face strikes her as a Janus head, which, after fucking, would turn and, while she was packing her things, bare its teeth. She foresaw it all. She wants the distortion, his ridiculousness, the giant image at the end of this pointless march.

In an alleyway he grabs her arm and pulls her to a stop. 'This is bullshit,' he wheezes, 'just another quickie somewhere.' He now looks at her from the bottom up, reproachfully—or maybe imploringly? His dark hair sticking to his forehead, drops of water beading off the hairs of his beard. 'I'm sorry about it,' he whines. 'About what?' she answers impatiently, 'That thing in the toilet?' 'No,' he says, now clearly offended, 'the story about the baby and the 5-mark piece.' She laughs, a few passers-by turn around; she could, but no, she no longer wants to stop. 'What's wrong with you?' he asks. The rain is streaming into her open mouth; it's burning her eyes, or is it the running powder? Instead of going to the gallery she should have just gone straight to the fashion house and she looks at her watch, just a little before three. Schiereisen unredeemed no doubt and on his way homeward, now the men from the Hansa-Werft and the Japanese propeller manufacturers would be impatiently waving their dollars and Siana would likely have already sent others and that, it continues in her head, will be the end of my career in the fashion house. She fishes a Tempo tissue out of her handbag and wipes it across her eyes and mouth; with the rainwater on her lips the, Lexotax goes down easily.

'My mother,' she says, 'died giving birth to me,' slowly her breath slows down. 'There were complications, and on top of it all there were the air-raid alarms, '43, all the rescue workers in town on duty.' 'Very funny,' Röcker says and attempts to cover his being offended, 'And your father?' 'God is my father,' she says threateningly and grins, they'd taught her that in the home. With a shrug of his shoulders first he points into the ever-stronger rain and then to the showcase of the little cinema just a few steps ahead trying to lure visitors with its posters. 'Movie?' he asks, and Marga wants to object, but he is already at the ticket counter and letting the coins clink down onto the tray.

They buy sweets, cola, lay their elbows over the armrests. The film that afternoon, which had just begun, was called *The Last Tango in Paris* and wasn't a dance film like she had thought at first but, according to Röcker, an outright scandal. During the first half an hour he hardly moved at all. His left arm was on the rest, his eyes equally fixed on the screen, only his right hand occasionally brought the cup of cola to his mouth, the bag of sweets having already disappeared under the seat. Suddenly feeling hungry she had tried fishing for it blindly between his lightly spread legs, then the cup slipped out of her hands and Röcker recoiled on account of the wave of cola; after that, they gave up on any other attempts at getting close. Now the floor was sticky, their feet were sticking to it under the seats, as was the short amount of time left in her plan to the guy who was sucking on his straw next to her although the cup was already empty before her last bus left. On the screen a brawny, already greying American who at some point must have been pretty good looking, she thinks, was rolling onto the small French woman with similar slurping and smacking sounds. She gives in to the flood of orange and red images, the colours of an endless sunset, which she not only finds awkward in painting but uncomfortable in film too.

In the smash hit *Gone With the Wind*, which she saw back then with Gila at the beginning of one of their nights, the main character, Scarlett O'Hara, she remembers, swears off the unhappiness which had been following her throughout the entire film and later, in front of the cinema, she, Marga, no, Mira, had raised her fist to the sky just like Scarlett O'Hara or, rather, the actress playing her, Vivien Leigh, but a sky which, unlike in the film, was not an angry black and burning one but a cloudy, rainy Hamburger sky: 'As God is my witness,' she cried, just like the heroine had yelled in front of that heroically flaming horizon, and Gila had laughed and even stuck her hand into the air, and together in the final words of the film they vowed—'I'll never be hungry again!'—up to the dripping gutters and into the face of an old man who was looking sullenly out of a window. And then smirking they had run to the club and into the arms of the doorman and night's enormous maw.

Recently she had learnt from her hairdresser in Zeeve that in spite of the vow and the film's immense box-office success, the actress had miserably gone to ground, depression, hungry in the midst of fame and luxury, so to speak, the hairdresser sighed, who knew a lot about the lives and the pain of the most important women, and she triumphantly nodded and had to think of that feeling of freedom and happiness as she had tottered through the neighbourhood with Gila, enjoying the desirous glances in the red and orange glow, lights that in the fashion house later would turn out to be the colours of emptiness, of boredom and of disillusionment, red-orange, not, as so many thought, black and white.

She would have liked the film more if it had been shot in black and white, clear lines, hard shadows, borders that couldn't be dissolved. Oppressive and pregnant with red light and the story too, told in a way as only a man could, about a down-and-out American in Paris who was interested in emotionless sex, dirty, empty sex in a dirty, empty apartment, but why? Aha, she'd been too impatient, here was the key scene, the

American's wife had just committed suicide a short time before, the man thereafter cold and numb with mourning, demonstrated in one of the next scenes on the floor of the apartment shimmering a red-orange in a Parisian sunset when the American greases his beloved's ass with a stick of butter, and her hand slid off the armrest and onto Daniel's knee, but his knees didn't close, only his fist, which pushed her hand back up onto the upholstery and held tight, as if both of them were sixteen again and this trip to the movies the big promise to get through everything together, that is, what the film, in the end, wouldn't show: the flagging faces and sagging genitals, the strife and frustration, the black and white after sundown.

Vivien Leigh, she remembers her hairdresser's words, first shot up to the heights of success but then rocketed down into the deepest night, into the hell of the mind from which even the electroshocks she was given only managed to zap her out of for short periods of time, but he hadn't really said *zap*, only *bring* or something similar, but the thought of a young man from close by who'd recently died, shot through Marga's head like lightning: Kar-Kar, Marianne Lambert's nephew, which made him a distant relative of hers too, and who in reality was named Karsten Karmstedter, had lived in the neighbouring village of Kleenze and was twelve years older than Dion, but had also been a stutterer, everyone called him Kar-Kar because he couldn't get but the first syllable of his name out, as a child already taunted into being crippled in speech and later, thanks to the terrible insults of his acquaintances and family, in soul. First, so the rumours around the village went, Karsten Karmstedter had gone to visit men in Hamburg and then, thanks to one of them, to a psychiatric clinic and its electro-cables while in between almost finishing beneath the wheels of an express train had it not been for the Lambert's farmhand downright beating him off the railway embankment at the northern edge of the moor one evening, that's how determined the poor thing had been to have his lovelorn head chopped off by the Hamburg-Bremen express but who—thank God! Marga heard Ilse Bloch say in her shop where she'd gone shopping—electro-therapy had pulled back into line, not *pulled* but *shocked* Marga had thought and eavesdropped on what Bloch was saying at the register, namely, that Kar-Kar's mind, full to almost bursting with unnatural sexual phantasies, at last had been repaired. Or executed—the poor man must have been sat up straight as a pin, Marga thought—and his speech impediment along with him. But Kar-Kar, Bloch continued, spoke not a single word any longer, not even with his own mother, Siegried Karmstedter, Marianne Lambert's sister-in-law, who he apparently no longer even recognized when Sundays she brought him his favourite *Bienenstich*, bee-sting cake.

She'd left the shop, her basket empty, and hurried back home to her boy in double-time, pulled him close to her in the kitchen and clasped his hand, as similarly distraught or embarrassed as Daniel Röcker had begun to work upon her own when in the film the American grabbed the French woman by her wrists and, while penetrating her from behind, forced her to repeat his so-called key phrases, those phrases which were to explain to the woman grovelling and panting on the floor why from then on she would or had to be fucked in the ass and indeed she cries and whimpers something about how a child, so the key phrase, will be tortured until its will is broken and its freedom assassinated, and once again Marga had to think of Kar-Kar, of how— before another train on another railway embankment took off his head and with it his pain just a few months after his release from the hospital—he must have silently sat in his chair next to all the other electroshock patients who had once and for all foresworn the colours, films and sunsets and given themselves over to the black and the white, the black of dreamless nights and the white of similarly imageless walls in the locked wing of the psychiatric hospital where Siegried Karmstedter tried to press the sweet-smelling bee-sting cake into her doubtful son's mouth, that stubborn and stray son who, as had always been her hope, after all the hard work, thanks to perseverance, motherly love and clinical therapy, had finally been set back on the right track and no longer bucked nor jerked. Marga got up from her seat and, stepping over couples' entangled arms and legs there in the red-orange cinema, walked out into the light.

As she stumbles out of the foyer into the fresh air, the sky is neither black nor white; for all intents and purposes, the day seems to have become stuck somewhere in-between, above her a ribbon of rain. She walks along the houses and onto the busy Holstenstraße; on the other side of the street the Kleine Marienstraße, where the fashion house is, branches off, now there won't be any other diversions. Two minutes later, Röcker catches up to her. 'What's wrong?' he asks, out of breath, and grabs her arm. 'It was fascinating!' She pulls him along like a stubborn child.

'Did you like that?'

'What?'

'How the whore stuck her finger into the guy's ass.'

She shakes him off and hurries on. 'She wasn't a whore at all,' he says; catches up to her again, marches in front of her, won't be shaken off any longer. On Holstenstraße she almost walks in front of a car, the driver gives her the finger. 'Red,' Röcker says, points to the light and apologetically raises his hand. 'You're right,' she grins and jumps back onto the pavement, 'men think that something like that's only fun for whores.' He pushes her to the pedestrian crossing where people are waiting for the green light: a group of tourists in rain capes, a woman with a baby carriage and a man with conspicuously indifferent eyes; she recognizes the world and light-shy eyes of men who have just left a strip joint or a porn theatre.

And what did she think about it as a woman? Röcker stepped from one foot to the other as if he could barely wait to make it over the street, finally reach her goal. She laughs and hisses the sound through her teeth; once there was a client who sometimes came to the fashion house, passable enough, she remembers, who, one would have thought, didn't have to go and pay for it. But with women he didn't have to pay, she couldn't explain it otherwise, he never got off. Instead of the usual number—jerking him off, blowing him, or doggy style—she had to generously wash his butt but not erotically and by no means in the nude. When she undressed the first time, as per usual, he had turned around, and without a word and an extremely red face, walked out the door. Only later did she understand what and how he wanted it. Ever the strict mother, she pushed him into the bathroom and bent him over the bidet where she routinely and rather disinterestedly soaped his rear end with a washcloth and lotion, just like a child; she had wiped Dion until he was in the third grade because of his odd quirk with the business of the toilet. When she urged him to do it himself, he just froze, huddled up on the lid, terrified that at the slightest moment he could tumble down into the pipe. So here she was, very careful to make her client feel comfortable; however, he would get nervous if she was too careful, would slide at the edge and moan. Her fingers were well greased because of the soap. She'd hardly be in to the second knuckle and he'd already be grunting and dripping into the foam without her having even touched his penis. It was a quick one hundred marks and she didn't even have to shower afterwards.

Maybe that's why she'd finally felt sick from all the splits and contortions of the Parisian tango as the French woman stuck her finger into the American from behind who, pierced in a way, forced out another one of the key phrases, a muddled babbling meant to encourage, no, compel her, his lover, to be fucked and vomited on by a pig, a fantasy which actually made the young, attractive woman excited, almost crying in her degradation and literally wriggling in the American's ass after sex with a vomiting and dying pig which made Marga think of those Thursdays—butchering day at the Lamberts'—when at noon death screeches would ring out over the Heidedamm, bloodcurdling sounds from the throats of the panicking animals the farmhand led into the hall and tied headfirst to the hooks then strung to rods and sliced open by a knife, which at one time the slaughterer himself used but now was done by a machine, over a tub. Before that they would lay the electric stunner against the temples of the animals, which, contrary to what the director had incorrectly written in the script, don't vomit from the stress of the dying process but, instead, just slumber painlessly into it, bottom line: after many years of observing life and death on the slatted floors, Marga herself could testify that pigs do not vomit, that is why nature made them pigs, they can utilize everything and turn it into fat and flesh, and she

pushes Röcker against the man in whose eyes the cheap
brothel window lights still were blinking.

Had he ever been with a prostitute? she asks and lifts
her index finger with the pointed nail. Terrified, the
baby in the carriage starts to bawl, its mother roots it
out and presses it to her chest. Röcker grabs Marga's
finger and places it on his throat again. With her child
the mother turns towards the tourists babbling away in
Bavarian dialect, but the baby is now shrieking as if it
had seen the devil and even Röcker seems exhausted by
this aimless wandering through the rain and the endless
circles around the definitive caress. The shadows and
streetlights ghost across his pale face. Even though it's
only afternoon, a little past four, she establishes with a
quick glance at her watch, it already seems to be getting
dark like in winter.

In half an hour she has to call her boy. The light
stubbornly remains red, time paused, the buildings of
Altona rise out of the still-stand, tower south towards
the Elbe River and in the west ever further out to the
sea, which, she thinks, would have been a better destination, you could make it in just under an hour, maybe
on the coast the cloud-cover would even have lifted a
little and the sun come through. A walk along the
beach, a trip through the salt marshes on his motorcycle, pressed tight against him, the flapping of the wind
in her ears and the soft creak of his leather jacket as she
lay her head against his back, her hands winding their

way under his clothes and up over his chest to his collarbone where later, when they were lying next to each other on the bed of some motel or other, a drop would be glistening. Somewhere outside there would be the sound of farm equipment, inside, the heater, and deeper still the blood in her ears.

But hadn't just such an image of a lover's trip to the sea turned out to be nothing more than delusion and deceit? That idea planted so longingly simply dissolved into a foggy night over the marsh? She bends forward to seek out Röcker's mouth, but, startled, he pulls back, not only his mouth but his entire body, and bumps into the woman who is still trying to put her crying baby back into the carriage and who then takes off past him as he emits a sound of pain—or is it mocking—and wipes his hand across his mouth.

Marga had also bitten more than pressed, that kiss on Dion's father's lips, she remembers, that kiss that she'd been saving for the beach at night, for a sky full of stars maybe and wishes cast upward and devoured, somewhere on the edge of the road behind Itzehoe where the engine gave out and he, Dion's father, who was usually quiet and not particularly gifted with conversation, suddenly began to drill into her with talk of giving up her work in the fashion house and beginning to keep the books for the farm and peat-cutting business, almost as if he had intentionally let the tank run out of gas just in order to have such a moment where she couldn't escape and for a painful thirty minutes talk her out of Hamburg and into Fenndorf until, exhausted, she opened the door and got out and then tugged him out of the car and led him through a fogbank and over a field swollen with rain, smacking under their shoes as if to give her a taste of life in the moor to come, and pulled the man who had been trying to keep her with promises of marriage and happiness into an inn on the other side where a light was still on and in a cold bed with stiff linen she laid her head onto his chest and pushed her nose against his throat as if she might still dig a hollow there. Still, she thought, he'd promised her her own atelier, 'A hundred square metres in the barn just for you and your work,' he said again, and turned off the light on the nightstand. She slid over him, turned the light back on and showed him what she had to offer in return; to paint and in between sleep with a man she desired but who would leave her in peace, she'd never wanted anything else from her future, it was a plan that seemed perfect now, a whole night long, just a few kilometres away from the sea, its constant rolling forward and foaming back, the waves rising, breaking and then rushing out within themselves while pulling away clumps of sand, removing pieces of the land and washing them ashore somewhere else, and in that unchanging movement of ebb and flow, remembering and forgetting, coming a little closer to the pair of lovers who, here, far beyond the dykes and in the fearful reciprocal eavesdropping of their thoughts, heard nothing of the surf outside, of the call and warning of the sea.

Looking back, she now believes, that must've been the night she'd become pregnant with her boy. The next morning his father had set off with a petrol can. On the trip back he hardly spoke a word, his silent face simply staring out into the low-lying, low-pressure clouds; at one point a long sideways glance at her so that they almost rear-ended another car at a stoplight. 'Your pride drives me crazy,' he said angrily and honked the horn, she still doesn't know what he'd meant by that, the light turned green half a minute later. But she had taken his unhappiness seriously and the same day had gone with him out to Fenndorf.

'Do we want to pick up your motorcycle?' she asks Daniel Röcker. 'In the shop,' he shrugs. She storms into the street and only comes to a stop in front of the entrance to the inner courtyard in the Kleinen Marien-straße, looks back, and finally shakes the phantom out of her back. In Röcker's slowly approaching, amber-coloured, undoubtedly beautiful eyes she now notices the daring sparkling of the successful artist and then, once he's standing next to her, the mistrust, the doubt, all the questions. 'I'm there now,' she says with a wink to the entrance and he: 'Me too.'

It was not even five hundred metres from the cin-ema to the inner courtyard where the delivery area of the fashion house was, tucked in between the dumpsters and exposed concrete loading docks, and, with the time spent at the light, maybe five minutes, yet by the time she stood at the threshold her legs were trembling as if she had not simply walked through the neighbourhood but an entire continent. And then the strenuously painted and passionately followed image of the wonderful life trembles and flickers before her one more time, flickers and goes out.

The next morning autumn unequivocally arrived in the village to set the fruit gardens, cemetery beeches and their edges all aflame. Until midday it painted muddy beards of leaves on the water-faces of the head-shaped willows, but barely beyond the ditches lost its passion. For a little while it continued to burn in the moor rosemary but only managed to create an ordinary brown in the wilting blooms. Here and there a few more dabs of red; the tiny cranberry, a rowan tree in bloom at the edge of the first flowing grasses but beyond the field of dried bracken the leaves of sundew simply did not want to burn. It sullenly tipped its viscous mixture over the reeds and a fair amount of black into the hollows and cracks. In the dampness decay sets in without touching the fallen-down. The plants darken in a kind of half-slumber of indecisive ephemerality. Fruit, if strewn about at all, rots between the rushes but without sowing any seeds; whatever makes it deeper into the earth becomes petrified in the acid of the peat. In the ditches the forgotten sod slumps upon itself or swells up into black monsters with the rain. Creeks now rush where earlier in the year the cotton grass stood thick, the sky motionless in the puddles, the wind blows an abandoned stonechat's nest in front of itself. Any trace of your flight becomes blurred in the morass which wells up and grabs after anything that displays any desire whatsoever, pulls it a bit into the boggy ground and, partially bitten, leaves it alone. At the arrival of night the drift of unfinished decay comes from the plain and only he who knows it knows that I—hissing within the cotton grass, creaking out of the woodland, gurgling at the edges of the ponds and silent within their depths—am at my difficult and laborious work for your future and against time.

You surface. I pull at you one final time then let you go. You think you are naked and in danger, a white feeling like the one from which Marga woke you in the morning. For a moment you do not know where you are. In the dream you were outside with me by the kolk, there where the sky and earth touch and the land flows into the water, where the two become one and only separate again once you have stepped over the horizon. You had seen the sky below you and the water above; you swam and at the same time flew, a body of peat. When, many years later, you recall this state in order to describe it perfectly in your book, you will write it was the day you died for the very first time.

People say that at the moment of death your entire life flashes before you as if it were a film. That the mind remembers long forgotten images: you see Tanja that morning standing before the classroom wrapped in her yellow jacket, only her gaunt face, cheeks dotted red from running, peeks out from the hood. She nods at you as if taking leave, slips through the door and closes it softly behind her as if there were someone sleeping there who you were not supposed to wake. At the same time she had smiled with her eyes, which seemed even bluer and more sickly than usual, as if the sky had set them aflame. When you are in the classroom and she watches you from behind, she can see that you are terrified of reading aloud. And although you tighten your belt, she can hear the growling of your empty stomach when Marga has forgotten to make you a sandwich for the break. Sometimes, at the change of classes, there's half a sandwich on your desk. But you can never repay the favour, for Marga, before she places it in your bag, always bites off one of the corners. Who would accept a sandwich with the bitten signature of someone's mother? You nibble to the edge of where the teeth marks are and throw it away. Tanja sees you and grins.

She has known, at the latest, since the time when you played ball together, your bond forged on the field in front of the ditches. You saw her, weak and limping, fall completely into the grasses and heard her grind her teeth in rage. Tanja was also one of the children who was always chosen last for sports. She never got too far with kicking the ball. Her face, you remember, was strangely distorted from the strain when the catcher placed the ball at the starting point, a circle drawn in the dust. While all the others screamed and ran away, she scurried off or dragged her leg, which had been without a cast for only a couple of days again. Everybody knew that Tanja would go and hide in the next bush but no one ever bothered to look.

You too, Dion, had already lost by the time it became your turn to be catcher. You're not a bad runner, but at the start the decisive call that signals the end of the game—*Bannabanna!*—just never made it across your lips. While you were running you'd yelled it numerous times in your head but then, right in front of the goal, ran straight up against the *B* like a wall. When finally you managed to get something like *Hannahanna!* out, the ball was long gone, or you'd stumbled over the names of the hunted, consonant chunks like *Bannabanna Kai!* or *Thorsten!* or *Danni!*; Daniela, you remember, who everyone called Danni, was the worst name of all. Not a single one of the village children ever lost against the Bloch's daughter who at that time was twice as big as now, no one, that is, except you.

Only *Tanja* made your heart pound even more, and not simply because of its initial letter in the form of a St Anthony's cross, that torture pole of the biblical thieves. You and Tanja cannot go out together thanks to the fact that you can't even manage to say her name. You could never say: 'Tanja, I love you.' 'Hannes, I love you,' *that* would work; the fact that the name of the Lamberts' oldest son begins with the only letter in the alphabet that's easy for you to say seems to be a sign or, at least, the wink of a higher power.

But now, oh laughing scorn of fate, you have just seen the two of them together. As you were coming home at twilight they were standing by the stump at the pond: she in her yellow raincoat, he still in his overalls, a cigarette in his hand, the glowing tip making traces in the dark tangle of the rushes. You couldn't hear what they were saying or whether they were saying anything at all. The wind in the alders and the blood in your ears overpowered their voices. You ducked into the bushes and observed them disgustedly from across the water, their silhouettes at times melding into each other, at times back into the darkness. You didn't want to see Tanja, who was now going out with Hannes. Hannes, who in no time would lay her down in the grass, just like he had Daniela right before the summer break. Your eyes wandered over the pond and up to the split bough. In the dim light it was only a shadow melting into the water. As if it had finally gone under. You had always awaited this moment and it seemed to you as if the branch had been waiting too: for the water, for you, for the instant it could submerge you.

On all sides the ditches trickled away. You made yourself even smaller in the underbrush and spoke with the branch in your mind. You hoped it would tear Hannes and Tanja apart and plunge you into the pond: the whole day, you imagined, the two of them would go looking for you throughout the moor. Now they pull you out and bed you down in the moss, your body wrapped in its skin of mud. Tanja places her hands underneath your head and Hannes, having already completed the first-aid course in ninth grade, his ear to your chest, then his mouth on yours in order to breathe into you. You spit water, slowly become conscious again, blink and see images you cannot put into any order: Hannes' questioning face, then Tanja's, in between a small cut of sky of the same unfamiliar glow as the four eyes looking down at you. The light no longer bright, night has settled down and with it something else, something darker, which you do not understand. They look at you as if they knew more than you, as if, in the time you were unconscious, they had learnt something about you that they would now be able to use against you.

Did Hannes tell her about that thing by the slurry tank? Suddenly he had been standing next to you with a shovel in his hand. The August afternoon, you remember, gleaming, cloudless. On the way home from behind the stalls you had heard the pitiful cries, different from those on butchering days, thinner, despondent, not the sound of pigs, but more like that of children in pain one orders not to cry. You had slid between the silos and over to the basins. The four little cats were floundering in the slurry tank, their mother walking back and forth along the edge, just at the point of pouncing, and crying. You knew immediately what had happened: they call the second litter of the hungry animals 'stubble cats', those cats which belong to no one and constantly slink away when you try to come close to them. Only the farmhands, who they are used to, can come within a metre of them. The Lambert's farm was full of these cats, which breed twice a year. The help often lets the May litter live so that there will be enough around to catch mice in the autumn, but the stubble cats, born at the end of July or the beginning of August, at the time of the harvested fields, the stubble fields, immediately meet the end of the shovel or are tossed into the ditch because, as you've heard the farmhand say, they'll never turn out to be anything. When autumn comes early they often don't even make it, they just get sick, crawl into the wheel casings of the farm equipment and cause trouble. At the end of August, when it's your birthday, the young animals are already a few weeks old. They frolic about in the muck behind the stalls, happily and clumsily dance around their own graves.

The sky was blank, nothing inside it that you could have described, not a cloud, no sign, your eyes blazing back as if from a mirror. A scream stuck in your throat. You tried to fish out the little cats with the board that was floating over the wastewater but they kept sliding off. One was already too far out to grab even though you'd leant as far as you could over the dirty concrete lip; it cried one final time then went under. The mother, who had darted under another tank, came back, its fur standing on end as if you had been the one who had drowned its child. Then all of a sudden there were boots next to you. Hannes grabbed you by the collar and shook you. You wanted to say something, mutter something in your defence but you did not even stutter. There was a different and new feeling in all the chaos: excitation or even arousal, almost a kind of thrill. Hannes in overalls, shovel in hand, his pale face reddened by work or anger, his closely spaced eyes like a clamp around you; you with your underarms full of pig shit and a scream in your throat but from which only a h-Hoppla! escaped as he pushed you and you tumbled backwards against the tank. Thanks to its soft initial sound the only word you could manage in your fear *hoppla*! like a little girl who's tripped over her skirt and all the while the cats screaming in their death agony.

Hannes mocked you in a feminine-sounding voice. 'You'd better understand it now,' he said, and undid his zipper. Even today you still don't know what he meant; together with this gesture it was a sentence which meant everything and nothing, full of insinuations that made the blood rush to your face together with a cold and shaming look which forced your eyes down, first to the struggling animals, then to the penis in his hand. He aimed at the mother cat, which walked away with her back arched, then at the tank. You wanted to turn away but from the throat downward it was as if you were paralysed, revulsion pulling you in one direction, curiosity in the other. For some reason the stream of urine was divided in two, one half went to the left, the other straight, but didn't catch the cat. All of them went down, one after the other. You went after him with balled fists even though you knew you hardly stood a chance against him, sixteen years old, already a head taller than you and wiry from farm work. You scratched against his bib and rammed your head against his chest while the sounds dribbling out of your mouth didn't sound all that different from those of the cats. He fought back half-heartedly, it seemed as if he didn't want to waste any strength and was only playing with you which made you even angrier. You threw punches and heard your hands thud against his chest; his stomach was soft and took your fists, he didn't even bother to tighten his muscles. His overalls smelled like the stalls and cheap deodorant when he took you into a headlock, which seemed too weak to you, just like the whole attack itself, awkward and casual, almost like a friendly hug. It was more the force of *your* resistance that clamped down your legs. Somewhere in your body something split, more of a tangible than audible sound tearing through the silence; even the last cat was now gone. He let go for a moment and stared at you, a glance which, so you believed, meant to leave you with something you didn't understand. Suddenly there was an unbearable feeling of heat in your face, as if you were standing near a fire.

Then you felt his grip again. His hands like a choke hold around your throat, then his boots between your knees, pulling your legs out from under you, and then, as you crumpled down before him, for a split second the tip of his penis pinched in his zipper.

From out in the plain you could hear the rasping of the cranes. They had come out of the north early this year, earlier than usual, it's not even September. Their calls increased like trumpets, came closer, grew louder as if deriding you because, yet again, you hadn't protested but simply swallowed your scream. When you looked up to Hannes you saw the bright strips of skin in the fly and high above his now ruddily flickering mane of hair the skeins of the black birds like a mysterious script. You couldn't decode what they wanted to tell you. The sky was high and almost white, high and white with emptiness, a bareness that hurt your eyes. At the beginning of September when the fogs rise, the grey geese pass over on the way to their winter homes. Floating in the mists like blurry silhouettes they dive into a space of blue and cast fleeting shadows. But before you have even looked, they've disappeared again. In these cracks between the fog and a higher, world-renouncing light no longer bound to earth but to space—it is no longer summer, but not quite autumn. These are the rare glimpses of a fifth or even more distant, more foreign season. The grey geese on their way south, the cranes arrive from Scandinavia and rest upon the wetlands. The chatter of the geese blurs into the rasping of the cranes almost as seamlessly as the fog into the light. At first you confused their sounds they were so similar. But the cranes' calls are longer and darker, less excited, less purposeful, the sounds of warning attuned with sad and serene echoes as if they knew that in the north, where they come from, there has already been the first frost. The grey geese continue to laugh, the cranes sneer. When their V-shaped swarms move across the plain, summer is over and all the stubble cats are dead.

Hannes arranged himself and with the same hand offered to help you up. 'Take care of your own shit,' he said, and pointed between the silos to the Heidedamm. For a moment he continued to look at the place where the cats had drowned as if to make sure. Then he disappeared back into the stalls. The mother cat had returned to cower around the lip of the tank, head hanging down, staring at you. Her lost glance and haggard body, her mangy fur with the black teats, heavy with milk, made you choke. You got up out of the dirt and went home, and with your shoes still covered in manure, up the stairs, into your room and onto the bed where you pressed yourself into the crevice deeper, longer and more violently than ever before.

And now Hannes had whispered all of this to Tanja? Had given away that secret meeting by the slurry tank which you'd sworn that very same day you'd never repeat out of shame and fear of Hannes' rage if anyone in the village should find out? A gust of wind tore the wooden fruit from the alders, the bough swayed on the water and you thought you could hear it creaking as it whispered to you with a nod: Well, come on!

Hannes and Tanja had come a bit closer to each other on the narrow path between the rushes, there, where in the mornings Marga steps into the water. Had they noticed you already? The thought didn't cause you fear but, rather, a feeling of having had enough and relief. But you were not sure whether they had seen you—you were sitting to the east, protected by the growing darkness, but they were standing in the west where the sky still was bright. And then, in fact, Tanja looked over—if you had had the eyes of an owl or a cat at the moment you doubtless would have seen a knowing smile on her lips.

Suddenly Hannes grabbed her by the arm. Or was it only a shadow falling over them from the alders? The wind wound through the branches, leaves spun downward. A twig broke under your shoe, revealing the secret alliance of your glances. Now Hannes looked over too. As you carefully raised your foot, the twig snapped as if breaking into shards. Then you were out of your hiding place and over the ditches out towards the field. The last thing you saw of the Heidedamm was the house and the black willow in front. Around you the landscape sank into the darkness and when you finally turned around again, by the yard, the pond had disappeared.

The film rips. When you move you hear a dull creaking but why, you wonder, could it be the moor? Then you smell her. Marga, her bath oil, the smell of cold cigarettes in the air. A harsh light in your eyes, you wipe your hand across your face, feel the warmth of the water, a crackling sound and something flaky on your skin—far too soft and light to be peat—crumble between your fingers. Slowly the shapes of the bathroom are peeled out of the mist. The mirror hidden, the window steamed, and behind it the night. You are not out in the cold brown water but at home in the bath.

Going under, you imagined me pulling your body gently down into the depths in slow motion, so that the film playing before your eyes as you lost consciousness would last as long as the summer of a dragonfly in relation to its own death. When in those final weeks the full-fledged insects return from the grasses to the garden, their lives have reached their end. In only a few months they have moulted, paired and laid their eggs. Though their brief summer unfolds in the isolation of the remote ponds, when it is time to die they seek out the company of human beings; on walls still warm from the sun, the last predators and mosquitoes meet. The dragonflies, as they say, stuff themselves one final time, then the first cold night comes and gathers them in. Yet at that second, as one image transforms into another at an extremely quick rate and they would like to see a slower film, at that moment of their deaths, in their eyes summer once more comes at a crawl. In your film you lived below the water with me in the mud like a larva that still has everything ahead of it: its dark time there, moulting, the moment of slippage, light and the freedom of the sky. In your dream of the life of dragonflies you learnt language anew, from the very first sounds onward, there in the still, brown water; not the language of human beings but that of insects, and as opposed to words you perfectly managed all your various voices, and your senses were the sharpest of all. With your feelers you could perceive the tiniest movement of air and through the bright colours of your body speak with the sun in an endless dialogue. And how you talked and talked . . .

The truth of the matter, however, is that no one from your class heard anything at all—how could they have? You turned around in front of the door and ran away from the disgrace of your presentation and out to me. 'The Lifecycle of Dragonflies' died away in the distance without a single word to remain your secret and our silent pact. The noise of the classroom and the hallway has always horrified you, but you have never been afraid of my silence. For half the summer you hung around the edges of the waters in the oppressive July heat and, notebook in hand, wrote down everything you saw: how the dragonflies would drop their eggs into the water mid-flight, insert them into swimming leaves or even go under for a few seconds themselves. Some female dragonflies still even form the tandem with their male partners. Other male members keep watch and protect the female from thieves and rivals, for even though they have already laid their fertilized eggs, so read the part of your presentation, the females are still courted by other males and even sexually attacked. The biggest challenge to the male dragonflies is to make the sperm of other contenders unusable. Female dragonflies carry the seed of many males in their so-called sperm-pockets at the back of their bodies. With the sperm of the strongest male the female then fertilizes the seeds herself, she has men in reserve, as it were, and with a grin here you'd have made the dumbfounded faces turn red: as far as dragonflies are concerned, the woman is spoilt for choice.

As you observed how the insects paired, many things about you and Marga became clear: in the words of human beings, this is how you put it in your notebook, female dragonflies are akin to sluts. They go crazy for a summer but only the best lover can be the father of their children, a selection process that over time leads them to producing the toughest insects. In one of your reference books on dragonflies, you found the scientific proof for your thesis: Dragonflies, it was written, are the perfect insect as they posses two habitats, the water and the air. Through their extreme adaptability they are superior to other insects that are sometimes dependent on one specific plant only. However, their means of flight is considered obsolete as, in contrast to other insects, they cannot fold up their wings and lay them along their abdomens. And yet, human beings modelled the helicopter after them and, as you sat on the banks of the pond, in the acrobatic screws and pirouettes of their feeding flights you saw the living proof for this claim: just like a helicopter a dragonfly can remain in place, abruptly change its direction and even fly backwards. The helicopter, this is how you formulated it for your presentation, has only existed for about forty years, the original form of the dragonfly for three hundred million. So, to sum up: first the dragonfly, then the housefly and finally the helicopter. Then, still standing in front of the class where not a single soul would continue to lob about paper-balls, you would have finished with this thought: nature, from the dragonfly through the housefly to the helicopter, has slowly evolved backwards again and, contrary to common opinion, did not realize its most complex creation only in the human being first. Nature, you continued, has no plan, it does not strive for the highest and best, and you intended to give an example from your Confirmation class where Pastor Deichsen maintained that God had made Adam in his own image and Eve from out of the latter's rib. Whoever literally believes what Deichsen says, you were going to conclude, and wants to have something to do with that love-thing must confront a problem: he will either have to break his own, or, Eve's bones, not a very highly developed form of propagation.

At this point you crossed out the paragraph, it seemed too daring; furthermore, your statements were getting away from the topic. In any event, to get back to the point, the dragonfly has always laid its eggs in the water. If it doesn't want to end up a fossil of an extinct species in a natural history museum, it has to secure its survival by collecting sperm. The best dragonfly mother is one that has many men, and again there was a little grin at the corner of your mouth as you uttered your next sentence, which would cause your classmates to grumble for quite some time: Only an uncaring, raven-mother, you say in Tanja's direction, chooses the first guy that comes along.

The fact of the matter is, however, that in front of the classroom door already Tanja knew that you would never say any of this. Not a single one of your classmates would learn anything about dragonflies that morning, it would remain your secret, or at least that's what you thought to understand from her eyes before she closed the door, softly but definitively, as if she wanted to lock herself within the noise of the raging students for ever, or you outside and into the silence of the moor. The truth, Dion, is also that no responsible female dragonfly would ever choose you to be among her lovers in the hard fight for survival. She would immediately recognize you as a stutterer from your sperm and thus there would be the risk of passing on your infirmity to her progeny. As you know, dragonflies communicate with each other through the colours of their bodies, which they use during mating season or for defence. A stuttering dragonfly-child would be colourless, every other dragonfly would ignore it. It would be unable to find a mate and soon be eaten. The stuttering dragonfly could at best hope to pair with another crippled dragonfly, for example, with one like your friend Tanja who suffered from brittle bone disease, a state which has made her shell not like the others' that are made of chitin but of paper or something similar, and would tear apart in the air. A stuttering dragonfly and a glass-bone dragonfly would have children that I would quickly kill off, for here outside it's survival of the fittest.

For that reason alone you cannot tell Tanja that you love her, for it would create a stuttering glass-bone child, a being broken both in speech and slowly within its own body, mute as a child and, as soon as it grew, in a wheelchair. Who would want something like that? When it would be time to play ball the child would have no chance whatsoever, it would simply be ignored, overrun and sent away, like Jakob Wendisch that time, who, as people say, is a mongoloid and who is now in a disabled peoples' home, which makes everyone happy, especially the village children, for he always ruined the Bannabanna game.

Can you remember? At some point the others, the healthy ones, just went away, annoyed, and began to play in the Voss' yard where instead of ragged moor brush there were thick conifers they could hide among.

But Jakob Wendisch wouldn't let himself be gotten rid of so quickly: although he was slow, he was tough and after five minutes was back at the ball. When speaking, if that's what you could call his mumbling, he made even more terrible faces than you and although he was fourteen already, always smelt a little like piss. Even his brothers, the twins in your class, stunk and with their potato-like heads didn't make it seem that their mother had collected the best seeds for her brood and a pair of them on top of it. She too had taken the first man to come along and that, as everyone in the village knows, had been her half-brother. So it'd have to be made clear and right away who the bigger slut in the village was: your mother or Brigitte Wendisch.

And this is the part of your presentation where you would have contradicted me. Nature, this is how you'd have thrown yourself into the fray for Marga, doesn't know such words and cripples can do it with each other, and do. The moor, you would have added, improving my nature, speaks a simple and therefore much richer language than the human beings who live along its edges, those who would condemn a woman simply for choosing the best of many men to be the father of her children. Your father had just not been good enough for Marga. She had acted completely in accordance with the nature of the dragonfly: she had wrestled away his sperm, had had him keep watch over your birth and then sent him away. After the shared laying of eggs, male dragonflies go back to their daily business in the groves and gardens where they go looking for prey, and you would have given further examples of the special features of dragonflies, which—as opposed to the relationships established among other animals like cranes or grey geese—were not monogamous but extremely gifted, nevertheless: how a male dragonfly would help its exhausted beloved back onto land when she came out of the water after laying her eggs; and how other species, the emerald damselfly, for example, even went down with her. However, you were never able to observe what happened then: the moor grasses are dark and with the oily film of dust and grass seeds often blind, even when the sun shines you can barely see a hand's length into the deep. From one moment to the next the flying acrobats change back into swimmers. A moment ago shooting through the air and showing off their beautiful, iridescent bodies to the sun, suddenly they take a breath and, though still close together, perhaps even embracing each other, for a second feel helpless and vulnerable at the mercy of the water and all of its threats: snakes, moor frogs and the mouths of all the ravenous larvae ready to catch their own relatives in order to survive in the barren world of the peat. When the dragonfly-lovers plummet down out of the sky and into the water, so the final sentence in the chapter on reproduction, for a single moment they are utterly, mother-soul-abandoned alone.

In order to be sure that this particular expression would fit within the scientific context of your presentation, you looked it up. You wanted to know just what aloneness had to do with a mother's soul. The dictionary explained that the expression *mother-soul-abandoned alone* was derived from *people-soul-abandoned alone* and served to emotionally reinforce the adjective. A being that has been abandoned by a mother's soul, you deduced, is one that has been abandoned by all others or even by the very soul itself and is, therefore, not only lonely but also downright damned to remaining forever expelled, with neither help nor home, speechless and therefore soulless, full of mute rage and yet filled to the brim with words that it would scream—just like you yourself would have screamed but instead only breathed as on the way home, with a choking in your throat, you had to recognize that Tanja had sought out Hannes' love, that man in the village who was not only the first to cross her path but the one, out of all of those who might ever come over the Heidedamm, who was also the best.

It's your own fault, Dion. You shouldn't have gone home, should have stayed out with me. You wouldn't have seen anything and the whole village would now be looking for you: they'd be combing through the bog myrtle groves and buckthorn breaks with their shovels and driving their dogs to sniff out a track that would only lead into the water but not the way out. Evening after evening your mother would stand out by the pond, waiting for the men to return at the onset of twilight with empty hands and dripping shovels. They'd turn in the direction of the village and tiredly shrug their shoulders as if to say: tomorrow's another day. In the Village Tankard, however, where later they all would gather, after the second or third beer one would say: 'It nicked him.' And a second: 'Whoever goes out that far is nuts.' Gorbach, your German teacher, who is also a part of the search party, shakes his head over his full glass and sighs: 'If only I'd known the boy was serious with what he'd been writing.' 'So what do we tell his mother?' another one calls over from a table. 'We'll chase her into the moor too,' Karl Lambert grumbles, 'then I'll finally be able to get the house back.'

In the meantime, his son Hannes will have snuck away from the kicker table. He will walk down the Dorfstraße, turn onto the Heidedamm and dive into the darkness where Marga is still standing by the pond, looking at the last strip of light on the horizon, and who, a shadow among all the black rising off the ditches, can hardly be recognized any longer. 'I know where he is,' Hannes says, but it could also only be the wind, a drone within the hollow alder boughs. The weeds whisper: Tanja gave him away. Somewhere a runnel gurgles, full with rain. Then it becomes silent for a very long time. 'I know where he is too,' Marga whispers, and looks at Hannes through the darkness. He looks around himself, for suddenly there is no one standing there at all and instead of words he only heard a small sound upon the water, a bubble rising at the point where many, many years ago a young boy drowned . . .

You raise yourself out of the bath, reach for the shampoo and lather yourself, first your head, then your neck and chest, then your hands go further down the slippery skin. When you press yourself into the crevice by your bed, a similar prickling sensation shoots through you: you feel yourself swelling as you stick your pelvis into the crack in time with the second hand on the dragonfly clock, instants stretching into minutes, until a feeling ripples through you which lasts until the next stroke of the dial, a small five-stroke eternity until some sound inside the house or a draught from the window forces the hand onward. You lie and listen to the scratching of a branch against the wall of the house, the soft tick of the clock, Marga's splashing about in the bath; in your body nothing more now than emptiness and silence. The bed has long since forgotten what it saw, it ends there where you flash one final time and only now does the wall on the other side return but old and deaf. But still you think the crevice has got to be full of that trickling which fevered through you, first your abdominal cavity, then, after a long pause that pulled your breath from out of you, down and out. But when you look into the crack you don't see anything but the dirty bumps of the ingrain wallpaper, a dried-out spider by the edge of the bed, bits of fluff, and further back only darkness and ambiguity. No trace in the bed drawer either, even when you pull it all the way out. It must dissolve within that empty silence into which you slide, then sleep comes, sucks it up and spits it out into the moor.

After the thing with Hannes by the slurry tank, you remember, you'd emptied yourself twice, once after another, into the crevice. There must have been a whole lot down there. Then you fell asleep; a tickling on your bottom made you awake with a start. At first you thought it was a mosquito that, attracted by the warmth of your body, was looking for the softest point of skin to bite; you were about to slap it when you noticed Marga sitting on the edge of the bed. She had come close to you with her face and was grinning as if she had discovered something there which made her laugh, and only at the end of that long and mocking look did you understand that it had been her hand. You shrank away from her like you did when you were younger, those times she came to you with a thermometer and you wriggled under her and ever deeper into the fever-hot sheets. But once again, just as in Hannes' headlock before, another force held you back and stopped you from moving, as if injecting you with a numbing poison. You laid still in the touch, felt the goosebumps wander up your back from out of the depths of the bed crevice that you, sleepy and long limp, no longer filled, felt a voiceless, knowing glance; and then, over your half-naked, slightly sweaty body, suddenly the buzzing of her soft and cold laugh, dark and superior as a crane. You held your breath and, as when younger, bit into your pillow—in reality, you never felt the thermometer once it was inside you but, as soon as she put it in, it was always ice cold in your belly, it was as if she had deep-frozen you with her hand. Even today that chill feeling is the worst thing you remember from your childhood, a black feeling that kept a tight hold on you even with your business about the toilet as well.

Embarrassing enough that that was why Marga could not leave the bathroom. While you hung tightly to the toilet seat, Marga would sit on the edge of the bathtub filing her nails, browsing through a fashion magazine or simply staring at you absently, which was uncomfortable, for she was there to keep watch, not stare. You would have loved to have sent her away but your fear of falling into the toilet drain held you back. How the cold came up from the water, not really, but in your imagination, and caressed you, an invisible hand arising out of the drain.

You have often traced the course of the pipe in your thoughts: after the bottomless shaft underneath the crevice takes the not uncommon twice-daily, dribbling white substance into itself, it runs out under the Heidedamm near the drain cover engulfed by stinging nettles and out into the open by the field. Camouflaged by the undergrowth, it tumbles out of the earth and feeds into a wide drainage ditch edged by bushes as it crosses through the pastures and leads the drainage water out of the peat-ditches and into the Jumme River. The sight of the tunnel holes from which—beneath the trails and tractor ramps—the black creek silently and, as it always seemed to you, a little grimly ran into the furrows filled you with terror even then. Like a toothless mouth it gaped in the bushes and spit the rest of your digestion out between the weeds that feed on the foam which accumulates into sponge-like, ulcerous shapes the wind rips into yellowish flakes.

As much as the drain and its seeping swill scared you as a child, it always lured you back; with a single hand you clawed yourself up into the pliable branches of a willow and stared, captivated, over the embankment into the abyss which led out of the blue summer day and into the depths of the peat. When you used the toilet, the drain's mouth threateningly appeared to you across the empty surface of the floor tiles. The thought that you could slip in and be whirled away by the flush of the tank always made defecating a nightmare for you. Even when there was nothing to be done, you sometimes lifted the seat and glanced into the bowl where there swam a sodden tissue or tuft of hair from Marga's blond mane. You would push the toilet flush button continuously, all the water gurgling away but then there it would be again, in the hole, as still, dark and deceitful as the drainage ditch all the village children are afraid of, for behind it is where I lie in wait.

Back then, however, your dread of me was useless. Even when you were a young boy I could barely trick you much longer, being well aware of my duplicity and attempts to deceive you with alder ghosts and horror stories of sinking and drowning. The trauma of the drain must have had its beginnings in kindergarten. You remember how David Voss, at that point already the most devious of all the village children, had thrown your favourite toy, a white plush fish, into the toilet. Marginalized from the role-playing group already, after your first failed attempts at speaking, for hours you had played with the silent animal, tugging it across the blue linoleum with the flutes or waves where you imagined the water reaching all the way up to the backs of the chairs. The smaller children still crawling about the floor were the dragonfly larvae, the slightly bigger kids the fish on the hunt for water insects. Or did you only add this image to your memories later? At that point in time, you didn't know very much about dragonflies.

But you remember David Voss' declaration of war very well indeed: the fish, like you, had to go home right away, he'd explained and pushed the flush button. You saw the water swirl and the stuffed animal come up for air once last time, then both were gone. The drain smacked its lips, or was it Thorsten Hinrich standing behind you, already David's henchman and thug, fat, sweaty and horribly gaseous just like today, only smaller. Then you went back to the others and were given the role of the stock boy in the shop, which meant you didn't have too say nor do very much, and so your eyes wandered to the window and were pulled by an invisible signal to the drain-mouths beneath the brush which at some point would spit the white fish back out into freedom.

Your first encounter with me was on the kindergarten toilet, the last—for the time being—this afternoon by the large kolk beyond the horizon and, as you had hoped, behind the last visible line of the land but which, instead, only turned out to be a bank of fog in front of the next wall of clouds, with me, the moor, as a border in between. The grass where you had laid yourself down, deathly tired, simply would not let you sink, for it is only in the stories that I devour lost children, an easily forgotten mistake, just like children are mistaken when they begin to question the fairy tales adults tell; a disappointed glance, a quick regret, then back out into the world. In the end, all of the shit from Fenndorf, yours too, Dion, comes to the community sewage treatment plant in Zeeve where the sewage authorities make no difference between you and the others.

Nevertheless, your mother sat on the edge of the bathtub until the end of your third school year, fixing her fingernails, seeking out new patterns in the catalogue or staring directly into the secrets of your body, for she also was in charge of cleaning you up. When she came from underneath with the toilet paper, on top you felt that heat and in your stomach below the chill, just like when she took your temperature. And just like when taking your temperature, that night after the thing with Hannes—which you had no intention of ever telling her about—you froze and at the same time sunk into her hand as she began to caress your bottom, at first over the small of your back, then deeper, as if she wanted to take your temperature or make sure you were already clean.

'Clean up the crap and come eat,' she said and stood up, and you didn't understand, the crap on your shoes, on the stairs or what was in the crevice. She had barely left the room when you moved the bed away from the wall. More withered spiders came to light, a dusty pencil, your long lost key ring and on the wall yellowish and faded traces, almost invisible, as if a long time ago moor water had run over the wallpaper. Although you had often stood at the drain and stared into the foaming maw, the white fish never appeared again, from either the drain or the bottom of your bed.

You grab yourself and bend your erection out of the water. According to the ruler you apply almost every day, you measure thirteen centimetres, thirteen and a half if you drive the zero into your skin until it hurts. David Voss wins with seventeen, but whenever you've looked over his shoulder at the urinal you've only seen a gold stream between his fingers, nothing else. Even the other kids from your class to the left and right of you at the trough have only measly and tiny things. Maybe you will soon have to move your bed a bit away from the wall in order to have more room. Marga, you've sworn to yourself, can't learn anything about it, from either the ruler or the crevice where it's hidden together with your notebook. That she'd compared your penis in both size and appearance to a larva that morning is, first, an insult, and, second, from a biological point of view, incorrect. Firstly, you would have had to tell her, as an embryo the human being is probably more of a worm but never a larva. A child docs not moult; on the contrary, its skin slowly grows together with the bones and organs and only in adulthood does it gradually begin to deteriorate. A dragonfly, on the other hand, once an imago, remains as it is until the end. You have already been collecting the exuviae for years and, furthermore, even the longest larva shell in your collection barely measures five centimetres. At the most, the body of a grown mosaic maiden, which was the largest dragonfly to be found in your area, would reach seven lines on the ruler. In the portrait you'd had to pose for over the last few days, she'd painted you with the little penis of an emerald or white-legged damselfly, both of which barely make it over four, and you straighten up while pushing your bottom simultaneously forward, beyond the limits of your flexibility, until your body forms a kind of wheel and with the tip of your tongue you can touch your glans.

Or just about. Tough luck, Dion, maybe you're just not crippled enough for that. Jakob Wendisch could do it blindfolded. At the swimming hole on the Jumme—just like that—the mongoloid was in the jackknife position. Shoulders to pelvis, mouth down onto his penis, at first the group around David Voss tickled him, then they simply kicked. While everyone was splashing around in the water on one of the last hot days of the summer break, Voss had stolen Jakob's swimming trunks right before he had to go back to the home. You already knew that the handicapped boy, who in the meantime had shot up and had quite a broad stature, was that flexible from playing on the meadow when, during races, you had knocked him out of the way or kicked out his legs so that you wouldn't have to lose to the village idiot on top of it all. Although you were a number of metres ahead of Jakob—who, instead of sprinting, jerkily skidded forward—once back at the ball the initial letter of his name, that friendly and benevolent, almost jovial *J* with its inconspicuous barb became a yoke around your spastic chin. Nevertheless, you found the torture at the Jumme to be unjust and mean; for, just like back then, as Jakob tumbled over your shin and plumped down into the grass without trying to catch himself once with his hands, this time he didn't turn against his tormentors either.

All the same you laughed out of the fear that you might be next. They punched him into the water and harassed him with pinches and pokes, things that had always made Jakob grin and chuckle regardless of whether it bothered or pleased him. Even the nipping and tugging at his bathing suit must have made him happy; when David Voss finally held the trophy up in his hand, Jakob protruded haplessly big and healthy. Could he blow himself? David yelled, grabbed him by his hair and pushed his face down towards his erection and further into the river until the water sloshed into his mouth and ran back out of his nose, first the dark Jumme, then bright blood. Heavy and bleeding Jakob walked over the sand and into the brush. It was the first time you hadn't heard him coo and giggle; suddenly somehow pushed with a sound like a wounded animal, he disappeared into the rushes. Morons, David Voss proclaimed to the group, always have the biggest ones but can't do anything with 'em. He stuffed his head into Jakob's trunks and hollered 'Mongo,' but no one was laughing any more.

As Daniela Bloch, the shopkeeper's daughter and class-mate who sat next to Tanja, joined in the shrieks coming from above the water as the girls saw what before had only been rumoured about Jakob Wendisch, Tanja sat motionless within the shade of a tree. You remember she wasn't wearing any underwear under her skirt or had taken them off before carefully wading out into the water up to her thighs as if, at least in that way, she could take part in the others' summer fun. And that's when you had seen that, in spite of her fragility and small size, for quite some time Tanja Deichsen had not been a little girl, but a young, maturing woman, full of fantasies and cravings just like all the others but with the one difference that youth's adventures would likely pass her by, which was to say, that none of her swaggering classmates would do the thing with her but instead would try to woo her friend Danni, what with her slipping bikini and skin-tight panties, and maybe that's why on that hot August afternoon, which you yourself would have rather spent reading in the shade instead of in the middle of the tumult, she, Tanja, had opened up her legs a little bit wider when she felt your glance but then quickly turned away as at that very moment there was the sputter of a moped.

The girls went quiet and even the boys' heads turned around. Everyone looked over to the cloud of dust rising over the reeds. Hannes, his chest bare, rolled the machine over the sandbank, handcart in tow with a case full of beer and a half dozen bicycles, which the group let clatter over the gravel. He jacked up his ride and looked over, a single glance enough to declare the area his property. Tanja wiped her skirt flat and bent over to whisper to Daniela who had sat back down next to her and now laughed shrilly. The clique noisily spread out. The sun already stood deep in the sky, now just barely over the whipping tips of the bulrushes. A smooth light melted upon the river where swarms of mosquitoes built themselves up into clouds. Over in the village the church tower struck the full hour, four blows barely holding together, hollow and lost as if from the end of the world. Hannes hefted the case of beer into the water. His blond hair gleamed in the sunlight, its reddish tinge flickering like a tiny flame. On his cheeks and shoulders the freckles had come out and given his reddened skin a dirty or crusty appearance as if the dust of the fields had settled there. The girls giggled as he splashed his face and upper arms with water which ran down his thighs in small streams and into his jeans, leaving bright traces on his skin. A few of the boys slipped away, but David Voss ploughed through the river right over to Hannes, spit and said: 'I want a beer too.' He pulled a bottle out of the case and threw it out onto the water. Before it sank the glass flashed in the backlight.

Tanja packed up her things, the others pulled the towels, cassette player and snacks a bit further up the bank. Hannes cracked open the beers with a lighter and handed the bottles out to his buddies. As Tanja awkwardly stood up and shouldered her backpack, he got in her way, handed her a beer and said: 'It's only seven.' The sun went behind a wall of cirrus clouds which had suddenly turreted onto the horizon. The sky became white, Tanja's face was bronze, her eyes dangerously blue as if made of copper sulphate. She briefly looked over towards you as if seeking your approval, then took the bottle and sat down in the sand; and before she turned her back to you, within that triangle of looks for a moment it was as if only Tanja, Hannes and you existed in the world.

The water rippled in the wind, the rushes waved, a duck flew off laughing and you suddenly began to feel cold, so you slipped on a T-shirt and lost yourself in your book. Voss turned the cassette player all the way up, the older students making fun of the oldies. From out of the corner of your eye you saw Tanja take a timid sip from the beer bottle while throughout the circle the lighters clicked and, in order to make a bonfire, Hannes began to collect branches, which he then broke over his knee in front of the stone-lined fire circle.

In retrospect, you believe that must have been the start. In the first weeks of school to follow, you often saw Hannes' moped parked in the church square, without a doubt not to go to Communion. When Tanja had to miss a week of school because of a complicated operation in a special clinic in Hamburg and then spend a second one at home in bed, her friend Danni had collected her homework. But I should tell you right away, Dion, that Hannes Lambert was the one who brought it to her. In the hallway he wrangled the folders away from Daniela and she understood; for, ever since that night on the beach by the Jumme, Tanja and him had been infatuated with each other.

Before the break, the Bloch's daughter had started to make, with kohl even bigger, eyes at the pig farmer's son, and barely out of the classroom would undo the two upper buttons of her blouse, both of which, however, left Hannes cold although Daniela already had more to offer than the still spindly Tanja. But that was precisely what seemed to excite Hannes, that boniness, those edges. Once Hannes' gang already had the third beer in them and the smell of burnt sausages lay over the sand, Daniela had changed her clothes on the beach, what no other girl would dream of doing, behind a puny birch which concealed nothing at all. But Hannes did not even look over once. You had him right in your sights without having once been exposed to his attentive eyes. In your hollow behind the tree you had seen Daniela's ass, the whole mass, because, so it seemed to you, she had intentionally got tangled up when putting on her panties so that Hannes would finally look. He cracked another beer and gave it to Tanja. The first bottle still stood next to her in the sand, half full, you remember, for the bonfire was already burning so brightly that you could see how much was in the glass.

Was she holding back because of you? The thought made you feel a little proud and you planned to hang around the bank the whole night and until the next day if necessary—that way you could show Tanja the dragonfly's morning dance. Around midnight Hannes would pass out, drunk, and that's when the moment of truth would arrive; you would slide over with your towel, carefully take the beer bottle out of your competitor's hand and let it clink against Tanja's who would now be smiling and taking the stuff down like she'd been practising. A cloud covers the moon, the shadows of the reeds grow a little higher into the air and offer the best possible cover, even that annoying frog would eventually give up defending his territory and you would finally, finally make a go of it.

The truth, however, is that Tanja doesn't drink any alcohol on account of the strong pills she has to take and is very disciplined besides. At the Advent's bazar where in the evening all the adults tipsily totter about and even the children are a little bit drunk because they've been emptying out the dregs of the leftover glasses of mulled wine, she just warms her hands around a cup of tea. But she had accepted a cigarette from Hannes. That's when Daniela, who had finally made it into her jeans, showed up in front of her. Would she finally be coming home now? she asked snappily, and Tanja put the cigarette out, but Hannes shook his head. You imagined how later he'd bring her home on his moped, she pressed tightly to him or already half-asleep on his shoulder. You jumped up quickly and went after the Bloch daughter angrily trudging away through the reeds; she turned around suddenly, pushed you and hissed: 'There's something going on between you three!' Startled you fell back into the rushes and straight into Jakob Wendisch's arms.

The mongoloid was sitting on one of the fallen stumps and staring at you out of his flat face understandingly before he spit out a gurgling noise, half-surprise, half-threat, 'Don't come too close,' or 'What do you want?' You remained standing between his open legs and eyeballed his massive shoulders and the hair ruffling out underneath. He smelt like sweat and suntan lotion, the messy white film gleamed on his neck. Had he gone home and then secretly come back? He wore a worn-out sleeveless T-shirt and shorts; you'd seen his pile of clothes and shoes back on the beach under the tree.

A crust of blood was stuck to his nostril. As you didn't move, he thought the danger was past and went back to his self-contained game: he was observing the mosquitoes which were landing on his arms in great numbers, would wait for one to bite him, and then kill it at that defenceless moment with an extremely agile hand. He'd rub the tiny drops of blood that remained behind to his skin together with the mosquito's body. That's how it went three, four times, on his underarm and then the inside of his thigh which was thick with white-blonde down; he even unerringly got the insect that landed on his cheek. Then, finally, you lifted your own hand. Jakob cringed and peeked out from behind his elbow; maybe he was even afraid of your fist, still frightened by what had happened down at the river. You laid your finger across your lips and ordered him with your eyes not to move. The mosquito on his shoulder was taking its time; first it crawled over towards his throat, then back into the soft fold of skin of his armpit. You squashed it at exactly the right moment. Jakob grinned and smacked himself on the chest so strongly that the imprint of his fingers with two mosquito corpses glowed white on his sunburn. You struck out and got him on the temples, he got up onto a calf, then your flat hand clapped against his shoulder blade, he countered with a hit on your arm. Thanks to the counter-attack the insects seemed to become vindictive and even more bloodthirsty. Jakob smacked your ears, you gave him a bump on the nose, a headbutt and push in the groin where there wasn't any bloodsucker at all. The staccato of clapping sounds mixed in with Jakob's excited grunts, the distant squawks from the cassette player and the sounds of the frogs in the din of a battle where the voices of the mosquitoes, if they could have screamed in mortal agony, would have been the most worthy of mercy.

But so was Jakob's sudden whimper. In order to have more space to fight he had bared his stomach, which had made his trousers slide onto his hip bones; your eyes—which rushed back and forth over his powerful, not in the least crippled body—suddenly taking in the flaxen bush of hair. With his fingers he had just laughingly smeared a mixture of mosquitoes and sweat under your shirt, now your fist shot past the insect wriggling about in the fluff around his navel and went directly into his waistband. The piece of flesh in your hand was big but soft and limp. Jakob let out a high-pitched, bird-like warning call, bent your arm back and hurled you to the ground. Then he stumbled away, wailing, through the buzzing noise of the stinging bugs and off through the reeds.

You were up and similarly off through the entrails, running blindly through the lashes of the cattails all the way home, your skin speckled black with mosquito carcasses and your face blazing with shame through the suddenly cool evening air rising off the river, onto the porch and directly into Marga's unpleasant grumbling as she sat impatiently at the table in front of the now-cold stew. 'It's your own fault,' she chewed; pinched and itching you could barely hold the spoon in your hand. She had nothing else to say about your unsettling experiences at the banks of the Jumme, and the rest of the evening your imploring glances mostly crashed against her back so that everything you wanted to stutter to her about your day—shivering, bitten all over but somehow still happy—you scribbled into your notebook instead after finally having fevered the urgency of your thoughts out of you and into the crevice.

You grab yourself even tighter. Rub soap into the hollow of your hand which is now lathered so well that it is a far better replacement for the missing body than the rigid crevice by your bed. You grit your teeth as the white, viscous strings glide through the water. The bar of soap springs out of your fingers and across the tiles against the rack where Marga's stuff is heaped, all the dishes with perfumes and powder between boxes of medicine, cosmetic tissues, sanitary napkins, things which have been lying there so long that you hardly notice them any longer. The steam has dissipated a little, in the mirror you recognize the outline of your face, the hair on the sides of your head almost as long as your chin for you don't let Marga use the scissors any more; your goal is to have a mop of hair just like Hannes with a fringe and coming forward around the nape of your neck to look daring. And yet, despite all your efforts, you'll never be able to match your uncle's red-blonde child. Thanks to your Lambert genes, you'll merely get a few freckles when you sit out in the sun long enough in August.

Otherwise in the mirror everything's the same as always. However, you cannot shake the feeling that between that morning at the pond and this moment there is a long and empty period of time, a type of blind patch in your memory as if you had slept through the entire day. Or had it been months and years? The young boy on the stump, who at that moment was still you, now seems distant and incomprehensible, you are almost embarrassed for him, hanging about waiting for a miracle and pleading with his mother, finger stuck in the moss. Whatever he felt and thought has become foreign to you. As if this morning you had taken leave of him for ever, you want to pull him towards you while pushing him away. You bend yourself out of the bath and fish Marga's pills out of the drawer. You turn the package around in your fingers and look at what's written there: the name of the medicine, Lexotax, and next to it the blue rhombus, or hexagon, and again the same in white with the word Roche inside of it, which you had always read without having understood. You spelled out R-O-C-H-E in your head and thought of rays, the flat fish on the bottom of the sea, but had no idea what the connection between the fish and your mother's pills could be. Then you sought out the chapter on the animal in your nature dictionary and found a picture. Its body was white, almost see-through. Its skeleton and inner organs shimmered through its skin. Even its brain looked like a shadow, and within it, the two eyes it carried on its back; being a flatfish, the ray did not have a head. In the photograph the light went straight into the water, and once you had stared at the animal long enough for the contours to blur, the eyes and brain-shadows together with the line of the spine and the triangular design of the viscera took on the form of a small person, a young girl in a white dress.

You'd quickly closed the book; now you believed you knew what the word *Roche* in the white diamond on the package meant. Over the following days you had looked in your animal dictionary again and again and observed the fish, its look tempting you like something forbidden and secret which now wanted to be deciphered and discovered. After Marga had pressed her goodnight kiss to you and closed the door, you turned the lamp back on, pulled the book out from under the bed and studied the ray. The longer you bored into it with your eyes, the clearer Marga's features arose from out of its insides. When on account of fatigue you began to squint, there no longer seemed to be any doubt: the little girl in the ray was your mother, and even David Voss must have suspected something like that when he flushed your white fish down the toilet.

As Marga loved the water—every morning in the pond and long evenings in the bath—you thought that the Lexotax would slowly turn her back into the little girl she once had been. But then you also understood why the water in the pond made her so much younger. Her insistence was thus only a tactic to drag you out into the cold even on days with awful weather. In truth, she was tempting the boy who had long lived inside the ray. But how had he got into its stomach? You considered the puzzle for entire days. Then, late one night while brooding about it in your notebook where the story was slowly taking shape, the sudden flash of insight: the girl had to have once been a dragonfly larva. Dragonflies, their eggs and larvae in particular, are first on a fish's menu. Evenings on the banks of the Jumme you'd often watched barbels or breams fall back into the river after having jumped after a lightning-quick insect. And finally you knew what the real reason for your year-long angst of the toilet drain had to have been: it was there that the white ray was lying in wait. At some point it had come up the Elbe from the sea, swum through the meandering Jumme to Fenndorf and carried your mother away; for in the moor there were no fishermen to fear who could have stolen Marga away themselves. From the river it had then made it through the drainage ditches and into the peat where it had hidden himself away with her. But it hadn't reckoned with your father who had managed to grab the fish with his hands. And so it had had to give Marga up, but now the ray was waiting somewhere in the sewer canals and ready to take her back. Shivering you had shoved your notebook with the half-finished story back into the crevice which at that point seemed deeper and more knowing than ever before. And yet, one question kept you awake: How had the larva ever come to the sea, there where everything lives with the exception of the dragonflies' children?

There was nothing on the patient information leaflet you pulled out of the package about any of that. According to the producers *Hoffmann-La Roche* Lexotax—which you read with a mixture of disappointment and relief—was a remedy for tension, agitation and anxiety, nervousness, inner unrest, insomnia and depressive episodes; in other words, for everything you did not like about your mother. You press a tablet out of the strip and—stuck between your index finger and thumb—hold it up to the light. You recognize the finely pored surface, the groove in the middle and behind it, as if through a broken magnifying glass, you yourself, just like the night before when you'd stood in her bedroom and all the blister packs had been strewn across her bed as if she'd wanted to swallow all the pills at once, an entire handful, which at the last minute she must have reconsidered. You know exactly what you had thought: if the story in your notebook had even a kernel of truth, with time the stuff would have to change you—the moor-child of the girl in the ray's stomach—into a dragonfly.

And, in fact, after swallowing the pill your body already began to feel lighter, for it was as if the invisible strings holding you to the ground had been severed. Everything shifted into the distance: the walls, the furniture, your own two feet; your upper body seemed to shrink while stretch downward like a kind of pole, like a dragonfly's body. It was if you were floating over the tiles, even if only a few millimetres, but still. Round after round you walked through the house. When you stretched your arms out, you thought you were sinking and at the same time somehow falling upward. At some point you landed on your bed where you could still feel Marga's mouth on your throat, cold as a fish. 'My poor darling,' she blubbered from out of the depths, and then devoured you, or you had simply fallen asleep.

You plunge your hand into the water, search for the stopper and wrap the metal chain around your finger; for a moment the plug loosens before it is snapped back by the suction. Just one jerk of your hand and you will be back down here with me, in the drain's mouth, in the fish's stomach, your story finished. You stretch yourself out and slip down into the water up to your chin. Your knees and shoulders create islands that slowly, but steadily, sink. You tense your abdominal wall and your thighs and imagine the moor enveloping you. In your head the film rushes past: suddenly Hannes is standing over you. Right next to you the stubble cats scream and lift their little heads out of the mire, you jump out and see the tips of moss growing out of the water, small, dark bumps and above them the circling of a large bird. A crane? As it comes closer, you recognize it as the short-eared owl, the bird of twilight, which you only meet here once you have left the last tree behind and stepped out into the void. It sits in the sedges and, as soon as you get closer, lets out a warning call which sounds like a cat's miaow. The owl's shadow glides across the water to you, then turns and rises into the sky where it disappears. Hannes too solidifies in the remains of a birch tree on the shore. A slit opens in the clouds, a sickly, death-scared blue; Tanja smiles one final time. In her eyes the flash of something like pride; she knows that this is right—you below, she above. Just like this, and nothing else.

The thought drowns and is not replaced. Relieved you release your muscles and give over to the sinking, this last, endless movement, soft, a stream, in the rhythm of your slowly exhaled breath, like a sentence without a stutter. As soon as you've spoken it—and this is your last thought before you pull out the stop—we have become one.

You hadn't heard her coming at all. Until now you had thought that dragonflies buzzed through the air. That is how it had always been: the black point of the insect still distant, you would look around and upward. The others heard a car on the Dorfstraße but you saw the dragonfly come in through the open classroom window and thought: Watch out! It's a trap! Now she's sitting and staring at you, motionless and beautiful, completely red. From the colour of her abdomen you recognize she is a blood-red darter. Even her forehead—which, unlike in humans, was not located above her eyes but below—was red as was her mouth, the mandibles as if painted with lipstick or the blood of one of its victims. To be strictly accurate you had neither seen nor heard her but simply sensed her with your feelers—the pressure wave in the air, the vibration of its wings, that she sought a man. Males are the first to approach the water and to occupy the territory. Only once enough partners have arrived does the female come to choose.

She had given herself time to observe you, perhaps even the entire day. While you were looking for your seat, she had had you in her sights. Now you have to hurry. You must approach her cautiously but surely, intentionally. Dragonflies are more complicated than humans. The male's sperm is produced by the sexual organ at the end of the abdomen, which in human beings would be similar to the testicles; the so-called copulatory apparatus, a kind of penis, is to be found much more to the front, below the chest. First you must bend the lower segment of your abdomen so that your body forms a kind of wheel. If at this point you were still a human being, it would look like you wanted to take your own penis into your mouth. But even this comparison isn't quite right, for in this kind of love, the mandibles are not used at all. Dragonflies do not kiss first but get right down to the business at hand.

You grab yourself and bend down until you form the wheel. She is still sitting there and watching you prepare your seed. As soon as you have collected enough, you shoot into the air. You corkscrew upward, rush towards her and with your abdominal claspers grab her around the neck. For a moment you both are in free fall, but as your film slows down within the compound eyes, you have enough time before impact. Right before the surface of the water you can tear her back up. She wriggles in your embrace and turns away; but this is only affectation, she has been waiting for you. Up until that point all the others had not been good enough. Now she bends herself into a half-circle and presses her long, thin, ruby red abdomen against you at that point where you have rippled outward. She will take everything into herself, check it and find the best so that you can become the father of her children. She will reject the others' sperm she has been collecting in her pockets up until then while you both continue to dance in tandem through the air above the pond, within the rays of a late sun.

Over on the stump the boy pulls his mother by the arm, points to the two of you and calls out: 'Look, a heart!' and the mother smiles, bends over and presses her lips—which still taste like a goodnight kiss—to the boy's mouth, the kiss he's been waiting for the whole day long.

TWO

Winter

When the snow comes, the stillness begins to move. The sky dissolves the clouds, extinguishes the horizon, only the crow on the tree stump is still stuck in white, one final stroke, soon blotted out. Above that, the mist creates a second layer into which the rime-enveloped birches tower, fleeting filigrees of cold and light. And then the wind. One final rustling from the bog myrtle, there the creaking of dead wood from beyond the ditch behind which everything seems to end, the children's games, summer's promises, autumn with its decaying sounds, here and there every echo silenced beneath the thin layer of ice that formed upon the water overnight, a soft gurgling, rising gases, a tiny hollow below the ice, winter's eyes. And finally, the bubbles' gaze within the blind sky, the crow's mournful cry as, with a piece of carrion in its beak, it takes off from out of the rushes, the heavy beat of its wings, a dwindling black trace in the clouds of snow, and then nothing, only the silence which slowly, ever so slowly, begins to fall.

This is how you remember me in your book: the beginning of the snowstorm—when they came to pick Marga up—within a spinning light that continued to flicker in the darkness, blue and silent. There was no need to turn on the siren again, no car would get in the way on the country road, no one in Fenndorf travelled anywhere nights after ten o'clock. They took her away silently, discretely, almost secretly, as if even the paramedics were ashamed to be with her. One of them pulled the grey blanket up to her neck. But all of them had seen her exanimated face, even paler in the blue light which continued to whirl for a time in the courtyard and that, every time it brushed the barn wall, reflected in the glass panel, as if serrated because of a crack, as if it wanted to burrow inside and direct the view onto Marga's worktable, into the centre of the tragedy the villagers had gathered around, shoulder to shoulder, to stare at the stretcher.

The shadows of the men bending over her turned gigantic and jumped over the walls when the light of the siren took hold of their bodies. They wore red protective clothing with silver reflective stripes that lit up in the rotating light and which still ignite your dreams where Marga is sitting again in the barn painting or at least trying to paint or maybe just hunched over, staring and guzzling away until the last bottle rolls into the corner together with a lost pill and the white canvas begins to bend in front of her eyes and dissolve into flakes, of snow the storm sets loose. But, in retrospect, doesn't the wind which came back that night tear at you more strongly now than before?

At some point the blue light flickered off into the distance. Those who were still standing around went back into their houses, their hooded faces turned towards you one last time so that you looked to the ground, to your naked feet beneath the seams of your pyjama bottoms which had already taken on the colour and feeling of ice. Only Marianne Lambert continued to stand next to you. Today you describe your aunt as smaller and more bent over than the boy had seen her then: you were a frightened child to whom, at that moment, she must have seemed giant-like and threatening, and although barely forty, already as shapeless as an old woman in her grimy robe and the felt slippers in which she'd tumbled out of the house.

She came even closer, grabbed your head and pressed it to her sourdough-smelling armpits as if by having you look into the dried leaves you would be kept from having to see the tyre-tracks, the stretcher being carried away, Marga's vomit-encrusted mouth with the breathing tube, an image like the fragment of a shattered happiness which had already been driven deep into your body and had begun to kill everything there; for, at the latest, that night—that's how it's written in your book—was the beginning of a long, possibly life-long, coldness. But is coldness even a word for the condition in which you have been frozen ever since?

The frost, in any event, had come early, after the storms that most often came down from the north around Reformation Day and swept away the last leaves from the trees, those leaves which were so fragile they crumbled apart on the ground and you heard the sound, pulled your head out of your aunt's embrace and saw her face grimace in shock or secret self-satisfaction before the bluish reflection on the horizon which refused to be erased and which perhaps was the first morning light, caught there in the willow branches swaying in the wind, naked, stretching into the air as if to pull the silence down to cover themselves. And then, in fact, it began to snow.

All of that just blurry shapes now, hesitant strokes on the sketch of a portrait you have to finish without knowing where it will lead or why you're the one who has to finish it. Marga herself could have painted it with her own technique which never had a concrete form and seldom allowed for any clear colours to appear. As soon as something stood out on the canvas, or one of her own pigments mixed with another to form a colour that a child from the area might have recognized, as soon as any thought arose in your mind of something you knew or loved, she would obliterate it with the sponge or quickly smear a new layer across the canvas.

You remember how sometimes you would become impatient or downright furious when you observed her painting as you pretended to rummage through the junk: a magician holding out a toy to you, only to whisk it away with a wink into her sleeve. The truth is your juvenile game did not do the trick any more. On one of the previous evenings, in spite of the cold, she stood out on the porch smoking in her negligee, you in front of her with the cotton grass in your hair and mouth. 'If it weren't for you,' she said, 'I'd end it all,' and you had angrily shrugged your shoulders and torn the moor-masquerade from your face; to you, *all* seemed as colourless as black or white, all was nothing, empty in the way her pictures often remained, or a mess of layers that sunk beneath their own weight.

But that is exactly what she meant. Her struggle with painting, which really did seem to mean everything to her, as well as her job in Hamburg, where she had stopped going. She maintained she was on sick leave, though she didn't seem sick to you, not like she had the flu. What the illness was you would only understand much later, and that you could not go on sick leave with something like that, or not back then anyway. Back then you still thought that maybe she finally wanted to give up smoking, for she had stared disgustedly at the cigarette and crushed it out; but you were familiar with such talk already. 'Tomorrow I'm done,' and then, sur-prise, the next one. Or was it really all the tedious housework, the eternal streaks of toothpaste in the sink and having to cook for you? Over the last few weeks there had not been any more everything-soup, not a sin-gle peeled potato, only bread with butter and a lot of cinnamon. She was interested in that much at least. You had considered every possibility, but not this one: blue light, paramedics, the vomit on your bed that stunk for days out of the mattress and turned your nights into deserts, sour, full of dead life. You write: like the moor.

In the end she still had blown a tuft of grass away from your upper lip, a bit bored. Pursed her lips, exhaled forcefully, or had it already been her final sigh, a kind of death rattle in which you should have recognized how burdensome everything had become, painting, the grind in Hamburg, the decrepit house with the as-yet-immature child, that apron-puller and speech-cripple she grabbed by the arm and said, 'But *you* still exist,' a sentence which was as much a relief as it was an accusation, and while you still had not known what she meant, you continued to play along at being the old man.

She'd pressed the old woman's kiss to you, and the following day covered a new frame with canvas, cooked everything-soup, with sausage even, and, as always, walked back and forth across the courtyard smoking; but then, two days later, with an entire package of Lexotax inside her, come to you in bed. Her stagger, the strange paleness, the claw with its fingers stinking of cigarettes and turpentine, the spit forth, almost gagged 'But I love you so!' on your cheek before falling over, which you did not actually notice because in the next moment you had fallen back asleep, a failing you still have not forgiven yourself for. At some point a kick under the blanket, her body convulsing, a groan you thought you could hear in your dreams, or really a blubbering, as if underwater, as if one last dive into the pond. Suddenly the flood of vomit onto the pillow, your panic, hands everywhere, her body now limp, slack, as if boneless, eyes closed, even after the shaking, even after the slap which echoed through the room, the eyeball in its socket completely white; it was the first time you had ever hit her, and then right in the face.

For a few seconds you did not know what to do. An indescribable fear rose up from your stomach, through your throat, and suddenly turned to ice at your temples; you shook and shivered uncontrollably until you did not want to do anything but sleep. But still, you went down to the telephone, in the silence the open line, a black hole devouring everything. And so you hung the receiver back up. In any event, you hadn't said a single word. Over instead to Farmer Lambert, barefoot, stones boring into the soles of your feet, their stabs almost outside of your body, at that time already a kind of phantom pain. Stumbling, still more stones, the somehow comforting notion of a trace of blood across the Heidedamm, but that too only came into the book later on.

The darkness between the tractors was almost liquid-like, a dollop, and the dog that didn't bark—whether deaf or knowing you already—rattled on its metal chain. An eternity until someone opened the door.

Hannes, in his pyjamas, hair a mess from the pillow. He looked annoyed and just stared at you. Looking into his open mouth, for a moment you were frightened because you had forgotten why you were even there. But he had already turned around and yelled: 'Mother!'

You even remained silent with Marianne, but she had already read everything in your eyes; in spite of being overweight and the inertia of sleep, she was very quick. She threw on her robe, dug through a drawer for a key, or maybe a flashlight, but why, on the Heidedamm there were already streetlights, and furthermore, it was her very own, familiar ground. Suddenly she turned around, shook you and yelled: 'Boy!,' this one word only echoing endlessly through the hall; your uncle Karl appeared on the stairs. The night now colder than just a few minutes before. Over to the house again, the flapping of Marianne's slippers, a soft cursing, maybe a piece of gravel in her shoe? In your memory she remained standing there, bent over, then back up, then the flashlight in her hand. You began to shake. In the hallway the receiver swung on its cord, you were sure you had hung it back up, had hoped Marga would have come back to, and called the emergency services herself. But she was still laying face down on your bed, her face turned towards you on the pillow, sleeping, as beautiful as ever. In front of it, like a wall of glass, the smell of vomit, a child's sleep, death. Marianne recoiled and yelled, 'Christ, Marga!' exasperated as if she had seen it all coming. She fell onto her, hoisted her up; Marga's head fell forward. Marianne held her chin, combed the hair off her forehead. Then her hands on Marga's heart, her pulse, for seconds a breathless silence, then another yell, 'A pulse!'

Where were you standing at that moment? Were you still in the hall, in the doorway or already back in bed? For some time the boy in these pictures doesn't appear at all, as if you had fallen into some hole in time, through your wide glances and into your own head: there is the house, brightly lit when seen from the pond, its jagged gable, the sooty clinker bricks, spots of light above them, almost like a fire in the moonless night, crushed beneath snow-heavy clouds. At the edges of the image where it frays and runs over into the next one, it begins to sleet.

Marianne's voice comes from the open front door; a silhouette standing in the hallway, she shouts the address into the receiver multiple times. She repeats the directions to a house in Fenndorf three, four times, before finally describing it as *the last house behind the pig stalls*. On the Heidedamm officially there was only Number Two, then the farm, and behind that nothing else, just the moor.

By the time she made it upstairs she seemed quieter. She stood in the doorway, motionless, almost reverent, like how, for a moment, you sink into an unexpected view from up on a mountain peak or a tower. Only her breasts swelled and swelled; she only seemed to continue to inhale, not exhale. All of a sudden, the boy is back in the picture: he is standing in front of the door to Marga's bedroom which he'd closed because of the empty packages of Lexotax strewn across the bed. Marianne shoves him to the side, pushes open the door, and groans, 'Oh no!' Between her fingers the crackle of a blister strip, the information sheet, reads it, she says, 'I don't have my glasses with me,' and presses the paper into the boy's hand.

Here is when you should've said something. Explained that she had been swallowing the stuff for years and that it had even made you wobble and tip over once or twice. But in your throat not a word, not even a single consonant, your tongue simply poked around in the gap between your teeth as you read the reasons for use under Indications again, why Marga had wanted to end it all, and were almost relieved not to find your name listed there; but that too is an idea from today and not what the child thought, a helpless attempt to find a point of light in a tunnel of speechlessness and fear.

'Well, come out with it!' Marianne yelled and ripped the piece of paper out of your hand. She stared at it for a long time, then pressed you to her chest and sighed, 'My poor boy,' a sentence that belonged to Marga. She rushed back into the room and pushed your mother onto her side. She changed the pillow, covered her up and went into the bathroom. You heard the water running and once again the sigh, you thought about the streaks of toothpaste in the sink and how Marianne would never have tolerated something like that in her home. She came back with the cleaning bucket and began to mop.

Here again the boy is outside the picture for a while, instead, the oversized dragonfly clock on the wall, which had been at half past seven, seven twenty-eight to be exact, ever since that day the hand got stuck on the bubble-like compound eyes. Marga had meant to bring batteries with her from the city, but then had never gone back. From the moment that time stood still in your room, everything had become different: the days were shorter, the sun rare, the nights endless, for she no longer woke you up in the morning. You tumbled into the classroom right at the bell for the break. Punishment, your first 'deficient' mark in homework, no one had given you the paper with the assignment, not even Tanja, who had eyed you challengingly during the lesson as if knowing all about your having failed.

On account of your tardiness, Gorbach wrote one warning after the other, which Marga did not sign, nor did put her initials on your classwork, but simply grumbled once, 'I didn't have a mother to take care of every shitty little thing.' Then the principal's summons, which she also ignored. On all future warnings you forged her signature, the M, it wasn't difficult. In a drawer you found an old alarm clock, its morning call cold and shrill. You longed for her lips on your forehead, her whisper, the hair that fell across your cheeks and tickled you into the day. But there was only the dragonfly and its blood-red head, continuing to stare.

As the moor too had supposedly showed its most hostile side—in other words, had ruined your exploratory exhibitions with rain and showers of sleet—in that late October you had been in the crevice a lot. But it too had seemed different to you, wider, as you write in your book, boring, no longer a tight, unimaginably deep gullet but only a crack, opening slowly out to the end of your feet, a tomb for dust, spiders, dried-out snot, the mysteries of childhood.

Outside the water rose with the constant rain, surged out of the drain onto the fields, gurgled under your feet at every step, lay in wait overall. The pond was swollen, a shimmering metallic bulge between the strips of peat, the cotton grass flat, the alders submerged. Lambert's farm help lay down boards and planks so that the tractors would not sink into the ditches. The Heidedamm turned into a string of puddles, then a dark lake which slowly began to eat away at the house. You saw the broth seep and slosh about the cellar, then the toilet became clogged, your shit would not go down any more. Embarrassed, you began to go at school and took care of the other business behind the barn where the rain washed it all away.

But when did Marga shit? Maybe she didn't any longer considering the few bites she still managed to take. She smoked even while eating now, spoon in one hand, cigarette in the other, but you already knew that from before, from the days when she would slowly turn to stone and you'd have to somehow get your mother-boulder up the stairs. Sometimes she confused cutlery and cigarette; she would purse her lips but instead of the filter, stick the spoon in between them or bite into the cigarette butt. You choked with laughter and drove the knife handle into your nose. 'Your mother's becoming a moron,' she slurred, and pretended to be an idiot. You nodded, relieved, and continued to eat.

In reality, everything was as it had always been. But it was precisely that *always*, over the years, changed more and more in your memory. In all of Marga's well-known gestures, in all of her too-frequently heard jokes, which you laughed at because you had always laughed at them, in every single one of your mother's glances today you see the ultimate one.

It seemed like even Karl Lambert didn't want to miss the finale. Suddenly he was standing in the hall, in a flat cap and overalls, as if meaning to go into the stalls. 'What's wrong with her?' he grumbled and pointed into the room. 'She swallowed this stuff,' Marianne said, and threw the empty package to him. He cast a quick glance and pointed to you, 'I'd immediately told his father back then that she was worthless.' Your aunt stood up in front of him, water spilt out of the bucket and across the floor. Both of them filling up the image, almost larger than life, their pale faces distorted by fatigue and questions, the oily, pockmarked skin on Karl's cheeks, the messy hair, Marianne's temples already grey. 'You said that she should go to hell,' Marianne hissed at Karl, 'and take your brother right along with her!' and then she makes a distracted movement towards the edge of the frame, halfway forward, halfway into the air, into an imaginary sky. Then all of a sudden she is gone, and Karl is alone. He leans against the doorframe and sinks a bit at his knees. In the bathroom now the gurgling of the toilet flushing, once, then, after a few seconds, a second time; your mother's vomit, the contaminated familial relations down the pipe and out. But the toilet, the young boy in the corner thinks, really is clogged; and in his mind he sees the black water slosh over the lid and the moor wash into the house.

When Marianne returned with a towel, she walked soundlessly past Karl. 'She was sick in the head,' he yelled after her, 'from the very beginning!' Marianne wiped off the bedposts, then Marga's mouth, opened the towel, it whipped through the air: 'Shut up for once, you ass!' Karl rushed forward, spun her around, 'You!' he yelled, 'you don't call me that!' She lifted the rag against him like a weapon. 'No?' she sneered, 'but *her* ass'—and she pointed to the bed—'that you didn't find bad at all!' She tore herself away, tottered a moment, then fell.

Enter the boy. He stumbled from some corner or other to the bed, and directly into Karl's hands. Karl's solid body swayed, his stomach absorbing the punches, kicks into air, a cry muffled by the large hand. In the end, a slap in the face followed by a quick blackout, as if you'd tried to cut something out of the film. 'You will not hit him as well!' Marianne yelled, pulled you away from Karl and to her smock. The sourdough smell, the black, flickering image, Karl's snorting for a few more seconds, a quarter of a minute perhaps where you thought about how the other day you were going to have to call Ute Hassforther to tell her that Marga had been sick for a long time, was sick again, still sick, an idea that choked you up. Was it the fear of the telephone that made you pause, or the fact that you would either have to lie or tell the truth? There did not seem to be anything else in between, no possibility to undo anything; only the black image on your aunt's breast, she who would now bring you over to her house where you would have to eat jellied meat and be the new brother to Hannes, Martin, Ole and the brutal Kerstin—who was herself almost a boy—would have to be the one to get a foot between your legs when kicking the ball. And the longer Marianne stroked your head, the more unbearable your craving for Marga's cinnamon cake became, you would have eaten cinnamon until the end of your days, just like Marga had done with her index finger, dusting the curd, the buttered bread, yes, you would've even rolled the peeled potatoes in cinnamon and, when the money for potatoes ran out, happily crunched the little glass tube between your teeth, would have done everything so that she'd open her eyes again, wink at you and say: 'Good morning, darling, shall we go to the pond?'

But, instead, when Marianne finally lets go of the boy, there is only the wailing in the distance or maybe no sound at all, only the snow in front of the window and the red men who all of a sudden were standing in the room. Maybe, you write, they had not used the siren on the way, but only the blue light, so as not to disturb the sleeping children's dreams.

Marga slams the book shut and shoves it away, disgusted, as if she'd been presented with something completely inedible. In fact, she almost has to gag, as angry as she is about the lies, the bitter insult rising up in her like bile. The truth is that on the November evening her boy describes the paramedics had indeed come to their house. However, neither Dion, nor Marianne, her sister-in-law, had called the ambulance. And yes, it's true, she'd had to vomit, thank God! That's why she hadn't gone unconscious, but had crawled to the telephone on her own or, she now remembers, thanks to his help, but even the word *crawled* seems to be one of those demeaning literary terms her boy now employed to denigrate her. Overall, his book a conscious slap in the face. So much for later insights and conciliatory hindsight!

She jumps up and staggers over to the window, numb, as if the slaps from the book had ripped her out of a decade-long blackout. She feels undressed in her night-gown, naked and bare before the city's invisible glances. He definitely means to denounce me, she thinks, and escapes to the wall where one of her self-portraits from her most recent series—nudes of a similarly naked older woman, the exhibition of a woman within her aging body—with the working title *Mira* is hanging. But even there the exposing glance rejects her. That could be, the old woman in the picture says and points to the table where the book lies silently, but, in any event, you still don't get it.

It is true that, as far as reading and writing are con-cerned, he'd always considered her stupid. What now appears before her eyes is not the scene as it really was, but the pages in her boy's book she cannot find again, even though she'd memorized the place, if not through the sound of the words, then as an abstract form which had presented itself at first glance from the print. That is how she had always found her way through books the best, she noticed the layout of the sentences and paragraphs on the page from passages she wanted or had to read again.

'So you believe him too?' she hisses at Mira, who is staring down at her with a mockingly puckered mouth from the work wall. Upstairs *Frau* Schäfer's TV continued to blather. She shakes her head. *Blather*, she thinks, that isn't one of her words, it too must have come from the mind of her boy. In her life she has always done what she's said. The single pensioner's TV gets *on her nerves*, as does the smell that often hangs in the stairwell when *Frau* Schäfer has forgotten her lunch on the stove; when the stink from burnt food crawls under her door, she, Marga, rushes upstairs. Recently, she got a copy of the key to the apartment, pure self-protection. She throws the charred fried egg in the trash, cleans up, turns off the stove, prepares a new one—a perfect one where the skin on the yolk is still glassy—and serves it to *Frau* Schäfer in her recliner in front of the TV. The old woman eyes it then complains that she's just had her supper. She's wearing her hair in a bun and two mismatched pairs of socks. It is three in the afternoon. The TV blathers on.

Every night the blaring TV tears her away from sleep, and she has to swallow at least two Lexotaxs just to be able to drift off at some point in the morning grey. Of late, she has been so upset by her boy's book that she can only manage with the pills. The book, together with the noise from the TV, has frayed her nerves and unleashed a storm of voices in her head. Above all, like blotting paper, her body seems to absorb all the scribbling that he, Dion, has mixed her into. You shouldn't pay any attention to a child's imagination, that he still is, she thinks, and certainly not when you're a mother.

That morning she had pulled the book out of the envelope along with a cool, almost formal letter that had been written on a computer. *Dear Marga*, then a few lines to tell her that he, Dion, would be on Sylt in August, the reason: the presentation of a literary award which he all the same *warmly* invited her to. Not a single question as to how she was, about her life or if she wanted to, or even *could*, come at all. The unease she immediately felt at the thought of seeing him again was commented upon with a postscript: *If you are ready to start over again.* As if *she* had deliberately left him, disappointed, like a cheated lover. In any event, he had been the one to tell the Youth Welfare Office this and that about her life and, on top of it, had added a thing or two so that the officials took her boy away as per court order and then and there gave him over to Marianne with all the rights and obligations of a so-called foster mother.

From the beginning, her struggle had been hopeless, the psychiatrists' ammunition too heavy, which, as a person suffering from 'Personality Disorder' as defined in ICD 8 Line 301.1, did not entrust her to lead a normal life with her boy, although thanks to a certain discipline and abstinence, she had improved—as she reassured those doctors who through medication, electroshock therapy and deep psychotherapeutic sessions had long tried to break her resistance—until her stubbornness, something which several lawyers had profited from for two years, was finally transformed into apathy, a condition in which the continuation of life would be, if not particularly fulfilling, at least possible. However, when the old fury re-emerged, the only thing she could do was smother it with two or three Lexotaxs, the only pill that had ever managed to give her relief, just like this morning when, after the postman had rung the bell and she had torn open the package, it had once again begun to boil inside of her.

She had truly felt ill, as if she had a fever. With trembling hands she clumsily pushed the letter back into the envelope and even tried to seal it again, as if in so doing she could get rid of the doubt that was growing backwards into the past, into that repressed and court-stamped file. She was not ready for a reunion, or had ever been after their violent separation, as she now realized while skimming the dust jacket, the summary of the novel's action which struck her as terribly familiar.

After graduating from high school in Zeeve, Dion had moved to Munich to attend university, as far away from Hamburg and from his mother as he could be; that is what she suspected at the time. Later, she received the obligatory Christmas card from West Berlin which is also where he had called her from on her birthday,

'Happy Birthday, Mom, how are you?'—'I'm fine'—
'You getting on.'—'Yeah, and you?'—'You have to—'
and so on; the boy, she remembers, had still had a
strong stutter, or maybe it had come back because of
all they would have wanted and had to say but could
not, were not allowed to, because the court order,
whether reasonable or not, had spoken nonsense or
because there was someone in the background listening
in, sometimes a man with her, or sometimes with him,
for Dion—that much he had confided to her—now preferred men.

But over the last few years he had even discontinued
those stiff birthday calls. In the end, whatever there
might have been left to settle, he had—without her
knowledge—put between two book covers; she even
found the title to be a conscious attack on her innermost feelings, her mother's heart which had been laid
on ice in the psychiatric ward: it was the very name she
had once given to her oil painting, the only one that had
ever possibly been worthy of a prize, the only one of
her early works that had been considered praiseworthy
by the Hamburger Art Foundation, a work, however,
which had been incinerated along with every last frame
in the old barn in Fenndorf, and which, until now, she
had never seen as a loss but as a liberation and possibility to start over.

But now, from one second to the next, the past had
caught up with her. Her mind empty from the Lexotax,

she sat in her chair until noon staring out into the blinding July day. The nudes glared spitefully down at her from her work wall. Most recently, her gaze out into the world had only been directed towards her own body whose decline she first projected in photograph-form onto a large canvas, then fixed in rough contours with a brush or spray paint, obsessed with the idea of its slow freezing and encrustation, with the idea that if there was no stopping it, at least she could present it unadorned— but, and this time she was quite sure, more perfectly than any of her works had ever been—to the eyes of the so-called art market. But the art market had never had eyes, bottom line: no gallery, in Hamburg or anywhere else, would be interested in seeing, as she'd recently lamented to her hairdresser, an old lady's vagina.

Only *Herr* Dröhmer, as they say, continued to make eyes at her. The similarly aged Personnel Director would cast long glances at her from the glass cube of his office in the warehouse where over the last few months she had been working shifts, stuck with a headset, which flattened her hairdo, in order to listen to customers' complaints for 9 euros an hour—gross. Whatever had to do be written, she typed with two fingers into pre-set computer programs, for even the German Studies students who were making their living in the call centre managed to mix up letters.

At two o'clock when her shift was to begin, she was still sitting at home and leafing through the book without reading a sentence. A call to Dröhmer would have

229

been enough, a slight cough, a slight strain in her voice and without any further ado he would have rescheduled her; a long glance back at him through his glass cube would have also made the idiot, who was not the first in her new employment relationship, forget about it the following day when she would have felt self-confident enough to take her place among all the students and young temp workers again.

But from one moment to the next, even a curt call no longer seemed possible. Now she'd probably lose this job too. So what, she thought, friendliness and patience just weren't her strong suits. And she wanted to quit because of Julius anyway, who had suddenly sat between her and Dröhmer one day.

He was the Business student who, after a few shared shifts, had chatted her up in the cafeteria and whom she, thanks to the charming way he had scrawled his number on a napkin and as she suddenly was happy to go to work before falling asleep, in the end had in fact called, on the agreed upon evening had brought her flowers, roses even, which she had always considered suspicious, and two bottles of wine. His shirt was open, and showed off a pronounced collarbone. As they ate their Thai curry and drank the wine in large gulps, he slunk ever deeper into the chair and stretched his legs out under her chair. Suddenly he pushed his plate to the side, stood up and looked at the paintings on her work wall, one after the other and from up close. 'It's really warm in here,' he said, which encouraged her to take off her long-sleeved cotton blouse when she went to the bathroom. When she came back, Julius was spread out on the couch, hands crossed behind his head. He looked at the thin tank top over her chest and made a face.

Did she have a cardigan? A grandmotherly-thing? She knew what he meant. And by no means was she to wear her hair down. He jumped up and pulled her freshly blow-dried locks into a kind of bun, 'Something like that,' he said, and came even closer. He found the only cardigan she owned, one from Chanel that had cost a fourth of her monthly salary, too elegant. 'Don't you have something left over from your mother?' He took hold of her hand and pressed his mouth ardently onto the brown mark which she had only recently discovered.

Here we go, she'd thought and, standing in front of the mirror, had begun to scratch at the age spot. With her pension, she had had to realize when looking over the last notice from the pension insurance fund, she wouldn't even be able to pay her rent, and even with social benefits it would have been a long way from being able to give herself over to cellulite while being protected behind the shield of status and affluence. Julius examined her arm. 'You don't have any others?' he asked, found the mole next to her armpit and licked it. She pushed him away. 'What do you want?' she asked. It was meant to have come out domineering, but instead sounded like a plea. 'I'm afraid this isn't going to work,' he said, turned around and left the apartment.

He did not close the door. The smell of burnt food drifted in. She emptied the bottle of wine, sniffed the roses, which did not smell, sank down into the chair and stared at her work wall where Mira, the naked one, the one with the disintegrating body of fuzzy brush-strokes, seemed to say: You really *don't* have any talent.

The storms that passed through the city over the following days cooled everything down. Lightning flashed silently in the sky, there was no thunder, the mist seemed to swallow all the sound, there were no longer any voices even from upstairs. When she arrived home after her late shift, the blue light from the TV flickered in *Frau* Schäfer's window. The silence unnerved her now. She went upstairs and rang the bell, the pensioner opened the door, traces of egg yolk up to her chin; flipping through the channels she had turned the sound off, but when Marga turned it back on, *Frau* Schäfer did not seem to notice the difference.

At the call centre, and thanks to the wet weather as well, she wore loose, cloth trousers together with something long-sleeved and timeless, which seemed to displease *Herr* Dröhmer; in his glances, through the glass wall to her seat, she thought she could see pity. When she ran into Julius in the hallway, he looked away. In the cafeteria he joked with the cook, an overweight, old woman who pushed flavourless chicken legs over the counter with her calloused hands. As he was now responsible for orders, during his shift he sat at the other end of the room, and so for days she only saw him from behind. Sometimes he would stretch his arms into the air, straighten up and expose his taut muscular back through his tight T-shirt, his torso like an ancient sculpture.

In the bathroom, she checked her hair. Because of all of the dying, it had become brittle, it was only darker at the roots; it would be months before the blonde grew out and the grey came back. She rummaged through the shelves in boutiques she had never visited before, but even fashion for the so-called more mature woman had become youthful. The old-fashioned cardigan which she finally found at C & A was only available in XL, the sales woman had to make a special trip into the stock-room, then came up to her at the mirror and attempted to dissuade her.

She rang at *Frau* Schäfer's. The pensioner appeared in a smock, blue veins pushing through her champagne-coloured nylon pantyhose. Did she have anything that needed washing? Marga asked, she was on her way to the dry cleaner's. *Frau* Schäfer declined. Then a ten-minute lament about her joint pain, the group flat next door, the TV programmes. Marga promised to take her out to the teahouse, in her, Schäfer's, finest gown, and pushed past her into the bedroom.

From out of the wardrobe came a musty smell. She went through everything quickly, checking material and cuts. When she came back into the living room, *Frau* Schäfer was sitting in front of the TV and following a talk show with a gloomy glance; the headset Marga had recently brought her lay on top of it, the cord attached, from the padded headphones the crackling of voices. She had found a pair of pretty things, Marga said, and presented her selection. *Frau* Schäfer complained about the sound interference, and seemed to have already forgotten about their trip to the teahouse. Marga carefully placed the headphones on her so as not to undo the topknot.

That evening she stood before Julius' door. She was wearing a heavy skirt and a cardigan made of grey merino wool, the collar scratching at her throat. *Frau* Schäfer's bra had not fit, she would have had to sew on two extra hooks and therefore she'd had to return to the department store. Julius opened the door, his upper body naked. He was breathing quickly, sweat glistened on his shoulders. Techno music came blaring out of a room, barbells lay in the hall, a hand towel on the linoleum. Without being asked, she walked into the apartment. It smelled of grease from the oven, from frozen pizza or pommes frites. She closed the door, the bass throbbed into her head, she would have liked some earplugs, headphones, something to muffle the sound, silence; the Lexotax which she'd just swallowed did not seem to have the slightest effect.

She asked where the bathroom was; he made a movement with his head. Once there, she looked around, even rummaged through the clothesbasket, found nothing that an even older lover could have left behind. She did not dare look into the mirror. She'd even adjusted the girdle. She pushed the flush button twice, then let the faucet run for a long time, did not want to hear how fiercely her heart beat in her Schäfer chest.

Julius had not moved from his spot. His glance now made her swallow. He stood there like an icon, smooth, cold, impregnable, an artwork. She went over to him and down onto her knees. With her foot she knocked a barbell, which slowly rolled in the other direction. Everything seemed to turn away from her—the dresser seemed crooked, the shadows fled into the corners, even the light suddenly seemed darker like when a slight variation in the current causes a bulb to flicker. The music ended abruptly but the bass continued to drone in her ears as if it wanted to fight back against the silence. From somewhere outside came a siren, closer, became threateningly loud, then suddenly silenced as if the ambulance had stopped in front of the building.

His track pants were made of blue heavyweight cotton with white stripes that reflected the lamplight. She could not get the knots in the drawstrings undone. His hands hung motionless over his thighs, balled into fists. She pushed her tongue into his belly button, felt as if she were falling into it with her entire body, that's how deep the hollow suddenly seemed to her, the artist's desire for the perfect picture, bottomless.

She pulled the waistband over his pelvis. His penis cowered beneath the V-shaped chiselled pubic bone with the carefully trimmed hair. It tasted salty. She breathed in the smell of *Frau* Schäfer's bedroom coming out of her clothes. She hadn't thought of wearing the right shoes and in the end had gone with the flat boots, a clash of styles. Now the hard leather wedged into her legs. She worked laboriously from a crouch. He did not once lay a hand on the bun. After an endless two minutes, everything was just like it had been before. 'What's wrong with you?' she asked. He pulled his pants up and tucked himself away. 'Come back in ten years,' he said, and went into a press-up over the hand towel.

After having them cleaned, *Frau* Schäfer's clothes smelt like lavender. She could mark the kind of scent she wanted on the order form: summer fresh, cedar, neutral. Lavender, she had thought, fits an old woman best, but now the smell reminds her of the bath fragrance she often used back in Fenndorf. At a certain point that one too had begun to make her feel sick; today she bathed without any at all. No substance had as of yet managed to bring her the promised relaxation. *Frau* Schäfer unwrapped the clothes from the plastic film. 'Ach, you can hold on to this,' she said, she was already too old for such things. She was wearing the headphones on her ears, the cord dangled in her lap. From out of the front room the TV blathered on, louder than ever.

She finally found the page again that had upset her so bitterly on the first reading, a heavily detailed and vindictive tapeworm of a sentence without any break, as if—under fire from his memories—Dion could not grant her any breath or pause, not a single line to hook herself into and offer any resistance. The truth is: on that November night, she had immediately regretted her suicide attempt. With the red marker she wished she could add how much her conscience had plagued her after taking the pills.

Admittedly, she had been drunk, exhausted, at the end of her tether; after Ute Hassforther had dumped her, painting was done with. She had finally given up staring at the ever-white canvas too, and only continued to go into the barn in order to spare you, Dion, from the heaviest and most terrible episodes of her depression. In her work corner she did nothing, if that small, inconsequential but all-powerful word could still be attached to an action that had come to a stop; for even a movement, however unintentional, requires and causes action, something which was no longer recognizable in her as she lay there on the old couch, listening to the pain in her back and letting her torturers go to work on her—those small, rather harmless metal springs boring into her back together with the large, invisible spikes coming down to impale her. The idea that it could all be over soon filled her with a kind of desire, the last emotion that a wretchedly, almost-dead person could feel, the final surge before the abyss.

And why should you continue to live without hope, she wondered, squeezed out a tear which, leaden from such thoughts, barely made it to her eyes, grabbed the wine bottle that had been standing on the worktable since morning, finished it off in one swig and walked over into the house. It did not at all matter to the abyss that the refrigerator had been empty for days; you, however, were hungry, and you were her child, you wanted your mother.

In his room, she remembers, the light was still on. She saw him in bed bent over his notebook, writing furiously, in the glow of the lamp. She pushed her face into the crack in the door, in her hand the bowl with the left-over stew she had found in the freezer drawer and quickly reheated.

You had remained still, hadn't looked up but just listened into the hall where for days there had not been anything other than the silence. Then you went back to your writings with a feeling of regret, a feeling that became filled with a kind of sureness, something clear, almost redemptive, like a cool draught of air in a sti-flingly humid room.

Now, at the corresponding point in your book, she reads that she did not want to come in to wish you good night; that, you write, had not been her intention, had never once been her aim in coming over to you. No, it was more of an issue of her lurking outside the door and waiting for you to tear her out of her misery with a hug, a kiss, the stuttered *Everything's all right again.*

But what misery? you ask yourself or her or me in the next line already. She turns the page, reads on with a choking feeling in her throat, cannot believe what her boy is putting out into the world about her: Hadn't she been cold and apathetic, only the shell of a person, an empty mother from the very beginning? The deaconesses' clothes hanger that beat the scars into her nothing but a symbol? The fantasy and crutch of a speech-cripple searching for words for something that cannot be described, without any weak spots, that simply is *nothing*? Did the clothes hanger beat the so-called soul, or whatever it is that makes a person loving, not out of, but in to her hollow body? Enliven her with pain so that she would be animated? In reality, he, her boy— she has to learn in the following paragraph—was the bruiser who consciously disfigured her in his book in order to find an explanation for her distance and coldness. There's a reason why she had to be the cuckoo-mother all too happy to throw her egg into a hole in the moor or at least in another bird's nest; in other words, Marianne Lambert's warm, well-incubated nest, Marga thinks, who with her heavy breasts and smelly armpits must really have impressed Dion.

Back then her sister-in-law not only saved her, Marga's, life after her suicide attempt, but ultimately, after the adoption, her boy wrote, apparently provided him with the feeling of security and caring that a child needs in order to make it in the world. She laughs bitterly at Mira. 'The butter cake!' she sneers. 'The steak! The walk to church Sundays at ten!'

She got off the hook easily, the painted woman says, and Marga thinks, you got that right!, and that Marianne, the miser, had been able to turn her pig stalls into a pig imperium by skimping on taking care of the children. She remembers how she had once tried the cake that Dion had brought home on a plate from the Advent's bazar, dry as dust! Baked not with butter but vegetable fat. With me, on the other hand, she informs the dubious one in the portrait, there was always butter, despite the money troubles! Don't you mean cinnamon? Mira shakes her head. No, no, boiled potatoes with butter!, Marga answers, butter sandwiches for school breaks, buttered cabbage, and her cinnamon cake, seeing as she was dishing it out, thanks to the butter had always been so succulent that it melted on her boy's tongue. From her stark colour-field Mira cries out: How about a little honesty!

A clothes hanger, she reads, would have been something. A deep, inner wound would have been enough of a reason for him to understand why she grabbed the package of Lexotax but only took a few pills in her hand and dropped the half-empty strip on the bed where he would, and was supposed to, find them. The only thing she had ever known, the last sentence of the paragraph hatefully reads, was how to cheat the nothingness inside of her for a tiny, sordid feeling of life, like a junkie getting ready to fix.

That's not true! She launches the novel into the corner where it lands with the pages open and gapes like a mouth. She'd always done everything for him! Shared everything with him! Had almost torn herself apart between art, cooking and career for him! 'What a special way to praise me!' she yells to Mira, but the latter only raises a thinly-painted eyebrow. 'Everything-soup!' Marga says threateningly and raises a brush against the painting, which she could destroy with a single stroke. But the portrait only shrugs its shoulders and says: You jerked him off! 'A six-volume *Nature Encyclopedia*,' Marga pleads over to the corner where the book is lying and the summer night drifts in through the window and blows through the pages where the same phrase sounds again and again.

But she really had been ashamed of her miserable condition in front of you. And had therefore tried to hide it from you as best she could: her unwashed hair, the sour smell of wine in her kisses, the tears that streamed across her face which, overwhelmed by doubt, in the next moment froze into a mask of stone, expressionless and cold, as if she hadn't cried in decades. But how can one conceal an absence, the nothingness? She had attempted to do so with defiance, and had even managed to get herself together at times, but maybe, she now thinks, that had been the problem.

After you had moaned her away a number of times when it was time for the morning kiss, she began to stay far away from your room. 'He's old enough to set his own alarm clock,' she murmured to herself, turned over in bed and swallowed another pill. His teacher's reprimands will make him wake up, she thought, and, with that, fell once more into the merciful blackness of numbed sleep. Why should she have to take responsibility for all of that? She later grumbled and pushed away the pen that you had tossed to her on the table so that she could mark the piece of paper with her *M*.

Exhausted as she was in those days, the emptiness in her head aimlessly stirring, for ever in search for the right words for a talk, she burned the everything-soup on the stove. Silently, heads hanging, you both sat before your plates. As soon as she had cleared her throat and laid her cutlery to the side, the look you gave her was so contemptuous, that she uneasily swallowed her sentence together with the burnt swill. At some point, you had pushed away the food, hissed *Disgusting*! without stuttering, gone upstairs and slammed your door shut.

After that, he didn't come to the table any more, she remembers that quite clearly. He would throw his knapsack in the corner, push past her and pull a piece of candy out of the drawer. 'Eat first,' she would say, and he. 'hI halready hdid hat hMarianne's.'—'Then why don't you move right on over there?'—'hI'm hin the hprocess.' She cleared his place setting, scraped the vegetables into the garbage, broke the plate in anger while washing. Later, in the barn, she squeezed the wound on her finger, which did not want to bleed. She did not know what to do with him any longer.

Goodness gracious, Mira groans. Marga walks past her. Did she really just say goodness gracious? Never in her life had a similar phrase crossed her lips. *Goddammit*! had been her phrase, *Fucking hell*! She remembers how Marianne had sighed the very same thing at the painting when she walked into the room that night. Marga had heard the cry for help the farmer sent heavenward before putting her hands on her blasphemous sister-in-law, playing with her life as she was, then awkwardly feeling for the pulse.

'Stop that,' your mother had said with heavy tongue and pushed Marianne away, she wasn't dead just yet. Then she had turned away from you to the wall. She wanted to spare you the sight. Contrary to what you have written, at that point she had not been unconscious. It was only in the ambulance that she slowly went under. She herself had called the paramedics earlier, and sent you over to your aunt's in case she suddenly collapsed. Had bent over the toilet and stuck her finger down her throat in order to throw up the rest of the Lexotax as a precaution, had drunk a few glasses of water, had even cleaned up the vomit-covered bed with her furry fingers so that Marianne would not have any trouble. Only when she had finished did she lay herself down on your pillow.

It seems to her that *Frau* Schäfer had turned her TV up even louder; the building was throbbing with voices. She was shaking herself and ducking under the bareness of the painting, as if only there she could still find some protection. The noise from upstairs—or is it the party next door?—had already caused the lamp to swing, and she was sure that she could suddenly notice the smell of fried eggs coming from under the door.

She not only scours the pensioner's frying pans. Of late she had even begun to dress *Frau* Schäfer, for which she naturally took a 50-euro bill out of her purse. No Pole would dirty her hands for such a price!, she thinks. She really had felt dirty afterwards, in spite of the gall soap and the brush, the stink no longer wanted to leave her hands. Or had her own skin, in the end, begun to smell? The old woman's stale air never left her alone, it would soon begin to accompany her everywhere she went, and she picks the book off the floor and digs her nose deep into the fold. Art doesn't smell, the painted one scolds her, and Marga shakes the book between her hands, turns the pages back and forth, yet page after page only finds a tiny piece of truth, the smallest trace of respect and love from her son, and that indeed only comes out in one single word, two twitching syllables— naked and miserable on the floor like a worm torn away from the protective crumb—that whimper *hMa-hMa!*, and she bends over the next page and, with trembling hands and stumbling glance, reads how her boy cries and writhes in his winter nightmare of a snowstorm over the moor.

You are awoken by a bang. The silence in the house as if made of corners and blades, it stutters you out of sleep. You cling to your pillow, pull the blanket over yourself, think you can hear it creaking, it has suddenly become so cold in the room. A blinking, blind spots before your eyes, then everything is there again: blue light, the red men, Marga's empty face. A clattering and a hissing, the grinding in the attic from either splinters or shards, the shreds of sentences from a furious outside, and you go upstairs and see me staring through the window, a throat of ice and snow.

But *Snow*, you think, and close your eyes again, is a breeze of a word, far too quiet and soft for the roar which is screaming you into day, 'hSnow' like 'hMoor' or 'hSea', loose syllables with long vowels, open at one end with a wide horizon and nothing but air within, a language of snow, that would be the solution.

Wrong, I say and, with a blast, hit you with the shutters; this is only the beginning of the speech-torture. Think back to Marianne's interrogation in her kitchen while outside the night slowly turned white: the piercing questions you doggedly answered by remaining silent although within you the words surged upward like they never had before. You would not have been able to stop speaking, a stutter-inferno unfettered, crashing and rumbling all the indescribable feelings that would have burst out of you.

'hLet hme hgo!' you howled against the wind as your aunt pulled you over the Heidedamm and into her yard. A veil of snow sprayed in front your eyes, and caused her features to appear coarse and mask-like. 'No talking back,' she yelled and shook you, 'tonight you're staying with us! Or where else would you sleep?' She let you go and hurried on with large steps. The rest of the way you went next to her, through the rapidly growing vortex, your head tucked in.

The snow fell quickly and urgently as if to cover up what you had seen, erase the tracks, which by then had been laid irrevocably. In the wild flurry you could hardly follow the path of a single flake. For one moment you held one with your eye as it spun down and tore you along with it, then the next one came and lifted you back up. Suddenly a larger and more beautiful one appeared. It danced towards you, quivered a while above your forehead, was caught by the wind and then spun back into the sky where it joined another before turning around again to fall.

And so it continued until you almost reached the door. Out into the night you flew, with the snow, through the white darkness, for a moment forgot all the painful questions: Where would the paramedics bring Marga, would they would bring her back, why had Marianne— your aunt who Marga so stubbornly avoided—suddenly been so motherly and would you sit next to Hannes at the table as his new brother?

You imagined what it would be like to live inside the snow, locked in by crystals of ice, which were similar to you and at the same time different from one another in the finest details: only a dragonfly with its thousand individual eyes could have seen that you were the soul of a snowflake, no longer speechless but simply silent, a pure, self-contained silence that had no need to force out any words. Within the snow you would no longer stutter; its movement from the sky downward, its slow, soft fall to earth would be the perfect syntax: the sound with which it settles on a branch or nestles up to the ground, that, to human ears, unnoticeable crackling, if not already too much of a racket for the microscopic consonants—the initial sound of the great silence that erases and liberates every word you have ever spoken or broken and within itself already supports every sentence still to come—if not only an insignificant tone in the absolute sound of your voice, for the snow had only just begun to transform the Heidedamm into a new, never-before-seen landscape.

Looking back you saw your house whiten before the night, the darkness pushing up against the edges, the naked image in which nothingness had already begun to break the frame apart. Marga long gone, the plain more an intimation and memory, I myself a silent, black-and-white rustling to the side of the path. When Marianne ordered you to brush the snow off your clothes and shoes under the awning, you decided to never speak another word.

But you ate the butter cake, which did not taste of vegetable fat at all, then drank the cup of hot milk with honey that she had made for you. A wicker carpet beater hung on the kitchen wall and next to it the cross; in your memory it was as if the instrument had become the unavoidable accessory to the eternal image of the farmer's kitchen, just as Golgotha was no longer conceivable without the thieves' St Anthony's cross, those two whose silent withering away and death was marvelled at by no one but had turned the central image of the son of God's lamentations into a metaphor.

You wouldn't respond to her questions. She wanted to know what Marga had done the night before, if she had had anything to drink. She also asked you what you had been doing, and whether anything had stood out recently. A new man, an unhappy relationship, what other reason could there be for this sudden distress? Then she began to delve deeper, right into the wounds; it was, as lost and full of urgent words as you were hunched up there at the table, the right time. Where was her car and why hadn't Marga gone back to work? Did you have any idea by what merit the two of you managed to live? That awkward phrase was precisely the

248

one she had used, and stressed, while slightly lowering her voice at the same time. She saw the shrug of your shoulders and looked at you reproachfully. 'Does she really never speak about your father at all?' She bent down and took hold of your hand. 'Pray for him now and again, Dion!' You scraped the honey from the bottom of the cup and blinked tiredly. 'And tonight,' she added with a look up to the cross, 'we will also pray for your mother!'

She exhaled heavily, sighed *my poor boy* again and pressed you to her; for a moment you heard her heart beating in her chest, two soft beats that hardly hung together. Then she stood up, cleared away the cutlery, tipped the crumbs from the plate into the palm of her hand and for a moment seemed to think what to do with them, then all of a sudden she stuck her fist into the pocket of her smock. 'Tomorrow everything will already be quite different,' she promised and pushed you up the stairs. The steps creaked with the same age-old sound as the boards at home, which had often announced Marga's arrival long after midnight, sometimes already the first echo of sleep. Through an open door you saw your uncle's outline on his bed, heard him snoring and asked yourself how and when he had come inside and if he had at all been at your house earlier. Maybe because of your exhaustion everything seemed to be confused and nonsensical, like a bad dream.

A smell of sleep slammed into you as soon as she opened the door to Hannes' room. She switched on the light; it hurt your eyes. Your cousin was bent and wrapped in his blanket as if it were a cocoon, one leg sticking out the side. You stared at him, blonde fuzz covered his calf, his shin grazed, you wanted to move backwards over the threshold but Marianne held on tightly and said, 'No talking back!' so authoritatively and loudly that Hannes woke up. From out of the depths of sleep his gaze seemed spiteful and full of crude plans. On the floor was a pair of house shoes, old, worn-out things like Karl Lambert also wore; until then you had only seen Hannes' feet in boots to work in the stalls, his proudly polished trainers or his naked, grime-blackened feet on the beach by the Jumme. You found the idea of the village hero's big dirty feet—he who always led the way of an entourage of pimply older students—in house shoes to be as reassuring as it was depressing.

And the stuffed bear or dog at the foot of the bed didn't fit the image of a guy who drowned stubble cats in the tank either. Maybe one of his brothers had forgotten the teddy here when his older brother began to demand private space and he had to clean out their shared room; nevertheless, the room certainly seemed large enough to accommodate the secret afternoon lives of two growing teenagers and as if it had been made for the two of you. Or were you the one who had placed the toy on the bed, later, in your book? There all of these memories will be full of details and, with every new look back, you will add another. At that moment, however, everything the thirteen-year-old boy, whose mother had just been brought to hospital, saw must have appeared desolate and barren, ripped out of the abundance of childhood. Every action, every step you take here is a movement from later on, initiated by your silence, threatened by stagnation and artificially kept alive by my voice, by the long, cold breath of your longing.

The teddy bear falls off the bed and out of the picture. Griping, Hannes turns to the wall. 'Go downstairs onto the couch,' Marianne says, and pulls off the blanket. But as her son's pyjamas have slid up on his stomach and uncovered some hair, she looks to the ground; the boy at her hand, however, looks directly to the pluck before Hannes grabs a pillow to cover himself, then gets up, out of bed while pulling the blanket behind him and cursing the intruder.

'Grab yourself some bedlinen out of the wardrobe!' Marianne calls after him and snatches the down blanket sliding off his shoulders whereby he grabs the boy's buttocks, which could mean anything: 'Bite me, I'm going to make a mess, I'll get the little guy's ass just yet.' 'For God's sake!' Marianne hissed, steadied herself against the bed and straightened out the sheets. Then she pushed you onto the mattress and said, 'Go to sleep!' But instead of closing his eyes, the boy in your book keeps wide awake and stretches his head—out of

Hannes' stale air, away from the images of his collapsing mother about to vomit all over him again—as soon as his aunt turns off the light, then sits up and looks towards the window and the dancing snow. She looks at her nephew questioningly as if she had forgotten something important, then bends down and gives him a goodnight kiss on his forehead. She says, 'You can stay here as long as you want,' not realizing that it will become months and years.

The boy is woken by a bang. The room is brighter than before, the darkness less deep, the snow outside multiplies the light, throws everything into his dream. The stuffed animal is staring at him from the foot of the bed with empty black eyes and an open mouth. Only now does he look up.

Hannes is standing above you with a strangely tilted stance, one arm in the air, at the same time his head pointed downward as if caught in the net of light-threads spinning out through the room from the window. 'Don't think that you belong here now,' he whispers, and the carpet beater hurtles down towards you, stopping right before your chest. You do not flinch, just lie there and stare. He comes even closer, lifts the beater up again, turns it around in his hand, then brings it down to almost the tip of your nose. You can smell the wicker, dust from the runners, all the dirt of his dreams. He presses the edge to his lips; you slowly wiggle yourself out of his grip, tongue heavy in your mouth.

You feel the wooden weave caress your cheek, then move up to your temples where it stops and exerts a gentle pressure. The grid twists in your hair, rushes upward, disappears for a moment from your sight— exactly the right time to escape or quickly fall back asleep. But you want to be awake now, receptive with all your senses, to see, to feel, to understand: the carpet beater again falling almost to your chest, like a dowsing rod seeking out the secret place on your body where wonder lived. You unwillingly jerk upward, open your- self up against the blow as if in so doing you could soften the act of violence by meeting it tenderly. Hannes lifts an eyebrow, his eyes flash something like, *You think so*? You sink back onto the bed. 'If you say a single word, you're going to get it,' he whispers, and slides the pole into his pyjama bottoms.

The night outside almost white now, the last grains of darkness at the edges. The boy is suddenly standing at the vanishing point, his silhouette slowly peels itself out of the background, step by step creates an axis. His squat body faces forward, his naked feet in Hannes' felt house shoes which are too big for him and which have become stuck in the snow; in one or two years' time he'll be able to fit, slip into them mornings and back out again in the evening, place them at the foot of the bed like all the Lamberts do.

The child turns around in terror as if afraid of being followed. In the background, the elongated farmhouse with the ribs of the attached stalls like the corpse of a giant animal that perished in the snow. The tracks lead back to the yard, and reveal the boy's flight. He wonders whether in his haste he closed the front door or, in order to avoid making a noise, left it ajar; the wind will now take hold of it, blow it against the wall and violently wake Marianne. She feels the cold draught, the room empty next to hers and shakes her husband who, moaning, pulls the pillow over his head, annoyed by the familial tragedy that simply refuses to end.

Now the yard disappears behind a wall of snow which rolls in from the moor. The boy struggles against the gusts and over to the house, which presently appears on the other side of the picture, at the end of the Heidedamm leading to it like a tunnel through the drifts of snow. Soon, he thinks, Marianne will have caught up with him, grabbed him by the arm and dragged him from the house back to the farm; and then over and over again the same images: the child in his aunt's hand, the butter cake, sitting in front of the cup of milk, later—for the child still refuses to speak—atoning before the crucifix and, finally, as it has not helped either, writhing and bending beneath the carpet beater that is trying to make him utter a word, any word at all, is trying to beat the truth out of him.

The house is almost obliterated, the secure home hardly perceptible any longer; the longing for warmth, sleep and stable, well-trusted shapes buried in snow. Forehead pressed against the storm, he walks into the yawning mouth which in the next moment has swallowed him. Only my voice continues, waving and waltzing, the white chant.

At this point in the dream you must have woken up. The images of the previous night still lingered, poking you with their angular echo. The next crescendo, gale force 9, rips the gutters off their clamps. You jump out of bed. In the window, the toppling shadow, but you wait in vain for the impact; outside, you only recognize a few lost forms: the thinned-out willows by the drain, hedges buried under soft hills, far off in the background the image of the pig farm like the relief of a levelled world. Streaks of snow blow off the slopes of the drifts in the ditch where the Heidedamm used to lead, which then, a flat trickle, loses itself in the nothingness. Evermore snow rolls in from the plain and over the village, climbs the tree trunks, piles up along the embankments and tractor ramps. On the ribs of peat by the pit I scratch the sod free in order to accumulate all the scum somewhere else. From the perspective of the pond, the house is far and wide the only elevation, your life within it the most capable of standing in my way. I am playing war. I've got my eye on you. A few more blasts, the insurmountable mountain of snow in front of the door, fallen trees across the drive, then I'll have finally pushed you off to the side. Even the tractor with the prestressed plough will have trouble making it through the drifts, which cut through the landscape like ravines, to reach you.

And Karl Lambert won't do a thing to get you out of here. He's sitting in the living room, staring out the window and puffing on one of the cheap cigars from Ilse Bloch's shop. In the early morning, I tore a corrugated roof plate down from one of the stalls, and nabbed a sow. He had to kill it and drive the rest of the animals into the adjacent stall, which is no better: rotten beams, walls cobbled together, everything too narrow and worn out, what he really needs, he thinks, is the Heidedamm, the new Dutch-style mass halls with steel pens and grated flooring, and then, instead of two hundred, two thousand pigs, his application for a grant was already with the Agricultural Ministry, all he had to do was wait for the green light.

'At least go over there and see if the windows are closed,' Marianne says and places the pot of coffee in front of him. Karl puts it to his mouth, says, 'She should've got the glazier.' He spits the coffee back out, 'Say, are you trying to burn me?' Marianne pushes the little can of milk over to him. 'Over in the barn the paperboard has been sticking for years now,' she says. 'The machines are turning to rust.' Karl pours himself some milk and says, 'If, in the end, the storm manages to knock over the sheds, then I won't have to do it myself.' She makes a dismissive gesture with her hand, stands up and goes into the kitchen and comes back with a carton full of groceries. 'Go on and bring this over to him,' and places the box on the table, 'if he doesn't want to stay here.' Karl looks up at her questioningly. 'They want to bring Marga to the psychiatric clinic tomorrow,' she says, 'and she won't be getting out of there too soon.' She pushes the food over to her husband and adds the rest of the butter cake wrapped in aluminium foil. 'And we have to feed him until then?' He rifles through the things, fishes out a bar of marzipan chocolate the kids don't care for. Marianne says, explaining the waste, 'In the end he's your nephew!' Karl stands up, goes to the stairs, and says, 'My back, I'm going to lay down a moment.' 'Then I'll send Hannes over,' she calls after him, and from upstairs, 'He has to clean the scalding tank.'

But after school Hannes wanted to go over to the parsonage. You could have beat him to Tanja with her homework. Firstly, the classmate who sat next to you, Benno Fendrich, was out with flu, then Tanja; finally, you noticed that Hannes was gone too, which seemed rather suspicious. Were they making each other sick, in love's fever, sometimes in his, sometimes in her room? Soon, throughout the rows there were gaping holes. You already had to read aloud twice; the eighth grade was terrible. You were supposed to bring Benno his homework, yet after school you didn't go over to the principal's bungalow in the new housing development with it stuck into your sweaty hand, but the parsonage.

You had hardly rung the bell when the door sprang open. *Frau* Deichsen seemed to be out of breath, a pail stood in the hall, water splashed. You opened your mouth while stepping towards the doorway. Tanja's mother put a foot forward and said, 'Careful, it's wet! The dog still hasn't been housetrained,' she sighed, and grabbed the puppy which had skid across the freshly washed floor to sniff at your shoes by its collar. 'Ronja, out!' *Frau* Deichsen commanded. 'Ronja, come here!' her daughter called from some other room. The dog jumped up your leg and snapped at the folder with all the homework. 'Ach!' *Frau* Deichsen said and called back into the house, 'Tanja, she's done it again!' The puppy barked in a thin voice. You ducked out of the voices whipping back and forth through the air, and went over to the dog, which had begun to bite the folder. 'Hallo Honja,' the sound barely audible over your lips. 'Ronja,' *Frau* Deichsen corrected you, and Tanja continued calling out to no one.

You whispered something about the homework; thankfully, the sentence began with an *H*. 'That is kind of you, Dion,' Tanja's mother said,' but Danni has already brought everything by.' When even the pastor's wife was lying! Shortly after the beginning of the school year, Daniela had gone to sit next to Yvonne, the barkeep's daughter who also hardly spoke with Tanja any longer. No doubt Hannes was crouching next to her bed and holding her fevered hand, you thought. The dog straddled your foot and peed on your shoe. *Frau* Deichsen picked it up off the floor, cursed and at the same time laughed, 'She's just so happy!' You backed up through that puddle of happiness, into the patch of dahlias, across the church square and behind the wall where you finally let out a curse when you saw the moped parked under Tanja's window. Shit happens, Dion, but your old rickety bicycle is barely enough to give you a leg up to look.

That was three days ago. Marga was still at home and in your world the essential things of life were taken care of. Now with another gust I rip the tarp off the wood-pile. It sweeps across the yard, flaps for a while against the fence then is gone. Soon the wood will be so wet, you will not be able to use the tiled stove to heat any more. After the snow, I will send the rain, then another low-pressure front to be followed by a heavy frost and so on, all the way through the end of March. You're fin-ished, Dion, in the end, you were always screwed. Your mother is lying in Intensive Care and after that shall find her way into the mental ward with all the other failed suicides; by Christmas, she will already have five more kilos on her thighs. Since the pills make her fat but not any happier, after New Year's the doctors will cable her to the electroshock-therapy machine. In February, your uncle will receive a 'Yes' from the Ministry along with the funding with which he'll buy Marianne her long-desired estate car. At the Advent's bazaar where she is serving warmed wine with Yvonne, Daniela will manage to snag a completely drunk David Voss, who the following day in the locker room will explain what titty fucking is to all his astonished pals.

It's your own fault, Dion, instead of primly undressing Tanja an entire summer long with your eyes, that time on the riverbank you should have grabbed her, it's no surprise that she's distant. Of course the girls enjoy boys' shy glances, but even the smallest and sickest of them doesn't simply want to be gawked at but at some point be kissed.

She presses herself into Hannes' clumsy embrace on the straw floor and Saturdays, as it has already been warmed for communion and there's always a little bit of wine in the closet, sometimes even in the sacristy. A wallflower? When you're around, she plays at being the glass-bone-girl, but with him she has long been the young woman who knows what she wants; namely, not ending up in a wheelchair at the start of twenty without ever having been touched, why else would she have consciously snuggled up against him, he who didn't let a single chance go, there by the Jumme fire? While the sacristan was busy studying the songs in the church, Hannes was pressing his hand to her mouth to quieten the sounds coming out of the room—or out of the long uncleaned pipes, thinks the sacristan above his keyboard, head tilted, ears sharp, in the process falling out of rhythm and messing up the Kyrie eleison—and that, Dion, not the little howling of the storm, is the real symphony of your decline.

I lay into the western wall, catch my breath for a few seconds, then three final beats of the drum. During the pause, the old woodwork creaks. To you it is as if the mountain of clothes on the chair was swaying from the shocks. Your nightshirt is on top. After escaping from the Lambert's house, you spent the rest of the night tossing and turning, but whichever way you turned, even with your head at the foot of the bed, the sour stink rose to your nose, and your mother's collapse was the very first image of your dream. At some point you climbed onto her cold bed with its faint smell of lavender, which later in the morning grey finally brought you sleep.

You grab the negligee from the heap and push your face into the silk. Climb out of your pyjamas and slip inside it so that Marga's smell takes you in a cold embrace. The shirt fits you perfectly, until now you had always imagined yourself to be smaller than she was. You wriggle yourself into the bottom half, stick your leg through, walk across the bedside rug as if it were a runway. The next blast of wind that whips against the ivy lattice is so strong, you can feel the cold on your skin from the window and I shake with laughter.

Offended, you turn away and prance over to the bathroom. Total chaos: clothes on the floor, toilet paper rolls in between, which Marga was always too lazy to get rid of, fixtures a mess, the sink with its perpetual streaks of toothpaste; perpetual, as you don't see any reason to wash them away when, as Marga has ordered, you are supposed to brush your teeth three times a day. Since she didn't want to look at them, you recently divided the sink up into halves: you spit on the left, she the right, and when cleaning up, she simply leaves your side alone.

You pick at a pimple between your eyebrows, a little bit of lymph wells out. 'Wait another day,' she would have said, her eyes already avaricious. Not only was she allowed to kiss you whenever and wherever she wanted but she was also allowed to take care of every pimple; in return, whenever necessary, you had to be her comforter. That was the deal.

You quickly dabbed something from one of her powders on it, a beige-brown, tan-like, the colour too healthy. The kohl pencil helps. The lead slides out and leaves a black streak across your cheek. Rubbed with a fingertip, it will turn into eye shadow, which looks like a sleepless night and sadness for your carted-away mother. With her brush, you comb your hair to the right, then to the left, cannot get Hannes' daring and windblown look quite right. Take the clip! I call from the window. You pull the hair at your neck and bind it tightly in the way she always did at the pond. A few tufts stand out, not quite as if blown by a storm but better than before.

In the mirror you see your chapped and crusty lips. It must be a shared gene that makes you both mangle your lips when upset, a bad habit, more disgusting than biting your nails. You've only inherited the worst parts of your mother. How much you would have liked to have her thick, blonde hair, almost Lambert hair if she wouldn't attack the curls with the iron all the time. But you had been left with nothing even though, you figured, somewhere deep in your body there had to be at least some trace of the farmer's DNA.

You look back at the window where the snow is sticking to the panes; I continue to unceasingly surge against you and the house. Do you really want to know more about what you have inherited, about your father's characteristics? It would be better for you to believe the stories in the village, then at least you'd still have a choice. You could distribute the guilt of his fate and yours on your own. Even Marianne's cardigan—in which, until now, you have only seen the good—is not entirely clean. Yesterday she encouraged you to pray for your father; back then, however, she herself had made, as they say, hell quite a hot place for him. The result was supposed to be heaven on earth, a tiny Eden there between the stalls and the moor. She wrote love letters, sent gifts, managed to get him for almost every dance at the village festival. Doggedly held the place in the church pew next to her free, where soon Karl Lambert would sit. During the songs, which he had never sung, he murmured his own song about his useless brother into her ear. How he had let the house and the land go to waste and how, in order to strike his peat deals, he disappeared every few weeks to Hamburg where, his brother whispered to the rich dairy farmer's daughter, he did nothing but whore and drink.

Marianne moved her lips along with the songs and now and again emitted something like a chirp which Karl took to be an expression of compassion. She did not reject the offer outright, as marriage would bring her closer to her potential brother-in-law. The younger of the two Lamberts was reserved and silent, but unquiet; and that aroused suspicion in the village. He seemed to be concocting something, devising plans with absolutely no regard for the others. And, in fact, your father did think big: his long-term goal was to have the moor drained, but not for pig feed. He sent offers to investors, factory owners, energy companies—if he were still alive, on the horizon you would not see the silhouettes of birches but the cooling towers of a power plant.

With the proceeds from the sale of his land, he wanted to go away with you and your mother to the south; the Hamburger exporter Rasmussen with his contacts in Spain was the right thing. Spain, the word rang in his ears; perhaps, he thought, he could go along one time in order to share his agricultural knowledge with the tomato farmers who were fighting a lack of water. Being a moor farmer, he was pretty knowledgeable about drainage and canal systems. He showed your mother a pamphlet of a white house by the sea; there they would finally work a bit less, maybe have a second child and you a sunny future. Your father, Dion, was a dreamer; you got that much from him at least. He could have had the large landowner from the next village over but, instead, he chose the street kid from Hamburg.

Marianne bit back her jealousy, continued to go to Communion and hung on to him in spite of everything. Every evening she saw the light in the windows and within them the silhouette of a very thin woman. Yet another girl, she thought, but she'd soon be gone like all the others. At some point her brother-in-law would have got it all out of his system, would finally have given up the unprofitable peat business, add his land back to that of his brother's and enter into the pig business. The house on the Heidedamm would give way to the new stalls and he would move back into his parents' home, onto her land, where there was more than enough room. The distance between his quarters and hers would not be great, the addition was already finished; there would have been enough chances, for Karl really liked to put away his schnapps at night. There just couldn't be any mistakes. She hid the little package of conjugal hygiene products she had purchased at a druggist's where no one knew her in the bedroom beneath a loose floorboard. With the passing of the years, mice gnawed away at the little square envelopes, cushioned nests for their brood with the soft rubber skins.

Or so goes the legend. Think about what's true or not, or go and find out yourself. Don't you trust me? I would finally like to come clean, tabula rasa, and not only in this mess of a bathroom, so that you can draw the lines necessary for a child to become an adult. Stop being so stubborn and let me in! Okay, your father does weigh heavily on my mind, but that is exactly why I bring in life from the outside.

You, however, pointedly turn yourself towards the mirror from which a frightened boy looks back, his pale features covered in his mother's make-up. You take the lipstick and trace the contour of your mouth, even your prominent upper lip comes from your father, that so-called Cupid's bow, and you cast me a scornful glance and pucker your lips. But is the Cupid's bow truly the real evil, that sharp, arrowhead-like V that sits beneath your nose like a clamp?

At the window the snow continues to whorl. If you could hear it laugh, it would sound like a rattle. The border in the sink is blurred, just like everything else that should establish clear boundaries between Marga and you. With the lipstick you draw a line straight down the middle, then the console too. The same problem on the trolley, a confusion and fusion of your belongings: a hair clip clinging to your latest *Yps* comic, your dragonfly guide too, your bathroom reading, all covered with her things. On the floor, pyjama bottoms and nightgowns tangled into each other and she'd already placed your deodorant—the same kind Hannes uses—on the shelf with the perfumes she didn't particularly like.

So, how to move forward? Wavy lines would end up winding through the entire house if you wanted to separate your life from hers. So pack up all the junk and throw it away! The two of you even share the bathtub, and so you draw a square all the way around it; from now on everything within those lines will be considered private. Then another restricted area around the toilet, marked in red and white. After that the lipstick is gone, you throw it in the bin. Sigh.

But I still have one last weak response for your new defences. Do you really believe, Dion, that your soft strokes will stop Marga in the future? She has always used the heaviest of ammunition when it comes to imposing her will, and not only at her job. Do you remember how she stumbled into the bathroom without any warning, and right into your intimate business? And on that September evening too, the last time she came back from Hamburg, she had been well armed. She piled up the editions of the *Nature Encyclopedia* she had finally got for you one on top of the other onto the trolley right at the very second you could not hold it any longer. The sound was like an explosion, that's how ashamed the silence made you feel. You kicked the trolley away in rage. The books crashed to the floor; with your vacant glance you counted only five. 'hAnd hthe hrest?' you'd mumbled and pressed yourself deeper down into the toilet seat. She stacked the books back onto the trolley and pushed the pile over to you. 'The more you know, the less you will understand,' she said and sat down on the edge of the tub. Her face seemed strangely contorted, stunned and full of disgust, as if in the minutes beforehand she had seen something that had upset her profoundly. You wanted to bark at her *I'm shitting*, the two angry words pushed against your tongue and might even have come out properly in the unambiguous, long-overdue order to finally grant you the respect you deserved along with your body, its needs and secrets.

She crumpled into herself, pushed her face into her hands and began to sob, soundlessly. You turned away and reached for the toilet flush; to you, it seemed the only way to escape the unbearable situation. The water shot up, and pulled you down into the depths. You felt the cold breath from below, for a moment the swirl of water licked against your bottom. You had to think of the ray, your childhood fear of the tubes, the old, unfinished story in your notebook. Had the time finally come? Did she really want to leave you alone now? What the hell had you done wrong again, overlooked or denied her that she would torture you so?

Below you the hole smacked its lips. In the bathroom now, only the suffocating weight of her despair. For a moment you hoped that in her rage she had simply failed to notice that you were busy and that any second she would sheepishly apologize, slip out of the bathroom and have a good cry on her bed, so uncontrollably and heartbreakingly that you would have no choice but to go over and lay down next to her.

She raised her head, tore a piece of toilet tissue off and handed it to you. 'Show me that you are old enough to do it now,' she said, in spite of the traces of tears on her cheeks her voice sounded hostile and sharp. She wasn't looking for consolation, but an attack. In her other hand she still held the clothes hanger from the garment rack in the dressing room which had brushed into a second one, the second into a third and so on, until her head was filled with the old, perpetual alarm.

Everything had been well prepared. Just like back then at the home, her plan for the great escape had seemed perfect, the image of her breakout just within reach: she had got rid of her gallerist and had Daniel Röcker in tow, the main prize. She pushed him across the inner courtyard of the fashion house and through the door into the hallway and its cold neon light, the great emptiness, the beautiful white. From now on there would only be this tunnel into the interior and posterior of her life, a moment she had already encountered a thousand times which always led back to itself, the eternal present. It had been, she thought as she dove in, the biggest mistake of her life to have once believed that painting could be a way out of this circle or this circle the doorway into art.

'Wait here,' she whispered, pushed him in a corner and nodded; the role of the girl from the home smuggling her conquest past the watchwoman and into her room began to appeal to her. She pressed herself against the wall and into the niche where a plywood door was mounted, behind it the mirror of the changing room, and silently swung it open. She parted the curtain with a hand and saw one of the girls lingering behind the counter, bored. Her boss seemed to be away. 'Who are you hiding me from?' Röcker whispered from his corner. Barely into the dressing room, he had put his hand on her ass. 'Wash first,' she commanded, and pushed him into the bathroom. He smelt his armpits, turned in front the door, ran his hand along the suits on the rack. 'A seamstress then?' he nodded over to her. She grinned and felt her face to be as old and immobile as a glass-encased masterpiece. 'Men's outfitter,' she replied, and he, 'Haha.' The clacking of boots on tile, the rattle of a belt, she heard the stream of urine, the flush, then the faucet, sank onto the bed, jumped back up, cleared her throat and opened the dresser drawer: condoms, lubricating cream, toys, the little envelope with cocaine for an additional charge, everything was there, the obligatory package of Lexotax for the refreshing sleep thereafter, and she faked a coughing spell, pressed out two pills and swallowed them dry.

'Everything straight?' Röcker called from the bathroom. She listened to her insides where nothing was straight, not the flutter of a single breath, her pulse faint, she hit herself in the chest, said, 'I think I'm getting a cold.' When in an emergency your heartbeat does not speed up but sinks, you have crossed the point at which fear is supposed to protect you from what is to come. She pulled her dress a bit above her shoulder, rumpled her wet hair with a glance in the dressing-room mirror, bared her teeth, stuck out her tongue, a green rag, like mould, had she really picked something up? With her head tilted back, she looked up into the mirrored ceiling where normally she saw the back of her client but instead now saw her head, her naturally coloured hair growing out from the roots.

'The time has come,' Wolfgang, her hairdresser, had said the last time she went to see him and with that had triumphantly plucked a grey strand; she'd eyed the thirty-one-year-old woman looking back at her from the mirror and with a ferocious nod declared war. 'From now on I'm going to be expensive,' Wolfgang grinned, and twirled the old woman's hair around his finger and unceremoniously yanked it out so that she gave a cry and the other little old ladies emerged from their drying hoods to look.

She stretched her hands up to the ceiling mirror as if to pull the fake one out of the glass prison of glances and into her arms—the one who, thanks to the fact that Wolfgang was also a make-up artist, you couldn't see when standing in front of her but could indeed begin to see from above—in order to make peace with her and, together with her, once again, or maybe for the first time ever, be a little girl, play at having love affairs, experience what it felt like to have a racing heart; but when the cold bodies pressed against hers, all she could feel was the emptiness in her chest and further below, in her stomach, no trace of butterflies but only nausea.

She pushed the old one back into the ceiling mirror, back into the blank, unforgeable sky where all glances end in the eye of the Lord, who, the deaconesses had warned them when in their Saturday night disguises, was the only one who could see everything. She hid her roots under a hastily twisted tuft of hair, reapplied her lipstick, followed up with her eyeliner, from the small bottle of perfume first spritzed her underarms, then her panties and cast one final scrutinizing glance into the mirror on the wall where she now saw life standing in its middle, at last pure and without the illusions of hope, the giant image.

She snuck over to the bathroom. Observed Röcker through the crack in the door, how he stood in front of the sink and soaped his hands, and then, after awkwardly fumbling around his fly, his penis, slowly and carefully, as if to win some time. 'Your ass too,' she ordered, and he looked quizzically over at her, grabbed the hand towel and put himself back away. 'I thought it was hot,' she said, and he, 'What was?' 'How the whore in the film fingered the fat bastard.' 'Whore,' he repeated, and came up to her, formed a pistol with his thumb and index finger, placed the barrel against her head, then with his fingertip, which was cold from the water, stroked her cheek, throat, breasts, suddenly went directly for her heart. She pressed herself against the stock. 'I won't do you the favour,' he said and turned, as the script called for, to the bed so that she slightly opened her arms, ready for the finale, the kiss, then a sigh, the closing credits.

But the scene didn't advance, the heroes continued to stand around, turned away from each other with raised shoulders and dejected eyes. Only now did she see that he had noticed the mirror over the bed in which he looked squat, a boy with too large a jacket in front of a girl in a red summer dress with her hair up in a bun. The room was windowless, time within it out of step. Indeed, outside it could even have been summer or another spring. After a sharp cut, all of a sudden the film jumped forward. They were on his motorcycle driving out into the countryside through May-green fields of wheat to a house in the moor that appears at the end of the road, a boy standing in front of it looking back at them with his hand shielding his eyes, the air warm and filled with a sharp, slightly medicinal smell from the purple blooming bog myrtle.

Then he saw the curtain, the staging, it was all fake; she saw that he had noticed the radiator humidifier, the little bowl with essential oils on top, the deliberate and contrived nature of its freshness. She stifled a sound that could have been as much of a laugh as a scream, bit her lips and swallowed both. Röcker rushed forward, grabbed her by the arm and bent her over the bed; it was the same movement Miklos, the big boss, had used to welcome her into the world of work.

'Who are you really?' he panted down onto her, 'stop fucking around with me!' Her jaw cracked, then the bedframe, somewhere in the middle of the image, within a deeper layer. It was the moment she had long been waiting for.

She tore herself away, beat Röcker's hands off of her, that final chance for an embrace. With her push, Röcker crashed back into the bedframe and the bedframe against the wall and then the first clothes hanger began to swing on the garment rack and knocked against the second and the second against the third; she seized. Too late. She already heard the clatter.

The door broke open, the stage was set for Siana, the madam. 'What are you doing here?' she roared in her harsh accent. 'I'm working,' Marga answered quietly and finally felt her heart begin to beat more quickly. She dragged her baffled client out of his corner and pushed him against her boss who grabbed him and pushed him back. Marga protectively put her arms around him, then thrust him back to Siana who raised her fists in defence. For a moment the bodies danced their absurd

274

ballet. 'Get out of here,' the Russian rasped, pointing to the door, and at the same time stretched out her hand to stave off the violence Mira, once her best girl, began to let loose. The clothes hanger hit Siana with full fury. She tumbled to the side and into Röcker's arms, who was suddenly standing next to Marga, staring at her and trying to cushion the next blow with his big, round eyes, those childlike, deeply disappointed and, at that moment, she thought, sympathetic, in the end truly honest eyes in which perhaps she could have stopped swinging and finally come to rest.

But Siana was already writhing on the floor underneath the blows of the clothes hanger, which first took aim at her sagging breasts and then, as the old woman turned her back as a reflex, between her shoulder blades, quickly, one after the other, and then no longer with the shoulder but the hook, again and again into the debauched, wooden body that began to burst from the middle, or seemed to, as the head and bottom gave way, her legs—like a broken-down nag—splayed out behind her, against the bedframe, to the rhythm of the alarm-beating wood.

The twilight is sticking damply between the walls, white concrete walls, which seem foreign and far too high to her. In place of the display window with the empty-eyed puppets where there was once the entrance to the fashion house, she only saw a gaping hole fixed with a bar. A car rolled out of the park house, the driver stared at her. She turned her back to him, why did she suddenly feel ashamed?

She hadn't been in the Kleine Marienstraße in more than twenty years and had even avoided it in the half-unconscious, half-defiant way you avoid areas where, at some point in your life, you left too much of yourself. She looks up and, high above the roof of the concrete block, sees the moon standing in a misty sky, a sickle, a hanger from which night hung down like a wet rag swollen with the day's dirt. She stretches out an arm as if to finally pull down that great, good star which, so they say, shields the dreamer, catch hold of some of night's wonder after so many years, that wonder which had been squandered; but in her hands she only finds your book.

At some point, she had left her apartment, had wanted to continue to read somewhere quieter, away from the exhausting blare of *Frau* Schäfer's TV and the party noise from the group flat next door, the battle cry of her guilty conscience, memory's frontal assault. She longed to be close to you, to feel what you really wanted to tell her at the end of your raging and roaring sentences, in the silence following the lost battle.

She took a long shower, soaped herself over and over again until the plastic bottle with the shower gel was almost empty. The feeling of being dirty or being stained, the smell of the old, thrown-away woman still clung to her. For a long time she stood in front of the wardrobe, eventually decided upon a short summer dress, far too light for the rainy July night. She did her make-up and blow-dried her hair, but didn't know why, no one was waiting for her.

Outside she drifted through a sluggish Wednesday in Altona beneath a sky coloured a sulphurous yellow the closer she came to the neighbourhood. She stayed off the Königstraße, wandered through side streets she hadn't been to in years. Hexenberg, Hutmacherhof, the tangle of back courtyards and passageways finally brought her back onto the Holstenstraße where on the other side of the street the body-addicted lights of the Reeperbahn blinked.

She crossed against the red, avoided the main throng and dove into the hazy light of the back streets. On the Paul-Roosen-Straße a small group of people were huddled in front of bar throbbing with bass. She caught a glimpse of her reflection in the glass, regretted having chosen the short red skirt, a colour that on a woman of a certain age was no longer seductive but vulgar. In the centre of her empty shadow she saw Julius. Even though she had long been sick and tired of the pills, for the simple fact that Lexotax eliminated anxiety she would have placed flowers on the inventor's grave—the man whose invention had almost killed her—for ever and all time. She pushed up the arms of her jacket so that the liver spot on her hand was clearly visible. Then she went inside.

He was with a girl. A fellow student perhaps? His girlfriend? They were holding hands, he in the usual tight T-shirt, she in jeans and a tank top over perky breasts. They stood straight out from her small body like two sugar loaves, and twitched over to him across the glass of Caipirinha, that popular drink made from nothing but sugar, *sugar*, the word bored into her thoughts, she didn't know why she kept on repeating it obsessively as if someone were hammering it into her head. 'Sugary sweet,' she said to the girl who was at most twenty and who was the first to look up. Marga took the clip out of her hair and shook out her mane. 'I'm fifty-eight,' she said, 'my pubic hair's not grey yet but, all the same, no one's fucked me in two years. And you?' The girl stared at her aghast. Julius frowned, annoyed, then his face smoothed out again and froze into its customary, idol-like expression. 'Who might this be,' his companion hissed. 'Why aren't you wearing your cardigan?' Marga countered. The young woman had taken her hand away from Julius' fist. She looked as if she wanted to say something, but instead only soundlessly moved her mouth which even without lipstick was attractive. Marga bent over her neck, smelled delicate perfume, fabric softener. 'He'll never get it up with that, little girl,' she sighed. For the first time she noticed the colour of Julius' eyes, a cold, glassy green. 'You're pathetic,' he said, avoiding her glance. 'But,' she answered, 'you've still never got a boner with her, have you.' 'What does she want from you?' his girlfriend cried in a shrill voice and grabbed hold of the edge of the table. Marga laughed sympathetically down to her and said, 'Come back in fifty years.'

The way to the exit was blocked by young bodies with perfect skin, a mountain of marble chests, ridges of muscle, collarbone hollows. She kept her eyes fixed on the distant door, hoped she wouldn't fall over before getting there. From one second to the next, the pills' disinhibitory effects had turned into numbness and dizziness. No one noticed her, almost no one gave her any space; she squeezed her way through the damp and warm openings filled with beer breath and past pointed elbows jabbing into her sides to the rhythm of the techno music. Suddenly she heard someone call out from behind her *Old cow*! Julius? Or was it the guy she'd just bumped into, spilling his drink over his chest? Or had her thoughts become audible again, over the noise from the bar, which was like a plug in her ears? She stumbled about, and within the tangle of bodies sought out the green, glaciated glance, then pulled up her dress to show him what he'd missed.

Only once she was outside did she allow herself to feel weak. She tripped over the step, tumbled down the pavement and past keyholes steaming out night's stickiness, past the heat of bodies, beats billowing, laughter. Across the street the stream of people slowly rolled down the Reeperbahn. She lunged forward, back onto the Holstenstraße and, with the red light, into the alley-way in front of the park house, finally at the end of a lifelong movement that had begun with the shuddering of a clothes hanger on its rod.

She opens the book to where there's a zigzag in the printed picture, the part where she'd no longer been able to handle the noise and had had to flee. She reads how the hanger she beat Siana with still trembles in her hand, *trembles and drags her on*, it says, she painfully establishes some kind of context for the words, feels her way along the lurching lines like she does when paint-ing and, painting the words more than reading them, struggles through your sentences while trying to follow the rushing string of memories, her eyes flickering, body shaking, stumbles on, reads how, shaking, you write, she stumbled on through the flickering streets, dragged along by the clothes hanger which continued to swing in her hand and drove her on through the entire neigh-bourhood, past the men hissing offers to her, and then she plummets into the next paragraph where the clothes hanger steers her past Stadthausbrücke Station and across the Mönkedamm and on past the gallery where it begins to throb in her hand like a divining rod but she holds on to it tight and hurries on past the elegant boutiques and hotels and onto the Mönkebergstraße and then into the mass of people streaming out of the stores with their bulging bags as if it were just before

Christmas and she thinks, wrong, reads in your book: it *was* Christmas, and that year she was supposed to give her boy something really special, for her birthday gifts to him had really been pitiful and the clothes hanger nods and leads her directly into the bookstore and unerringly to the shelf with the bound encyclopedia set and the sales woman who's hard on her heels sees the client with the clothes hanger tearing a nature encyclopedia off the shelf and manages to catch the first volume, then the next and the next, all six copies falling down onto her until, with the hanger, the client directs her to the counter, the sales woman all the while balancing the entire stack while slaloming between the tables and when at one point she thought she was going to crumble under the weight she felt the metal hook between her shoulder blades while another client waved and called out, 'A detective novel!' and another yelled, 'Love story!' and another, 'A hiking guide!' But then she finally made it and let the books slide into a paper bag, sweating, but in the corner of her eye could still see the clothes hanger in the mad woman's hand, the hand which only let go of it once, briefly, in order to dig some money out of its purse, the woman pushing crumpled bills over the counter with the tip of the wood and into the fingers of *Frau* Mayrisch, as she was known by her nametag, a woman with glasses and a turtleneck sweater who held her, Marga, to be a cheat as, at this point in the book, *Frau* Mayrisch puckered her mouth and shoved the money back, it was, she said, unfortunately too little, deliberately too little, she thought and felt as if she were being robbed when the client raised the hanger towards her and, Marga reads, did not simply ask but *barked*: 'How much?' and that she had then attempted to blackmail her, the sales woman who she could, in fact, barely remember, in order to get that final volume which *Frau* Mayrisch had unceremoniously taken back because of the missing 20 marks and after a war of words in which Marga had growled at the woman, so the book says, but in which she, she now remembers, had only asked politely whether she could come back with the missing money a little later, for the wilfully malicious sales woman had taken back precisely that volume beginning with the letter *D* which had more than fifty pages on dragonflies and it was precisely that volume which was of particular interest to Marga, wrong, her son, she begged, she wanted to give him this big, costly edition for Christmas but in his novel at that point there was nothing about the politeness and decency and humility that just such a situation demands, there was nothing about Marga's pleading and supplications and the tears of shame and rage that filled her eyes, instead she only hears herself hiss and complain and rumble and emit other animalistic sounds as with the pack of books in one hand and the hanger in the other she did not simply elbow her way to the exit, no, but, as the next paragraph says, violently jabbed the other shoppers who were standing around with her hanger and even managed to find her seat in the bus in the same manner, first poking an older woman who was herself heading for it, the only free seat left in the bus, then batting her away with the encyclopedia or, rather, the bag of encyclopedias and then for the rest of the trip biting off the other little old grandmas who begged for a seat, you old ladies hang around the whole day on your fat asses, in the book again she *barks*, and took up the seat next to her with the encyclopedias and even in Zeeve, where she had to get off, she had first abused the bus driver—who out of fear or pity had let her on for just half the fare—then the armrest of his seat with the hanger that only stopped shaking after she had wrenched herself down the Dorfstraße and over the Heidedamm into the dark house and through the front door which, she remembers, had been locked, her boy's bed empty so that for a second she was afraid he might have been ripped away from her or had finally taken off in anger at the call she had once again forgotten to make in the late afternoon at a moment when she hadn't been able to think about anything else but fucking Daniel Röcker, you write, but not the painter, no, him, it had been her very own son instead who she'd taken between her fingers after bursting into the bathroom and sitting down on the edge of the tub next to him, her shitting child, with a piece of toilet tissue in her hand to get the thing done and over with cleanly and without a spot, just like she was used to doing with her clients when she had to jerk them off.

She did it casually, almost as if she were a little annoyed, the same way she always slapped something together to eat in the kitchen while smoking and thinking about her paintings, or nothing at all. She didn't even look at you once. You felt the cold creeping up from the toilet lid, the black feeling in your lower stomach growing taut while your insides seemed to be pushing out and into the pipes where the white ray lay in wait, hungry after all those years of banishment to the outer reaches of your consciousness and nearly forgotten. But now he had finally returned to retrieve what was rightfully his.

She enveloped you even tighter within the cave of her hand—or was it already the mouth of the fish? The thought that you would soon have to go with him down to the dark and cold place from which she came cripplingly and unavoidably seized you; and if there had been a language within you, for that which was now happening, without any doubt your scream would have been stutterless. But at that moment the feeling was silent, its colour unclear, hardly perceptible, it was something raw and incomprehensible overcoming you and tearing you away with a great, annihilating wave.

You had opened your legs wider, had felt the trickling in your stomach, water running in or was it out of you, as if your skin were only a sieve. She bent forward. You saw the sweat stains under her armpits, her scabbed lips, the smudged make-up, her utter desperation. As close as she now was, so brutal and predatory, you found her repulsive and foreign. Was this, you ask at this point in your book, really supposed to be your mother?

Then her face too began to warp, to turn white and flat. She felt you begin to come and slowed down. Unyielding now and glassy, her eyes rested on you while going through you at the same time, soullessly, you write, like an animal, like the cows or horses out in the pasture staring at you when as a boy you walked or, rather, slunk along the fence with that feeling of having somehow been caught, as if you had had to hide something from them, and behind the drain—which divided the meagre meadow and its shooting violet cones of green-winged orchids at the edge of the pool from the moor—you felt the black eyes that mirrored the emptiness and extent of the plain upon you, felt them follow you indifferently, see who you truly were without, however, recognizing you.

'My poor boy,' said the ray, then tore its mouth away and put its cold lips over you whole.

She closes the book and lifts her head out of the mire of your memories and into the foggy air above the balconies of Altona where, no longer hassled by any human face or member of the human race, she has finally found some peace upon a park bench, the view open onto the Köhlbrand Bridge which joins the south and north Elbe to the greater expanse of water and which here are no longer rivers, but not yet the sea.

High up in the pale dark, she sees the hanging lights of the harbour, to the left the inner city with its buildings shining into the sky over Hamburg and away, and in the west, where the Elbe rolls out of its stony pen of dock walls and jetties, a black horizon without any lines, the levels of glittering water and the glittering land both losing their lustre to the devouring mist, night above the distant coast like a gigantic sponge, sucking up the world.

Of all places, Dion, that's where you wanted to see her again? She had always avoided the sea in the same way as she had hated the empty plain behind her house in Fenndorf, in truth, any landscape that she found to be unpaintable, image-less in its deepest being, for it no longer gave away its gaze, enticed one to come into its shapelessness, or tore one out of its anchoring in the body and thus, directionless and removed from all knowledge and desire, devoured it. And so, beaten back by the bleak image of night's horizon, she decides to leaf through your book once more, for the din of your insults are less painful to her than the oppressive silence that creeps over her when she thinks that, in a little less than four weeks, she will see you at a path through the dunes where you have agreed to meet; but just not on the beach, she thinks, she would have preferred a cafe, maybe even the dim hotel bar, a niche where you could sit quietly in front each other and endure the stare of the other's eyes.

On the sea, however, she thinks, her eyes would only flee from him and out onto the water, while the waves would throw back everything she would want to say to her boy about his book—response and refutation—with that wordless roar that she wouldn't be able to oppose with anything other than her as always defence-less, far-too-lightly-dressed body pressing stubbornly against the wind; and so, forging ahead through the storm of your reproaches and lies, that storm which drives her on to the next page where she can barely read what has been written but only fly across it with her eyes in the painful hope of finally finding the part where her boy—a novelist, she thinks, who is allowed to and must outwit the so-called truth, things as they were and are—gives her if not, of course, his real then at least his fictional mother, just one more sentence so that she could retroactively take back the irrevocable and make their shared past different and better. But, at this point, I would either have to throw away this entire story, or take this already well-advanced winter and rewind it, spool back not just the previous autumn but all the sea-sons lying even further back in the past: the moor at first flat and white, then rust-red and steppe-brown in its slow decay and, later still, flecked with the violet and pale pink flames of the blooming bell and rosemary heather until spring inflamed the purple fire of the bog myrtle blooms before the light green of the birch trees, similarly sprouting in between the last crusts of ice. And then even the snow falling upward into the heavily

bellied clouds which billow, shrink, then suddenly—
after the water from the week-long autumn rains has
streamed back into the sky from the overflowing
ditches—crawl back over the fruit-heavy rowan trees
into the horizon where the world-distant blue of
September is slowly filled up by the hazy heat of late
summer and so on . . . spool back the whole laborious
process of growing and becoming, millimetre by millimetre, against time, which has made your home what
it is today, a cultivated secondary landscape with artificially protected biotopes in which the old and original—which people have always thought is better—are
protected against the onslaught of the present, the consequences of your memories and my narration. So, how
many years would we have to go back? To which point
of your life? What exactly must happen so that in that
crucial summer—towards which everything here is running—the reunion with your mother, as she envisions
it, will be the most peaceful and conciliatory it can be?
And, in fact, she finds the point in your book, the sentence, on which all her hopes are pinned: There is a
knock at the door.

Mama! shoots through your head, as well as the fact
that yesterday in your excitement you forgot to push
her the house key under the wool blanket and into her

lifeless hand. On the trolley a jar trembling, the glass in the window frame. Again the knocking, now already clattering. Dion, open up for her, would you? Or is she supposed to stay out there freezing on the porch in her blouse and thin house slacks, which Marianne had managed to quickly pack into a bag and push into the ambulance driver's hand? Oh dear, your aunt probably thought, the poor thing doesn't have anything on! Soon she will be coming through the door, pale and exhausted from all the stress, '*My poor boy*,' her voice still hoarse, her throat hurting from the tube with which they pumped her stomach. It doesn't matter, the important thing is that she's back at home! In the afternoon she will sleep long and deep, then get rid of all the coal the poison sucked out of her body on the toilet, and after that make an everything-soup overflowing with extras. She can still barely get anything down but for you there'll even be steak. Cinnamon pudding for dessert, then the first shy, somewhat contrite words promising you that from now on everything will be different and better. Well, let's go then!

On the steps you almost swoon from emotion, in the crown-glass window you see her slender shadow. A dog begins to bark; at first you hear the voice outside, then its echo multiplies out of the rooms downstairs as if a pack of snow dogs had made their way into the house—beasts with frozen lips and icy tongues. Had she brought you a mutt as a reconciliation gift from the animal shelter in Zeeve? Your eyes fall into the wardrobe mirror where a made-up boy in a satin dress with a girl's mouth and blown back hair beams back. An umbrella and a beard of cotton grass blooms would have been a better outfit to greet her with—then you would have immediately earned your kiss. But, starting today, new costumes have come into effect, other rules, you are the mother and she the needy child, the role reversal long overdue; and so that now *she* would be the one to stutter helplessly and *you* to simply smile tiredly, she should read you something from the church newsletter, the saying for the week: *Suffer the little children to come onto me, and forbid them not; for of such is the Kingdom of God*—Mark 10:14.

Her word in my ears; a gust of wind has barely blown the door against the wall when I push Tanja into your arms. The puppy in between and barking. You open your mouth—'Watch out, trap!' I yell—and the greeting freezes upon your lips. Or is it a sound of disappointment that it's not Marga who's embracing you? The decision you made yesterday to remain silent is the premise for everything that is to come, the seal marking our covenant: you shall give me your longing for intact speech, and in return I shall fulfil your dreams for which you cannot create the words. Here is Tanja, but keep your mouth shut!

'It's life-threatening out there,' she says, and points out to the waltz and welter of the snow. Ronja wriggles and sniffs at your neck, her black-flecked red tongue moves across your chin, no monster from the cold with pointed teeth, but a puppy, a German short-hair, Dion, what are you afraid of?

Tanja looks at you and thinks the same thing. If only he were one or two years older and wasn't so inhibited. And that stutter! The poor girl who goes for him all the same will have to literally shake the 'Yes' word out of him at the altar. Without a doubt, as far as love is concerned, he's still completely clueless. Instead of experiences, he collects dragonflies out in the moor. But still, she likes his eyes, their deep, sad gleam. Totally different from Hannes' braggart eyes, which make her freeze. Freeze and sweat at the same time. But does he know, she wonders, that Hannes and I . . . ?

Of course you know! And how angry it makes you! It fills your head with flickering images that refuse to go out for entire nights. Jealousy bathes your fantasies in a dull yellow light, a colour like the feeling itself. How they huddle, body to body on the straw floor, barely moving, now and again one of the two simply stretching out a leg, changing the position of the arm supporting their head. The straw crunches, the planks creak when she shifts her weight onto her other buttock where he still hasn't placed his hand, although it is lying there, open, ready to take her up, for Hannes' hand is large, strong and inviting; and she presses the air in her lower stomach as if she could become round and easy to handle, as supple as Daniela, but he doesn't move. Down below in the stall the tired grunting of the pigs; sounds from a warm, red-glowing inside, outside the crackling of the frost.

Wouldn't it be better to go to the sacristy? Being so late, she thinks, her father wouldn't have to come back, and they would be undisturbed. The small room smells of moth powder and extinguished candles, during Advent on pine needles, as the branches for the large, heavy wreath are already stacked up in the corner. The Communion wine is hidden away in the closet where the cassock and collar also hang, ironed and reinforced by her mother. The idea of her lying in Hannes' arms on the runner in front of the closet, the eavesdropping silence of the pews in the room next door, the image has barbs and thorns and it painfully bores into your chest.

It would be better to leave them alone in the straw, they don't trust themselves to get down to it there. The help could come in at any time. Hannes winds a piece of straw around his index finger, pulls it taut to his other hand where he's holding a cigarette. He ashes impatiently onto the ground. His hands are too powerful, even the last joint seems to strike more than flick the butt. The ember alights, his face glows red in the half-light, but you doubt it is from either shame or shyness.

Tanja herself may even be wondering why he is glowing. 'Isn't it dangerous to smoke in here?' she asks. He shrugs his shoulders, burns the piece of straw and says, 'Of course.' She sighs, feels the warmth from her mouth spread across her fingers, the rest of her body cold, numb in expectation. A draught comes through the crevices, the straw gives off a damp smell. She told her mother that she and Daniela would be practising for the concert that the confirmation candidates would have to give at the Advent's bazaar, she, Tanja, the flute, the Bloch's daughter on the piano.

Say something, she thinks, just don't show how uneasy you are. Did he also play an instrument? Hannes shrugs his shoulders again, says, 'If anything, then drums.' He crunches the cigarette out on the wood, the smell of something burnt. Threads the straw between his fingers. 'And Katthusen, the one from your class,' he says, 'what does he play?' She stares off into the darkness, over to the slat-wood wall where the glow of the lamps from the yard pushes through the cracks like a thousand tiny eyes. Suddenly she has the feeling that you are looking over; no, it's more that you wish that at the moment she was thinking of you, that she believed your eyes were watching her.

'He also stares at you,' Hannes says, the straw now stretched to snapping, 'He's not quite kosher.' Her head sinks onto his shoulder but only so far that she can feel his cold parka on her temples. 'Ach, Dion is pretty cute,' she waves, hoping to provoke him. He grabs her by the elbow and pulls her over, 'Did he say something about me?' She can smell the cigarette on his breath, his deodorant, which he had sprayed just a little too heavily. The points of light had all gathered around his head. The pain in her lower back now straight and sharp. In spite of the straw she feels the hardness of the boards, deep below an even more distant collision in one of those dreams in which you fall but never shatter. The kiss so close she can see the cut on his upper lip. Hannes pauses, then moves, his goal seeming to be something else. 'He knows about us,' she whispers, in order to fill the space between their mouths, which now seems insurmountable, with some kind of secret.

Down below the door creaks, a light flares. The farmer calls out for her son. Tanja holds her breath, in the straw his hand balls into a fist. Marianne's voice calls out a second time, then the door closes again and the darkness sinks back into its gloomy silence. Only a couple of pigs paw at the ground louder than before and through the cracks the eyes are bright and cold. She feels as if she has committed some act of betrayal, but doesn't know what or to whom.

But you are not stupid! Indeed, your eyes are every-where and can see how she is playing with you, enjoying your jealousy and flirting with her big catch. Why else would she be looking at you now so sneeringly while you are trying to quiet her dog in your arms? 'Ronja, enough!' she calls as the rough tongue once again licks your chin. Her mother had been against getting the dog because when it's big—and she makes a gesture at about thigh level with her hand—it could knock her over and break her bones. Sharp sounds cut into your skin: the dog's whine, Tanja yells 'Sit! Stay put!' the door bangs against the wall. Thank you, Dion, I am inside. Now, are you ready for the biggest game of all?

She finally pulls the dog off you. Ronja jumps down, crouches and pees with happiness in the doorway. Tanja brushes the snow off her jacket, there is so much that the puddle on the floor is hardly noticeable. Then her face suddenly disappears in the long shawl she unwraps from her neck. Ronja grabs hold of the end and pulls it away, spinning Tanja like a top out of the wool. You want to help her but the game seems too dangerous, it could pull her onto the ground and hurt her; but I hiss, Hands off!, and spin her out of the loops against the chest of drawers. 'Homework,' she says, out of breath, and hands you the plastic bag. 'The school bus had got stuck in the snow, half of the class didn't even come, but Gorbach,' she sighs, 'wants another personal-experience essay,' and she winks at you, as if she had known about the amusing piece I want to study with you here for a long time.

Does he suspect anything? she wonders, he looks so strange. Maybe I shouldn't have come by. But where else should she have gone after the fight with her mother? She doesn't go to Daniela's any more. The only other option would have been her cousin in Zeeve who would've kept her mouth shut, but with the weather as it was there was no bus.

'And what's that supposed to be?' she grins and points to your costume. Has he been crying? His eyes look red to her, the rings underneath them dark even without make-up, the rest of his face pale as a corpse. He looks distressed, no doubt because of the thing with his mother.

In the thin, half-see-through nightgown you suddenly feel naked, you take a furtive glance at yourself, wish you were out of the rags. Or could you at least throw the jacket over it all? But between you and the wardrobe there is me, the wall of cold and snow blowing in, o woe to the killjoy! the whistling of the storm pushes back. Look how well Ronja is already performing her role! The shawl writhes its way up the steps, a yellow python with red diamonds and brown whorls, when her mother had knit the thing it had been a lifetime's achievement. Up at the top of the stairs the puppy battles with the beast's raised head.

'You still have to practice a bit with the kohl,' Tanja says, bends forward and shows you the razor-thin line under her eye. On her cheeks a gleam of powder, and the storm had created just the right amount of disorder in her hair.

Until just a few minutes ago, she was the ugly and sick little duckling you had to cuddle and love so that it wouldn't eventually annoy you. Her mother wanted to force a caretaker with her on the way to school, although her shinbone fracture was as good as healed and the bone had been strengthened with an implant which, however, still caused her pain. Nevertheless, she had already begun to practise the light exercises during physical education class again, which angered her mother who would rather pack her into the wheelchair; since the operation it's been flipped open in the corner. If it were up to her mother, she wouldn't be allowed to leave the chair in the sitting room either, her grave would be right there between the mountains of pillows towering up in front of the TV. The last straw was at lunch. *Frau* Deichsen got rid of Hannes on the telephone. Tanja threw her spoon down, soup spilling out of the sides of bowl. 'I know what is good for me!' she yelled with a voice that made everyone start. After school she had taken a painkiller, had wanted to go with Hannes and his clique to the indoor pool no matter what. How excited she'd been when he grabbed her in the hallway and asked! She hadn't been expecting that at all. Many of her friends couldn't wait to be grabbed by Hannes at the edge of the pool in Zeeve and thrown into the water. She still had to look after her, her mother said, and ladled out more soup. 'I should be looking after *you*!' Tanja yelled and kicked the chair against the table; her sister just stared. Then there was the slam of the door followed by the flowerpot I blew off the porch; as a prelude to the afternoon play to come, in the normally quiet Deichsen house I decided to already take care of a few humorous scenes.

She locked herself into her room, cried a little, then sat around sulking and, finally, gathered a few task sheets. When she heard her mother downstairs in the basement at the washing machine, she slipped into her jacket and snuck out of the house. I immediately snatched her towards me and dragged her down the Dorfstraße and onto the Heidedamm where, to relax her, I knocked her down. On the frozen field I blew into her with gale force 10 to make her fall over, if softly, into the snow. The birch splintered behind her; it will be a few days before Farmer Lambert's moor saws are able to clear the way again. Yet by that time any help will be too late. Here is your new girlfriend, Dion, look how beautifully I have made her up for you!

But you remain standing there like the trees outside, swaying, windswept, naked and freezing under the white robe. Ronja hops down the stairs, the head of the dead snake in her mouth. 'This is boring now,' she barks, 'let's play something else!' Little tree, change yourself, I growl, and brush the hem of your nightgown up; the snow blows up to the chest of drawers. You rush out and shut the door in my face. You goddamn bastard! That wasn't part of the plan! I want to play, just look at what I've brought you all: glittering splinters of ice, funny gusts of wind, a crackling and crunching for the lurid gag!

With four hands and two unexpectedly strong bodies you press against the door and push me back. I howlingly hold my own against you, the hinges groan, Tanja giggles, and you too now bite back your laughter; then the lock clicks.

'What luck!' Tanja pants and leans back against you, exhausted. You have never felt her so close before. Her eyeballs are not only blue below the eyelid but also bend outward as if she were wearing contact lenses. Across the two benches that separate you at school she had always seemed bigger to you, if delicate, but still somehow lanky because of her spindle-shaped body. Now she reaches just barely over your shoulder and even slumps a little as she peels off her jacket and in so doing puts pressure on her knees, which looks dangerous, like an arc bent to bursting.

She is more fragile, but also more flexible, than the others and in spite of all the nailed bones, quite nimble. Under the birch tree she had skilfully wound herself out of my hands and when Hannes turns her into a woman today, he will simply bend her into shape: legs into the splits, arms over her back, head into her neck, 'And now,' he'll say, 'try to meet me with your pelvis,' and little by little she will slide herself over Hannes, who will push her leg even higher until she fans out into a wheel, her knees at her ears, the sensitive point overstretched and he will begin to moan with excitement, the sound coming from out of their insides, finally released from his oppressive fantasies.

'You go to hell for that,' she pulls you out of your thoughts. You look at her, shocked. Does she know something about what you just imagined? She's right, Dion, I drum against the window, those kind of images, as you paint them, definitely come from the devil, 'I mean,' she cuts me short, 'It's a sin to try and take your own life.' *Frau* Deichsen, the pastor's wife, had said so.

By breakfast-time she'd already known. What Dion's mother had done was against God's will, she instructed her daughter, her father nodded and looked at Tanja who sleepily spooned marmalade onto her bread, already having noticed that something strange had happened.

'Life is a gift,' *Frau* Deichsen said and added an exclamation point to the statement with a serious glance. 'And my illness?' Tanja chewed, 'was that a gift too?' Her mother froze in her chair. 'God doesn't make any distinction,' her father attempted to smooth everything out, 'between the sick and the healthy. On the contrary, whoever is sick . . .' 'I'm not sick,' Tanja began. *Frau* Doctor Burgwarth, her doctor, spoke, rather, of a hereditary defect, *autosomal dominant*. She turned to her mother and yelled, '*You* caused this shit to happen to me!' The pastor slammed his fist against the table so decisively that the candle fell out of the brass stand. Tanja broke it in two and threw the pieces to her mother. Then she shouldered her knapsack. I clapped and knocked the shutters against the wall. The overture seemed to have gone pretty well.

'I think it's brave of your mother,' Tanja says challengingly, 'the others are cowards for letting it go so far.' You want to contradict what she's saying, our pact; all the same, you would have gladly known what, in her eyes, Marga's profit from last night's horror had been as well as your failure. She fishes two pills out of her pocket. 'A painpill,' she grins, 'Just two and you're light as a feather and a little drunk, it's like flying.' She tosses one into her mouth, hands the other one to you, and then sticks out her tongue where it sticks. But I punish little sins immediately: she chokes.

You knock her carefully on the back, it feels hot and a little wet, maybe from the stressful march through the snow. 'The collagen's broken,' she coughs, that's why her eyes are so strange and she sweats constantly. She sniffs at her armpits. 'Does it bother you?' You quickly shake your head. 'And this?' she bares her teeth, which are almost colourless, more grey than white, on top of it a number of them are broken, which reminds you a little of shards of glass. 'It doesn't affect me when kissing,' she steals the answer from you, and everything else was just like with other girls, totally normal; the youngest in the class, she had got her period one year ago already but she didn't tell you that. Because of the tampons, she had had yet another argument with her mother who recommended instead that she wear pads, those thick things that make you look like your shit had slid into your pants. That's what she had told Danni when she was still her friend; on top of the crap she'd had to hear about becoming a woman and her mother's fear about her hymen. Then the two of them huffed and puffed, tore the tampon packages open that she had picked up in the drugstore in Zeeve and tried out various sizes.

In the end, her hymen hadn't been broken by the o.b., but by Hannes. Although he had been careful, she had still bled a lot. Her legs were smeared, his hands too, and although it all looked like an operation and had also been quite painful, he squeezed her and groaned '*Man-o-man!*' the entire time. Afterwards, she wiped herself with a hand full of straw, but did not know what to do with it. Outside, the rain beat down upon the roof.

Tanja pulls her sweater flat over her chest, where there is barely anything curving out. 'With Daniela everything's so big, it's no wonder,' she sighs, 'everyone is interested in her.' You nod and shake your head at the same time and hope she takes your answers in the right order. 'When I'm grown up, I'm going to have saggy breasts.' She says it brashly, almost as if it were an accusation against you. 'Because of my connective tissue. Look!' She pulls her sweater up and pinches her skin. On top of that, the last test suggested that she was already a little hard of hearing. 'All right, tell me the truth'—her glance is now suspicious and aggressive—'do you still find me attractive?'

There's no more saliva in your mouth, nothing but the dried-out T of *totally*. Tanja lays her hand against her ear, now in the form of a shell, mimics the deaf old woman and croaks, 'I can't understand you!' You wince. Where did she know that old-person's pantomime from? She begins to cough again, you lay your hand on her back and caress her spine as if you could steer the pill that was stuck in her throat all the way down. Through the crown glass I see two silhouettes in the hall standing next to each other, ready to merge. Damn it, kids, let me in! When the pill makes it to her stomach, you quickly pull your hand away. And now, Dion?

Everybody upstairs.

Ronja knows the way already and hops on ahead. Hey, I call out behind you, you can't just let me stay out here! and throw myself with such force against the door that for a moment I really do lose my breath.

Outside, everything that still is protruding halfway stands up straight with a groan: the gable relaxes, the barn with its bent ridge points out of the lee of the house, the birch and alder branches become untangled and shake off their shells of snow. A crow uses the lull to flee towards a better hiding place. It shoots out from a bush, reels through the air and leaves behind a black scratch in the picture which is almost completely white already, nearly perfect. I grab the bird and spin it to the ground. For a while it crouches by a mound of earth, ruffles its feathers and hacks into the snow with its beak. I let loose an avalanche from a grain chute, a wing is torn off, then the crow is gone.

In the moor, the lines begin to break; the geometric pattern of the ribs of peat with the almost level mounds of sod which have not yet been transported, the flat furrows of the drains between the paths and farmland useless. In the pine woods, the branches snap under the heavy white weight of the spitting, all-devouring waves rolling in off the plain and from the large kolk where the air is so sharp with splinters of ice that you can hardly breathe. And even the soft peat moss is threatened with suffocation by the masses of snow arising along the edges of the mounds, they harden under the weight and, only in April, when the last crusts have melted, will they show the traces of their own destruction, the sear of frost in filigreed braids, flaky brownish spots just like the ones the wood workers' feet leave behind who, with a single step, can eliminate an entire growth of peat moss; and so, once the broken trees have been removed, at the end of winter, it will look as if an infantry had marched across the highest point of the plain which at the same time is its innermost and most serious core, its massive, black peat sponges burrowing seven metres down into the earth. And, over the next few weeks, when at night the temperature sinks into the double digits, they will freeze through down to their very last pores, more slowly, but also for longer than the sandy ground of the meagre meadows and adjacent pastures. Out here by the kolk, on the treeless knoll where my power multiplies unhindered, next spring the peat will still be frozen, your memory of the heaviest winter storms of the decade imbedded within my cold heart.

I am gathering strength for the next coup, scale the west wall where the bedrooms are, break off the first roof tile. Soon the house will be naked and vulnerable, the protective roof over your heads gone. Later, in the village it will be said that the two of you were not responsible for the accident, which is what everything revolves around here; no, once again the moor will be at fault, that child-addicted monster, its ancient and evil powers to blame for your misfortune. By the end of today, you will know what it means to take blame upon yourself, but you will be acquitted and I once again will be accused. I, who here in Fenndorf must pay for everything: the meagre, leached earth, the bad weather, the hard winters and the region's poverty, even your father's death—everything comes back to me and, in the end, on that everyone in the village agrees.

That being said, Karl Lambert played right into my hands. 'How long have you been doing it with my wife?' he yelled into a clap of thunder from the storm just breaking loose as your father was tying down the peat under the tarps. By then the others had already been asking him, Karl, down at the pub. Your father looked to the house where he thought he could see the shadow of your pregnant mother in the window. He turned around and said: 'I'd rather fuck one of your pigs than your wife.' The next moment everything crashed and splintered, but not from Karl's fists, which were busy beating his brother down to the ground. An alder branch broke off from the tree where I hurled a bolt of lightning in order to prepare an end to this village farce, an action that turned out to be more effective than I had planned. The branch that rattled down ripped the two from each other and knocked your father into the pond where, after a few helpless rowing motions and suffering from a serious head injury, he lost consciousness and sank, right about there, where today the dead branch you, not without good reason, describe as a claw doggedly keeps the truth concealed so that even your mother with her daily swims can do nothing but stop and, at a loss, stare down into the depths when she reaches that point, there where the legend of your father lies stored; and you too, Dion, will only vaguely remember my violence when you let it burst forth once again in your book. Distorted, punctured by forgetting but full of a wealth of invented details, the moment you led Tanja into the bathroom and poured water into Marga's toothbrush holder, a gesture she first answered with a crooked smile but then, after she had finally washed the pain pill down into her stomach, rewarded with a quick kiss on the cheek, and a wave of happiness rose from your stomach up into your throat, all the knotted words and hardened sentences melted away and filled you with a feeling of intoxication and freedom or simply with the stupidity of an infatuated boy who takes a deep breath and without a stutter says: 'I love you.'

'What?' Tanja and I call out at the same time. Traitor! You're not sticking to the terms of our agreement! And she thinks: Shit, now I have to tell him the truth. He's a good guy who doesn't deserve to be lied to. She lays her hand on your cheek. 'My dear,' she sighs and says it in a mother-like tone just like Marga's *My boy* or *My darling*. She pauses, and eventually, in an extremely delicate voice, says: She had a lot of love for you too, like a brother. Then adds: She knows it sounds pathetic, but she wants and can only do it with Hannes.

Naturally, it is not true that he took her virginity on the straw floor. No one has yet, which is why the thought of Daniela bleeding in the straw and of Hannes being difficult to hold on to will not leave her alone. She didn't quite believe it; even if her friend had recounted the details so vividly, there was no way she could have thought of it all on her own. It was unimaginative, just like her personal-experience essays where most of the time she walked away with a simple passing mark, while she, Tanja, on the other hand, shone, although both had written about the same thing. And so, in her thoughts she had stolen the role of being deflowered from Daniela. Instead of the Bloch's daughter, she herself was suddenly sitting with Hannes in the hiding place. While Daniela bragged about her night of love, Tanja could trace the secret movements she whispered to her, she even thought she could feel the pain in her lower stomach, the pricks and pains, all the blood.

That was before the summer break when the two were still more or less of one heart and soul; which is to say, thought, felt and suffered everything together. Since kindergarten, the shopkeeper's girl had been Tanja's closest confidant, a girl who played alone most of the time, heavy and awkward as she was with that oozing psoriasis on her skin. Then all of a sudden the ugly duckling became a swan, all the fat shifted to its proper place, and the scurf changed into pimples which could hardly be seen beneath the delicate pink powder she began to use. The first arguments, weekly leg and breast comparisons, betrayals with Yvonne, the pub owner's daughter with whom she was allowed to serve drinks at the Village Tankard during school holidays for a little bit of pocket money and, even more importantly, the glances from the boys at the kicker table.

When Hannes had wanted to pay for his beer once, Daniela supposedly said that it was on the house. It had been, she later admitted to her, Tanja, not just one but four beers, the entire night's wages gone just like that. Nevertheless, it had been cheap, Tanja answered defiantly; but she didn't know who she was supposed to be jealous of—Hannes, for having stolen away her best friend, or Daniela, who was now going with the farmer's son that, until then, had been of no interest to her.

She avoided her glance and, instead, stared into the corner of the room where there was a pile of stuffed animals they had once separated according to sex; the new, still-fluffy ones were always the women and the worn-out ones the men who had to go out to the fields while the women-animals cooked and paid for tiny packages of Persil detergent or Maggi with pfennig pieces that were larger than their paws.

Then all of a sudden one of the long-legged cats fell in love with a day labourer; of all things, the ugly plastic pig, which otherwise was only ever given the role of the brute. Daniela insisted on having a wedding in a farm made of building blocks and with the lovely Steiff bear as a piglet. That had been the beginning of the end. The celebrations finished in an argument, for the cat required her maid of honour, the mouse, to clean up the pillow cave in which she, Tanja, was lying. Ousted by the false cat, the grey mouse brooded upon revenge.

If there really was a whore in the village, she now thinks grimly, then it wasn't Dion's mother but Danni. No man was as big down there as Danni maintained Hannes was. First it was as long as a pen; then, a week later, it was already a ruler. That was a bit much for her. Dion would do it slowly and carefully, of that she was certain. He was not the type for a quick number. He was also looking for a big love; Hannes, on the contrary, never burnt long, and was known for it. He'd been after her since that night at the Jumme. Held the door open for her at school, something no one had ever done. Even the teachers quickly slip through the door while she bumps into the glass. Hannes, she thinks, had to have seen that once. Since then, however, he'd been hanging about in front of their house on his moped, and today even invited her to the indoor pool. Then she had once again begun to imagine scenes with him. She was proud he had invited her, her—a real disaster for Daniela. But at the thought of him following her into the changing rooms, sliding in behind her, closing the door, and then, with his ruler . . .

'We could be like brother and sister,' she says and sees you take a breath and open your mouth to protest. 'One could steal horses with you,' she says to you in a soft voice, pursing her lips and kissing you in such a child-like and chaste way that your mother's affections seem like salacious bites in comparison. 'Didn't you ever want a sister?' she coos and grabs your hand.

No! Never! Get going, Dion, scream that in her face, all your frustration at this defeat; but in your throat there is only the pressure and further below a feeling as if your own skin no longer fit and that your body would shrink down to a miniscule point, the smallest shared sound of all of your miscarried words.

You choke on a sentence that should instead make clear that you want her honestly and without any ulterior motives, so that through your love she, you wanted to promise her, would have a long, protected life or could at least recover; for the handicapped were, in truth, far ahead of the others. Whereas the healthy simply walked past all and sundry towards an uncertain goal, the lame could see the flowers on the side of the road and the stutterers hear the buzzing of the insects;

you, Dion, and she, Tanja, could hear and see the courtship dance of the stuttering-dragonfly with the glass-bone female who have now joined each other in a wheel, as, between them, it's irrelevant whether or not the children born of their union stutter or have brittle bones. Dragonflies do not speak, they are made of chitin and do not have to tear out their hair over any other kind of deformity; and, come to think of it, your children wouldn't even have any hair, neither flaxen nor moor brown, they would simply fly and fuck in the air, full stop.

At the end of all your struggles, however, just one unfortunate sentence, 'It takes at least two pills to fly,' you stammer and hold out your hand. What he says, I whisper to Tanja, is true! And she is already punching out two more pills from the blister strip. You swallow and then rinse your mouths out with the water in the toothbrush holder. This is going to make him tired, she thinks and will win her some time.

'But with such a cool mother, you wouldn't need any siblings!' she says to rationalize her manoeuvres and lies. Her grin doesn't seem to want to work, her mouth hangs down, seems pinched and small. But she's right! I say in agreement, Marga always let you do what no other child was allowed to do: go out into the moor alone, stay up until after midnight watching a film on the late programme—how you could have let loose during school breaks with your knowledge about sex scenes and brutal murders! So don't complain. Other children had worse parents; Hannes, for example, who is being groomed by his father, as per tradition, to become a pig farmer, and Tanja, whose mother has never tolerated your being around. So do it with her as a sister, that's no problem at all for a dragonfly!

In fact, Tanja has a very high opinion of your mother. She had smiled at her recently from her estate car. Had even given her a lift for a bit, for Tanja was still in a cast. *Frau* Katthusen had been at the wheel in a miniskirt, she remembers, even though it was cold, further down she'd noticed the fine stockings with the embroidered leaf pattern, which she thought were gorgeous. She herself was wearing a long, tiered skirt which she had sewn together from a number of colourful coats, sometimes there were some real finds in the Goodwill collection. Dion's mother, she thinks, who was an artist, had to have immediately recognized her talent. She had complemented her on her skirt, she seemed to like her hairstyle too. While driving, she had run her hand across Tanja's head and undone her hair tie. More attractive to the boys that way, she said, and that she too had once had such nice hair, back when men still wanted her.

In front of the shop, Daniela's mother was pasting up special offers and staring inside. Surely, Tanja thought, Dion's mother wouldn't have anything against me living here for a while. She had driven me up to the door and even invited me to come over in order to try out clothes and hairstyles. Only when *Frau* Katthusen had bent down, and pressed her finger to her cheek in order to get a kiss had she been able to smell the schnapps. She, Tanja, was something special. She pushed open the door. 'Listen to your heart,' she heard called after her, 'not your parents!'

A dull blow to the house. 'What was that?' Tanja strains to hear what's happening upstairs. I've torn the second tile off the roof, and am now worming my way through the hole and looking around the attic. Beams that will not give way, no matter how much I shake them. The battens are well made, the old tiles, however, already somewhat broken. It is here that I shall begin my work. Downstairs I can hear Tanja chirping.

'Come on, let's do something fun!' She pulls out a brush and a make-up stick. With a few hand movements, she turned you into the spitting image of a brunette. Then she begins herself, here a spot, there a line, teases her hair, a little hairspray on top, in the mirror she snuggles up against your temples. Lesbian love does not exist between dragonflies, I gnash between my teeth in a fading tone and go into the bathroom. A cold draught of air blows beneath your nightshirt.

Frightened, you turn towards the door where Marga's clothes are swaying on their hooks. In the hallway, the shadows are swaying too. Is it because of the pills? Tanja bends over laughing and throws away the cotton pads. But what, she wonders, will he do when he realizes that I'm lying? Where will I go when he throws me out? She must find a way to become his best friend. 'I'm not in love with Hannes,' she says and looks at you challengingly. Was that good? she asks herself, does he believe me? Don't worry, I reassure her, that was precisely the right tone for something intimate, sister to sister. Out with the truth! you yell in your head and, as if she had read your glance, in an imploring voice she says, 'It's just fun with him.' Fun! the word echoes through your head, the code word for let's-be-friends, swimming at the Jumme, unpronounceable for someone like you.

He did everything with her that, because of her illness, she wasn't allowed to do: drink beer, go to the indoor pool, ride his moped. 'Look!' She pulls a piece of her sweater over her shoulder, points to a spot and grins, 'That's where I had a bruise from him!'

Looking back, it all seems to her like it had long been planned. Around the end of September he suddenly showed up one day, shortly after the big fight with his girlfriend. He wanted to take a spin on his moped, she says and can feel how the story winds you up. It had been coming down in buckets. Thankfully her mother had been at choir, her father in Rahse where there'd been a death. Only Jule, her little sister, she remembers, had peeped through the door, looked at Hannes curiously and shrieked: 'Mama says you're a lout!' Then she'd placed her doll on her head, skipped on down the hall squawking *lout, lout*, over and over again. Tanja locked her into the bathroom.

'His face was totally red,' she laughs, 'his ears had really glowed.' She grabs the lipstick and jauntily draws a line on your ear. Then it suddenly became cold and there was another shower, and it made it into the hallway. Jule banged against the door in the bathroom. Hannes pointed to his moped out on the square and said: 'Go for a spin?'

'No one goes around outside in weather like this,' she had said, and delays the punch line. In your flashing eyes she sees how you want to know a lot more, all the details, the whole story. 'He explained the gearshift to me,' she says darkly, 'as if I was his best friend.' She herself even drove a little bit, on the Heidedamm, puddles shooting out under the wheels.

In the half-light behind the veil of her pill-heavy eyelids she can once again see the moor waver around her, once again feel his hands. 'He was sitting behind me,' she murmurs, 'and gently pressed into me in the curves, like the professionals do.' 'Professionals' you repeat in your thoughts and already understand just what she means. 'It was really dangerous,' Tanja nods.

Hannes lifted the moped up in front like a frightened horse. Daniela's window looked out onto the peat hollows, and so Tanja could imagine how she jealously watched Hannes and her on their ride through the moor, but she doesn't tell you that. He suggested riding over the paths to the pond, said it would shake less. 'Giddy-up!' she cried and the wheels spun; behind them a fountain of mud. 'We went full speed,' she laughs, 'over the bump.' She hopped up and down on the nag and was only a little bit afraid.

But that is really only half the story. The rest, which she is hiding from you, you saw from your hiding place among the alders. They were there in the reeds—because Hannes wanted to smoke a cigarette, Tanja will no doubt maintain. But you know better, want to counter, tickle the truth out of her: Hadn't he lured her into the rushes with an excuse? I brush across your mouth with a cold breath: Remember our pact! That is to remain your secret!

Naturally, she had followed him, though the pond was sinister to her. It was always dusky and there were animals. She likes horses, sheep, because everything else bleats, and cows too, when they look over from the meadow, they caused her to shudder comfortably, as if extraterrestrials had metamorphosed into cattle in order to collect information about humanity and transmit their knowledge back out into the universe. But it was not the reeds or the looks of any creatures that made her feel uncomfortable. She knew from Daniela that

Hannes had already done the business with her there. Only the birds up in the trees could see down into the reeds, yet they would transmit it to the cows over on the meadow and the next thing you knew, her mother—who had quite a good link up above—would know.

You make a quizzical sound when she takes your hand and places it where the haematoma had likely been. Okay, I can no longer get to you with such infantile stuff. Nevertheless, she'd turned back towards the village while Hannes pushed ever deeper into the rushes, which the wind split in two. No one was supposed to see what was about to happen. At that point in time she didn't realize that over in the alders there had already long been an observer. Hannes, who was almost 1.90 metres tall, towered over the reeds and that was the moment you had noticed them.

'Look,' she says, and drives your finger into her skin, she wasn't as fragile as everyone thought. 'I came into the world with broken bones already, what else can happen?' She looks at you with expectant eyes, inches closer; the snake, that's how she did it at the pond with Hannes too.

But she only wants to be a little bit nearer to you, to receive a little comfort and the certainty that you mean well. 'It doesn't matter,' she sighs, and presses your thumbs even tighter into her bony shoulder. Back then, she remembers, the spot had been violet and as long as a finger, and stretched from her armpit almost to her chest. She had showed it to her mother, not really, but she hadn't hidden it from her when she was in the bathroom; in fact, she'd almost been a little bit proud of it. Where had she got it? Her mother grabbed her arm, which was truly dangerous—as an infant, she always reminds her, she had carried her about like a raw egg. Then and there Tanja had had it. She yelled into her mother's face that, with her illness, she should never have been allowed to have children, that she had only had children in order to please her god. Her mother had put her onto the chair, and she, Tanja, had placed her arm through the backrest and wound herself up like a knot. She remembers how it had cracked. Not her arm, but the wood; she'd had no idea she could summon up such strength when it came down to it. Her mother was in shock, completely pale, as if she were about to fall unconscious. Instead she smacked Tanja's face. She'd seen the welts in the mirror, the unmistakable proof. She pointed to the bruise and cried: 'It's from you!'

That was how she was going to tell the story to *Frau* Doctor Burgwarth. Instead, her mother sent her to an adolescent psychologist who asked her strange questions. How she saw her own body, too thin or too heavy? Just right, she had answered, and that Daniela was so mean to her now because she herself had grown too fat. The psychologist—a pudgy type with glasses and a moustache—kept at it, what did she mean too fat?; and what did Daniela have to do with the subject? That's when she served up all the lies: that Hannes and her had been doing it on the straw floor and in the sacristy and thanks to the various positions they were trying out, it could easily have happened that he grabbed her too roughly.

The therapist took notes, and now and again would take off his glasses to rub his eyes, two small slits, his eyebrows above them like bristles, a mole.

Whether her boyfriend, Ha-hannes, he read from his notes, had already told her that he loved her? She nodded meaningfully; she thought that is what he wanted to hear. And when one day he didn't love her any more? She hadn't understood the question. He gave her a speech about her illness, everything she already knew: that her body was not growing like other girls', that other girls were quicker, straighter, healthier and so on, and Ha-Hannes, he stammered again, he too would grow older, and how old was he anyway?, and that he might very well at some point then prefer the other girls. She had shrugged her shoulders and said: 'Then I'll just end it.' 'With Hannes,' he nodded satisfied, and she: 'No, my life.'

'That's not all completely true,' she says, and looks at you guiltily. She has left something out. She takes your hand and lays it on her chest where your heart hammers against the pressure to tell her what you had really seen from your hiding place. She places her hand on top, 'Swear,' she whispers, 'that you won't tell anyone!' Her mother could never learn of it: how the moped had broken in back in a muddy rut and she had been thrown off the seat. You hold your breath, then let the air stream out through the cracking and splintering sound, 'hBro-hken?' In fact, you think you can hear the sound again when Hannes had pulled her to him, and you ran out of the underbrush and back home. She lifts her shoulders expressively, her voice sounds almost threatening, 'It still hurts,' and with her left hand she plucks the knot of your intertwined fingers from your chest and pushes it onto the invisible wound; and so that no one will ever find out that at the moment Hannes had bent her over the stump Tanja had already seen you on the other bank. I too lay my own cold hand on her heart and the lie of that afternoon into your mouth for ever. A rumbling above in the fly loft. Tanja starts. 'Where's Ronja?' she cries.

Exeunt omnes.

Even your mother takes flight before the performance begins. She jumps up from her secluded loggia seat on the park bench of Altona's balcony and hurries off. And that is when she begins to feel the pounding in her back again, the stabs between her shoulders propelling her through the streets while urging her to finally come to a stop at the next corner, to not utter another word. And once again that well-known feeling to fight against an obstacle that, as soon as she paused, would catapult her back to those places she had freed herself from through year-long struggles, overwhelmed by a pain that she would only be able to endure if she yields to its violence.

That's how she'd left all the stations of her life behind: the girls' home, the Heidedamm, the Ochsenzoll mental hospital, a name which back then even the deaconesses had used to threaten the unruly girls; a name that sounded like cages, whippings and even more severe drills. At the same time, of all things she had discovered moments of relief there, almost a kind of happiness when she considered that she had come to a place she didn't want to stay but that she was allowed to leave. Her mood swings became less pronounced, that persistent movement from numbness to a crash which at its outermost point led back into stasis began to stabilize. And, strangest of all, in the quiet and emptiness of those hallways that smelt of chlorine, she no longer felt the compulsion to paint, and swallowed the medicine that clipped those thorns with gratitude and humility, twice a day a little plastic cup full of the mercy of an almost all-encompassing listlessness, and state health insurance paying for the whole thing, where else could you get such a good deal?

For all that, she'd even accepted a fat ass. After the ward doctor—a young guy with wide shoulders and a soft, passionless, so to speak, merciful voice—had proven himself immune to her looks, she'd been willing and with grim delight, in the end, even swelled out like yeast dough, happy they'd managed to pull that last thorn out too. In Ochsenzoll, she had been able to get some rest for a few months. She stretched out in bed, listened in on her ever-expanding body—and heard nothing. The antipsychotics had slowed down her metabolism to a bare minimum and wrapped everything else that still pinched and pricked in soothing padding. The electroshock machine, which after insistent discussions they cabled to her temples three times a week, brought the pendulum back into swing. Or had it been Daniel Röcker's unexpected visit?

She ran on. Back to Fenndorf, and after that once again to Hamburg, the group flat in the Susannenstraße, the Pulverteich in St Georg where she had managed to live for eight years at least. Even the prostitutes, cast out by the redevelopment measures in St Pauli, had moved and had begun to hang around her street at night. Then one year in Berlin, right after the Wall came down; a few months later she realized that she was there only to be closer to her boy. One of her more or less forced reunions—only two hours in a cafe—then her flight back to Hamburg. Ochsenzoll again, almost half a year, that time they let her stay. The ward doctor was long gone, the modern medicines and the regular fitness programme even kept her fellow patients, who were long past menopause, in shape. They sent her to art therapy classes, really pushed the idea of *reconciliation with one's inner child* in deep psychological talks and, after five months, excused themselves in a friendly manner: there just really wasn't anything else they could do for her now.

She moved to Eimsbüttel where she lived with Kathrin, a lesbian, not far from the old girls' home, which was now a hospice, modernized and, as she had heard, outfitted with a palliative care ward. That's where she'll return one day, she thinks. The circles still haven't become a line, just grown larger, spiral-like they spin out of the scar on her back and at the end of all their meanderings lead back to the start again, there between her shoulder blades and within her body, which, of all places, is the only one, even after all her repeated betrayals, that has stubbornly stayed by her, although, she thinks, it would be about time to once and for all get it behind her, as a woman at the end of her fifties, to leave her body with dignity, that flimsy container, before it was too late, and she rips open her door and stumbles into the house.

A smell of something burning hits her, more threateningly than ever before. But it doesn't seem to have disturbed the party in the other flat at all, young people are lingering out on the staircase and toasting one another. She takes the stairs two at a time, wheezing, she clings to the handrail in front of her apartment door. Her back pain bends her over the balustrade, for a moment she doesn't think she can move another step.

She feels herself slipping, and longs to see her body break apart on the ground, the young and beautiful clapping; but, in reality, she hasn't moved a single millimetre. To fall to pieces, yes. To burn, no. She'd always been terrified of a death by fire or, even worse, to have to live with a face like out of a horror film; either softly while asleep or a quick and painless fall.

The flames are already surging out of the pan, or, more precisely, out of the hand towel that *Frau* Schäfer must have tossed inside before simply forgetting her dinner. The stream of water hisses onto the smouldering junk which has turned into poisonous smoke. Why doesn't she just let the old girl suffocate? In her position, at that age, she would be thankful to have a younger neighbour who out of pity would just let the fried egg burn.

Dead tired, *Frau* Schäfer was already lying in her chair in front of the TV where an old crooner was singing a schmaltzy tune from his on-demand concert *You only have to look around / Mountains up to the sky from the ground* . . . Marga rips the plug out of the socket, the tubes silence with a snap of light, continue to crackle. The room now as dark as a burial chamber, in the corners the furniture crouching like beasts of the underworld, eternal night flickering in through the window, white noise.

The old woman sighs and dreams of Florian Silbereisen, the cheery angel and joy of all lonely widows, who Julius, Marga thinks, even somewhat resembles.

She sees *Frau* Schäfer's blue-veined hand, her eyelids, the corner of her mouth, liver spots, the whole package that has been laid out and ready for collection twitch to the rhythm of the melody which continued to echo in her head and burrow its way deeper and deeper inside. 'Let mercy prevail!' the blonde hosts sing, 'For your mother too, Dion.'

But you continue to write Cerberus and the snakes of the Gorgon into her head. They stare out of the holes, crawl closer, shadows like tongues shoot out of buildings, wind about her calves. She reels. The third Lexotax had been one too many. The room seems to have grown smaller, the walls press inward, the ceiling bulges down; although the flat is on the third floor, she suddenly feels like she's in a cave, deep under the ground, beyond time. In paintings, the mythical Tartarus is protected by an iron wall. Here the chest of drawers is oak, it creaks and spits out the drawer with all the old photographs that put *Frau* Schäfer in a melancholic mood. Marga has to open it up for her every time she has one of her nostalgic days. Over there is her boy's book which she, coughing against the hellish smoke, had thrown onto the dresser. *Every blossom and every tree / Every laugh and every dream* . . . an echo from out of the novel, she thinks, wrong, from out of the drawer! No, a woman says from the TV, and Marga spins around but the TV is off and is now the quietest and blackest thing in all of the quiet and black that encloses her like the inside of a coffin, and outside the night's noise, the sparkling lights, *Stars as bright as diamonds / And the endless, beautiful land.*

Then, just before the furniture crushes her, she hears the drops. A tiny, but real sound within the chaos of artificial voices that continue to whirr through her head, and before she sees it and before she truly hears the drops falling from the skirt to the floor, she knows or, rather, smells that *Frau* Schäfer has completely pissed herself.

She snaps the floor lamp on. Cowering, Medusa and the hounds of Hades retreat into the corner, then freeze in place, their mouths open. A puddle spreads across the parquet. *Frau* Schäfer snores softly; her lips expand then fall back into her toothless mouth. She had lost her dentures the last time Marga visited, and though Marga had even crawled under the bed to look for them—the dust of twelve years' loneliness scattering between her fingers—and in the process come across a row of empty miniature Sekt bottles, they were nowhere to be found.

Frau Schäfer! Marga falls upon her, grabs her arm and pulls her out of her chair. The heavy body falls back into the urine with a slam. She wipes her hands on *Frau* Schäfer's cardigan, presses herself against the furniture with all her might. The carpet gets tangled up in the wooden legs, after two metres she gives up. 'Erika, please!' she pleads with the sleeper who now opens her eyes, looks at her in panic and says, 'Did I not hear my alarm again?'

She tips the confused woman out of the armchair. She skilfully grabs hold of the doorframe and toddles into the bathroom and over to the tub while, as she'd practised in the previous weeks every evening, holding onto the bath rail, which Marga had picked up from a medical supply company for two hundred euros she had found, not in *Frau* Schäfer's wallet but in the box she'd dug out of the pile of Sekt bottles under the bed, an old jewellery box that hid even greater things, gold coins, rings, savings books. With the change in her pocket and the sturdy thing under her arm, in the end she had gone into a boutique; considering all the emergency duties she'd performed, one hundred and fifty for a new dress seemed like loose change.

Erika Schäfer placed her slippers on the step. 'Get undressed first!' Marga calls, grabs the tottering body and peels off its clothes. She undoes her waistband, the hook on her bra, and, as the stubborn woman slaps about herself, finally tears open the hose—which in the scramble had got caught up in the zipper—with a nail file.

The way she's lying in the bathtub, naked, helpless and embarrassed, at least now, thinks Marga, she, the younger woman, who in fifteen, at most twenty years— if she managed to do it at all—would be overcome by the same fate, should at least muster a little bit of sympathy for her senile neighbour. With all the riches she had in her little box, why didn't she hire a Polish woman? She would indifferently handle the showerhead, cold or warm, all the same. I, on the other hand, she thinks, am a sensitive woman with heart and mind and know how much the old woman is suffering. She strokes, pats and pushes until the trembling woman slowly begins to relax. The hot stream of water pours out of the spout onto the ashen skin, turning it a fire-red. Marga washes her back, her breasts, stomach and genitals with their sparse white hair. *Frau* Schäfer struggles, finally lets out a sound that warbles in Marga's ear. She runs the washcloth between *Frau* Schäfer's legs, struggles against the knots she feels in her own shoulder blades, which force her down over the old woman, as if that would be the ultimate position of her life, the one to stay, visible to all, written down for ever in your book: Until her very last breath, for ever bent over other peoples' genitalia.

Here, she is the pensioner's hard-nosed nurse; there, the terrible mother from the moor who ditched her son. In her head the mean word from her boy's book continues to resound, and *Frau* Schäfer's whimpers and cries echo the insult, which perhaps would even mar her tombstone, *Jerked off*, the one phrase which shall remain.

Yes, she's got to admit it, it happened. In retrospect, she had been so ashamed that for weeks she could not look you in the eyes. In the end, that was even why a few weeks later she had overdosed; you were supposed to see that she was also suffering because of it.

She had burst into the bathroom without a knock, yes, and? What did you have to hide from her? She had already had your penis, as you yourself described it, in her hand when it was still only a larva. Why all the sudden such a prude? she supposedly said, and more too. In your book she had to read how, at the end, as if to prove her motherly power, she had taken a piece of toilet tissue to quickly wipe away the proof of your love and devotion and throw it in the toilet.

What rubbish! In truth, the moment she had pulled his hand to her, the tears had already sprung to her eyes. She knows quite clearly: how she had pressed him to herself and, so that he would hold her tight for just an instant, laid his arm around her neck. Or *forced* as it says in your book, whereupon she supposedly said something like: *You could at least be a little nice to your mother*. Because of me, she thinks, and that her accusation was even justified, he had given her the cold shoulder for weeks. But that she'd forcibly slid his hand onto her body, and, in the end, even under her dress, never! That's how she offered herself to him, he vilifies her in his book, and *Frau* Schäfer, tickled by the wash cloth, squeaks.

It is difficult for her to pull her fist between the old woman's thighs, who suddenly seems to be bounding with strength. The showerhead flicks to life, a fountain sprays into the tub. She forces the old woman, who's trying to escape, back into the tub. Under the water her eyes seem even emptier, even bleaker; then they are completely gone into the other, better, Silbereisen-sung world. And yet, her face, so panic-stricken and drained within the tiny swirls, suddenly turns lively again, almost youngish. Her bun comes undone, grey strands of hair spread across the water. Bubbles filled with the shreds of melodies rise from her lips, bright, bell-clear voices from blonde angels with hard biceps dressed in blue billowing silk who are sliding their hands over harps: *I believe in God, I believe in the man / I am indeed a part, a part of his plan . . .*

She didn't want that. It was like an obligation. An unavoidable movement, a reflex. Suddenly the feeling that she would only be able to live on just there: in this closest of caresses with her son. How much she loved him at that moment. 'Truly loved!' she yells down into the gurgling water.

And so, as always, she had come with her mouth. With her muzzle, as you stated in your book, as if that were the only way she could force life—towards which she felt nothing but nausea and apathy—to come to a climax, press that small squirt of love out of you which all the others had until then refused her despite her

330

cunning and craft, you write, despite a whore's heart and a mother's jokes.

She jumps back and tumbles out of the bathroom, the noise of the showerhead continues, now the only sound in her head, an ever-present reverberation as if from a distant sea. The living room seems smaller than before, it's as if the furniture had not quite returned to its proper place. The monster of an armoire's doors gaping, no, maw; but the white porcelain vases inside of it do in fact remind her a little of dull teeth. In the glow of the lamp, the Medusa's head emerges out of the vacuum cleaner in the corner with its twisted tube. The TV stares silently, Silbereisen already off to celebrate, fucking the angels by now. Outside, the headlights of a car crawl over the front of the building without a sound. In one of the windows across the street, a blue flickering. She longs for a cigarette; in a few seconds the desire will become a torture. For almost ten years she'd managed to keep her fingers away from the smokes, then a few pages of her son's memories and now this. She wants nicotine, alcohol, Lexotax, the whole programme. *Frau* Schäfer hoards the fresh little bottles in the bottom of the chest of drawers; the lukewarm swill foams in Marga's mouth. She takes the book and closes it with all her might. The sound echoes through the silent flat like the lid of a coffin slamming shut.

If only that too were over with. She had recovered from his insults no more or less damaged than before. But would she now have to go even further, away from Hamburg, and out of the country? She shook herself. Disgusted, she fires the bottle into a corner. No, this time she would not run away! She will not go to the grave with this dishonour about her. She will read on and in the end be able to discount everything. With honesty and dignity, that's how she will meet him on the island, above all, his gossip and banalities. Ever the mother and he the child. Will still have to explain the world to the forty-one-year-old, steer and guide him so that, when it gets to that point, he will be able to wipe her ass one day in return.

In the desk overflowing with odds and ends she finds stationery and envelopes, even a little book of stamps. Focuses all her attention and writes with impeccable spelling and her still-childish handwriting: We will see each other on Sylt, but on one condition—we will not speak about your book, but about us, and underlines the last word twice.

She doesn't really know any more if she really worked you until you came that evening. Probably not. And if she did, she thinks and signs the letter, the M with its spirited point, if what he writes is true, then he was lucky enough to have his first time with a woman who understood her handiwork.

It is only back in the stairwell that she notices her dress is sticking to her, wet from the struggle in the bathtub. She should throw something over herself, she thinks, or else that night death would truly come to get her. In her hand she is bending the letter, which she has expanded by a few sentences, nearly insuperable words that she practised before scratching on paper: I am as happy as I am afraid. I hope that you are too. In a final step, she had copied his address from his letter which was still stuck in the dust jacket of the book. She went to great lengths to find a neutral kind of handwriting in block letters; no one was to see how anxious she was with the most serious words that she had ever put to paper.

Frau Schäfer's cardigan is lying by the doorway of the bathroom. Marga throws it over herself, but doesn't look over to the lapping and splashing. 'I'll be right back,' she yells, and that she should use the medicinal gel. She pushes a slipper into the crack of the door of the apartment, and goes downstairs, stepping over a young man passed out in the stairwell. The rest of the partygoers have gone back into the flat, music and laughter. She takes the beer bottle out of the sleeping man's hand and downs it in one gulp. Goes through his pockets looking for cigarettes, finds only a lighter and a little bag with a clump of hashish, which she takes. The guy—a haggard type with a fuzzy beard—tips to the side. Right before he knocks his head, Marga grabs him and leans him back up against the wall. She pulls another beer out of the case and softly steps away from the noise.

The door is already closed when she remembers the key in her handbag, which is in some corner of *Frau* Schäfer's apartment. She jiggles the knob, rings the bell of the group flat where through the open window she can still see silhouettes melting into one another. No one pokes their head out, the bass just continues to echo through the narrow gully of a street. Someone or other will open up, she thinks and walks out into the night.

The post box is two blocks away. She considers the shortcut through the little park, but, in the end, because of all the dog shit in the grass, sticks with the longer route. A man with a shoulder bag catches up to her, hurries past, smoking, tired out from a late shift. She clears her throat, asks for a cigarette. He grudgingly turns around, looks her over with tired eyes, mid-forties, she recognizes his after-shave, can guess how his apartment's decorated, a tiny roll of fat above his belt. 'I locked myself out,' she says, he shrugs his shoulders, mutters something about a locksmith and fishes the pack out of his jacket.

'Can I take two?' she asks, 'who knows when they'll come,' he rolls his eyes. With one hand she sticks the filter between her lips, with the other clutches the bottle, could he open it for her? He snaps the cap with his lighter without taking the bottle from her hand; she drinks, holds it out to him. Already half turned away, he shakes his head, she puts her naked foot in his way, taps the cig.

The lighter doesn't want to ignite in the wind, she cups his hand, inhales deep and long. The nicotine explodes in her brain, a dizziness almost takes her to the ground, throws her into the soft, billowing plunge, the best feeling in years. 'A friend of mine lives over there,' she points down the street, 'I should probably go over to hers.' 'Well, then,' he says and paces impatiently. 'You don't live far from here,' she grins, 'I've seen you around.' He pulls his bag closer and disappears around the next corner.

The letter slides into the slot, is now irrevocably on its way to you. She's overcome again by dizziness, a different one now, more wrenching, life catches up, accelerates madly, plummets, she grabs the box. It doesn't matter what she does now, it's all downhill. Now that there is no going back, she's suddenly quite sure: it's a trap. Her boy's initiated his war game, vindictively placed her in front, a tactic against which she'll be completely helpless and destitute, checkmate after just a few moves. The old childhood game of Klabberjass she always won lies deep in the past, the rain pantomime too, the old folks' routine, her good night and morning kisses, the whole mother-theatre ineffective; from now on, tougher rules were in effect. Newspaper articles, interviews, if possible, even on RTL, their story a feast for the scandal-hungry mob, a story as if made for the TV station for those who'd lost out on life.

She begins to shiver within her damp woollen sweater; soon her entire body begins to tremble in the tinge of death that arises from *Frau* Schäfer's smock. What is he up to? What kind of theatre piece has she fallen into? What really strange family drama in a country where they once gave a medal of honour to the best mothers? And she sticks her hand into the postbox's mouth, which has already bitten up to her fingers.

She washes the phrase that she had expressed better in the letter and which would have allowed her the first counter-attack back and forth in her mind; for everything that he implies about her—the lack of education, her poor spelling, professional training in the red-light district—no mother, she thinks, not even the stupidest, would get tangled up in such a rotten, nasty and vulgar plan, and she stuffs her hand even further into the box's all-devouring throat.

The most important thing was to get the letter back! Her new, revised version would reverse the signs under which the reunion stood in four weeks' time, with better chances for herself; and furthermore, she wants to meet at a place she's familiar with, not some rich person's island where the cost of the hotel alone would ruin her. No, here, that's what she'd inform him, here in her little hole in Altona, that's where'd they'd meet,

336

with the smell of *Frau* Schäfer's piss and burnt food in the air, the collection notices piled up on the table and under them the interest settlement from the bank which owed her money; in the reunion scene she envisions, she holds the piece of paper with the 10,000-euro credit under your nose. In that very place, she says, where they are now honouring you with prizes for your success, if you had stayed by my side, I would have had my own gallery and with the proceeds—and here she comes up close to you with her mouth—would have sent you to the best university, and, she whispers, if that hadn't been good enough, then even bought an apartment in the city, wherever you wanted, just for the two of us, she whispers into your ear, kisses your neck and swears that she would have painted the red sun sinking into the sea in front of Sylt in the cheapest colours and at the speed of an assembly line, everything, I would've done every-thing, she threatens, and holds the book under your nose, just so that this would not have happened!

The letter she fished out of the box was from a cer-tain Peter Hufschmid and addressed to German Telekom. She throws it into the next bin. The telephone company, she thinks, would now have to send reminders, then a collection notice, would turn *Herr* Hufschmid's life into hell. Just one missing letter would be enough to ruin everything. Maybe the sea would have put her back on her feet. Inspired her with its vastness and raw beauty, as they say, awoken a spirit of life in her, or simply planted spirit and life in her at all. Instead, the moor had held out its mirror and turned her life into a dead and constantly numb desert, and as she runs back through the shit-strewn grass, for the first time in decades she feels the urge to see Fenndorf again, to feel the unsteady earth behind the house—which she had never visited again after her exodus—beneath her feet, and she jumps over the grass, splashes through the puddles and sinks into the soft topsoil between the rosebushes with their intoxicating smell, walks ever-more quickly back to you, for she hasn't yet finished reading your book and sent her letter, she thinks, prematurely, long before the end where no doubt everything would turn out in her favour, a final scene in which you release her from her guilt and take the weight you've built up and imposed over hundreds of pages off her shoulders so that in those last few pages her back pain—which has come back to stab and drive her homeward through the rain-swollen park—that old, incurable wound, would turn into something like humility, a new, expansive and never-before-known feeling through which she would swing, take leave of her past in peace and finally be able to move on, with quiet steps, thanks to her boy who with his book had brought her to this path and, suddenly buoyant and weightless, as if this hope had given her wings, she glides out of the green dark into the brighter-lit street and in front of the locked building, sees the partygoers in the window and hears the doorbell plead, but no one takes any pity, and she throws herself against the door and the door throws her back, she rattles the handle and it tears off a fingernail, she beats against the wood that seems to grow harder and thicker the greater and more doubtful her desire to read on becomes, her desire to be close to you again and to lead you out of that frozen night in which she had abandoned you and into the light, into the warmth and the spring over the moor, which would then, having come to the other and better side, no longer be a malicious and threatening wasteland but a flourishing and blossoming garden; and yet, no matter how much she scratches and hammers, begs you to let her in, bows down before you, you leave your mother out in the cold.

'Who's that knocking at the door?' Change of scene, quick conversion. Your room: wardrobe, desk, shelf with its marmalade jars and the empty dragonfly-children inside them who have bewitched the dog with their bubble-like eyes. Whimpering and wagging her tail, Ronja knocks your collection down on the floor. A few of the containers break open. On the label *Leucorrhinia dubia*, white-faced darter, and *Lestes virens* which once held the exuvia of a damselfly, but no trace of either any longer. Ronja licks her lips, paws about the wreckage. Tanja pulls at the pup's collar while ordering her 'Out!' and 'Sit!' but the dog continues to chew happily at the shell of the blood-red darter, one of your finest specimens. But so be it, Dion, your childhood treasures have long been lost.

Sounds again from downstairs, a blow, then a drumming. Tanja looks over anxiously, even the dog tucks in her tail as if she can already sense the scolding to come. Mother!, the thought shoots through the three of your heads almost simultaneously. Has this cheerful scene already come to a close? All our revels ended? But where will all the costumes go? And how can we resolve the chaos so quickly? And just what lie would be a way out?

The best thing to do would be to hide, Tanja thinks, and begins to look for a place. Until now, the plan had seemed perfect, the adventure endless: the house was so big and full of corners, Dion's mother's wardrobe so full of beautiful clothes, she would have tried on her jeans and miniskirts, even had her own room. But because of the strange noises at night, and being afraid, she soon would have moved to your bed where the two of you, pressed up tight against each other, would tell ghost stories.

You liked the vision a lot as well. Tanja's parents would go around talking to relatives and schoolmates, then would eventually alert the police who would begin to comb the train stations and Autobahn service areas, but she'd be safe with you. No kid from the village had ever sought refuge here. Outside, it continues to grow colder, the snow piles up high against the windows. The two of you are cut off from the world. Mother-soul-abandoned alone.

I shake the door again, nibbly nibbly mouse, a scratching from outside, who's nibbling at your house? You anxiously grab each other's hands. Being a descendent of the wolf, Ronja knows that fairy tales told from the animal's perspective end poorly and therefore answers with an aggressive bark before running from the room and growling. 'Tis the wind that blows, as round about the house she goes. You want to command the dog to come back, but her name crosses your lips far too late. Tough luck, Dion, instead of messing about with consonants, you should have learnt the language of dogs!

The heavenly messenger turns out to be a squall from hell thrusting Hannes inside, a crate in his hands. 'Fodder,' he says, and kicks the door shut. He rummages through the supplies, sticks the marzipan chocolate into the one, the butter cake into the other pocket of his parka which is dripping with snow. 'From Mom,' he says, and slams the package down onto the chest of drawers and grins at you.

You'd never been so ashamed of yourself in your life. You wish you could have been out of that silk rag and into a T-shirt and jeans, or, better yet, Hannes' worn-out overalls that Marianne had laid out for you the previous night. 'Why did you run away?' he asks and, from between cans of food and packages of noodles, pulls out a bottle which he unscrews and hands to Tanja. She drinks, relieved that her mother is not standing in front of her, but there is something else, a kind of feeling of triumph, pride even, that Hannes has entered into her plan, as if his arrival had been the real highlight of her escape, the climax everything was moving towards.

She spits a fountain of foam into his face. Only after a couple of slow-motion seconds in which I whipped everything that wasn't tied down against the house, does he wipe the drops away and say, 'Grandma's homemade soda.' Tanja breaks into shrill laughter. 'Your Grandma rides a motorcycle through the pig stalls,' she sings, and lurches towards him. With the second sip tears shoot into her eyes; through the veil his owl-like face with its hooked nose and his square body seem downright soft and beautiful. How light everything all of a sudden is!

Your heart, however, is heavy. Jealousy the yellow feeling pinching your eyes and warping Hannes' fine features into a grotesque mask. A girl and two lads, and one's on his way to the bath, I whisper the looming disaster into your ear and push you down the stairs and right into Hannes' gaze, which envelops all your bodies, the unambiguous shadows below your nightshirt and Tanja's made-up lips and eyes, the lovelorn plaster of her face.

So he *had* thought of it immediately! The two of them sure got to the point in no time at all. Shortly after he'd called, from his window, he saw Tanja walking across the Heidedamm, reeling through the snow as if drunk. Couldn't go to the indoor swimming pool indeed. Always playing the wallflower with me, but the stutterer can do what he wants, he thought until staring into the storm made him dizzy. Then she fell. A branch crashed down right behind her. Although visibility was poor and there was the windowpane in between, he thought he could hear the sound *Thunk*!

He flopped down onto his bed and leafed through his *Batman* comic. Laid his finger on the hero's thigh, felt the muscle twitch beneath the skin-tight costume. He hadn't missed a single issue. He listened to the living room downstairs, pressed himself against the wall and pulled the comic book right under his nose. He smelt the paper, his own breath, the onion sauce from lunch. Another dreary day, he thought, the help was in bed with a fever, so he'd have to go into the stalls, and later on the silos, at mid-morning a delivery of feed had come. Batman stood rigidly in his frame, had no interest in jumping or fighting. This shitty little backwater, Hannes thought, they're all idiots, and a whole life wasted away in the stalls. His father called his name from downstairs, Hannes with two 's', just like he always did when he was angry. Hannes had also failed to clean the scalding tank.

And after school the fight with his mother. 'To the foreign legion, what a crazy idea!' she'd yelled and pressed the supply crate that he was supposed to bring over into his hand. 'Spared no expense,' he said, looking at all the treats, chocolate, cookies, the expensive instant meals from Ilse Bloch's shop, but here, he thought, we have to count every pfennig twice. It made him sick. 'When will I finally get my allowance so I can get my new moped?' he asked and banged the carton down on the table. 'Two more years, then I'm gone.' Marianne sighed, heavy and sorrowful, and, as she always did when the children expressed their pain, she wiped her hands and said, 'Your father has big plans. He's counting on you. You'll go to the army like everybody else then you'll come back and take over the farm!' He'd turned around and gone straight up to his room where he cursed his parents and dreamt himself away, as far as possible, to another country, a hot, desert-like one where sweat-covered bodies wrestled in training camps. The idea had come to him after seeing a report on the foreign legion on TV. He'd imagined himself down to the smallest detail, pitching in with the men's collective that was responsible for good things somewhere in the world.

And Batman fought evil too, in his bat-suit, which gave him power and supernatural strength. I'm going to be like him, Hannes thought and waited until it was quiet down in the living room again. Then he pushed his pants down to his knees and grabbed himself. He could feel the nylon crackling on the warrior's body, the flat, cool bat-mask on his face, the impact of life-threatening jumps and acrobatic manoeuvres. He stretched his knees apart and opened himself above the comic book until it hurt. The figures jumped out of their frames *Zapp*! *Swoosh*! *Zonk*! the crack of his hero's punches knocking criminals to the ground, a rhythmic cracking and smashing of his opponents' skulls and bones, as elegant and graceful as a dance.

Batman won. He kicked the last rival out of the way with his foot and triumphantly raised his fist. Suddenly Hannes was standing in front of his idol, dressed in Robin's elastic green and red outfit so that Batman would trust him; that was his mistake. 'My courageous friend!' the victor called out, stretching out his hand. Hannes struck, spun Batman around and with a sharp *Cronk*! broke his arm.

'I want a costume too,' he said, and pointed to your disguises. Tanja looked triumphantly up at you. Now's your chance, Dion! I whisper, give him your hand! You do as you're told. Through the bannister he hands you the bottle, your fingers touch at the tips, by chance just a second too long. Grandma's soda is a white-hot schnapps that sears your throat. Your tongue is numb, as if it has been burnt clean. You begin to sing the old toast and Tanja joins in: 'Hannes' Grandma is a real clever . . . sow.' She doubles over with laughter, Hannes grins with a lopsided glance, and I bow with a quick curtsy. Then I set the mouth of the storm onto the hole in the roof and suck you all up the stairs and into Dion's mother's wardrobe.

'It's all whore's stuff!' Hannes says. Tanja's eyes light up. She holds miniskirts, fishnet stockings and corsets up to her body, fishes the red dress out of the pile and throws it on. Not a single clothes hanger is in the wardrobe; everything is folded and layered in stacks. On the floor, a pile of used clothes. Hannes rummages about with pinched fingers, Tanja picks and pokes, you stand there with slumped shoulders and an ever-greater feeling of betrayal, and Ronja gets herself tangled up in a bra.

From the furthest corner Hannes pulls out the black bundle. 'That's awful,' Tanja says, 'your mother wears something like that?' A reflection of light tremors across the latex, shoots from Hannes' eyes which are now glassy and small; on your way into the bedroom, you'd handed the bottle of schnapps back and forth. You feel the giddiness, the cushioned feelings, the room sloping away from the walls and lengthening into the ground where the movements begin to pile up, your glances become caught. Come now, Dion, how does it feel to be drunk?

Hannes bends down into the wardrobe once again. His sweater inches up his back, his belt with its slits and sharp studs, over that the edges of his spine, somehow animalistic, you think, the ridge of a reptile. Tanja has something of an animal about her now too, the way she goes through the clothes, giggling, grabbing and cooing, makes you quite tame. Hannes pulls out the whip. The plastic wrapping has flaked off, the handle is slightly bent, the end with twirly leather ribbons. 'Hop-hop,' Tanja cries, spreads her legs, grabs you by the shoulders and mimics a rider. You all seem to like the toy. My plan is working.

Hannes throws her the latex dress. She makes a sound of disgust, your throat scratches; you don't want to imagine your mother in this outfit. In your thoughts you force her out of the thing, back into her bathrobe and onto the bank of the pond, white and enshrouded in fog, in the colours of morning.

Hannes sees completely different images: Tanja pressing her pointed limbs into the fabric, folds curling up, seams crunching. He likes the glowing garments beneath which every cord of muscle is drawn. He would gladly have Batman's costume, the night-blue one with the black briefs and the tight vest emphasizing every rib.

'Put it on,' he says, almost groaning. His eyes move even closer together, move over the small of her back. He's already pretty drunk, I whisper to you, the odds would be favourable! He stretches his neck, relaxes, bares his teeth. 'What kind of game does your mother play with this then?' he grins at you. 'Five marks if you put it on,' Tanja says and fishes a 5-mark coin out of the pocket of her trousers under her dress. 'Ha ha,' Hannes says, and Tanja, 'No joke.' You dive into the wardrobe through the trusty smell of laundry on the ground, long forgotten days—in a time without images or memory—when your mother must have travelled to Hamburg with this stuff on her back.

And then you find the gloves to match the rubber dress, arm-length, battered things. You toss them to Hannes, whisper, 'hTen,' and run into your room where you finger a pair of coins out of a jam jar holding your allowance. Back in front of the wardrobe, you lay your bit in Tanja's hand. She says, 'Bought,' and lets the coins jingle. This will be fun! Applause from the window. I sling snowballs and frost flowers onto the stage.

Hannes touches the gloves, slips inside. The rubber fits snugly around his joints and fingers. Batman, he knows, wears the same things in blue. He imagines him grabbing himself and making himself hard, first his own body, then the one he's overpowered. Through the latex, touch is dulled, almost masked; between that which the hand does and the impulse which controls it is a margin in which a dab can become a deadly blow, and every caress of his inner hand is, on the outside, a bending and a breaking but without his fingers performing any violence, because it is the glove that guides it. Batman is able to summon up his supernatural strength only when he is in the costume; without his disguise, he would simply be a man like any other, one with weaknesses and the fear of pain. In his second skin, however, he is powerful and free; just a few millimetres between inside and outside in which the unthinkable is possible.

'The bottle,' he says, and you hand him the schnapps. He drinks, gives it to Tanja who does likewise and so on. Youth has its rituals. But this is all taking far too long for me. The meteorologists have predicted my climax for the hour between five and six. Although my power is great and free from any schedule, it will not last for ever. A snowstorm, like all natural catastrophes, is a singular event. It swells, destroys and then subsides. The hole in the roof is already a chasm sucking the sky into the house. So, come on, children, let's see a bit more nerve!

Schnapps bottle empty now, the first blast of wind violent gale force 11, the next tile gone. Hannes is in the bathroom. To him the square tiles look like empty comic-book panels, the red lipstick bars around the bathtub and sink the borders, the house a new, as-of-yet-unwritten issue. He moves around the toilet in a magic circle, poses in the restricted zone of the tub, conquers the magic space. Bends himself over the halved sink, divides the mirror into similarly large panels with the make-up stick. In the one above left he gets undressed. In just four frames, the farmer boy has transformed into the black knight.

You are already swaying before you take the next drink; the ground of the moor had never been so sponge-like. Tanja grabs hold of your arm, asks: 'You okay?' her voice just at the edge of collapse now too. Of course you are, Dion! and I grab you from the other side and punch you to the bedside table where your mother keeps her medicine. In fact, in the drawer there is a blister strip with the last two Lexotax that she would have had to have swallowed for her soul to take flight.

You press a pill into Tanja's hand, but she hesitates, has already been at the limit for a long time. 'So that we all take a hop,' she slurs and anxiously looks at the tablet. 'Hop!' you cry, throw the Lexotax into the air and catch it with your mouth, a small, white, intoxicating word, as weightless and stutterless as death. The snake that Ronja lays at your feet is also halfway there. Tanja bends down and tears the ball of thread, which had once been Marga's most expensive bra, apart. 'Would this fit me too?' She hangs the chewed thing around her neck, sticks her fists into the little cups, pouts, struts through the room on imaginary pumps and shows off her non-existent curves. You grab her arm and pull her hands out of the laundry. 'Leave it alone!' you shout, your tongue a bitter film of schnapps, painkillers and Lexotax, a mixture that allows you to speak seamlessly.

'Why?' Tanja looks at you pitifully. 'It's no secret that this is what your mother does.' For a few seconds her fists lie in yours. 'Does she really have to take every guy?' She kneads your hands as if in so doing she could inject you with courage, vaccinate you against everything that was to come. You want to pull her towards you, and at the same time beat her away; now would be the right time, Dion, to give the little one who's talking badly about your mother something to think about!

Tanja bites her lips. She's got to be careful with what she says. She can't blow it with you now. 'I think it's good,' she sidesteps, and as you are now looking at her with even more distrust, adds, 'Your mother does whatever she thinks is fun.' I give a loud, impatient groan. That won't convince him at all, I whisper to her, fake it! But you beat her to the punch. Wrench open her fingers, flick the 5-mark piece into the air and catch it before Ronja, who rushes up like an elastic spring, does. 'If you are really my sister,' you say with a speed I can barely keep up with, she could also show you, and you point to her skirt. Tanja looks at you aghast, even I have to catch my breath. Dion, did I just understand that right? Do you really want to see her snatch?

Slowly the dumbfounded look in her face softens into a grin. She pulls the hem up to her knees and says, 'Ten marks, but only if I get to see yours too.' You exchange coins, glances, caresses from pointed fingers. You lift the nightshirt, her panties have a flower pattern. Her mound is fluffy, a bird's nest of down, not as bristly as your mother's. I impatiently take a breath. These are the facts, Dion, she's a woman and you're a man. And so?

We need to play something else and quickly, Tanja thinks, and palms the skirt flat over her knees. 'Can you do this too?' she snaps like a pocketknife then she's straight again. 'It was Hannes' idea,' she whispers, and points to the bathroom. They had made a bet, but he could only make it to here. She nods towards the right-hand corner, puffs up her cheeks and blows. Again you feel that yellow feeling which undermines every objection on your tongue. He makes you do that? Had the farmer really won her over with those kind of games?

'Twelve marks to whoever can hold it longer,' you say and imagine a tangle of bodies, circular or heart-like, a tandem. You pull her body straight, just a chest-length away from you, your pelvises parallel, heads to the side and knees straight; dragonflies' thoraxes and, above all, their slim abdomens are extremely manoeuvrable. That's the only way the male can deliver his semen from the genital opening at the end of his abdomen to the copulatory organ under the chest.

You take her hand, and count, 'One, two, three,' then bend over her from the hips. Tanja is already over her bellybutton with her nose. You turn your face towards her and stick your tongue out, she does the same; for an instant it looks as if you could exchange the first flying French kiss that humankind had ever seen. Right before the end, your heads crack into one another, you both tumble backwards, arms flailing. The nightshirt balloons in the wind. Next to you Tanja rushes upwards, her red dress spreading into wings. Her arms gracefully circle through the air, spin around their own axis quicker and quicker until you can no longer see her individual fingers, just the whirring wheel of a propeller.

And so the two of you fly through the room, up and down, past each other and back, a blood-red darter and a white-legged damselfly that have both survived the frost. But be careful, there are enemies: with a quivering, ripped-open mouth and her floppy ears as a sail, the dog jumps up into the air while outside I am getting ready for the most powerful and coldest blast yet.

From the bathroom, Hannes can hear the two of you whooping and crowing. It's just about time, he thinks, they're putting themselves in position. The latex dress is skin-tight; almost legless, it coolly encircles his bottom. It pulls at his back, squeezes his penis, encases his body in its spell of tightness. He can hear the stitches rip, he rubs and plucks but cannot stop the bulge below. He cannot get rid of the bubble over his chest where the breasts are missing either. Daniela would manage. Danni, he thinks, can push her tits through the hatch in the straw floor and fill it out.

He poses in front of the mirrored cabinet, raises his hand and with a single punch sweeps the bottles, toothbrush cup and brushes into the bathtub. That's how he'd imagined it back in the barn when Daniela started to be annoying because he didn't want anything from her any more. A twist from one's own axis, attack, counter-attack, *Zonk*! But, in reality, everything had stood still. In the attic it was dark, the shadows hung heavy above the bales of straw, Daniela's big, white breasts like two fat moons, the cow, he'd thought, and as it was somewhat embarrassing to him at the same time, he murmured something like *too tired* into the cigarette filter he'd been biting the whole time. She snorted and jumped up. 'Bullshit,' she said and sucked in her stomach; at least, he thought, she'd recognized the problem herself. He quickly looked away, somewhere, just not at her. She angrily gathered up her clothes. The filter tasted bitter. 'What's wrong now?' he asked. While getting dressed she flicked the arm of her jacket in his face. 'So it's Tanja, right?' she answered, took the cigarette and threw it to the ground where a piece of straw began to glow. For a few seconds they both looked at the bright point. 'And?' Daniela asked suddenly, the shadow before her feet all at once small. 'Are we still seeing each other?' He waited for the piece of straw to catch fire, then stamped out the ember with his thumb. The tiny pain rose in his body, chased the numbness out of his head. By the time he looked up, she was already on the ladder. A sharp sickle moon cut through the hatch, ripped craters into the mountains of straw, sharpened them into bones and blades.

He observed the chaos on the fixtures, the traces of domestic life in the lipstick-drawn boxes, here a pair of hose, there something to bleach your hair. Issues of *Yps* and scouring cream, a mother's things, kid's stuff. He pouts into the mirror, smoothens out the wrinkle over his stomach. His nipples press through the material like Batman when he's ready to fight. A person might be tempted to twist them. The comic doesn't show that, but Hannes can see it all the same in the image that pops into his mind while flipping through it, and he fills in all the missing details the illustrator had left out because of the minors.

He pulls out a black, silver-lined sleep mask from the trolley and puts it on. The velvety material slips softly over his forehead, smells of perfume. 'Katthusen's a nymphomaniac,' his mother said. She'd only had Dion because of a slip up. Back then his uncle didn't let a single one get past him. She never said that, of course, but everyone knows he'd had his women. And Dion was only an accident. I can see that. It's in his eyes. Just a beaten dog. He lets the whip crack through the air, pushes the sleep mask halfway over his eyes with the handle and, when the black knight stretches his hand out of the frame in the mirror, strikes.

Tanja plunges down and lands softly on the mattress. I better not move any more, she thinks, or I'll be ill. It already tastes sour in her throat. I should vomit, then everything will be out. I've also really got to pee, and she feels her shoulder burning again. She listens to the point, hears a grinding within her as without. The plaster seems to be trickling off the walls, the floor crumbling, her body out of control and in spite of the pills her leg now hurts. She doesn't feel too good about the whole thing. Her mother had been right with her misgivings. She'd know what to do now. A cold press on the forehead, a salty broth, drops for her stomach, sleep. At the thought of her family, she feels reassured, her chest warms. Could that be homesickness? The wave takes her away from the house's threatening unfamiliarity, down the Dorfstraße and onto the church square where her mother is standing with open arms, her good face full of worry. She forces herself up and looks around, but no one is there.

You sneak across the floor like a thief. Tanja cannot know what you have in store: you are going to wrangle her guy away, steal those caresses that belong to her. The leg-in-leg and arm-in-arm in the thicket by the pond; the touching of those small, deliberately exposed spots of skin where the wind causes gooseflesh to rise; merging lips, the locking of tongues, not knowing where to look . . .

To the bathroom! I call to you. Go up to the door! I urge. Sneak a peek through the crack! Look how Hannes is squeezing himself into the rubber dress, the rough farmer in your mother's rags. See how he stretches and bulges. You did indeed listen to Tanja and now know how it goes. Nothing to do with the splits, the jackknife and jumping jacks! The exercise has a very different end in mind now. Do they do it with their tongues? But where does the air go then? Through the nose maybe? Can you breathe when kissing? You would've gladly asked her that too. You wanted to know everything. Everything about Hannes and her. Being so drunk, she would have told it all to you straight. But suddenly she lay there completely still, passed out between the mounds of clothes, almost on her feet.

Your head is spinning too, the schnapps sloshes about in your stomach. My dear boy! I cry out of your room, knocking the last jars off your shelf. The dragonfly larvae scatter, dance in the storm, entrap the wind in their empty bodies. You walk around, see the keyhole gape, spit out screams, grimaces, shreds of memories: Marga as if dead there in bed, Marianne swinging the cleaning rag, Karl his fists, the boy in the corner, the red men bent over your mother and in the window the snow.

Suddenly she's there again, bursts into your thoughts. How free the last hours had been! Mature, gruesomely beautiful. Where did they bring her? Why doesn't she call? And if she's able to come home today?

You begin hear your name, distant and thin as if from out of a long sunken world. You turned around, frightened, but I hold on to you. It's only Tanja.

Your mother, Dion, isn't coming back. She's clogged up your mind long enough, cooked the mush, wiped your ass, Marga's boy, Marga's darling, Marga's joy and Marga's need, here a kiss, there a slap, Marga only for everything and ever, and now your mother's gone, just like that! And Hannes has stepped right into the void! That young, luscious body into her whore's dress!

The hallway seems endless, it's warped and serpentine and with every step the walls waver, bow and scrape and bend downward as if the house were bursting apart. Don't turn around! If you look back now, it'll get you. Onward, onward! You've got to keep walking! Onward, or it'll all come back up! Can you see the door, the light, the trembling shadow? It's Hannes, he's waiting for you! You begin to run down the white, hissing throat, teeth tight together, fist on your mouth.

Ronja pulls on her little master's skirt one last time, then gives up. She looks at you disappointedly, and barks. The noise again in the attic, up there, it seems to you all, a new game is waiting. She wags her tail, but the children are busy, one is asleep, the others are ignoring her, no one's paying any attention to her begging. A dog in a bad mood, an irritating whimper. I whistle another time. The puppy hops up the stairs into the attic, sees the flickering snakes of snow between the smashed tiles in the draught, wags her tail for joy. Good dog, now go and get it!

The house jettisons everything. Flayed, it protrudes from my hands, the gable scalpelled, beams like broken ribs. It wants to be airy and open to all eyes. It hands me roof tiles and building stones, the plaque of mouldy plaster, the hammered and the forced, all the useless ballast. Soon it will be unmasked and disembowelled, it will whirl away as ash and dust. The stubborn walls forgotten, the whispers therein, the decay in the cellar, the mushroom spoors and the moss, the sprouts of the past sown against time's assault, traces for your memory: woodlice, spiders, rodents traipsing, rustling, dried tears, screams fallen silent, a child's snot and a boy's cum in crevices, all the stuff it hoarded in order not to forget itself.

Finally set free, it moans and casts itself into the storm. For thirteen long years it has given you stability, protection, a home and kept watch over every one of your steps, even those you thought only you could see. Now it wants to serve as something other than your history, which it is fed up with, fed up with all the way up to just below the bursting roof. Then will come the water, which the wind will scoop out, the spring carry off, the fire, freedom.

At this point in your book you suddenly have to vomit. You write that, at that moment, the house had shaken so violently that you tumbled into the bathroom and right in front of Hannes' feet. Only later did you understand what had gone through his head, why he had come by your house that afternoon in the first place. Not on account of Marianne's fodder packet; not because he all of a sudden wanted to be your friend, something that you, at the beginning, had really believed or hoped. Sure, there had been that thing at the slurry tank, that creepy visit with the carpet beater the night before. But it was only later that you made sense of it all. At that moment, however, you'd only been choked by the feeling that you were about to vomit and that had been bad enough.

Hannes sees you—there, on the floor, in the square that you had drawn around the toilet that morning with lipstick—as a safety zone. The way you writhe in the frame unwinds in his head like a comic strip: Batman against Robin, enemy against friend, the bat and the beaten, that innumerably won game rehearsed throughout all the empty afternoons there in the security of his comics. He stands above you and, spreading his legs, gets into position.

And yet, at that moment you only saw the bowl. Full, you write, up to the rim. No one had repaired the drain. Whether at that moment you really thought about the ray inside that was blocking everything, today, with so much distance, you can't really say for sure. Maybe this idea first came to you later, just like how almost everything in your book, in truth, is not the exact thought or feeling of that thirteen-year-old boy, but the considerations of an adult; chewed-over and biased memories, unavoidable truths wrestled away from forgetting, a fairy tale.

No one, Dion, this must be stated once and for all here, had ever pulled a fish out of the moor. Insect larvae, yes; the skins of garter snakes, tyres tossed into the reeds.

Lost love letters, engagement rings, the clay jugs of the Germanic peoples, the Ice Age boy, all of this is fact. Sunken treasures that in the light of the present have a particularly mysterious glow. But a ray never ever lived down here below!

Of all things, he is supposed to be responsible for the whole drama. In your distress, you write, you did not know where to direct the flood that at any moment would shoot out of your mouth. The bathtub was too far away, the sink too high. Then Hannes suddenly grabbed hold of you.

Did he want to help you? Not force over the drain opening, no, he had picked you up, like a mother lifting up a child when the lid only reaches to his chest. Secretly you had hoped for more touches, soft words by your ear, his comforting. An unexpected kiss? In his eyes you had sought the expression that had not left you alone since the thing at the slurry tank: that half-shocked, half-surprised look, that foreign writing, enigmatic and full of promise.

This, Hannes thinks, is how it's got to be: the victim has to struggle, it's part of the game. The other surrenders, he waits until they begin to beg, then: *Bang*! He stalls. When he feels you begin to yield, he thinks he's made it. You stop resisting, even push yourself a little into his hands. The moment has arrived. From then on, you will do whatever he wants.

In hindsight, you could only put together what happened next through great effort. For a moment you forgot your nausea. Within the chaos there was suddenly another feeling. Only later, when you were writing your book, did you understand: you wanted to shake off and at the same time savour his touches. Today, these feelings which then had torn you from all sides have come asunder, splintered into a row of more or less nameable sensations—fury, unconsciousness, shame, longing—words that can indeed describe what you felt then, but not call it back to life. Today, you write, no doubt about it, Hannes had waited weeks or months to involve you in his sadistic fantasies while you longed for his closeness. To you, the grown-up, it is clear and would have been clear from the beginning. The boy, however, continued to believe in the mysterious sign of the group of cranes which he had once seen in the sky above the slurry tank; and, for him, the white ray continued to live in the drain.

Hannes had considered it all: that you would scratch, bite and spit. He calmed and quieted you, showed you that you could trust him, then grabbed you even tighter. He had planned every step. But one! He means to jump to the side, but the stream of vomit splashes against his leg. He stumbles backwards, then forward again, can no longer control his movements, the dance he had rehearsed one hundred times and more. Everything slips. He grabs you by the collar, hoists you up, 'What the fuck!' and hits you harder than he had ever wanted to hit anyone before.

Maybe, you write, it had had to do with the tears that came to your eyes, the blood that shot out of your nose; as the pain exploded into your head, for a moment you really saw the fish in the dirty water. But then everything went black. You had longed for help and wanted to call for Tanja, but there was only a gurgling in your throat.

Hannes looks at you in shock. He catches a glimpse of his face in the mirror, tied up in the dress, sleep mask on his forehead, skin bulging in the slits, he finds the costume ridiculous. The rubber is squeezing his chest, it cuts into his skin, he struggles for air. I've got to get out of this thing! he thinks and wheels around.

Tanja had heard something. Was it the storm? She opens her eyes, for a second didn't know where she was. She was huddled on a bed, half-lying down, half-sitting up, between a pile of unfamiliar-smelling clothes. Like the red dress she was wearing, the chaotic room, the afternoon in fragments, incoherent, a debris of images, gestures, laughter as if in a crazed dream. She listened to the hallway. How eerie the sounds in the house were. And how cold it was all of a sudden. Outside it was already growing dark. Was her mother looking for her?

By no means should Dion say anything if she calls. Or maybe she had already? Where was he anyway? She slid off the bed, stumbled as soon as she felt solid ground beneath her feet. In her head a carousel. Somewhere a floorboard creaked. 'Dion?' she called, a croak. Then she heard your scream.

How you managed to find the strength to grab Hannes from behind is still a mystery to you today. At that moment you felt nothing, thought nothing. Your body was numb, your mind empty. Even today, you write, sometimes you are consumed by an unprovoked rage when you drink too much, an urge to smash something. Today you know that it was this nearly unbearable feeling of disappointment that you wanted to smash: Hannes' brutal rejection, the inextinguishable slight. From one moment to the next you were once again the strange kid all the others avoided during recess, alone next to the column where your eyes sought out the sixteen-year-old who, in return for your admiration, first cuts then thrashes you. That's when you laid into him with your fists.

Tanja sees you in the door wrestling with Hannes and throws herself in between. She feels responsible. She stirred up your jealousy, fed you with lies and incited you against him. Did she really go too far with all of that? She hadn't wanted a brawl. 'Dion, let go of him!' she yells and pulls your shoulder. Hannes feels the plucking, the pull of the rubber on his skin, the sharp elbows in his stomach, wants more, wants everything now, the whole game until the bitter end. In his head the film speeds up, the comic now bursting with life. He imagines the bodies merging into one another, a snarl of limbs, hair and whimpers. That's how he wants to crush them, spin them above the floor, stick one into another, at first rib for rib, then neck by neck, very slow, so that nothing breaks just yet. Hold, caress, plead for forgiveness, and then, only at the end, within the embrace, *Cronk*! Finally taken care of.

'Let him go,' she yells, 'he didn't do anything to you!' She wishes the afternoon wasn't gone, all the fun games, the laughter, that exciting life in costumes, the boys' lingering looks; she doesn't want to go home for anything in the world. When everything comes out, when it's all in the open, it'll be over, she'll have lost everything. Dion will be angry, Hannes will make fun of her and will tell everyone. She would go back to being the sick, bent girl no one wanted, and Daniela would be the winner. She has to fight back against her fate, against that shitty illness, her shitty mother with her shitty prayers, that shitty god who would have her small and meek. With all of her strength she tears you away from Hannes. Or was it Hannes away from you? At that last moment she feels strong and determined, full of power over her life.

Which hand got her? Which arm hurled her away? In your memory you see the fight from outside, a confusion of bodies where, at that moment, not a single glance was possible. Within that knot, you write, you had only seen shreds, felt skin and heat, Hannes on the one side, Tanja on the other, at times above, at times below you, their faces close. Looking back, you can bring this moment to a stop, even turn it around. In reality, however, the next second Tanja was lying on the ground.

Today you believe you could perfectly describe the sound she made when she fell backwards against the bathtub, hitting her head against the tiles. You heard Hannes gasp and the blood in your ears; otherwise there was nothing at all beyond the sudden silence after the slam.

Hannes stares at the motionless body on the floor. Stop! he thinks. Start over! Everything back to the beginning! It was only supposed to be a game; hunter, hunted, winner, loser, Batman, Robin, then the comic book closed and good, in the end he would have released them, would have invited them both over for something to eat. Of course, he tried to convince himself, it's only a temporary blackout, she just fell over, too drunk, she's a lightweight, she'll be back any second. A slap, a cold shower, then everything will be back to normal. And then we'll continue.

But she doesn't move. He wants to jump over there, pick her up, shake her, but he cannot break loose. The dress as if made of concrete, this goddamn dress, he thinks, it's the dress' fault. In his thoughts he tears it off his body, but the real one doesn't let him move.

I leave the house alone, I'm finished. That was some pretty tough work. The battle is over, the game won or lost, it doesn't matter. The gusts of wind ebb as abruptly as they began, what remains is the trace of devastation which moves through a new, never-before-seen land-scape. In the attic, the gaping hole is edged by moun-tains of snow. Floes break and thud onto the wooden floorboards. On the west wall, the snowdrifts climb up to the windowsill, the yard is buried. The drainpipe is sticking out of the corner, twisted like a dislocated limb. The plain has slid over the Heidedamm and created hills and hollows that are broken only by the white-clad trees arising out of the drifts of snow. Everything that once was angular, coarse or raised—the fences, walls, the mounds of sod and the landfills—I have smoothed down and wrapped up, I have stamped and whited out every well-known face. Here a small avalanche slides off a branch, there a doe ventures out of its hiding spot and, driven by hunger, takes its first, cautious steps.

Lone flakes whirl through the air, float aimlessly about for a while, sink down somewhere else. Then even this last movement flows back into the stillness. My strength is spent, the weather forecast for tomorrow:

bright and cold. The day thereafter the local newspaper will take stock: The storm, one of the strongest in years, tore the roofs off numerous houses, knocked over power poles and uprooted many trees. Many villages lost power and remained cut off from the access roads. Damage is estimated in the millions. Two people lost their lives in an accident on the main road, in Fenndorf a thirteen-year-old girl was seriously injured by a falling roof tile. But why should any of this still concern me?

She didn't look hurt, you write: as if sleeping. Rushing to her, you still hoped it was only a joke. She'd soon be on her feet, would burst out laughing, pull her dress straight and suggest another game, something a bit quieter. You never saw any blood, no wound, her face peaceful and sweet. But then she had hung limply in your hands or, rather, sagged through them, like a bundle, something boneless. You cannot find any image for it. You called out her name multiple times and the louder and more desperate your voice became, the more oppressive and definitive your awareness of being at fault. What had Hannes done?

'What do you mean, me?' he snaps back. '*You're* the one who came after *me*!' He wants to scream or to laugh, very funny, should I also play dead, you guys thought you could scare me, you little pieces of shit—ha ha. Instead, he sees your pale face, the tears in your eyes, that stunned look you cannot fake. He sinks into himself and doesn't move; inside of him everything slides away. The dress, that shitty dress, is still holding him and binds him into your fear.

And so, face to face, for a number of seconds the two of you did not move or even breathe, you just watched each other and were afraid. You wanted his face to smooth out again, whatever was mysterious and admirable in it to return, you wanted your life with the mystery and admiration for Hannes to go on being just like it had been before. Then the telephone rang and tore the two of you apart.

Hannes winces at every sound, listens in to the hallway, wants it to stop. He counts to three, to four, to five. Each time, the space in between appears to grow longer. At some points, he gives up hoping that Tanja will move. 'Not a word,' he says, 'do you hear, not a single word or I'll kill you!'

Today, you write, you can barely remember the ringing. It was a rare sound in the house. Ute Hassforther was the only one who ever called, every few months, twice a year the coal merchant to give notice of the delivery date, and every Wednesday afternoon Marga from Hamburg. You always longed for that call while ignoring all the others, or leaving them to your mother out of the fear that when picking up the receiver you'd have to say your name, which never worked.

Hannes kneels down next to Tanja, pokes her, lays his hand on her forehead. She is warm. He doesn't trust himself to open her eyelids, afraid of the white or a dead blue. He lowers his ear to her chest, listens, hears only the telephone and the emptiness in his own head. He sees the puppy in the door, a roof tile in its mouth.

Ronja droops her head. What's going on here? She pads in, lets the quarry fall onto the floor next to Tanja, looks at her expectantly. Whimpers, licks her hand, pushes her head between her paws and makes, if a dog can actually do such a thing, a disappointed face.

Hannes pets the dog's head, says, 'Good.' Lays the shard in Tanja's hand, closes her fingers around it. Tries to locate her pulse in the soft hollow below the base of the thumb as he had learnt in First-Aid class. He feels the blood pumping, counts the beats to the rhythm of the telephone, something mechanical as if from a machine, buzzing or rasping—

And the louder the noise grew, the closer you came to the telephone stand, down the stairwell, step by step, winding endlessly down into the depths, and more unrelentingly the idea choked you that it wouldn't be Marga announcing her imminent arrival through the static of the connection in a distant, still somewhat weak voice, but Marianne, Tanja's mother or the police in a harsh and threatening tone. Never before, Marga

reads the final sentence, had you ever been so afraid of
the phone.

That she loves him. Now, in the stillness, it occurs to
her again: those are the words that still are missing at
this point. Exhausted, she closes the book. The party is
over, all TVs off, even the distant street sounds have
faded. Through the window falls a thin strip of grey
morning light. At some point a group of drunks had
tumbled out the front door, she had barely had to wait
fifteen minutes. She had quickly grabbed the book and
her handbag from *Frau* Schäfer's flat. Now she wanted
to be alone. The light was still on in the bathroom, there
were water sounds: a lapping, the sough of the spray,
the dull squeak of skin on enamel as if someone was
taking a leisurely bath. Or had it been a groan? she now
wonders. From the hallway she had called out a loud
Good night! to *Frau* Schäfer and, when no answer
came, softly closed the door.

Now it seems just a bit too quiet upstairs; in this
deathly stillness, she almost misses the noise. Should she
go and look one more time for the TV license and see
whether *Frau* Schäfer had turned off the water? Today
the old woman had seemed particularly shaky and confused. Should she stand in the doorway of her room for
a few seconds and listen to her breathing in order to
make sure that she was asleep and dreaming?

She too would have liked someone to have been at her bedside keeping watch over her back then at the hospital in Zeeve when one moment of madness ended and another began. Why doesn't her boy write about what she had assured him on the telephone? What would it cost him? It would not have hurt his book, but it would have been essential to her. Only three little words, they could change everything.

She remembers perfectly: the nurse had pressed the mouthpiece to her lips. She had just awoken out of unconsciousness, an oxygen tube stuck in her nose and connected to a blinking machine. A stylus scribbled her heart-curve onto a piece of paper which was stacked on a shelf. The nurse turned it off, said, 'Make it quick.' She was not to strain herself.

She was not at all sure whether Dion was even there or whether he could hear her at the other end of the line, which rang monotonously. It had rung for an exceptionally long amount of time, she counted the rings, the long intervals in which she was threatened with sinking away and was startled each time the next beep tore her back out of the abyss. Was he even at home? Had Marianne already taken him over to her house? Or did he refuse to go out of defiance and rage? Her heart beat more quickly, she could feel the pounding in her throat, the pain of having had her stomach pumped. The machine gave a shrill sound of alarm. She groaned. 'Quiet now,' the nurse said, 'you can ring again tomorrow.'

But she had pushed the hand away and pulled the receiver back towards her lips; after the crackling in the line, suddenly there was another, deeper silence, as if a space had opened up. She did not hear Dion, no clearing of the throat nor breath, just this expectant silence, its distant presence. He had never answered the telephone with his name. At that moment she knew that she was with him at home, in the hallway where he stood by the little table and listened into the receiver. She whispered the sentence, the only one of all those she might have wanted to say at that moment, the one that seemed the most important and just.

The nurse smiled down at her, finally took the receiver from her hand and hung up. 'Sleep now,' she said; her face was friendly and good, it was a mother's face. Marga faded away.

'It becomes you,' Julius says and pulls at the cardigan. She sits up in her chair. Is she dreaming? Is she still reading? How did the jerk get in here?

He shrinks into the corner, looks up guiltily, now the little boy who must admit to having played a stupid trick. 'What do you want?' she snaps through half-opened lips. 'You,' he bites back. She dodges his mouth, turns away, 'I want to sleep now,' she says, then smiles: And anyway, she was no longer the youngest. She feels his eyes in her back, enjoys her punchline, leaves him to court her. He creeps into her hands, into the blow that is already beginning to vibrate in her shoulder. She rips his jeans down to his behind, Julius cries out. 'I bet,' she hisses into his ear, 'your mother jerked you off for the first time when you just started school.'

'Seven,' and he squirms in her grip, he'd just turned seven, but his penis already stood up. She pulls the cord from the floor lamp out of the socket, doesn't want to see it. In the gloomy dark she thinks she can hear the rushing of the water again, a trickling and dripping from a thousand veins and canaliculi.

'But then you deserted her,' she chides him and pulls out his belt. 'She died old and alone, you didn't even pay one single birthday visit more to your mother!' Julius tries for the buckle with his mouth, says, 'There must be a punishment,' and sticks out his ass.

The blow breaks the silence. The boy falls full length down the hall, crawls on all fours over the runner. 'Ten, nine, eight,' he yelps, arching himself up to mother with every number. With the second blow she feels stronger, more penal, younger, she grows back into her body, her back like a tank now, powerful, upright, free from pain. At six he begins to beg for forgiveness. What was he stuttering? 'Speak clearly to your mother!' and Julius, in a press-up, whispers, 'hI ham hso hsorry.'

Then, right before the number four, which Julius is pleading for, her strength leaves her. The buckle clatters to the floor. 'What's that supposed to mean?' he moans, 'If you give up now, it'll all have been in vain.' He stands up, pulls up his trousers, goes into the living room and falls open-legged into the chair. Now she had to tell him she loved him again. 'Otherwise,' he mumbles contritely, 'I can't come.'

She laughs. Hadn't he sat there once already, in that very same pose, with those very eyes? Even his shirt, she thinks, was the same the first time he had come over and observed her self-portraits and begun to get excited; she feels how her hair, just like with Mira, knots itself into a bun and her breasts hang heavily down onto her stomach, 'Your mother . . . ' she begins the sentence, breaks off and straddles him, her legs those of an old woman, as if painted, the skin white and porous, covered with blue veins, a masterpiece, finally complete after so many years of excessive toil. At that moment he already had the larva in his hand. But she doesn't lend a hand, stalls, for seconds she hangs motionless over his shuddering body, hand on his throat, the burning and sucking of his gaze on her lips, his hoarse pleads for the word *Love* in her ear, and behind it, like the echo of a child's howls, distant and at the same time deep within, the sound of water, a moment, which appears to her like the end of all movements, the point that everything comes down to.

At first she feels it in her face, then in her shoulders and arms. It pours down the walls in steadily growing and rippling streams. She only has to get this behind her, she thinks. Mete out his deserved punishment. Just make it through this paragraph, struggle through these last lines, then slam the book shut, tick off another chapter of her life. When he is even with her and she with him, she'll go and drag Erika Schäfer out of the tub, towel her off, blow dry her hair, pull it up into a nice bun, get rid of her deathly pallor with a little powder and lay her out in her Sunday dress.

No one will be able to prove anything. On the contrary, they'll be understanding, and feel sympathy for her and thank her, even praise her for being such a good neighbour. 'My goodness,' she sighs, she'd always warned *Frau* Schäfer not to bathe alone. How considerate she had been, her neighbour's health her greatest concern. Help getting in. Fresh vegetables from the market as a change from the perennial fried egg. Twice a week scrubbed her back. Ordered the most expensive gels from the pharmacy so that her eczema would finally heal, and she wipes a tear from her eye. Dementia, and in addition to that, severe diabetes, there is nothing you can do to stop that, the doctor reassures her and lays his hand on her arm; and if it would be any consolation to her, Marga, *Frau* Schäfer died without any pain, she just peacefully fell asleep in the warm tub.

She'll mourn a bit nonetheless; after all, the woman was the only person she had become close to over the last number of years. Then she would get herself together, for life goes on. The landlord will agree to transfer *Frau* Schäfer's rental agreement over to her, renovation is long overdue. The costs of the water damage will be covered by the building's insurance. Any other bills accrued will be taken care of from out of the box. On the morning after she moves in, she will make breakfast, coffee substitute with lots of sugar. After that, she'll clean out the wardrobe and give things to Goodwill. Finally stop dyeing her hair. Leave the plucking and filing alone. Look on as the spots on her hands increase in number. Get fat. Continue to bathe only with Julius' help, everything else will be too dangerous, she could slip and fracture the neck of her femur. Cook everything-soup from the few things in the pantry. During the musical request show she'll hum along with Florian Silbereisen until Julius comes home, his Business Administration degree finally in his hands whereupon she'll open a mini bottle of Sekt.

The water rains down from the lamps, crashes over the furniture, is already at their bodies. 'Say it,' he begs in her ear, 'Say that you love me!' Cascades plummet down onto his shoulders, spill into his open mouth. She presses her lips onto it, kisses the silent sentence inside that she does not yet want to give him, maybe later. The water is rising on the floor, is licking at their legs. She feels his hands knead her breasts, she sits down onto his penis, closes her knees around his hips, brings her mouth up close to his ear. 'My poor boy,' she whispers, and he, 'hMama, no!' Then she presses him softly, but assertively, into the depths.

The silence swells, becomes a roar, muffled and dark, a sound like at the bottom of the sea. Why doesn't she say anything, you wonder, and press the receiver tighter to your ear, she's there, you can hear her breathing. A creaking behind you, you turn. Hannes is standing on the landing, Tanja in his arms. With one hand he is supporting her head, with the other he's holding her under her backside. The way she nestles her forehead into his shoulder, her legs draped over his underarm, she looks secure, sleeping and protected; you're almost jealous that she can lie like that with him. The dog is jumping at his leg, happily wagging its tail; the children's games seem to be continuing.

'Who's turn is it?' he whispers down to you. You shrug your shoulders, listen in to the telephone again. Any second she's going to say it, you think, just after this breath. But there is no breath. Not this knowledge of Marga's presence, her arms opened wide to you as soon as you need comfort, her body the eternal place that, on those silent afternoons, whenever you knew that she was somewhere in the house or over in her workshop, was a part of your world. There is nothing else, only the roaring.

Hannes comes down the stairs, step by step, pearls of sweat across his forehead, eyes full of questions and fear. What are we going to do with her? He holds the motionless body out to you, and only when you see the haematoma spreading out in her neck from under the knot of hair that has fallen to the side do you know that no one is at the other end of the line any longer; not Tanja's mother, who had seen through your game, not the police, who were already on the search for the culprits, and not Marga, who still had to utter the sentence that could save you from this calamity.

Out on the Heidedamm—which at one point was the last sturdy path before the courselessness of the moor but which is now no longer the case—a birch tree bends under the weight of the snow. The slow jolt, the letting-go and abandonment of its only, irreplaceable place without a sign of violence; gentle, almost dream-like the tree bends—whether rotten, too old or its trunk already hollowed out by the erosion of years—into a slant until its fall is inescapable and it gives itself over to gravitational pull, contrary to what it wants, to its tireless and, up until now, well-fortified aspirations and desire to move upwards.

Of all things, it is the soft, light snow that eventually causes the birch to fall. And yet, it still does not topple. Insulated from the snowdrifts piling up around the trunk, the roots snap silently and, apparently slowed down against the stark background in which the speed of any indications the eye could still measure have disappeared, the tree sinks to the ground in a stately, almost ceremonial fashion with a self-forgotten and self-redeeming movement downward, humble and epileptic but without any sound of impact, only the mute break of the crown and its simultaneously methodical and incidental order of branches, boughs and forks; in their middle over the scrawny winter silhouette of the birch the once, perhaps mistakenly, too quickly or sickly grown—and therefore, at the upper part of the trunk, dead—knottily projecting stump which rips, up to the very last metre, if without the desire for destruction but with serious consequences, the telephone wire down from the pole.

You hear the crackling in the line, hear me exhale, the day's final word. Then nothing, only snow, the great silence. Now you can speak.

THREE

Spring

They are flying water into the moor. Helicopters are making their way in front of the glaring sun, the shadows do not stand out against the ashes. Even more oppressive than the noise of the machines is the weight of the silence in the air afterwards, the rustling of the wake-like whispers within the burnt rushes, as if the plain wanted to make fun of their trying to put me out with a few vats of water.

They've encircled me, I have been cordoned off from the outside world with ribbons, guards and warning signs, the areas which were already doubtful before, now mortally dangerous. Hikers are sent back, curious onlookers pushed on, paths beaten into the grass; on the maps grids marked as already lost or acutely threatened areas. The specialists claim to have everything under control, but under the turf I continue to smoulder, burst out again in other as yet unmarked places, lead the firemen astray.

The farmers are worried and herding the livestock into the neighbouring fields. Their mistrust is great, their resentment towards the authorities immemorial, their land sacred. They do not want to protect the moor but their houses and stalls, the children who are standing around the freshly excavated ditches that have been flooded by hydrants and looking at the fluorescent fire-extinguisher canisters which, instead of paper kites, are rising into the sky to welcome the spring. The brave ones have crossed the bridge, no longer any willow faces under the wobbly planks, only a dull layer of mud; over there the ground is solid, it doesn't split, but crackles drily beneath one's soles. Like every year, the cotton grass blooms at the beginning of May. In billowing rows the little white flames flicker out into the low-lying water, eat through the dry grass towards the edge of the ash, which pulls a second, unequally close horizon onto land.

You're crouched on top of the tree stump again, shoulders hunched, hard shadow in your face, picking the dried moss from the bark, it crumbles into dirt between your fingers. Next to your feet your knapsack. You packed it several times then emptied it out again. Balanced the beloved against the necessary, toothbrush and pyjamas winning over *Huckleberry Finn* and your dragonfly guide which you will not need in the city. Maybe later you will; it should only be a few days, you said to yourself for courage. You wanted to ask for help in the hospital, you had no other choice. There, you thought, they'd still remember her from the winter.

Everyone would know what there was to be done. You wanted to get a room somewhere close by. In the wardrobe you found 50 marks in one of her coats. This time you would stay with her, would not leave her alone for so long again. If, as in winter, she prohibits visits, you nevertheless will stand in the doorway every day, bring fruit, magazines with colourful pictures to take her mind off things, maybe even flowers. Force her to accept that it simply doesn't work without you. That had been the plan anyway.

While you are tying up your knapsack, these thoughts go back and forth. No doubt in winter it hadn't been her choice; the doctors must have convinced her that she had to keep her distance from you. As if you would wear her out. So that something like that would never happen again, you had decided to talk with them. The sentences are in your head, some already formulated in a new notebook. With facts from the past week, you want to prove that she simply cannot get by without you.

The thing with Holland will make it clear to them. You will describe Holland down to the last detail. It was there that she really showed you how much she needed you. In the Dutch clinic you were the only man among all those distraught women. In the hall you saw one crying who was much younger than Marga, almost a child still, you will say. No one would have been able to comfort her there. Who, if not you? You walked proudly through the corridor, which smelt fresh and healthy. While you were waiting for her to come out of the examination room, it became clear to you that she was doing everything only for you. For the family, you add. Later, at the sofa-bed where she was supposed to rest a little while, you held her hand for a long time.

The doctor looks up from his notes, clicks his pen. But why, he wants to know, of all people had she brought you? Did she not have any girlfriends, a sister? And what was the situation with the father of the child? You avoid his look, look to the window. The light is falling in sharp cuts through the white shades, blinds with vertically adjustable slats, typical for doctors' offices where the healthy must be clearly separated from the sick. The pattern on the linoleum is regular, its geometry calming and appropriate. You think you could trust the man with his bright, friendly eyes. He only wants the best for you and your mother.

You consider your words for some time. The sentence sounds different in your notebook, more hopeless and angry, but now you say, 'Leon, the one we had to leave behind.' The doctor wrinkles his brow. 'My little brother,' you add, 'who'd stayed behind in the room.'

And what was with the child? The psychiatrist wants to know, stands up and adjusts the blinds with a cord. It becomes comfortably dark. Only now do you notice how bright and loud it has been around you the whole time. You take a breath and say, 'She maintains that it was our child.' In the sudden silence, with the dulled sounds of the city, so far away from me, it occurs to you that you did not stutter once the entire time.

That is how it was supposed to go. After you told them everything, they would have sent an ambulance to the gallery to pick up Marga. Everything would have worked out when the doctors convinced her to take her medication.

The therapy schedule had still been hanging on the pinboard until recently. She was supposed to mark how she felt on a chart, from one to ten, but since Daniel had left, she hadn't made a single cross. At the beginning, her mood swung between five and seven, with a tendency towards going up. Then, for a long time, nothing; it must have been when she believed she didn't need any of it any longer. Then all of a sudden two crosses next to the ten on the days she began to paint again. Then more holes. A cross next to the one—big, threatening. Then all the way up to three. And then, finally, far below zero. On the following day, the chart was in the rubbish with the tablets and the reminder to get her blood test done, which she refused to do. From her arguments with Daniel, you knew that the drug level in her blood could not be allowed to drop whatsoever. Even the slightest fluctuation could catapult her upward or downward. You had fished everything out of the bin and glued the leaflet in your notebook; just in case, you wanted to have the clinic's address.

With the appointment pending, you had woken her up at the same time that she used to wake you in the mornings; the dragonfly clock on the wall still stood at seven thirty. It had been winter in your room since September, and your bed had remained just as cold. For safety, since Daniel had moved out, you'd been sleeping next to her in the other half of the bed where she used to pile up her clothes. When you opened your eyes, a bright spring sun was shining through a slit in the curtains. You had bent over and carefully pressed your mouth to her forehead; being woken up always put her in a bad mood. Most of the time she shooed you off, grumbling, and pretended to sleep; you pull her out of bed by her feet.

But that morning her eyes rested on you for a long time, scrutinized you doubtfully and questioningly, like waking up after being drunk and looking at a stranger next to you. What were you thinking, she snapped, about waking her up so early, she had slaved away the whole night, someone had to come up with money again now that you had—the word hit you like a bullet—disgusted Daniel out of the house, and so on, as so often lately, she continued to fire off pointlessly into the emptiness. Eventually you had begun to stare at the ground where a shaft of sunlight burnt into the wooden floor; in the dust you saw edges and strange structures as if under a microscope. She had to go give blood, you heard your voice say, which splintered off from you, cut into the green half-light behind the closed curtains and right into the middle of the confusion of shadows, blankets, hair and glances, the naked skin between sloppily bleached strips of wallpaper, buckets encrusted with paint and the old, long dried-out hopes of that spring.

She didn't say a word, looked at you horrified, as if she had only now recognized you, suddenly stuck out her hand and said, 'My darling.' You reluctantly slid over to her. 'hI'm hcoming too,' you said, three miserable, whistled words that made you wince; but it was not only because of the breaking of your voice that the pitch of your words were no longer under control. At school you were excused from afternoon lessons, a doctor's appointment, you hadn't lied, but Gorbach, still suspicious after all your absences back in autumn, wanted written confirmation. But who would be able to do that for you and why?

She caressed your wrist with her thumb right at the point you take a sick person's pulse. 'It's sweet that you pay attention to me,' she said, pressed your shoulder, came closer. Until then you had always done everything together; her mouth sought out your ear. The shaft of sun had crawled a little bit further, was now exploring a knot in the wood. 'And now give me a kiss.' She turned her face towards you. You wanted to do anything to get her up, dressed and onto the bus with you to Hamburg. They would be able to tell from her blood test that she wasn't taking her medication, would draw their own conclusions, therefore, deduce that it couldn't be going well for you either.

You were disgusted by her saliva, by the moist places of her body in general. Her kisses smelt again like they did last autumn, the smell of her breakdown still in your nose. But you were aware of their effect and could handle them. Any resistance would have just made things worse. Her tongue sought a way through your teeth. You had just barely given in and opened your mouth a crack when you felt the quick, sharp bite. You jumped up, she looked at you nonchalantly, then there was something like a malicious joy in her features, or was it the twilight seeping in through the curtains, poisonously dimmed by the bright green linen fabric she had picked up with Daniel in Zeeve and sewn into a smartly bordered drape?

You had wiped the drops from your mouth. 'Give them some from yourself,' she said, 'we've got the same blood group.' And with these words, she threw herself back into bed, dug her hands under the pillow and didn't move any more. In front of the mirror in the bathroom you dabbed at the wound, which no longer was bleeding, where perhaps there had never even been any blood, only a misunderstanding of lips; she had wanted to cuddle, you had wanted to talk, an unsuccessful kiss, like one between a young couple that has demanded too much of the moment. And so the tangle of your tongues had been a way to enquire of the needs of the other even without any words. But now she had literally bitten through even this last connection.

The one looking back at you from the mirror was a stranger. You saw the dark fuzz on your chin, which you soon would be able to shave; a new pimple between your eyebrows which had long been ready to be picked but which hadn't interested her at all for quite some time; the rings under your eyes which you could no longer sleep away. You scratched away a flake of skin from your lips, addicted to the pain. A whimpering came from the bedroom, the light in the doorway green. When you walked over, she stopped. No doubt you'd misheard. It had only been one of those sounds that sometimes startles one in the house and, after a while, resounds in the ear, the echo of a tone which has long since faded away but is caught in one's head. A whistling of the wind, the roar of water, your mother crying.

No one at school noticed the injury. When you went to the bathroom, you only saw a slight swelling just like with Benno who sat next to you and suffered from herpes. And if someone had asked, how would you have explained it? At one point, the opportunity had indeed been favourable; after the bell had rung for break and everyone streamed towards the door, Gebhard, your biology teacher, had called you to the lectern. Playing with the chalk, he asked how you were; recently, he carefully weighed his words, you had seemed rather distracted and your class results . . . Sighing, he leafed through his register. 'Earlier you had been so interested in science class, your dragonfly studies,' he said, 'were unique.' 'Naturally,' he added after a short pause, 'the thing with your mother . . . ' She doesn't have anything to do with it, you wanted to interrupt, but the first word came out too late, he had already finished the sentence, 'was very difficult for you . . . ' 'She's doing better now,' you managed to say. Your interests now lay in other subjects, and your one in German would balance out your five in biology. Gebhard did not seem to have any argument against that, he only shrugged his shoulders perplexedly and threw the stub of chalk into the bin. In the same movement you floated your way out of the classroom. 'If you need any help,' you heard the teacher calling after you, 'you can come to me any time,' and you wouldn't have wanted anything more than to turn around, close the door and slowly begin to talk, struggling for the right words and the right moment you could begin your story. But even in your diary there were only a few helpless formulations for something that was much more painful and incomprehensible than a bitten lip, and nothing but blank pages, for that which was to happen a few days later in the kitchen.

'hIt's hthese hor hme,' you'd threatened and held out her pill box, after lunch, when, as always, she hadn't eaten a thing. She looked at you derisively, threw back her head and ran her hand through her hair. In the sunlight the red seemed too sharp again, just like the laugh that contorted her face, starting with her eyes, then screwing her entire body up into the air until she was bent over you, had snatched the box out of your hand and with a voice that could never have belonged to your mother punched into you like a machine, 'Then-the-tablets.'

With her sharply filed nails she had painted black she picked one out, looked at it against the light as if it were something precious, laid it into her palm and closed her fingers. 'Look here,' she said and pointed to the grooved pill, 'this is where my life line ends.'

Yet another one of those games, you thought, intended to punish you, transfer the responsibility for her state onto you. She turned on the faucet. The water streamed into the sink. Of all the sounds that filled the silence in the house, or first made audible the numbness your days were packed into like a thick clump of sod, the sound of water was your favourite. It usually signalled an improvement: when it rushed into the bathtub, for example, she was finally back from Hamburg. When you were still a child, the gurgling in the toilet had kept you safe from the ray until the next time you had to go; the beat of the rain in the eaves was the start of the morning's rain pantomime and she always thought up new punchlines to make you laugh. But, by now, even the softest of all sounds had transformed into noise.

The feeling of defeat was green, acrid, the feeling of spring. Since her return, you had barely felt any other. 'hMama, no!' you cried, and in fact she stopped, did not, as you had feared, put the pill down into the drain but filled a glass instead and sat down at the table, upright as if about to eat. 'Your word,' she said and swallowed. Behind her the water continued to stream into the sink, down the pipes, ever-downward. You took a thankful step towards her, even wanted to take her in your arms, but by then she already had the entire contents of the box in her mouth, after a movement, which today you can barely remember—like the majority of gestures in those last few weeks, which from one second to the other changed everything—had played out in quick motion, with a speed that only the eye of a dragonfly could have managed to follow.

But your body, which had always been a bit sluggish against time, had become trained to all her—by then—unpredictable actions. In the next instant your fingers were already in her throat. With one hand you pulled her by the hair and with the other hand wrenched open her jaw until you had managed to scrape the last pill out of her mouth. She leapt up and vomited into the sink. Your fingers glimmered with spit. Where she had got you was evidenced by the mark of her teeth. The water roared long and loud. 'I'm going to get fat from them,' she shouted, and tore open her blouse, 'These'—and she pushed your hand into her flesh—'these tits were once the best thing about me, and as for this'—as she pulled down her jeans and panties, her voice again like the punch that had sunk into your bones—'men used to stand around in lines,' and she punched you in the chest, 'But if I continue to munch these things,' and she swept a few of the spit-out pills from the table, 'if you continue to force me to swallow this shit,' and she pulled your hand out from behind her back and closed her thighs around it, 'then you will be the only guy,' she wept, 'who'll still want me!'

Everything as if in quick motion again. It's just in your memory that you can slow down the confusion of movements, calls and glances. Suddenly you saw tears. You quickly stepped out of her embrace and backwards, your arms bent behind you. The kitchen seemed to be a kind of cage, your mother within it the rabid animal writhing on the floor. 'Is that what you want?' she yelled; in the corner of her mouth where the slope of her lipstick had run off, the dust of a bitten tablet. 'Did that turn you on?' she pressed your hand into her crotch. Between your fingers, finally, the edge of the cupboard, the broom in the corner, behind it the doorway, freedom. 'That's why you chased Daniel off,' she kicked into the floorboards, and long after you had slammed the door to your room shut and thrown yourself onto your bed, from downstairs you could hear your overheating mother-machine rolling and stamping.

Like every afternoon when you did your homework, the sun stood naked and unveiled directly above the pond in a gleaming and immense sky. Only occasionally wrapped in a light mist as if beneath bright silk, it had been shining with growing strength since the March day Marga had come back from the hospital, and the warmer its rays became—tempting cats out of furnace rooms and into yards, driving dogs back into their sheds, licking the runoff in the ditches and making the dust on your desk more visible where, instead of doing your homework you doggedly scribbled into your note-book—the more you recognized a new characteristic: its spite.

It was the eleventh of May, Mother's Day, you added when you pulled the notebook out of the crevice to record the date and how over the last few weeks you had been noting her mood swings almost daily as if she had been your patient and the notebook a file. If no one were to actually believe your diary, you thought and began to write with an even more trembling hand, you'd both be lost. Were you really aware of what day it was? Suddenly she was standing behind you; sunk into your notes, you hadn't heard her come in. You don't react, and why should you? She hated Mother's Day; as if they were all holy while alive, that had always been her verdict. And so she had spent the day like any other Sunday: painting in the barn, smoking in the porch, up and down throughout the house, sometimes she'd driven off without telling you where she was going. When one of those times you nevertheless had placed a freshly picked spring bouquet in a vase, she had embraced the weeds with feigned dismay and cried, 'O beauty, on account of me you had to die!'

Now she was bent over the page encased in a cloud of perfume. 'Sick mother?' she said and tried to pull the book away from you. You fought her off and covered up what you'd written with your hand. How had she been able to read so quickly? And would you perhaps want to take a day trip on that particular day with your *sick mother*? She had got dressed up, touched up her lipstick, tied her hair up, even put on a smart dress, the ruby red one, which clashed with her orange mane. 'hHomework,' you lied. She mockingly repeated the word, the only one that had come to you, closed the notebook and stuffed it into the crevice. How did she know about the hiding place? In her eyes you thought you could read triumph. It was such a lovely day. Her voice sounded darker now, it resonated with regret or melancholy, something seemed to have touched her all of a sudden. She turned towards the window but without recognizing any of that which might have made her happy: the sun, the spring air, the new grass, the swallows above that had only been back from their winter quarters for a few days. 'In ten minutes,' she said, 'we're going to Hamburg.' She gave you the kiss and left.

With the green feeling in your stomach, you had put the pen away, changed your house trousers for your best pair of jeans, combed your by then almost-shoulder-length hair, put on some of Daniel's aftershave that he had forgotten on the shelf, laced up your white trainers which you saved for special occasions, threw a final glance into the wardrobe mirror where you made a face; everything slowed down awkwardly against a sheer and insurmountable inner resistance, like an ill person preparing themselves with great pain for a trip to the doctor.

When you went to pick her up from the barn, she was hunched up on the stool in her high-heeled sandals, with her legs tucked under her, and continuously dabbing at the same spot in the extremely red picture which she had been working on for weeks without it having undergone any noticeable change. Only the colour seemed to grow harsher with every passing day, more bloody and baleful. She didn't once raise her eyes as she said, 'I can't do anything about the fact that you don't have any friends.' And she placed the end of the brush like a scalpel on the point and narrowed her eyes, 'Go to the village, it's full of kids.' Your eyes pouring with water, the sun laughed as you ran into the open, and out into the burning moor.

✳

But here at the pond you do not see a thing from me. Not a single sign of flame or ash at all. A fresh wind from the northeast even makes its way through your jacket lining. Timid blooms dot the alder branches, and further away, the birches shimmer in their otherworldly, almost hallucinatory, efflorescent green. In a lowly row before them, the blooming bog myrtle glows a rust-coloured red. Above that the glassy May vaults against the sun.

The fire that smoulders here is wintry. My flames rage within the hidden black layers of peat beneath the grass, along the thirsty roots; the peat cutters only hit water at one-and-a-half metres this spring. The last rain fell at the beginning of March. The cranberry is still in bloom, the earth already stews. I slowly seethe and burn my way towards you, below the sod and along the gaping edges of the drains; without any hint of the spectacle, all of them stretch their necks out to see: the children, the farmers on their tractors, the tourists from the city who have read about the burning moor of Fenndorf in the paper. They all stand behind the barricade tape amazed at how peacefully the land lies under the beautiful, burn-threatening sun.

Hidden by an artic wind, it sinks and shrivels up the peat moss, dries the low water out into dust-white crusts. Every drop of dew acts as a burning lens that can set the weakest blade of grass aflame. No tiny explosion like a match, only a slowly burning point at a precarious part in a plaitwork of simmering grasses. Because of its low heat conduction, on long sunny days the peat heats up like an oven. At night, the surface layers only reluctantly cool down since by early morning they will be rekindled by the sun. Out there by the kolk, on the treeless summit of the raised bog, in the steppe of grass and shrub, where the sun is wasteful with gusts of wind for twelve hours at a time, I have begun my work.

But the farmers blame the careless city folk for flicking their cigarette butts onto the footpaths. In one way or another, however, I had long been ready for the catastrophe. The feverish nerve burns through, sets the flesh aflame, the soft, forever slightly melancholic face of the plain warps into a scowl, turns black and breaks open. The moor has a sunburn, as will your skin and forehead, Dion, at the end of this day of wandering here and there throughout the city. After that, the blisters will burst, peel and allow a new, white, but still oddly vulnerable young man to emerge, yet you will have definitively got rid of that much more dangerous boil, your mother. She is finished with you. Is waiting for you to finally be grown up, and to get lost. At the crack of dawn already she had driven to Hamburg, and you know from experience what happens when she hides her trips from you. While you are busy brooding and procrastinating, she is busy begging Ute Hassforther to give her a new exhibition. Do you really want to go through all of that again?

You breathe in deeply, feel your breath quiver, blink with glassy eyes against the sun. Go on, have a good cry. This kind of goodbye isn't easy. Feel the pain, recognize what it means for your life, then be a smart boy and take a decision!

You sink deeper into your winter jacket, in your eyes the pressure mounts. How now so melodramatic? As a child of the moor and a dragonfly expert, you know that from time to time I must create new relationships. Even in the animal, in the long run, incest leads to the degeneration of the group, and so, at the right moment, the hatchling that will not leave the nest is thrown out. What are you still waiting for? Don't stand around, get the bus to Hamburg, find your mother and bring her—with a clean conscience—to solitary at Ochsenzoll.

Back there of all places? you think and wipe away your tears. When she came back from the hospital on one of the first sunny days of March, she was ruddy and fat. Maybe it had to do with the clunky motorcycle outfit in which she looked just as heavy as Marianne, who had stepped up next to you. Material had never been strained on your mother's body before; the belt around her waist had always been buckled to the next-to-last hole, the skimpy blouse sewn even tighter. Now the ass she was swinging off the machine was wider than the seat.

In your memory, she arrived alone. You would prefer to see her coming back to you by herself, riding a chopper out of the empty, winter-bleak plain like a heroine crossing a heroically survived battlefield. She took off her helmet, shook out her flaming hair, looked at you, then nodded to her sister-in-law and said to you both or to the space between your shoulders where the evening sun was dazzling, 'My boy!'

In reality, however, *he* had brought her there. You had recognized the man from the toilet stall immediately. Had she been hiding her lover from you all those years? Had she already known him back then, at the Sparkasse Bank's award ceremony, and spent all those days you waited for her at home with him instead? You feel relieved at the thought that her weariness with you had not been the reason for her getting sick but her being unhappily in love; and yet, there was also another, more powerful feeling which began to press down upon your chest. Only later, in your book, would you call it 'jealousy'.

He stepped out of her shadow and gave Marianne his hand. 'A friend from Hamburg,' Marga said nonchalantly but immediately took hold of his fist, he said: 'Heyya, Daniel Röcker.' In retrospect, the scene is complete. Today you know that she sat tightly behind him, her hands around his hips, her head nestled against his shoulder, dreaming of a family while the wind reddened her face.

'So are you doing better now?' Marianne asked and moved closer to you; the yellow light on Marga's face disappeared. 'I'm doing great,' she answered and looked at you encouragingly, and said they had put her to rights. The phrase did not belong to her, it seemed as if it had been memorized, as if she were being forced to say it, just like all her movements seemed to be more awkward than before, remote-controlled, clumsy, even her eyes flew restlessly from one person to the other; your mother entirely behind a mask which you could not penetrate.

The sun sank in the horizon, grew larger and turned red. Then her voice suddenly changed. 'Brainwashed!' she laughed, and you heard Marianne cough slightly. 'It was an excellent clinic,' Daniel hastily added, standing protectively beside her now. They had immediately recognized what was missing there. 'And what are you missing?' Marianne asked without looking at Daniel at first. 'Something endogenous—it's genetic,' Marga explained and pulled his hand even closer. You had never heard such terms from her before. In hindsight, many of her words from that time seemed too big to you; she couldn't complete the phrases, sentences like *I have to isolate myself*, or *I have to be alone with myself now*, always with an emphasis on I, this pressure to prove herself in front of Daniel, to be of a different opinion than he was, later, when they argued about the so-called *solution*.

'Genetic?' Marianne repeated doubtfully and laid her hand on your shoulder; you pulled away. Marga, it seemed to you, registered your resistance with satisfaction. She reached her hand out to you and said, 'Let's go!'

Marianne tightened her grip. You looked to the ground, onto the soil where you were supposed to have dug out the bigger stones. Like every year your aunt had planted the garden patch with potatoes, lettuce and cabbage. A grub was crawling between the clumps, then dug itself back into the protective topsoil. With the tip of your boot you pushed it onto a steppingstone where it bent itself into a ring. The tiny legs wriggled, could find no footing.

Marianne coughed again, you felt her hand grabbing your shoulder. 'Maybe you can ask him first if he wants to,' she said. Marga let out a squeaking noise, something between a laugh and a threat; it was a little like the jarring call of a black-tailed godwit, that bird you often hear in the moor but have almost never seen. The grub continued to crawl aimlessly around.

'Ask him.' Daniel whispered to her. She let go of his hand and punished him with a look. That's when you took the shovel and cut the insect in half. At that moment it was so still, you could hear the grating of the metal. You even remember what it was you thought: That thing will never turn into a May bug, or something like that. Then you kicked the cadaver halves into the ground.

'Maybe *you* should have asked him earlier whether he even wanted to move in with you,' Marga said and pulled you away from your massacre. 'Before that,' Marianne answered quietly, 'you should have asked *me* whether I *could* take him.' She knew what the situation in her family was—all of a sudden Hannes had wanted to study further, because of his asthma Martin had to take a cure again, the funding from the administration still hadn't come through. Her voice was composed, only its pitch had increased, it shook as thinly and brittlely as when she fought with Hannes.

Marga smelt of cigarettes, petrol and leather. Her boyfriend smiled at you chummily but you looked away, past your mother and into the moor. Gusts of wind bent the rushes, shrubs and tops of the willows to the west, towards the sun, a cold hole of fire sinking into the earth and reddening the chuckling and crookedly brushed birches in their soot-spotted white coats at the last minute of the day, as if they were already standing in flames.

'Thanks for everything!' Marga reached out her hand to her sister-in-law. She nodded, did not take it, said, 'The door is open.' Without looking at you, she took the shovel out of your hand. Marga pushed you to the motorcycle; Daniel helped you up.

You were allowed to drive the way home yourself. In your notebook you wrote how that March day your first impression of her new man was *Okay*. He explained the clutch and the gas, pointed out the brakes a number of times, you had to be gentle with the machine like it was a virgin. Marga said, 'Don't screw up my boy here,' pulled you to her and squeezed the perfume-smelling helmet onto your head.

You pressed the ignition, let out the clutch; the motorcycle gave a jerk forward, flooded. Marga squeaked and clung on to you. After the second try the Honda began to roll. The speedometer slowly began to inch up to forty, you hoped that Hannes would see you from his window.

Everything was once again how it had been: Marga big and protective behind you, her embrace tight, familiar and inseparable, as if she had never been gone; the Heidedamm a shoddy old road, to the right the moor, to the left the thin meadow and the freshly ploughed fields, in the rich sunset the house like a sparkling palace and Daniel almost forgotten. For a hundred metres you were happy with your new mother.

It was when you turned off the motor that you heard and saw the cranes. They had returned from their winter camp and were flying through the enflamed sky above the house towards Rahse, to the north, their V-shaped squadron in several lines, one after the other, the writing strict and clear and yet still encrypted somehow, their distant, trumpet-like calls a kind of laughter, as if about to make fun of you for once again falling into your mother's trap. For already in the kitchen the squalor began. A strip of wallpaper had peeled off of a corner of the ceiling; in the sink there was a whole stack of cutlery, studded with black plaque. Someone had walked across the tiles with muddy shoes, the track winding its way upstairs.

'You two live in this hole?' Daniel asked and looked around. 'My hole is your hole,' Marga answered, grunted over her joke and kicked a dead mouse out from under the chair. 'You really weren't living here?' She looked at you reproachfully, you asked, 'hWhat hfor?' 'She could have easily cleaned up a bit, that miserly broad,' she hissed into one of the dirty corners, and you knew that she meant your aunt who had often sent you to the Heidedamm with a bucket full of cleaning products, sighing that she couldn't take care of two houses at the same time, in her voice the underlying accusation of being overwhelmed which resonated throughout all of her instructions and rebukes that she gave to you as her new foster child. Every single time, you turned around right before the front door; you did not want to do either Marianne or your mother the favour of taming the chaos in which they had left you behind.

Daniel opened the refrigerator then quickly shut it again. 'Let him come back home first,' he said and stuck his hands into his pockets. Marga snorted, 'Come home?' It was his home. 'Then you should do a little something about it,' Daniel drew a line in the dust with his finger. She went to the sink and threw him a cloth. 'Why me?' she said, her voice shrill with the *M*. 'You live here now too,' and with that she looked at you as if she were already sick of you again.

'Go on, show me how you did it,' she ordered. 'Did what?' he asked. How he had cleaned up the oil in his father's garage. The sentence's sharp vowels clawed into your temples. It had been his artistic in-i-tia-tion, she shot over to you. The word toppled into a falsetto. 'hInitiation,' you corrected her.

Daniel began to laugh. At first only his face contorted, then it split out of the frame of his full beard, expanded and grew coarse. Marga froze. As if a kind of counter-reaction, her features smoothed out. You saw her back tense and authoritatively straighten up, knew the menacing gestures from *Frau* Härtel, the English teacher, when she lost control of the class. Daniel bent over laughing, a quarter of a minute or longer he punched the back of the chair he was holding on to. 'Hilarious!' She'd actually believed that story! From the corners of your eyes you saw her clench up her fists. She hissed, 'What?'

Did she really not know who his father was, 'Hartmut Röcker?' His face slowly slid back into the frame of his beard. His eyes were glassy, his forehead red and covered with small beads of sweat, he looked drunk. Marga began to busy herself with the kitchen table. Why should she be familiar with some auto mechanic from Hamburg? The cutlery clattered in her hand. Daniel wobbled the chair. 'He was the former director of the Theatre of Hamburg, and my mother'—

the still chuckling voice suddenly sharp and aggressive—'is Therese Giering, the well-known actress,' and he let the chair bang against the table. '*Film* actress,' he added, 'in case you didn't know that either.'

Marga knocked the dishes into the sink and said, 'Asshole.' In his face everything was now back in the right place. You liked the beard, it gave his gestures something strict and clear, almost fatherly. Any talk about his woodcut mouth will only come up many years later. You'd also noticed the way he occasionally looked at you—not like an adult with the annoying child who stands silently in the doorway while its parents fight, no, but friendly, as an equal, including you. As if he were seeking your approval.

'Why don't you clean up your own life first?' Once again, her sentence, which she had half-spoken in your direction, seemed to come from someone else. In her frightened face you saw that she herself didn't believe it. 'Then get going,' said Daniel and threw her the dishcloth back, 'I'm going to have a look at the roof.' He took two stairs at a time, the floorboards creaked, upstairs the attic door slammed. As she turned around she began to cry. But even her tears seemed forced. Perfectly shaped, they rolled across her cheeks. Her mouth was turned slightly down, as if she wanted to cry but couldn't—a poor actress in the role of the unhappy mother.

Today you ask yourself where you were standing. Sometimes you see yourself at the table, then in the open door, behind you the garden, the dyke, the escape route back to the Lamberts' house. With distance and all the disappointments that came afterwards, you would react differently—wouldn't hide away in the corner silently and shyly but be tough, bang on the table, get some things straight. They had acted, it says in your book, like little children. It would have been better to have followed Daniel who had already learnt how to take your new mother, or to have walked over to Marianne's where the soup would already have been steaming on the table; your stomach, you remember, had growled loudly, but that was the only thing in you which rebelled.

You pick a stone off the ground, throw it into the water. It tears apart the peaceful image of the spring day mirrored on the surface. Small waves dart to the banks. She lied to me, you think. Promised me siblings, domestic bliss.

Bliss? I press. Come on, Dion, you can express it better than that! It's time you finally defend yourself!

You stare at the water where the ripples whisper, angrily throw another stone. It cracks against the trunk of a tree. Leaves from last year sail down, a crow takes flight. Go on! Trust yourself! The truth is that she played at the perfect family so that you wouldn't move back over to Marianne's, her rival.

Be done once and for all with *Mama*, think *Malicious*, say *Monster*! be the molested, bruised son!

You turn away to the alders; you have always looked to the alders, run into the moor, when you refused to see who she really was. You were always her 'dear boy', the picture-perfect son who bore his mother in his hands, defended her against the world, kept every evil at bay: there was the claw-like branch that loomed above her when she went swimming, so you carefully kept an eye on her. Quickly handed her the towel to protect her from the threatening cold, threw her bathrobe over her for the villagers were already staring, let her lie to you and were offended on her behalf, and even after the scene in the kitchen, when you should have recognized how much she manipulated you, you still managed to find words of comfort for her.

She already had that rigid look on her face again and was chewing on her lip; you thought it was because of you. But she had only been back for half an hour. You had waited for her all winter long. She couldn't begin to cry again just now. You took a deep breath and sighed more than stuttered the first coherent sentence, 'Of course his father's the auto mechanic.'

She turned around. There were no more tears to be seen on her cheeks, not even a trace. 'hThe hmotorcycle,' and you pointed out to the yard, 'he knows his way around machines.' She looked at you in disbelief, bent her head down and shook herself. Her hair had grown over the winter, reached almost down to her shoulder blades. You would have liked a hug, at least a smile, a trusty old wink, but she just laughed at you. 'You're right, you're a sharp little guy, director's sons,' she said, 'drive Jaguars and not rickety Hondas.' She grabbed you by the arm and pulled you onto the chair. 'Should he stay?' The three of you could make a family. Father–mother–child, she giggled, her eyes standing a bit out of their sockets. You said you weren't a kid any more; you'd struggled with the statement for a long time. 'Ha!' She tilted her head backwards again, a movement that she would repeat often in the weeks to come, as if she had to get rid of something, squirm her way out of an invisible shackle.

'True,' she said, 'you're a man now.' She flicked you in the thigh with her finger. 'Down there too long, up top still too short, but that will sort itself out in time.' You pushed away her hand but she didn't let go, ruffled your hair, something you've always loathed. 'What'd you think of him?' She looked at you challengingly. You shrugged your shoulders, she pulled you closer, wrenched approval out of you, you said, 'hOkay.' 'Hokay?' she repeated. Should she tell you why she also found him *hOkay*?

Now, at the latest, Dion, you should have been upset, got up and gone, out into the moor like always when she hurt you, or over to Marianne who felt pity for you and your stutter. You should have just left her sitting there, growled something like 'Bite me!' just like boys your age do when their mothers get on their nerves.

She had never aped you before, had never, like all the others, impatiently or embarrassedly looked to the side; on the contrary, whenever you failed to manage she had protectively stood in front of you and with her steadfast gaze and an encouraging nod steered your every word until it had finally come out. You would have forgiven her everything; her making fun of your body shooting into the air, the guy you now had to share her with, even the lie about the family. But that tiny little letter, an airy, completely unnoticeable H before the *Okay* had got you at your weakest point.

'No doubt you've already gathered your experiences with love,' she nudged you in the side, added, 'Since your mother hasn't been around to control you.' You felt yourself blush. What did she mean by that? Did she know something about Hannes? The wafer-thin wall between your rooms and the crevice that had quickly sprung open in your guest bed as well? Your cousin hidden within it who, in your thoughts, you had touched when you heard him cough over there against the creaking slatted boards in ever shorter intervals—cough–creak–cough—until all was suddenly still and, in the moment you both emptied yourselves at almost the same time in your imagination, you bit back the noise in your throat and turned yourself onto the mattress while over there too it creaked one last time before all the secret sounds trickled away inside the wall which shimmered white and empty in the dim light together with the metal crucifix that redeemed those tortured stares onto your damply gleaming penises. Eventually sleep indeed poured over you both and soon pulled your bodies back into the bed crevices, with each other, in each other, coughing and creaking, something that no one else could hear.

'Go on and tell me,' she pushed. 'Who was it? . . . A girl from the village? Nothing good's ever come from over there, and don't you dare say Kerstin, Kerstin, that hussy, I wouldn't serve her at my table, wouldn't open my door to any of the pig farmers, don't make the same mistake I did,' she said and punched you, a punch like the electric fence on the cow's pasture where kids would often stand and shove one another against the wire, equally frightened as entranced by the painful shock.

'I'm going to find out,' she sulked, 'Mothers have a sixth sense.' It grew dark in the kitchen, only in the window the scattered fair-weather clouds continued to glow like coals thrown into the void. In the twilight they looked even stranger, larger, older, who was the woman who'd come with the motorcycle, this Röcker in tow, and who wanted to credit you with a girlfriend you didn't have, did not want to have? And even if you had had her, or had even done the thing with her, you would not have—as they say—let her, Marga, whom you no longer recognized, in on it.

If she had still been the old Marga, you might have told her the truth: Hannes. And, having admitted it, and your mother having taken a solemn vow of silence and understanding, that sixth sense she supposedly possessed would have allowed her to understand just what her child needed in such a situation: comfort, consolation, understanding and so on, all that in one single sentence—whispered or kissed into your ear—that only mothers can and are allowed to say because in those moments they are indeed somewhat holy and know more about their children than their children themselves, like Mary, who, so Pastor Deichsen had explained to you in Confirmation class, had only been chosen by God because before Jesus' birth she had accepted her fate, had accepted that her son would have to die for the sins of humankind, as well as for those of his mother, in order to survive for many years in poverty and isolation.

'hTanja,' you said.

She looked at you disappointedly. True, she did have something, she was talented and smart, could even be quite pretty if it weren't for those eyes, and so bony, she sighed, she would have hoped for a different calibre, Daniela, a real looker, or at least Meike from the new housing development, she had a terrible overbite, but in compensation a rich father, a paint and varnish manufacturer, that would have been all right with her, he would have taken care of her with paintbrushes and turpentine her whole life long. She said, 'Tanja's sweet, but sick.' A light shot through her eyes, gleamed in the reflection of the sky on the glass of the kitchen cabinet and sowed two tiny flames through her pupils. You needed someone to show you what the deal was—boys in puberty were often disoriented.

In a sudden image that flared through your mind you saw her sitting in a white, tidy room in the hospital with her legs crossed in a comfortable chair, maybe next to a rubber tree, across from her a doctor in glasses who said that exact sentence: *Show him what the deal was*. Now you understand why you had often felt so speechless during the telephone calls that winter. Naturally, you were afraid of the device which only transmitted your voice but would not let itself be tricked or distracted like people. When a word sticks in your mouth you quickly turn so that you can then eject it when you turn back around, or you simulate a cough attack that will catapult the phrase out without any consonants. With jolts and twitches you can always muddle between the speech wreckage and in the best scenario the person across from you won't even hear your stutter but think you're just a bit fidgety.

But it wasn't only the telephone which hung pitilessly on the next word, no matter how much you squirmed. With the receiver in your hand you had remained on the little bench in the Lambert's hallway, on the wall across from you a bouquet of dried flowers which you dissected with your eyes, from the stems tied with a velvet cord to the delicate veins of the leaves when Marga would tell you about her daily life in the hospital from the other end of the line twice a week in the evening, mostly Wednesdays and Sundays, would describe the *grub* they'd had again, the names of her fellow patients, Gisela, you remember, Astrid, who'd already put on eight kilos and had started to smoke again, and her roommate Birgül, a Turkish woman whose husband would bring her stinky food wrapped up in aluminium, but otherwise everything was quite all right. She told you about the crazy people, their chaotic babbling, and that she no longer had to get angry about losing her lighter which was, she had laughed a bit too loudly, chained to her table.

You nodded often, smiled sometimes, it always occurred to you too late that she couldn't see you. When in these conversations you brought out the only complete sentence, when she would be coming back home, she would go silent for a while and then say something about the doctors who were of the opinion that you both needed a bit of distance from each other. You would have gladly torn the dried bouquet down from the nail, it was ugly and dusty, a monstrosity, would have tossed it into the rubbish right then and there.

Only once did she add a sentence that you now have to recall again; it included the terms *puberty* and *disoriented* which were not Marga words at all. She had corrected herself as if she had suddenly noticed that someone had been standing behind her and listening, 'I mean,' she said, '*I* must learn to let you go.'

Marianne, who was cleaning up the living room, would come to you and take the receiver. She shouldn't worry herself at all, she said so loud as if she had to bridge the distance to Hamburg with her own voice. He was doing quite well. She nodded at you vigorously; you would get your appetite back, help out in the stalls, in the meantime even get your own room, 'Yes, indeed. Sorry? What do you mean, the junk room!' she said, meaning your new sleeping area, your grandmother's former room where she had prepared everything—you had it nicely put together there, bright and quiet for your homework.

The line crackled, your aunt shook the receiver, called out your mother's name a number of times and finally said offended, 'She hung up!' But you knew that the coins for the phone had simply run out, and you imagined it on the wall of a white corridor flanked by endless rows of doors overseen by the strict-looking nurses in their white uniforms with bonnets on their knotted hair, which the idiots would tear at, wind around their fingers or chew on apathetically in the corners while playing with their exposed genitalia and their dirty fingernails. Indeed, Marianne always described the hospital where your mother was being taken care of more or less favourably as compared to the asylum David Voss did, for scarcely had the piece of news made it through the village that November, been trumpeted across the school playground, it was said that Katthusen was now there where Kar-Kar, the Karstedter's speech and sexually disturbed boy from Kleenze had been brought; in other words, the nut house.

Kar-Kar, you knew that much from the stories, had tried to take his own life many times. Lambert's farm-hand, from his tractor, had supposedly seen him on the train tracks and dragged him to the police, Karsten Karmstedter, the world-weary man, he suspected, had tried to kill himself on the rails. It was said that he had often hung around in Hamburg with shady characters, drug dealers some said, rent boys others. He'd always been a bulldyke, you had heard Ilse Bloch say to a client in her store a few weeks after his death. You wanted to know from Marga what a bulldyke was, and she laughed and asked you who came up with such stupid words. When you told her what you had heard Ilse Bloch saying, she looked at you thoughtfully, suddenly grabbed you by the shoulders and with a serious voice explained, 'Karsten Karmstedter was gay, which means that he did it with men. On top of that, he was a drug addict, a junkie who'd started to whore in order to get money for his stuff, but that's not why he died.' 'The reason . . .' she added after a pause in which her thoughts must have wandered quite far away from the point, for she shuddered as if after a nap when she looked at you again, pointed to the kitchen window, in the direction of the village and said, 'The reason he wanted to die is them.'

You still remember it clearly: you were ten years old when the news of his suicide made the rounds of Fenndorf. In the previous years you had seen Kar-Kar a few times at the village fairs; he was twelve years older and, more often than not, drunk. Although you never exchanged a word with him, had even been a little frightened by his red face, always a little bit contorted and as if swollen, with its flickering eyes, in a certain way you had felt yourself drawn to him with a quiet sort of complicity, most likely because he also stuttered; when Kar-Kar would order a beer he'd tilt his head backwards and kick the word with his boot against the stand.

At some point he had gone to Hamburg and rarely showed up at the fairs any more. His father, it was said, had kicked him out of the house. In the end, on Sundays Siegried Karmstedter would drive to Hamburg with a basket of food and visit him in a hospital where one would ostensibly help him. On that day, as always, he had brought his mother back to the main train station because she was afraid of getting lost in the city. Then, so it was said, the unhappy guy jumped in front of the next city train.

And what if those doctors who could not save Kar-Kar had failed again with your mother? How were you now supposed to take care of her, you thought and anxiously stared at the strange woman, or the one who had grown even stranger, by your side. From the attic came a crash followed by a short cry. Through the walls you heard Daniel cursing, Marga sighed, 'Not worth much as a handyman.' You stood up and mumbled something about your things that you wanted to get from Marianne's, but she held you back, 'Would you prefer a sister or a brother?'

You defiantly pulled your hand away. You had always wanted that kind of family, the kind that on evenings, at the fall of twilight, would sit around the kitchen table, father and mother at each end, children on the sides, in the middle a pot of soup or a plate with sandwiches garnished with sour pickles, the cuts of pork sausage eaten with a fork and knife; that's what you'd seen through the illuminated windows of the village. Marga would be sitting next to you, and on the chair with all the post, Hannes, elbows bent, who would always come a little closer, just like around the table at the Lambert's.

At Marianne's there'd been a kind of everything-soup too, a nourishing and filling meal from which each member of her clan ate as much as they liked. Just like Marga's stew, your aunt's dish became your favourite meal, a quickly prepared dinner, at every moment replenishable and reheatable; the farmer's daily schedule was carefully regulated between the stove, the stall, the field, the market stand and her choir. With her leftover stew she kept her brood happy and full: Kerstin ate only the meat and despised anything green; anything solid, on the other hand, was anathema to Martin, he would spoon out the broth and scoop the remaining fluid from what was at the bottom of the bowl until Marianne ladled out more of the broth and added it; and so it went until he'd had enough. Hannes threw everything wordlessly and hungrily down, and Ole loved to line up similar looking pieces of vegetables and ham on the edge of the bowl like cards in a memory game only at some point to shove them all into his mouth. You didn't like the celery and, therefore, loved the meat that much more; and as you watched Hannes—who sometimes ran the back of his hand across his running nose or the broth streaming out of his mouth and thereby spread his elbows so wide across the table that through the cut arms of his T-shirt you saw the aromatic hodgepodge of muscles, skin and hair—out of the corners of your eyes, you didn't eat as much as you could but certainly saw more than your fill.

Across from him at your secret table you had placed Tanja; Tanja would be the perfect sister. You would share all your secrets with her that you couldn't trust Marga with or didn't want to tell her simply because she was your mother; for even brothers, that's what you'd observed in your host family, stole from each other and squabbled. When Hannes caught his five-year-younger brother Martin with one of his comic books, there was trouble. He wriggled in his big brother's headlock, spit and cried for his mother who punished not the thief but the one who was robbed with a smack on the head—which Hannes avenged by eating up all the younger one's pudding after dinner. Karl Lambert had the troublemaker leave the table, Kerstin, ever-playing at being the boy she wanted to be, refused sweets and shoved the cheated one her dessert. You always saw the two put their heads together. In spite of his asthma she took Martin, not you or Ole, with her into the chicken stall to the brooding hens, and they would disappear for hours. When she would put on her roller skates, her brother in turn would pedal his bicycle over the Dorfstraße where she had drawn paths and obstacles with chalk. Martin was never allowed to even ride a single course alone. But he didn't complain; at penalty kicks Kerstin therefore stood round after round between the beanpoles and caught every shot.

Tanja and you would be just as inseparable. You would have rolled her to the table in her wheelchair every morning, from there through the village past all the swaying curtains to school where you would push her across the playground and through the hallway. Everyone jumps to the side when you drag the heavy part backwards up the stairs and even David Voss has begun to hold open the classroom door for you and spares you the stupid comments. For longer stretches Tanja follows Kerstin's example and holds on to your bike rack. No step would be an obstacle; you would have literally, as they say, carried her everywhere, done everything so that she would forgive you.

The truth is that *Frau* Deichsen turned you away a number of times when you wanted to ask about Tanja. At first she said she was still in the hospital, then in a physical-therapy clinic. When you sheepishly asked whether you could visit her there, the pastor's wife closed the door, leaving just a little crack, stuck her pointed face through and answered, 'Do you really think that you would be doing her a favour?' And she held tightly to the dog, which bared its teeth and growled, something it had never done before.

Then in the village they said that Tanja was back but she didn't come to school any more; the building was an old, frequently modified thing with steep stairs and narrow doors. One evening in February, Marianne told the story at dinner that in the future Tanja would go to a boarding school for handicaps, and with a side-glance at you, 'Naturally you both will visit her there.' Hannes threw down his spoon. 'It was an accident,' he yelled, how often did he have to explain that to her? His voice cracked in the middle of the sentence and after *accident*—that lie of a word—fell away. 'I'll drive you over there,' Marianne answered, it sounded like an order. He jumped up, tore his jacket off the hook and slammed the door. You wanted to go right behind him, but one look from the farmer was enough. She ladled broth into your bowl, the soup shot onto the oilcloth, the children spooned it up in silence.

A few days later you were standing again in front of the pastor's door and, when it opened, immediately stepped into the suspicious crack. *Frau* Deichsen defensively put herself in your way; Ronja snarled, then seemed to remember the fun winter afternoon and led you with a wagging tail past the mother-block and into the living room.

Tanja was sitting in a wheelchair in front of the TV, sunk into a comedy show. She laughed at every joke, kicked her foot, which she apparently could move again, against the footboard, finally looked up at you casually and chuckled, 'This is so funny.' Her mother came in and cut you off once more. She didn't find it to be a good idea at all, she warned her daughter with a voice that rang of control. 'It's all right, Mom,' Tanja answered, ordered *Frau* Deichsen out with a glance and you onto the sofa. She had put on a little bit of make-up, her lips shone mother-of-pearl, but the soft pink shadows of her cheeks wiped out all the softness and the sweetness from her face, which had never seemed particularly childlike to begin with. Your heart was beating into your throat; it was the first time you had seen each other since the moment the paramedics had loaded her onto the stretcher and shoved her in the heli-copter. There had been no chance for the Red Cross ambulance to make it through the snowdrifts. In all those years, the emergency doctor had never been called to the Heidedamm, not once at the death of Hannes' grandmother, and then suddenly two days in a row. Once again the villagers had stood in a line in the knee-deep snow while the emergency medical technicians took care of Tanja, who in the meantime had awoken and was screaming in pain. Hannes was stammering and in his excitement—or because of the still snowy winds—was fire red in the face and walking back and forth, here and there, between the men, Marianne and Tanja's sometimes-crying and sometimes-cursing mother who suddenly grabbed him by the shoulders and let fly, for a pastor's wife, some rather offensive and abrasive insults which worked Hannes up, in his desperation, to outline the course of events over and over again, the suspicious noises in the attic, Tanja, who had wondered whether there was an animal or maybe even an intruder, he, Hannes, who had warned her, you, Dion—and he pointed at you threateningly—who had, however, egged her on to go and inspect the space where there was already the gaping hole in the roof and right at that very moment, as Tanja wanted to get a glimpse of the truly breath-taking spectacle of the snow, the tile came crashing down, the '*Tiiiiiile!*' he yelled again and again against the roar of the rotor blades which whipped the unlucky word with the wailing vowel into the night so that he had to start the story over until Marianne silenced him with a smack and the helicopter twisting up into the air provoked a short, powerful snowstorm that, as in fast motion, blew the whole violence of that afternoon over you, out into the softly undulating night landscape which had been so peaceful and untouched under the snow until just a few moments before but now already destroyed by the first tracks, footsteps, which, as the villagers trudged back to their homes, expanded into circles and loops in the middle of which Hannes stood with raised shoulders, a bowed head and a trace of tears upon his cheeks which had already frozen.

As the evening news began, you finally risked the question you had been silently chewing on for fifteen minutes: How did she like her new school?

Tanja shrugged her shoulders, shovelled a handful of gummi fruits into her mouth and handed the bag over to you. The sweets softened your stuck jaw, and were like smooth, melting vowels on your tongue, your heartbeat slowly calmed down, her lopsided grin dissolved your stupor. 'And the other students?' you chirped with the sugary film on your tongue. 'Over there I'm the fittest,' she laughed, 'There're some real freaks, you wouldn't believe it.' She imitated the uncontrolled skittish movements of a spastic, then one without arms, making her fists disappear into the sleeves of her shirt and pressing her elbows to her flanks, 'Many are the accident victims,' she said, 'and more than half are in a wheelchair.' She needed something cooler than this old thing if she wanted to score with the boys, and she punched her ungraceful vehicle.

You could feel her confidence, the artful, slightly scornful forgiveness and forgetting that echoed in every one of her words, her smile now mischievous, now challenging, the blue-enflamed eyes rested unblinkingly on you, more alert than ever before. Finally, you too managed to smile.

'hWith hthe hboys?' you repeated and reached quickly back into the bag of sweets, the consonants threatening to clump together yet again. In your imagination the handicapped school in the south of Hamburg had once been a home for girls; but boys your own age—if possible without any of the contortions in their faces you knew from Jakob Wendisch, Hannes and David Voss-like blonde teens curving about the corridors in their wheelchairs and playing wheelchair football in the gym, something you never would have been able to do even with healthy legs, no, that was something you had just never imagined, just as you had not imagined that such true rivals to you, to Hannes, to whatever guy in the village you want, might exist, no, and your hopes, which you had bound to Tanja's new abode, in the end, had nothing to look for there.

She rolled closer to you, her face sharp, a bit mouse-like, by now you know the expression when she wants to share a secret with you, some forbidden story or other. Her mother came into the room, cleared her throat, she said in your direction without seeking out your eyes, Tanja had to get a little rest before the family doctor's evening visit.

Tanja ordered lemon soda, casually and surlily, the way one sends away an annoying servant. *Frau* Deichsen's face first became patchy, then extremely pale, before she left with a stiff turn. Hardly one minute later she brought glasses and a bottle of lemon soda, which she served on a tray with two pieces of marble cake that Tanja commented upon with a rolling of her eyes, on top of that she raised her voice, which until then had been just a whisper, about a paraplegic in the ninth class who could only move his head, or really only his face, she sighed, but it was really stunning, framed by dark curls and eyes as black as coal, and then she pulled out the picture of her new crush while *Frau* Deichsen awkwardly folded the napkins and opened the bottle and said, 'Maybe he's half-Italian, or has Spanish blood in his veins,' and whether those veins, which in cripples are cut off from the nerves, that is, the feelings, could nevertheless fill with blood in the appropriate place, 'Think about it,' she snorted, 'him and I caught in our wheelchairs, who'd be lying, I mean, sitting on top, who'd be on the bottom . . . and how am I supposed to have kids with the guy who'd still be healthy, God willing,' she yelled at the pastor's wife who had spilt the soda in shock, 'Oh my goodness, I'll bring a new one.' 'But I'll definitely kiss him,' Tanja triumphed and with a seemingly routine movement turned the wheelchair back in front of the TV.

A game show had just begun, 'Dalli Dalli,' Tanja crowed, 'I love this one!' Then she went quiet for the next fifteen minutes. Sunk into the mountain of sofa pillows and with Tanja's twitching, flatly glowing profile in the corner of your eye, you followed the quiz show, long minutes in which you neither wanted to nor had anything to say—after a certain point, the emcee called out 'Top!' and jumped into the air and remained standing there on a magical point of great lightness—which until then you had always missed in your life. That is how you would have liked to sit with her the whole night long and every evening thereafter.

Her mother never brought the new soda. In the middle of an exciting game Tanja suddenly turned her head and looked at you in surprise as if she had only then seen you sitting there. 'And you?' she asked, 'Have you already made out with Hannes?' In the tempest of words which instantly stormed onto your tongue even the most impertinent and quick-witted mouth would have broken down. The moderator in the frozen image was stuck with a grimace in his jump; after a cut he was once more standing at his place and jabbering away, no tottering or stumbling in between, not a single moment of insecurity. Tanja was staring back at the TV and seemed to have long forgotten her question when you finally got around to shaking your head.

'At any rate,' she said, 'I'll ask him.' Hannes? you wondered, alarmed, but in spite of the airy initial sound you couldn't form the question. 'His name's Marco, by the way,' she added. 'The next chance I get, I'm going to ask.' She was speaking quietly again and lengthened the words, weighed them, a bit mysteriously, as if she were discussing her plans with the TV. She didn't have any more time to wait. *Top*! Hans Rosenthal called out and jumped forward as if he wanted to embrace her. The audience applauded.

Would she ever be able to walk again?—of all the questions you had planned in your head before your visit, this was the most difficult, dangerous and insurmountable one; and until this moment you had been certain you wouldn't be able to ask it. But now it came across your lips almost without any interruption. Tanja finally looked over to you. The fresh sheen on her face was extinguished, her make-up now seemed lacklustre, her face tired. 'If some day you don't stutter any more,' she answered, broke off but after a few seconds started again, 'Assuming that no one will stop listening to you when you talk, no one will look to the ground out of embarrassment for you.' She rolled to the TV and turned it off at the climax of the show. 'If all at once everyone were to listen to you,' she now said almost a little threateningly, 'would you even have anything to say?'

In the sudden silence, the soft crackling of the cooling cathode ray tubes was the first and last sound in the stuffy, upholstered living room. Behind all the heaps of pillows, the world appeared mute, deaf and motionless. At its exit stood her mother who, arms pressed into her hips, bellowed, 'It's time!' so that you couldn't do anything but jump up and follow her out of the room without even saying goodbye.

Halfway you heard her call out your name from behind. She had rolled into the hall, rummaged about in her pockets and eventually held her hand out to you, for only a blink of the eye, but long enough for you to recognize a roof tile shard. At the end of the hallway *Frau* Deichsen held the front door open, cold air blew inside. At your last glance, Tanja nodded to you like she used to in front of the classroom door when with the presentation in your knapsack you were struggling with your fear, but Tanja knew that you would remain silent this time too.

And now? Had Marga read your thoughts somehow? Heard your innermost desire with her sixth sense, that mother's sense they had sharpened and trained through therapy so that in the future she could take better care of you? She barely knew anything about you or the things that had happened over the last few months. In your telephone calls you had only mentioned the essential: your grades, Marianne's cooking, the weather in Fenndorf, only rarely your homesickness and the longing for the old times. Why had she suddenly come up with this idea of having another child?

In front of the empty kitchen window her eyes were sightless. The red reflection in the glass snuffed out. 'I should be able to pick one out,' she said in a hushed voice, in the way one instinctively begins to whisper when it becomes night. She sighed, seemed to consider something for a time, or was she consciously turning it into a secret? 'Another boy,' she said eventually. You barely saw the movement of her lips. 'Boys are difficult when they're young, but later they're low-maintenance.' In the darkness her words sounded lost and unsure, almost imploring. She saw you move away from her, she slid after you, 'I'll ask Daniel if he also wants to,' and she indicated the stairs.

You looked to your wristwatch with the phosphorescent clock face, a Christmas gift from Marianne and Karl. You had to get over there for dinner now: in the dark your voice seemed deeper and harder. She did not react. The way out was like a tunnel. In the west, one single cloud still aglow on the horizon. Behind it the sky and moor already one.

The helicopter lifts up off the meadow by the fire station where there put the village fair tent in July. The rotor blades whirl in the air, whip the alders down, which, so bent, seem even skinnier and sicklier. The skids flash in the light, with a panic-stricken flapping of wings a duck flies out of the reeds. The din roars in your head, but you withstand the pressure to press your hands over your ears, stretch yourself into the mind-numbing noise and hope to blackout.

Over the last few days you had followed the fire squadrons on their search for the moor-fire everyone was talking about. You know the crevice where the barricade tape ends and none of the guards go. In its familiar, unchanging back and forth of hollows and crests, moss-covered mounds and low-lying water the moor lay beneath the skyline. But the stillness was a different, more complete one, freed from all ghost calls, dream confessions and children's oaths; you had stood at the gate to your childhood kingdom for a long time, on the look-out, listening to the silence. The fire, you thought, must be raging in another part, one still unknown to you, which lies beyond the kolk, in the heart of the moor, which is at the same time its end. On the other side, bit by bit, the world begins again, trails appear between the swinging weave of the bracken, wind along the grass into the forest, then into the thin meadow which is enclosed by electric fences, streets, yards, a village; in the glittering air another two, maybe even five, kilometres away, you saw the church tower of Rahse.

You gave up the search, turned around and were startled: not far from the way you had come, only one hundred metres away, behind the belt of reeds which had earlier blocked your sight, the plain was black. Shot through by the skeletons of a pair of charred birches, the carpet of ashes was spreading out to the east where beyond the burnt areas the clinker brick houses of Fenndorf could be seen. A helicopter was getting closer, but still without a sound; then suddenly, as if it had made it through an invisible wall, the noise began to swell. The watchman who was standing over at the barricade tape began to blow his whistle. You ran more quickly out of the fear that the flood of water could crash down onto you at a place where the soil was already burning in your footsteps; at some points the pockets of fire had eaten up to ten centimetres into the peat, smouldered patiently beneath the grass cover and waited for the wind to spark it according to a principle of chance that for days had driven the firemen haphazardly across the plain. Underneath the moss that carries you, along the track that guides you, and with the selfsame goal that should save you, I cling to your heels.

When did the moor begin to burn? What day did the mood turn, and what was the moment you took the decision to go? Your memories of those final weeks blur into a succession of hopeful, often cheerful, hours mixed with the moments you hated Marga. With a hard cut the sunny days turned to frosty nights and the starlit darkness again into glittering morning light, without a pause for breath or the calming boredom of a rainy day they moved onward, staccato-like, towards summer while spring turned into a desert.

She uttered sentences like: *We're building ourselves a palace*, or, with a glance at her coming birthday to which she wanted to invite the whole village: *May makes everything new.* The house truly shone. She filled up buckets, soaped off the furniture and pushed the floor cloth with a light in her eyes that you had never seen before. The mildewed wallpaper was to come down, the linoleum in the kitchen be taken out and replaced with tiles which she herself would paint. She ripped the nicotine-yellow curtains down from their rods and rolled colourful material across the floor, which she then sewed into new ones. She gave you free rein to choose a colour for your room. You spent entire afternoons scraping the wallpaper down, the leafy forest populated by little birds, which, on days you were sick with the flu as a child, you'd tramped through for hours until you had recognized a system in which the motif—double leaf, forked branch, nest, single bird, cooing pair of lovers—repeated at regular intervals. At some point Marga would arrive with new wet compresses or a bowl with grated apple and lead you back out of your fever-jungle.

When you threw tubes of black paint into the shopping cart at the Do-It-Yourself shop in Zeeve, she took charge, the ever-caring mother, not wanting her growing child to have too gloomy a bout with puberty. You, however, wanted your room to be just like Hannes'. Right before leaving the Lambert's, he had painted the wafer-thin wall next to his bed—where all the secret noises were hidden—black. When he was out and about on his moped in the afternoons, you had snuck into his room and sniffed his bedding. You threw his clothes over your head in front of the wardrobe mirror, fingered things which had often gone through his hands: pens and rulers from his desk, a comb with hair, a pair of underwear which had been kicked into the corner, the stack of comic books hidden in the drawer beneath things for school.

The main character who in almost every frame was fighting crooks or jumping acrobatically over cars, was an angularly drawn hero in black boots, a dark blue body suit, briefs and bat-mask; a—so you imagined—blonde, most likely green-eyed boy or young man who you would also have gladly seen without the mask.

You felt his face and then, maybe thanks to a sudden change of the light, it was as if the mask might slip and Hannes emerge, eyes close to each other, chin a rough edge, everything about his body more angular than it was in reality. Downstairs the door opened, and heavy footsteps shuffled over the floor.

Later, stretched out on your bed, you had sniffed your finger but it didn't smell like anything. And yet, in your imagination it had smelt like Hannes, that smell which had been sealed in the wall clung to it, and, unable to breathe it in nor lick it off, after a quick, half-desperate, half-enraged touch you relieved yourself. Over in his room, Hannes turned his music up full blast.

Since having applied the new black colour, even the noise seemed suffocating to you somehow.

Hannes had come to the annual masquerade in the gym dressed as the black knight. Lips painted black, he wore a tight shirt over black Lycra trousers and a blue cloak—he'd likely to have found at a second-hand shop—over his shoulders, its velvety material fascinatedly fingered by all the girls dressed as fairies and witches. Only Daniela, the half-naked belly dancer, crossed her arms and said, 'Total fag.' Hannes stole the jewel from her belly button, held it up into the crowd and bawled, 'Even the stone is fake!' Daniela threw a punch at his face and took off with Yvonne behind her, an androgynous black girl with heavily red-painted lips and shoe polish across her laced-up chest.

While the others were taking their places for the polonaise, Hannes began a kind of pogo, spinning, his arms appearing to conjure up unseen spirits, a seemingly demonic dance. A circle of respect formed around his bent body as it rolled through the gym. Only David Voss, the lion in his mother's ermine coat, now and again unexpectedly fell into the arena and bent himself in similarly ecstatic figures, less out of abandonment than drunkenness; but he was soon pogoed into the corner.

In the past, Marga had always sewn an outfit for you—often in an intoxicated state of daring ideas—so you had already won the prize for the best costume twice. But the box in the Lambert's basement had had nothing more to offer than the worn-out Saint Nicholas' mantle your uncle showed up in every year at the Advent's bazaar, for your new siblings had already snatched up the best costumes. In the end, the sought-after trophy went to the hermaphroditic African and the oriental whore.

There was almost no one standing in front of the stage as the school representative reached for the microphone. The crowd had gathered out in the playground around the blue light which spectrally cast the shadows of the hats and witches' outfits across the walls. It had begun to rain. By the time you battled your way through the brooms, swords and shields to the front, David Voss was already climbing into the ambulance, helped by a paramedic. His face was wracked with pain, his lion's fur on the ground. In between the maintenance man and Knoor, the physics teacher with the clown nose, stood Hannes. He was explaining something with wild movements, the crowd's chatter swallowing up the words. He held his Batman-cloak in his hand, the dye ran out of his coloured hair in dark streams over his face. The maintenance man made a dismissive gesture; Knoor took Hannes by the arm and led him back into the school building. Music echoed from the gym. Halfway there he turned around, and it seemed like he was looking directly at you, but without having to look for you. Then the ambulance came in between. Through the rear window you saw Voss bent

437

on the stretcher. That Hannes had given your tormentor
a lesson filled you with a feeling of satisfaction and an
almost painful one of connection.

The next day at school it was said that Hannes had dislocated David Voss' shoulder in a fight. The eighth
grader had suddenly gone off on the older one, some
said, the other way around, others maintained. Someone
said that they'd seen the two of them earlier out on the
tartan track, amicably toasting one another. You had to
think of the moment the two of them had collided into
each other on the dance floor; there the pogo had
already resembled a scuffle. At one point David had
crashed into the stage in full swing, in the same way as
three months earlier, in the middle of your brawl, Tanja
had fallen down in in the bathroom.

The whispering in the playground stopped when
Hannes appeared at the goalpost. The students lined up
in a row. You pushed yourself a little bit to the front,
out of the line but he avoided you. At lunch he avoided
your looks which sought to defend him from his father
who would not tolerate having a violent criminal in his
house, even his mother was now talking about boarding
school; in the army he could let off steam, but as long
as he was at home, manners and respect for others
would rule. Marianne ordered him to go to the dentist's
house that afternoon and to apologize properly.

'Why don't *you* do that?' Hannes had answered
indifferently, after all, she was still his mother and

responsible for his upbringing. Karl Lambert bent his cumbersome body in a strangely acrobatic way from one end of the table to the other, but the slap had somehow lost its force along the way. Hannes grinned at his father tiredly, then turned to Marianne, 'You see,' he said, 'that's exactly what I mean.' Ole began to cry silently. The very same day Hannes painted the wall black.

The sombre, however, had no place in Marga's new concept of family. It consisted of light green, like young birch trees; she nudged you to the checkout, and one day later was mixing the new colours, the spring look. Little by little you had brought your possessions back from your aunt's and up to your room. As you silently pulled the paint roller over the plaster, Daniel was balanced up on a ladder whitewashing the ceiling and humming along with songs from the radio which he seemed to turn up just as the silence started to become more oppressive. He had rolled up his shirtsleeves, his tendons twitched, his veins jutted out when he stretched. Little white flecks of pigment nestled in the hair which reached all the way to his knuckles; the hair as well as his thick beard were similarly sprinkled. Again and again your glance drifted up to him, crawled into his collar and studied the wiry curls that coiled from his chin down his throat, away over the Adam's apple which protruded sharply and bounced up and down to the rhythm of the melodies. You'd trim your beard the same way, you thought, if the fuzz that was sprouting on your chin and upper lip ever thickened into something you could shave or cut.

Marga came into the room and dispelled the stillness which, in spite of the light-hearted music, still weighed on the room. 'Food for my boys,' she said and brought in salami sandwiches and cola and a bowl with those juicy liquorice snails from the plastic jars in Ilse Bloch's shop, which had always made your mouth water. She placed everything by the stepladder, dipped a brush into the paint tray and dabbed your nose just like how she had used to cockily stick her foaming toothbrush into your ear during your toothbrush wars in front of the bathtub. 'I know what my men need,' she said and Daniel grinned down to you and reached after a piece of bread with sausage. Marga stuck it into his mouth, stood on her tiptoes and spurred him on. He bit after the piece, which she only let him have once he had given a paw, arched his back and wagged his tail, a long-handled brush that went up his back which he had stuffed between his thighs, in so doing, almost falling off the ladder. 'Poor little tomcat,' Marga said and stroked his fur. At first he hissed, then he purred, bit the little woman on her neck and went on to paint the edges of the ceiling.

After the next liquorice snail you began to feel ill. The cola tasted flat, the bright sunlight exposed your work to be a mess, there were trickles and drips everywhere.

Marga was painting Daniel's toenails birch-green and cream-white, then slowly made her way up his calves to his knees and under the edge of his cut-off jeans, before finally pulling him down off the ladder and disappearing with him next door.

Continually rolling the same piece of wall where even after the fourth layer you could still see the dark flecks below, you noticed the spatters and sap of the sauce in the cracked masonry and listened to the soft voices drifting out of the bedroom, a tittering and cooing that, interspersed with irregular pauses, slowly turned into a series of long spread-out sighs which became louder and grew into a cataract-like moan before reaching a climax of mutual cries that immediately ebbed and flowed into the exhausted stillness that reigns in rooms where a child who, having long held out against turning off the light, has finally fallen asleep.

You flung the brush into the bucket and went out into the spring, under the midday sun, which burnt the streaks of paint on your cheeks into imitation tears just like the ones clowns and Pierrots stick under their eyes in their tragicomic pantomimes.

That was all barely four weeks ago. Marga finally seemed healthy again and Daniel was the man who had got her moving once more. He would sprawl about in chairs with his legs open, lie on the sofa reading, or be bent over the junk in the yard he had hauled out of the barn to turn into art, hammering loudly or dancing around with a power drill. What Marga liked to look at was not hidden from you either: the tight muscles, his thin, often dirty or paint-covered hands, the bushy armpits with their cat-like smell, his penis, which would point out of his ratty shorts when, reading the paper at breakfast, he scratched his crotch.

You'd quickly looked away, over to Marga, who was blowing cigarette smoke and waving to you, in silent agreement with what you both saw. Your—at that time—always slightly pinched eyes registered every change: her often uncontrollable movements when she cleared a cup from the table or walked into some corner or other and suddenly froze as if she forgot what she had been looking for; her voice, which sometimes squeaked in a way that you had never heard from her and then unexpectedly broke into laughter; and from that laughter which was just a little too loud the fleeing glance that would suddenly come crashing down on you . . . all of that seemed to belong to another Marga, the autumn mother who had wasted then fallen away from you like a dead leaf from a tree.

Everything that seemed foreign to you about her was duly noted in your new notebook where, instead, you tried to write her back into familiar and reliable forms and patterns of behaviour. But nothing seemed to fit any more; the mother of your memories, which you attempted to tailor on the new Marga from out of a bundle of cut-up sentences, stuck to her like an old dress that had grown too tight.

Even her cigarettes smelt different now. Daniel rolled them for her. He'd sit in the chair, would lick the paper, pull out some tobacco and crush something on top of it that came out of a little box he always carried in his pocket next to his loose change and his motorcycle key. Then they'd inhale, he'd take three, she two drags, and go back and forth continuously. As soon as he'd stamped out the little pasty cigarette, one of those, as Marga called them, *blue* evenings would begin.

The blue feeling arrived as soon as Daniel put on a record. She'd pull him off the couch, get him to dance, he'd let himself be dragged, then she'd punch him away and shake a leg with you until you too stepped on her feet. 'You all want to be guys?' she called, jumped up on the living room table and mimicked a stripper. Blouse and bra flew into the corner. Daniel sprawled out on the cushions and hooted at her, you pelted her with peanut crisps. But before she could undo the zipper of her jeans, Daniel threw his arms around her legs and carried her out of the room.

You put the record player back to the beginning and watched the needle wander from groove to groove as it played the Rock song three, four times in a row, always the same trajectory, until you lifted the arm from the turntable and, the terrible scratching sound at an end, from upstairs heard Marga scream into the silence.

Once all three of you danced together. They took you in the middle, and Marga laid Daniel's arm across your shoulder. 'Come on, don't be so difficult,' she mumbled, from her wry look you couldn't quite understand whether she'd meant you or him. She nibbled at his beard, began to kiss him and all of a sudden forced her lips on you. Daniel became clumsy, let himself be guided, his elbows bore into your back. 'Now you two,' she said and pushed your heads together to kiss. 'You kidding?' he snapped, pushed her away, fell into the chair and took a drink. Marga called him a square, 'You're as repressed as your paintings,' she yelled and tore the wine bottle out of his hand. 'He's your son,' he hissed, and she, 'But you aren't his father!'

On the record player she changed the blues to The Doors and staggered through the room. Jim Morrison sang *Father, I want to kill you, Mother I want to . . .* 'Fuck you!' she shouted with delight in a jarring voice, balled her fists in front of her mouth and imitated the love-crazed groupies, in the end, even collapsed in a corner. Daniel let the resinous and thick smoke stream out of his nostrils, grinned over at you and said, 'Your mother's not all there any more.' He yawned happily, hummed along with the refrain, *This is the end, beautiful friend / This is the end, my only friend, the end,* then the record got stuck. On the floor Marga twitched in time to the rhythm of the endless, cracking loop. You had to think of her convulsions when in autumn she'd vomited on your bed, you went over to her and shook her, *Bluhuu!* she laughed and bit the blue feeling back into your mouth.

You no longer played Klabberjass for 1-pfennig pieces; she demanded larger bets, your allowance jar, Daniel's chequebook, and, when you both refused, your clothes. You ran into your room and then back into the kitchen wrapped up under three sweaters, a shawl and a cap. Marga bent over laughing, then disappeared herself and came back as a kind of Siberian tsarina in a fur coat and stuffed with so many skirts, blouses and scarves that you'd shamelessly yelled out, 'Fat!' She poured a box of musty smelling men's clothing over Daniel. 'Like your father!' she joked, came over to you as he sat there at the table in the old-fashioned things. 'Show me what you got,' she called to him aggressively and grabbed the cards from his claw.

He was the first to be sitting there with his upper body naked while you still had your T-shirt and Marga, sweating underneath the fur, won one hand after another. 'I'm going to get you both naked,' she said, her eyes flashing with a fighting spirit. Or was it already the first glimmer of insanity? 'You can get that sooner,' the tomcat hissed and grabbed the wrong sable from over the table. You had insisted on the rules of the game but they engaged in a brutal cloth-throwing fight before, in the end, simply giving up, she with the fur tail as a whip, he purring about her legs. Tired from the half bottle of beer Marga had let you have, you went to bed but couldn't fall asleep for a long time thanks to the sounds from the room next door, which, with your hands over your ears, you accepted in exchange for that blue feeling of family.

Wake up, boy! I tear you away from such saccharine memories. What does all this toking and fucking have to do with family? The heavy soup at the Lambert's table would've been better for you, would have filled you not only with calories, but with that which makes family truly worthwhile. Stability and unconditional love had never existed at Marga's table, there where a successful everything-soup was the highest expression of feeling.

The helicopter returns, the empty fire-extinguisher canisters attached to cables. But instead of landing on the meadow, it turns. They've given up, I bellow to you, they're leaving the flames to you! You jump up and, in fact, now back on your feet on the horizon see a mushroom of smoke. It grows quickly out of the plain and frays into wisps which slowly rise towards the sun.

The local council is meeting at the mayor's house. Everything, according to the specialists from the fire department, depends on the direction of the wind. Rahse is protected by the meandering of the Jumme, but Fenndorf, on the other hand, is only separated from the nearing fire-front by a few small, hastily flooded ditches which any spark can easily leap over. But they continue to waver. Hope to get the fire under control before the change of weather which has been forecast. But what do their plans, their emergency procedures, mean to me? Just like the winter storm which dismantled the house, I am also a part of the plan which you want to attach yourself to. Dion, get out of here already! There's no going back. When the soil is leached out and the peat can no longer provide, I shall set it all alight and within hours destroy what had been the result of centuries. Nothing is more fertile than a burnt moor. In the nutrient-rich cinders the purple moor grass will be the first to sprout. At the deeper layers the stolons of the bracken will have defied the surface fire, after only a few days small, hard points will begin to point out of the ashes. A stonechat broods over a new clutch. The algae multiplies within the low-lying waters, a pair of Mallards which have come from the Jumme strain the water with their beaks. Rabbits pull up fresh clover in the burnt-off birch woods. After the fire, the plain is even richer in species and greener than it should be.

I sent your mother away beforehand and brought her to safety, to Hamburg; by the time you woke up this morning, she was already gone. The only thing she took with her was the painting she had continuously been working on over the last few days, a masterpiece, she was convinced of it this time too. Between us, Dion, it's not worth a thing. But today she will finally understand that she is as hopeless an artist as she is a mother. Yes,

Dion, she sold your childhood for fifteen thousand marks, which is the sum Karl Lambert paid to her after she had the house and property transferred to him by the notary.

Don't be shocked, don't take it the wrong way, look to the horizon, far and wide nothing but ashes and death. If you stay, soon it will be really dark. Swallow your pain about the break, go ahead and whine about what you would call home, barely having lost it, but it's worthless if you never come back. Vent your anger, write your book, before you suffocate. What do I care about art?

When the noise of the helicopter finally dies away, you sink back onto the stump, exhausted. The desolate view into the distance closes, beneath the alders the pond lies deceptively still, just like the way Marga last painted it. That image is the only thing she saved from fourteen years in Fenndorf, a wild painting in acrylic, the manic confusion of delicate and tiny red strokes a kind of fire, impenetrable even for you who had often seen more in her work than she was comfortable with.

It was a sketch from the heap of discarded works and if the motif hadn't somehow been familiar to you from the beginning, you would never have recognized the pond. At the beginning there was only a scrawled black prong on a white background; you could remember it was the last thing she had finished in autumn before deciding to put an end to it all. Recently, however, she had begun to work on it again as if possessed. Layer upon layer with the thinnest of brushes, at the end even using individual strands of hair she had torn out of her own head, while the centre of the painting, the black bar fraying at the top, had always stayed the same. Then, at some point, you finally recognized what it was: the alder branch.

It had only been a fleeting glance as you went through things in the barn once. At first, the branch floated over the swirl of colours, then, when you looked closer, sank into it. You couldn't establish any clear perspective or fixed point of view through which the painting would have allowed itself to be opened up; you looked ever deeper into the abyss of lines. For the fraction of a second a pair of eyes blinked back, then a mouth, a chin, a dark shock of hair appeared. Finally, the frame dropped out of your hand from fear, but no matter how much you rotated and turned the canvas thereafter, your face—you were sure it had been your reflection—did not reappear.

You look to the point where the branch once was. Without the alder claw, the once-magical space now seems empty. The November storm had broken it off and cast it into the water. If the wind weren't so cold and the water not blacker than usual, you would, you think, even dive in to look for it. Pull the branch out of the deep and hang it back in its rightful place. Re-establish the old times; repair the ruined image of the pond. But do you really think, Dion, that a dead, half-rotten piece of wood can really tell you what you should do now?

The truth is that, since her return, Marga has not gone down to the pond with you because she is not interested in juvenile things any more. She was half a year older again and with all the fat around her thighs, not necessarily any more beautiful: neither the water of the moor nor your childlike gaze had ever made her any younger. She had gone there only one more time but not with you.

Instead of being behind the school desk, early mornings you crouched behind the alders in the hope that, with such nice weather, you might be able to observe a dragonfly moulting; the constant sunshine could have quickened the process in which the young insects—enticed by the rising water temperatures, the light and impact of a never-quite-aired secret—leave the mud. But the sunny days had not made the dragonfly larvae high-spirited and reckless, only your mother. In reality, admit it, the insects didn't matter a thing to you. The yellow, gall-like feeling, your jealousy of Daniel, had guided you away from school and into your hiding place.

She had come with him over the meadow, barefoot as usual. She was wearing her bathrobe, tied sloppily, he was in jeans and a sweater; in her hand the bast fibre bag, which would have been your part. Her hennaed hair ablaze in the glare of the low-lying sun, she put it into a ball and tied it with the hair clip. As she awkwardly and prudishly made her way into the water, he sat on the stump smoking and driving her on.

You had ducked into the undergrowth behind leftover leaves. As always, she swam her usual round; from the bank to the mouth of the drainage ditch, which was already dry, along the roots where the sun scared the shadows out of the hollows, then on her back and with sweeping arms towards the middle of the pond, which she reached precisely although the branch no longer stretched out over it and steered her. There she held still like always and called, 'If you want to be a man, get on in here!'

You had crouched even deeper into the brush; had she meant you or Daniel? Her hair slid out of the clip, her eyes flickered in the bright light that burnt the silhouette of her body into the water. The way she was floating there, the strands of her hair like brown algae around her face, her flat, pale bottom, her downward protruding limbs, fin-like in the warp of the water, for a moment she really looked like the white ray from your natural encyclopedia, waiting for its prey. She turned onto her stomach and looked to the bank. Now he was standing between the rushes, taking off his shorts, made no attempt to hide anything. His winter-white body was filled with hair from his neck down, between his legs it was black, bushy. You had always had to look to the alders when your mother was naked, but now the perspective had changed. Another had taken your place. Only the trees were aware of the mistake in the picture. They stood silent and all knowing; you were mesmerized.

He descended into the water. As he swam out to her, she egged him on, called out phrases which, in light of the stillness that had always reigned over the pond, seemed rather shameless. He circled around her, grabbed after her, but she kept him at bay, playfully and temptingly in a kind of courtship dance until he grabbed her by the calves, pulled her thighs over his shoulders and buried his face into her lap. She stretched out her head and dipped it back into the water, her laugh gurgling. From somewhere an alder shadow pushed itself over her. The movements became blurred, here an arm darted out, there a foot, bubbles rose. When she came back into the light, he was gone. She continued to lap at the water for a few seconds, rattled by the last laughs, gasped, 'You passed the test.' Then she went silent and stared into the depths. The reflection of the sun swam an arm's length; next to her, a flickering, white sliver.

It was now so still you thought that she could hear your breath, the hammering of your heart. The snap of a twig under your shoe gave you away but she didn't look over, simply swam to where the branch had once hung and stirred the strip of sunlight, which would not be wiped away, into the water.

You felt yourself turning to stone. Had she pushed him under? Lured him to the water for that very reason, just like she'd once done to your father? And was it not Karl Lambert but she who had him on her conscience? She didn't want any man at all, not until the very end. No one would ever lead her by the hand only to betray her and leave her when she was old and ugly. And so now too Daniel had to go down into the mud. It was immediately clear to you why the stump had always been your favourite place at the pond; your father's gravestone, this is how everything was coming together in your mind, the remains of an alder tree that he had felled as a symbol for the future, the happiness of his family. But her goal had been to remain beautiful, young and free; guys were free to come and enjoy her, but then had to disappear as soon as the meat began to taste bitter.

You were not yet at the stump when Daniel shot up out of the water, puffing and snorting. He climbed up onto shore, spit a few times, shot you an annoyed glance and wheezed, 'What're you doing here?' You quickly grabbed the bag and handed him a towel. He must have been under for one, maybe two minutes, long enough for you to have thought about his death. Marga swam back, trudged through the rushes, pushed you to the side and snatched the towel out of his hands. 'Very funny,' she hissed, ripped the clip out of her hair and launched it into the water. Then she grabbed his jeans and squeezed herself into them. When she threw his sweater over herself, the arms hit you in the face.

'Hey!' he yelled and spun her around. She punched him in the chest, the sound muffled by the tree trunks. He fell onto the grass, laid there with a lopsided grin. 'Is this what you've always wanted?' Marga asked you, and only because of this glance which applied neither to him or to you but went out onto the water or into the emptiness above it where there no longer was any branch, you later understood why that same day she had begun to paint this picture in which the alder claw drowned you in the burning pond.

'How'd you manage to live with her for so long?' you heard Daniel snort while you stared at her until she had disappeared in the yard. When you finally turned around, he was sitting on the stump, shivering, knees pulled up, the towel around his shoulders. You threw him the bathrobe. He grunted, put it on, tied the knot and stretched his feet out towards you. You recognized his toes and their black bushy tufts, the little bearded men, the dirty edges under the nails their grinning mouths, five of them in the window of their slanted, chapped house. They wiggled their heads and waved at you. You were now very sure that these men-feet, which were one of your only memories of early childhood, had belonged to your father, and if not him, then a man who could have been a father.

'Why does she do that?' he asked; you just shrugged your shoulders. You had never got any closer to the why; how and what had always been the pressing questions; *how* will you get her to open her eyes again, breathe, smile, and *what* will you tell Marianne who you had to wake up in the middle of the night, how should you call it, and what's to be done, those were your concerns when back in that autumn she had died in your hands.

He pulled you close to him. 'She should start taking her pills again, tell her that!' His voice now sounded jealous, dulled by a feeling that he had no right to be so, and with those thoughts in your head you had torn yourself away. 'It's all a bit much for her,' he added, when he saw your doubtful face. Then he spoke about the clinic's success rate which she had to uphold, and that they had pretty regularly run electricity through her head in order to get her back to normal. He pressed his fingertips into his temples and hissed a sound that was supposed to resemble electricity.

So he had been allowed to visit her while they kept you away from her with excuses. In the end, was it perhaps not the doctor who had driven all these strange expressions into her but him? 'I've known her for a long time,' he said, as if he had read your mind. He believed in her talent but she would have to decide what she wanted to do with all this, and with a vague gesture indicated the pond, the house and you. 'I'll gladly help her with that,' he added and came close to you again. 'But she trusts you a lot more. You know her better. Make sure she takes those damn pills!' he said and shook you, then suddenly seemed to laugh at himself and punch you chummily in the shoulder; he must have read the plea in your eyes.

'Ha,' he said, 'But don't start calling me Dad. I'm your friend, get it?' He stood up, pulled the bathrobe tighter, grinned once more about the cross-dressing. 'Come on, soldier,' he nudged you, 'time to go back into battle.'

That's when you gathered all your courage. Today the sentence seems to you to be the most difficult that you had ever had to say. You stared at the pond for a long time, then suddenly took a deep breath and with the help of the wind coming from the plain asked whether it was true that she would soon be having a child. Already halfway through the sentence Daniel had understood what you wanted to say; his face slid out of shape. That was just another quirk of hers, he brushed it off, 'What kind of ideas has she put into your head?' At the moment he was focused on totally different things. People were ripping—these were in fact his words—his paintings out from under his ass, a situation he had to take advantage of and had to get away from canvas and paper and onto new shores, more modern ones, more radical ones, closer to life, painting had long been too elitist, dead, could you understand that at all? He grabbed your arm again, but you had already stopped listening and, as before by the alders, once again were frozen. Was it disappointment or simply emptiness now?

Something definitive, irrevocable began to spread through you like a crippling poison, a kind of unconsciousness you recognize from the last day of holidays when you realize that summer's promises had not been fulfilled. But even flatter and more unsuccessful was the by-now green feeling when it became utterly clear to you that there was never going to be a family.

'Don't you have to go to school?' Daniel asked, let go of you abruptly and went across the meadow to the house, white clothes wafting just like the mother once upon a time with her child.

Do you really still believe, Dion, that a baby would have saved you all? It wasn't only his father, she'd also given short shrift to you after the dream of having a family had definitively gone out. Think back to the evening before the trip to Holland; the whole day you had consoled and supported her, which was actually Daniel's job, but that very week he had had to go to Munich for the vernissage of his new exhibition, which promised both success and money.

He had sent the five hundred marks with an express messenger, signature required, which you had provided. She was weary of leaving the kitchen, so at first the courier didn't want to hand over the envelope to you; why couldn't your mother take it from him personally, she was, most likely, at home, and he had stretched his head into the hallway curiously, the whole thing unnecessary, embarrassing, and, even for someone who didn't stutter, the word would have got stuck when all of a sudden she was standing behind you, laying her hands on your shoulders and ordering the postman with her eyes to hand you the letter. 'If you knew what this money was for,' she said, 'you wouldn't even wipe your ass with it.' The envelope in your hand was stuffed full; you hadn't believed the thing would be so expensive.

Your ticket had been calculated in the price. It would even have been enough for the promised side trip to the seaside because Daniel had added another one hundred, a tribute to his guilty conscience. In the afternoon, she had stood up on the chest of drawers, agitated, and called Holland. Daniel had got the number for her through Ute Hassforther. With her finger she twisted a strand of hair taut up until right before her skull, hissed a sound of pain or insult, whereby she looked at you and nodded. Would someone definitely be waiting for her? She asked the person at the other end of the line, who apparently spoke German, the train could be delayed. She seemed to be happy with the answer, hung up, dialled again. Now she seemed to be connected with information and was asking to be connected with the tourist office in Groningen. Again the person seemed to understand German as she asked about accommodation, a double room, yes, she waved over to you, wrote down a number, said at the end, '*Tot ziens*.' Once again the rotary dial rattled. Now she was twisting a lock of hair from the other side of her head; unwashed, it hung in greasy strands, no longer brown, not yet blonde again, you couldn't find a name for that which was barely a colour, this woman on the telephone hardly had anything to do with your mother.

The other one you found that evening slumped out on the landing, a burnt-out cigarette between her fingers crinkling ash, you just wanted to get rid of. You touched her shoulder, and the ashes fell off onto her bathrobe. Although her face was very pale, something within it seemed to burn; was it the red eyes that gave her that fiery, inflexible expression, the fever-like, sharply delineated spots on her cheeks, like a just-bloomed eruption, or the hair with its noxious copper hue, which framed this image of misery?

You could have simply taken off. Finally got away from her, hThat's henough, hgoodbye hMom! You could have lasted a few weeks with the money that Daniel had sent. The bills lay strewn across the floor, poured out of the packed travel bag between clothes, toilet articles and a book that you wanted to read in the train. In the living room, the record-player speakers boomed, in the last few hours over and over again the same song *This is the end, my only friend* an endless loop.

Now the record, which had been broken in two, was wobbling on the turntable, one edge brushing the needle, making little explosive sounds. Your hands simply did not want to open when you commanded them to let go of Marga, to run back up the stairs, she should just stay there until she rots! She sobbed without any tears and with a dry voice that swelled up, for a moment lowered then faded, like those of the cats which would howl out on the Heidedamm once night had come, drawn out its mournful sounds.

You pulled her foot off the floorboard and pressed it onto the next step. 'I don't want to,' she protested, her heel slid out again. She couldn't do it, no one could expect that of her. 'hWhat?' you yelled and punched her ankles. What was it exactly that she suddenly no longer seemed able to do, it couldn't be the stairwell with its few steps? Ridiculous! Even the procedure which was scheduled for the following day was in reality a piece of cake, that birth on the other hand much riskier, she had herself quoted the doctor who, like all Dutch abortionists and abortionist assistants, seemed to have a perfect command of German.

The cold flesh shivered in your hand, the wrack, you thought, the whole mother a heavy, unmovable monster, her child tugging at her, telling her he only wanted to help, the millstone around her neck. She shook you off, continued to snivel, spit out insults and threats, but it didn't seem to you that she meant you any longer, but someone else, an absent one, Daniel maybe, who'd left her hanging, all the men who had ever snubbed her, you really didn't know all that she had gone through with you, and the thing in itself was not immoral, only the way that people treated women like her in Germany who could not afford the three hundred marks, and she reached for a bill on the floor.

'That's how much money, darling,' she suddenly whispered, almost tenderly, and laid her hand on your cheek, 'you cost me every month,' and could you even imagine what it would mean for her and for you to have to take care of two children, forget studying, you could get out into the fields and bring home your pay each and every day, and she grabbed you by the shoulders and shook you, 'for thee hundred marks a month, your aunt will probably take you back,' and she threw the bill into the air before slumping down.

'Then come down!' The words came out without any hitch at all, barely more than a whisper, only a bit out of breath, with a moment of panic thereafter, two, three seconds long until over in the living room the record finally turned again and its broken edge went against the needle and shattered the silence; then you let go of her. The next moment she would fall over backwards and apart, the child in her stomach along with her, then you wouldn't have to go to Holland and would even have saved some money. 'No!' she yelled, grabbed your shoulder and steadied her whole weight against you. She wouldn't do you the favour and did you really want to leave her alone now? The doleful tone had disappeared from her voice, she spoke clearly, even a little bit threateningly.

How quickly she changes sides when you don't obey! She took your face into her hands and pressed it to her breast. In spite of everything, she smelt the same as always. When you dared to breathe again, the memories had covered over the bitter aftertaste of her words. She sucked in her lips, bent her back, played the helpless old woman, demanded the pantomime. You didn't like her any more, she mumbled and stuck her nose in your ear, while wrapping your arms around her thighs where they hung down into the abyss of the deepness of the stairs that pulled you downward as if your body had suddenly liquefied, without muscles or bones, a membranous sleeve filled with gloomy thoughts and blurry sensations, a frail child's body in pyjamas, you sunk back into her arms.

Who had pulled whom onto the stairs? Even weeks later there is still this bubble inside your head, which had suddenly surrounded the two of you, a dark filter covering the movements which had forced you onto the steps, a reciprocal pushing, maybe a quick battle, blurry, heavily and strangely slowed down, as if underwater. She was sitting on top of you, legs spread, her hands clenching your underarms, a position you'd often seen in scuffles out on the playground when the stronger one won. 'You won't be able to get rid of your old mother,' she laughed, or did she whimper it again, her voice suddenly sounding strange, she had now completely become the other who had absorbed and annihilated the rest of the Marga you had always known.

You wrenched your head out of her clasp, you had long given up. Her chest pressed against your face, her breath burnt in your ear, scratched at the delicate place on your throat. The edge of the stair dug into the small of your back, a gradually expanding pain that split your body into two halves; while your arms continued to flare, from your pelvis downward you already felt paralysed, as if your body would suddenly end with your trunk, there where she had begun to finger. If you had pushed her ankles over the edge of the step, which was balancing her whole weight, you would have got rid of her. Just the smallest movement, automatic, a reflex to the thrust of her hand between your closed legs which you did not want to open. Not give her what it was she was grabbing after, keep it small, retract it, squeeze it away, she hissed, 'Don't make a fuss!'

In her hand you saw the small, wrinkled thing, wormlike like, a rolled-up larva that you dug up out of the deepest earth. Now she would lay it in her lap where it was supposed to thrive and then hatch, pro- tected and warmed by her stomach which, arched over you, all of a sudden did seem somewhat fat, swollen with water that had backed up in the air bladder of her womb and could no longer flow so that they would have to cut her open to make sure that the child would not drown inside her, the one they would save at the right moment, with the tube, she had explained to you, they would simply vacuum it away, the body, amniotic fluid, the moor water, a small, white, ray-like creature inside, pump out the still blind little eyes in the lumpy head, hands and feet like tiny flippers into the tubes and you'd looked down the stairs, just four until the floor, barely a metre. Earlier, when you were still very small, you had found the depth to be threatening, had wished that she would take your hand and lead you. 'Do you like me again?' she whispers and right before it plunges, the child screams, 'hMama, hno!'

Naturally, she hadn't been interested in the little trip to the sea any more. On the way back, the train was stopped in the middle of the track for a long time because of engine failure; at the border station their connecting train was gone. By the time they finally got off the bus in Fenndorf, it was already dark. She quickly buttered a few slices of bread in the kitchen, pushed you the plate, 'Eat,' she ordered and poured herself a glass of wine, it had been a stressful day. You held out a piece to her, she shook her head, watched you chew, then with a quick movement did in fact steal it, bit her signature into it, gave it back and smiled at you for the first time in days.

'Tomorrow there'll be everything-soup with pork,' she said, and even her voice—from which the hard, clashing tones had disappeared—gave you hope that everything would once again be as it was. She stood up and cleared the dishes although you hadn't yet finished. She had to be alone for a bit now, she said, suddenly reproachfully as if you had been too much of a strain on her during the trip. Without a glance or goodnight kiss she was out of the kitchen, teetering a little. You followed her at her heels, half-angry, half-afraid that she wouldn't be able to make it up the stairs again. In front of her bedroom she abruptly turned around, looked at you tiredly and said, 'What do you still want?' She went inside and pulled Daniel's bed linens off the right-side mattress under the window. She threw the pile into your arms, then, as if she regretted the brusque gesture, tousled your hair, which, at that moment, made you particularly hate her. You disappeared between her and the doorframe and hurled the bedspread back onto the mattress. She laughed out loud, now there was definitely a glassy tone in her voice, and her movements also seemed too quick: she came closer, built herself up, took a deep breath as if at any moment she would start to scream, then grabbed you by the neck, pulled you to her, almost pressed her mouth to yours, only a millimetre of distance between you where her breath stopped. She couldn't take any of it any longer, she said softly. The sentence surged into your mouth, it tasted sour and old, but familiar from distant, black, almost forgotten feelings, the memory of her collapse back in fall—was it starting all over again?

The Dutchman, you thought. The stranger she had met in Groningen. Just someone she had spoken to and for that reason had got his telephone number. If Daniel wasn't going to be around, then the two silently agreed you would turn the Dutchman into a father; he'd be your brother's step-father, that brother you wanted so badly to be back in her womb at any price.

On the way from the station to the clinic, she had stopped in front of a cafe. 'Weeping German women attract attention here,' she said and pointed to her troubled reflection in the large glass window behind which you could see young people sitting shoulder to shoulder. She blew her nose, ordered you to wait outside and went in. You leant against a street sign and observed the chatting groups of people standing around in the doorway. Ten minutes later she still hadn't returned. The appointment had been scheduled for one o'clock, your wristwatch showed ten minutes till. There was a lot of traffic in the street, pedestrians hurried past, no one paid any attention to you. You listened to the snippets of conversations, the sizzling and shuffling sounds of a foreign language that you assembled into rows of letters with soft consonants only. Would you stutter in Dutch too? you asked yourself. Every movement of the heavy glass door startled you. You almost did not recognize her next to the large, blond man. She was wearing make-up and had had her hair done, when she looked over to you the sun reflected in the lenses of her black sunglasses. The man bent down, whispered something in her ear, she laughed, gave him her hand and said loudly, '*Tot ziens*.'

You spoke the word again in your head, with German consonants it sounded more angular and harder, more like a call to slaughter: *Tott Zzienz*! She came over to you, pulled you away from the metal pole, took your hand and said, '*Let's leave it behind us*,' in an exaggerated Dutch accent so that only a few seconds later you understood what she'd said. You continued to turn the word around in your head, again and again until it sounded just as smooth as the singsong of the fragments flying to you from the people passing by who now all turned their heads to curiously look at the German mother with her young lover by her side following her into the abortion clinic while from all sides the whisper *Tot ziens*! and, in fact, that evening you found a crumpled-up piece of paper in her handbag with a long telephone number, a foreign dialling code and a quickly scribbled salutation: *See you soon*!

The countdown is on, the time bomb is ticking, a siren wails in the distance. They are clearing all the buildings on this side of the Jumme, the Kliewe farm and the lumber warehouses, for the wind has changed direction. The sun is still standing powerfully at midday, the villagers are at their tables or bent over their work, no one is looking towards the pond, no one would see you; the moment, Dion, is advantageous. Your wristwatch shows just a bit before one o'clock. Your bus is leaving in fifteen minutes from the church square. If, as planned, you want to get on two stops later at the fork in the road in

Pellhof where there isn't ever anyone waiting, you'll have to get going. What are you procrastinating for? You have already thought through, ordered and considered the relevant consequences of your decision.

But it's better to make sure one last time with a final glance. Over there the plain, the grass, the breaks and birches, the low-lying water and mounds, the monotonous up and down of the lines, unchanged throughout all the years, forever the same from your place on the stump, green, brown and only sometimes red in an unspectacular blooming, sometimes bare, sometimes in leaf, full of figures in the fog and invisible behind the walls of rain: the moor as you know it.

You turn your eyes away from the horizon. Stand up, shoulder your knapsack, turn around.

Hold on, Dion, haven't you forgotten something?

You hesitate but nothing, no one gives you a sign. Eventually you fish the pack of cigarettes out of your jacket. Lighter tucked in between the filters. That had numbed you with fear; in her anger she forgets everything: the key to the font door, her wallet, the post at the agency where you had had it sent, she'd even forgotten you one whole winter long. But when she hasn't given a thought to her smokes, then her state must truly be life threatening.

You sniff the tobacco, stick a filter between your lips. Flick the lighter. The death-addicted grass crackles underneath your shoes. You puff at your first cigarette just like she did: your two fingers spread, a quick glance at the end, then the energetic inhale. The smoke bites at your throat, takes your breath away, tears shoot into your eyes. Whatever was it that she saw in all of this? You wonder and spit a few times. As an adult at some point you will loathe all smokers, but now with the second drag the cigarette already tastes like her; her mouth, the goodnight kiss, like childhood.

After the third cloud of smoke your lungs no longer hurt, the tickling in your throat is gone, your head feels loose and wide, your body drunk, your steps bounce over the ground; the floating bog mats had never been so wobbly as they were on that, your last trip back to the village. Behind you, where you had tossed the butt into the grass, a blade snuggles up to the ember.

What you remember of spring? A sky that continued to glow long after sundown, the horizon fire-yellow and orange, merging into the mother-of-pearl emptiness of the zenith and slowly drowning itself in the inky night-blue of the east where it suddenly went out only to ignite once more eight hours later.

Half-green walls at home, open cans of paint in between, filming over, crusty brushes that no one wanted to clean up.

The insanity of strokes on Marga's painting; a red which began to harass you, grew more aggressive every day since the time you understood that it had gone that far again; she had once again given up being a mother.

Daniel's face, in which you could no longer detect anything father-like at all, which was now only a mug, hard and always with the same offended expression as if cut into wood.

Her mouth had begun to gnaw at you again ever more often, the less often it was turned to Daniel, the more vehemently it went for yours, mostly when the other had turned her away. And then it tore open, distorted into a pair of jaws, spit out cruelty or rumbling laughter when Daniel persisted in trying to find a *solution*, and Marga, suddenly lipless, would answer, 'If you are looking for a solution, what exactly is the problem?'

Her goodnight kiss, which was no longer short and sharp but long and searching, halted breath and probing tongue. The nights when Daniel stayed in Hamburg, she would crawl under your blanket, pull your hand out from under her back and place it on her stomach. That you had to stay with her, that she was now counting on you, he couldn't give you a brother, it wouldn't be his child, and she caressed your underarm and stared into the darkness.

Her body beneath your hand haggard since she had yet again begun to hardly eat anything, simply drag at her cigarettes hurriedly, push the crumbs back and forth with her fork and take long drinks from the wine bottle which Daniel once ripped out of her hand. 'That way you'll ruin yourself too,' he had yelled, and poured the rest into the sink. 'This time it won't cost you anything,' she answered, stood up, went to the cupboard and slammed the next bottle onto the table, which no one opened.

Boys' names she whispered into your ear: Demian, Robert, Victor, no, she didn't want a Victor, no warrior-types but, rather, a soft dreamer like you. She ran her hand through your hair, which by now you accepted, you didn't bother to pull your hand out from between her thighs any more either, the moist embrace. For a long time she said nothing and then, 'Leon,' what you believed to hear in your sleep, 'Dion and Leon,' it echoed through your dream, two, three times in a row, first the one, then the other name out of the house and over to the pond where she had already begun to swim.

She stops beneath the branch, reaches into the water and pushes something down into the deep, which, if it could surface, you imagine would be black and intact, nameless, never before seen, something long forgotten, conserved in the peat. 'Dion and Leon', the echo once more from the house where Marga is suddenly standing in the yard and waving at the pond which now lies quiet and red between the rushes, shaded with ripples and the rays of the morning sun trembling through the alder leaves and which for the fraction of a second sketch your face on the water. 'Dion and Leon!' she yells and parts the rushes, in the claw of the branch the dead child.

By the time you started up from your dream with a cry, she was gone. You thought you could hear a whimper from the other room; you carefully pushed open the door. She was rolled up next to Daniel who must have come back late from the city. Her face was pale, and her mouth was not distorted by crying, but pretty, almost smiling in the moonlight, or was the room actually dark, and you only hung the moon into your memories later on?

In this light you see Daniel jerk when you move up to the bed and the floor creaks. You duck down behind the footboard but he does not wake up, just turns to the side, closer to her. Now she threatens to wake up. Her mouth, upon which only the shadow of a strand of hair had drawn a smile, curls up, you hold your breath. She grumbles something, stretches her legs, turns over and continues sleeping, her face now at the same height as his, between their eyes which are turned towards one another an arm-length of darkness, soft, warm and inviting there between their bodies, as if made for a child.

You climb onto the bed and lay down between them. He puffs, she mutters, they come closer and reach their hands out towards each other, groping your shoulder until they interlock and then one pulls you into her arms from the left, the other from the right. She presses her chest to you, he his pelvis, she shoves her hand between your thighs, he lays his heavy knee onto your penis. They seek out each other's lips, they crawl over your cheeks from both sides and find each other on your mouth where you first steal her, then his, kiss. Just before their contact breaks apart and each sinks back into their lonesome sleep, you stick your tongue into the chaos of skin and beard, lover and beloved, father and mother.

Perhaps, the boy in your book thinks: This is truly my family; not the being-together at the dinner table, a sister locking you into a chicken coop and a brother kicking a football into your stomach, no portrait the village rooms or yards had ever seen, but she on the one side, he on the other, and ME in between, held by the two of them and caressed, at that moment for the first time ever—loved.

They both woke up at the same time. Another two, three seconds, you write, her face was the old familiar one again, the one you knew from her goodnight or morning kiss directly before or after sleep. Then it cracked, starting with the mouth as if from a crevice.

She began to laugh, at first in slow, convulsive shudders, then louder, more clankingly, until she fell onto her back and writhed beneath the salvos. Daniel pushed you away and leapt out of the bed. You think you can remember him standing naked on the runner, staring down at you both disgustedly, suddenly grabbed her by

the hair, pulled her and seethed, 'You fucking bitch!'—
which only encouraged her. She was gripped by such a
shrill sound that you could no longer hold back either.

You had no other choice. The only possibility of making
it out of that moment was to agree to laugh Daniel to
death, to become her accomplice. In your book, you
write of such an infectious and rampant laugh eating
its way through your body, like an aggressive virus
caught through a tiny drop of spit, destroying everything that had still felt good and right in your three-
way embrace.

Daniel pulled the blanket away, which made your
laughter turn into a blood-curdling screeching. Then the
outbreak began to trail off, her moaning slowly became
softer—you didn't know any longer, so it says in your
book, whether she was still laughing or had already
begun to cry.

From that moment on you did not feel anything else.
Your insides a pile of ashes, as if after a blaze, annihilating and liberating at the same time. At some point
you both left each other and turned on your backs, each
on their own half of the bed where, just like a pair of
lovers after climaxing, for a while you lay sweating and
quivering until you fell asleep.

She pulled you to her, pressed her hot face against your throat and dozed off. For some time you had listened to the darkness with throbbing temples, maybe ten minutes long, until behind the din of blood in your veins you could hear the sounds of the night—the wind through the ivy on the wall of the house, the irregular flapping of the tarpaulin which still hung from the scaffolding around the attic, outside in the plain the cat-like scream of a short-eared owl, from your room the creaking of the slatted frames soon followed by Daniel's snoring, in between again the wind, the bird, your mother breathing into your ear and eventually nothing more, only my voice, which slowly sank into your dream.

The pond lies abandoned, no one there to disturb the play of light and shade on the water, no one sees a face, no hand. The boughs are dead or sprouting, the stones bake in the sun, the larvae crawl through the mud, roots jut out every which way. The rushes are straight then bend slightly to the east, followed by the thinner branches. A few leaves swirl up. The sun stands high up in its white hole. The stump cannot remember who once sat upon it. The desiccated pillows of moss will turn green again after the next rains, someone will bore their finger into them and find the caress tender. The sky is a bright blue and open. No clouds, no smoke on the horizon, not a single helicopter in the air. You are already on the Landstraße when the tiny flame whips out of the grass.

At a certain point you had really seen a fire from the moped. Where Hannes had laid off the gas, and the Landstraße abruptly swings to the right after having run dead straight along the dyke for kilometres. Behind the little pinewoods through whose porous rows you could see into the shimmering bands of moor grass, in between dark mounds, sometimes a small, deep sunken stream, flashing for a moment in passing and then blurred out by the waving coniferous trees at the edge of the embankment which guides one around the plain in a wide arc, then, at the end of the curve, almost in the opposite direction again as if the street would indeed turn into the area only to bend once more to the left, at the last moment, where the first rifts in the earth below the embankment begin, to the west in the direction of the Jumme, you look around.

Grassland behind you, a whiskered, silvery flickering band between the trees strung to the rigid horizon line with the pale, in the dusty air slightly tremulous edges of Fenndorf's church tower. Here, seen from this end, the moor seems a lot smaller than from the other side, at its entrances behind the alders at the pond when, on your forays, after just a few hundred metres, your village already lay out of sight, and you were soon the only human being in an uninhabited and pathless wilderness, just an optical illusion maybe, you now think, as Hannes suddenly turns and your eyes lose themselves in the woods.

He steers the moped into a tunnel-like lane. It instantly turns gloomy and cold. You have never been afraid of dark woods or unmarked paths before, you know the uncomfortable feeling only from the playground or in the middle of the loud games at the swimming spot. You cling to the luggage rack which cuts into your fingers with its sharp metal edges.

Already a few kilometres from the bus stop your hands had begun to hurt, but you didn't trust yourself to loosen your grip or even to put your arms around Hannes, your head between his shoulder blades to protect yourself from the wind as you'd often seen the girls from the Tenth Grade do when evenings they stood by the little waiting shed where their boyfriends would pick them up. Only once, when the moped stayed even along the Landstraße, did you let go, balancing the swaying with your upper body you even stretched out your arms a little, in the excitement of speed a sudden happiness which was at the same time a feeling of fear; aware of the danger, so close to Hannes, you surrendered to him, his way of driving, a destination that only he knew, a blue feeling, deep and open as the sky which, when you looked upward, raced past without changing, only becoming ever-bigger, ever-emptier, the further you got from Fenndorf.

The thoughts of Marga which had previously weighed so heavily upon you fluttered away, were now more like the tree trunks flying past in an irregular staccato, hard, black cuts before an endless space of light, seen, thought, forgotten. And if Hannes were to take a sharp curve or, thanks to a sudden bump, toss you from the moped, and your head hit the asphalt—because you are not wearing a helmet—what would she do? Where would she look for you? Would she even cry at all if you were dead? And you began to see yourself from above, out of this blue, completely open and completely homeless feeling; you raised your arms higher and slowly turned your palms outward but then Hannes suddenly hit the brakes.

The moped careened over the slope. Your head hit the helmet, you unwillingly grabbed his shoulders. Where the path ends in the undergrowth, he puts his foot down on the ground so that you both don't tip over. You knead your fingers, which have become quite stiff, you'd held on so tightly. This is your place. Here you will touch him for the first time just like you had always imagined. The path lies hidden behind the trees. It ends at a pile of treetops, torn branches, the remains of the winter storm, a pile of earth. The ground is torn up, trenches and ruts lead here and there, young grass grows in the tracks the excavators have left behind. You could hunker down here. The wood will no longer be picked up. Those who had worked here hardly remembered where it was any more. It was a place like any other off the side of the road.

Only deer or the Heidschnucke sheep that, thanks to the danger of the fire, had already been sent into stalls a long time ago, might cross the slender cattle track that led deeper into the thicket. But now the two of you would follow it, one after the other, here to the right, there to the left, with lowered heads, your hands which want to go to the other still dug into your pockets until your steps grow slower, your fists sweaty and one of you grabs the other. There are still ways through the moor that you are unfamiliar with.

But he doesn't get off the bike. He remains motionless in the seat, hand on the throttle as if he wanted to immediately start the moped again, and only when you follow his eyes do you once more see smoke behind the jumble of pines. He crawls over the peat to where the brush opens. Above it the plain glitters, hardly a ray gets through. As soon as Hannes turns off the motor it becomes very quiet. Somewhere the rushing of wind, or the noise of traffic. Now you see smoke at another spot, a dull speck between the flashing stalks then all of a sudden a number of sooty specks, but still quite far away.

'I'm going to go put something out,' he says, swings himself off the moped and presses the handlebars into your hand. The front wheel flops to the side, the machine threatens to slide away from between your legs. You dig your heels into the soft earth which is covered by pine needles, but do not find any footing. If you fall over now, and the thing with you, he'll think you're a weakling; then, with one push, he had the moped jacked up. His hand, for a moment on yours, is dry and raw. He takes off his helmet, hangs it on the bars, runs a hand through his hair.

'Be back in a second.' The touch begins to cool on the back of your hand, a lifeless, oppressive feeling; why didn't you hold on to him? You should have grabbed him immediately when he picked you up at the bus stop, simply put your arms around him; then the motor started up again, 'Okay, let's go!' You remember how the girls would shove their hands under their boyfriends' jackets from behind, would wriggle through the mess of material until reaching their naked stomachs. Hannes had been on his way to Zeeve, supposedly on the way to visit a friend. But the backpack he pulled off the luggage rack and tied to the handlebars seemed to have been a bit too full for a simple afternoon visit.

Twigs snap under his feet as he begins to investigate the stacks of wood. He glances back, stops, then takes a few more steps back towards you. He doesn't look at you, but you know that his gaze includes you. You feel the moped beginning to slip from between your legs again, the heavy backpack falls to the ground. The tangle of branches and trunks, the erratic gusts of wind, the drifting smoke make the image hazy and blurred, your eyes cannot find a place to rest anywhere. Now you think you can smell the smoke, resinous as fir logs in the fireplace. And then he is standing by your side, looking out to the burning field, and only when he unzips his fly do you understand what he'd meant by *put something out*.

But he doesn't pee. He just stands there, tugs at his belt, digs the tips of his shoes into the ground and kicks the wood to the side, as if wanting to create a place for the two of you. Now you too feel the pressure on your bladder once again, like you had earlier at the fork in the road to Pellhof, there where you didn't trust yourself to go behind the waiting shed, when he suddenly came through the curve in the road. You tighten your abdominal wall, back on the road a car rushes past, for a split second its body flashes in the sun. No one would see if he suddenly tore your legs out from under you, put you in a headlock behind the woodpile. Not a soul looks into the woods here. The curve in the road is dangerous; everyone is familiar with the wooden crucifix standing at the embankment, it is always decorated with fresh flowers although the Mayor of Rahse's son has been dead for over five years. If Hannes decided to finish you off here, you'd be lost. You'd lie there in some brake, possibly unconscious. That's why you only gave a quick glance over to him; you only wanted to see how he held it and why the stream of urine was divided again, like back at the slurry tank. 'Don't look at my cock, you fucking faggot!' he snarls, then strikes.

For a long time the rattling of the motor continued to hang in the air. You cannot stand up because of the pain; you crawl across the ground, the woodpile suddenly steep and tall. While trying to make your way around to the other side, you see the wave of flames rolling towards you from out of the underbrush, sparkling pine branches at its crest. Below, in the glow, pine cones pop and burst.

What's with all this shit, Dion? Hannes is no thug, he's only a bone-breaker and sadist in your darkest dreams and even the death of the cats at the slurry tank was nothing but the product of your imagination, an unfortunate accident just like everything else you make your cousin responsible for. The cats had been doing gymnastics on the board that was stretched over the edge of the tank and fell in because of the weight, that's the vile truth. Even the most hardened of people would never go willingly into the wastewater hole which, bubbling and foaming from the oxygen that's pumped in, supposedly to speed fermentation, would swallow up even the best swimmer. Was Hannes supposed to have risked his life for a few animals that no one needed? He had done what he could to save the unloved children from the hired hand's shovel.

Just last week you saw him in the moor, there by the meadow near Kleenze where the milk farmer's cows graze. Although there was no path through the plain leading up to the fence, he had come with his moped. It had been propped up in front of a field of ferns. You had followed its tracks which wound from the pond through the grass mats. Snakelike, sometimes through a dip, dust-white with dried mud, avoiding the higher mounds, it single-mindedly ran close to the fences; Hannes seemed to know his way around the pathless part of the moor just as well as you.

He was crouched down in the grass and waving his hands as if trying to scare off some insects. Then you heard the mournful cries, and once you had carefully unscrewed yourself out of the bog myrtle, in slow motion, so that there was no snapping of wood, you saw the four little cats, two black, the others black and white, exactly like the stubble cats the previous year at the tank, but much smaller, each one hardly a handful.

'Go away!' Hannes yelled, and wagged his hand, 'Go on!' He placed the little bodies down into the grass and poked them, but they fell over, wound their way squeaking between the rushes, crawled here and there, stretched their little heads on the search for their mother's teats. Hannes made a sound that was as much of a miaow as a cat watching its children die. 'Shitty little creatures!' he said and shovelled the wriggling things through the electric wire to the cows who were standing there in a row. They continued to chew, stare and transmitted whatever they saw to a higher power.

He pointed to Farmer Öhlke's barn and hissed, 'Over there! There's food for you there,' unnerved, but not without tenderness in his voice, as if he were reproaching a group of disobedient children. But the animals turned around and crawled back under the fence and into the shelter of his lap. He grabbed up the puling, black-white throng and stuck the cats one after the other back into the sack that lay next to him in the grass. He swung it over his shoulder, once back at the moped tied it to his belt, climbed onto the seat and turned the ignition. On the field the cows sunk their moist, glistening nostrils into the grass.

You came out of your hiding place as relieved as you were upset about the unsuccessful exile, but also a little bit proud to have seen Hannes at such a weak moment, one that seemed to embarrass him so much that, instead of taking the short way to Kleenze on the Landstraße, he had taken the arduous and dangerous detour through the moor. You did not know what you were supposed to regret more—the unknown fate of the May cats, Hannes who was now responsible for them or the desolate field of sundew which shot out to all sides under the wheels as he took off with a roar, the sack of cats flapping at his thighs. And now, Dion, you're about to piss yourself because of such a sissy?

A sound pulls you out of your thoughts. Hannes is standing closer to you again, a stick in his hand. You jerk back, he grins with a crooked mouth, flicks the split end into his palm, tests the strength, smells the wood then breaks it in two, a crack that shoots straight into your bones. 'It's burning here like a match,' he says, throws the pieces away, comes another step closer to you. Your need to pee becomes painful, you strain your abdomen, feel a drop escape. 'Wait,' he whispers and lifts his hand, 'Don't move!' The pines have come closer, are taking hold of one another's boughs, ready to conceal the performance. You hold your breath, tense your muscles against the hit. Over at the edge of the woods the midday is radiant, a white hole between the trees filled with sun and smoke.

Don't worry, Dion, it won't hurt for long. Just a quick pain that will rip you out of your numbness. You sink down, then back up, take a breath. You have not screamed for far too long. The village is far away; you have finally left it behind you.

Someone on the Heidedamm has seen the smoke. Behind the rapidly darkening clouds, the house looks even further away and even more abandoned, turned away from the village, an inaccessible place far out in the moor. The fire department is in another place; by the time they make it to Fenndorf, the villagers are already standing on the street, children walking behind the cars, trying to avoid their mothers grabbing after them. Between barn and peat ditch, the grey, billowing wall which swallows up their glances. The wind whips glowing embers onto the porch, the dry plaster blazes on the wall of the shed. Police are pushing onlookers back, blocking off drives. The men in fire gear are unrolling hoses which lie like empty snakeskins in the grass, then swell and rear up. The nozzles shoot blindly into the sooty cloud; in the barn, a windowpane splinters.

Police cars are patrolling. They circle around the plain, controlling every path in search of smoke. Binoculars focused. Your location has already been marked on the finely detailed maps. In front of the police station in Zeeve, radios are crackling. A few more minutes and they'll be here. The red and white ribbons will flutter between the trees where you are standing. Looking back, it is now a restricted area, until further notice entering the premises is prohibited. Forgetting looms.

Hannes wipes the dragonfly off your shoulder so quickly that he barely touches you. 'Got it,' he grins and holds his fist beneath your nose. When he slowly opens his fingers, the insect is lying motionless in his palm. You were ready for everything, had been awaiting the worst: his punch that would knock you to the ground, then the inescapable clutch pulling you towards him, so close that you would be able to smell his chewing-gum breath but the very next minute he would push you away and hurl you into the underbrush, yelling: Now it's your turn! His revenge would be brutal, his fury boundless, for, having been the oldest, everyone has blamed him for Tanja's accident.

Although nothing on the spindly insect seems to be broken, you think it is dead. It is a young blood-red darter which quite possibly moulted just a few days ago; though the head, back and segments of the abdomen are dyed yellow like the majority of young ones, you recognize the strangeness of the black legs which distinguishes it from the common darter. Not a single one of the filigree-like limbs is bent. The finely veined skins of its twin pair of wings are unharmed but do not move, although you can feel the wind on your cheeks. Even in the eyes you fail to find any sign of life, but they do not really seem dead; large and pupilless, distributed across thousands of individual glances, they stare into the emptiness caught in another, many times over slowed-down time and are hidden behind a slightly glassy film reflects the pine woods.

The hole in the brake where the path opens onto the plain no longer gleams; smoke has drifted in, has mixed with the pine needles to create a blinding twilight, swallows up every sound. The feeling of pressure still throbs in your body although you no longer have to pee. The dull pain has wandered upward, becomes stuck in your chest, pushes into your throat, a feeling of immediate distress like right before a scream.

'It's alive,' he whispers and slowly raises his hand until the dragonfly is standing right against your face. The way you bend forward softly, in its eyes you can see a tiny movement, but it is only your own shadow making it appear as if the insect were looking at you. At the same time it lifts up, cuts out over your head and in the direction of the road, a small, unstable point disappearing within the stillness, and it is the nightmarish soundlessness of the dragonfly's flight that tears you out of your immobility.

You jump off the moped and stumble down the path. The smell of the fire becomes numbing, knocks you back. You climb onto the pile, sink down, grab after a dangling branch, pull yourself back up. Beneath you the flames blaze knee-high. Something rushes past your head, a wisp of ash or a blade of grass whirled upward by the heat vacuum, but then, when you look up, you see them: first two, three, then more, an entire swarm attempting to flee the fire. They shoot out of the brake and over you and disappear between the tree trunks, their tiny bodies hardly visible in the twilight and soundless.

You had always thought that you could hear the flight of dragonflies. Far out in the plain where on windless days the crackling of wood resembles an explosion, on the ponds sunk deep into the peat whose water, often covered by veils of dust or an oily film, creates a kind of membrane that even the most miniscule movement sets to vibration, the only sound which made its way to you had been the dance of the dragonflies, perhaps less of a tone than this voice of light made to move in the reflection of the water like the amber-coloured flickering of the sun's rays in the deep, the silver sparkling of the blades of grass, the tireless movement of clouds above, their shadows that wandered through the plain, the distant glimmer of the horizon, an oppressive silence within it, your secret.

Hannes starts up the motor and waves at you. The drone continues to swell. Through a hole in the tops of the trees you can see the helicopters circling in the sky, and you jump from the woodpile onto the soft moss. 'Let's get out of here,' Hannes yells and presses the helmet down over his head. You swing yourself onto the luggage rack but he doesn't move; instead, he turns to look at you. In the tight shell his face seems even slimmer, his small eyes pressed together, seemingly pupilless. 'I mean, let's *really* get out of here,' he says. When after a few seconds in which, despite the noise, you thought you could hear your heart beating you finally nod your head, he takes off so quickly that you can't do anything but grab his shoulders.

The sudden change of light at the end of the tunnel hurts your eyes. The sun is not warm but you can feel its strength. On the sandy, rutted ramp onto the road Hannes brakes, the moped slides, and at the same time you both put your feet onto the ground. There is a police car at the edge of the road. Someone rolls down the window. 'Fire!' Hannes yells and points back into the woods. The police officer observes you from behind a pair of mirrored sunglasses then disappears; on the passenger side you make out a second person speaking into a radio. The car turns onto the path. 'And where's your helmet?' the driver calls to you but at the same moment Hannes fires the machine up the embankment. You drive your fingernails into his jacket. He turns onto the road, stops again, stretches his head over his shoulder. 'It's better like this,' he says and wraps your arms around his stomach. From the bend of the road, you see the police car disappear in the woods, then, on the bridge over the Jumme, everything fades.

Somewhere on the open road you stop and pee in a field, separated from the traffic lane. No one even looks. Nevertheless you cover yourself. The stream shoots out from behind your hand and splits into two, trickles away between the pale green blades of corn shooting out of the ground. Instead of stopping at the train station in Zeeve where Hannes had originally wanted to drop you off, he kept on going. The rows of houses end abruptly, wide fields stretch out along the embankment, most of them already sown, some still fallow, speckled by dark spots of forest alternating with small developments of black or rusty-red clinker brick and thin apple plantations where hardly a tree is dead or in splinters.

At the large intersection you turn onto the highway that leads to Hamburg, full of lorries, and at times running parallel to the Autobahn, and into a horizon pierced by electricity pylons, factory chimneys, bridge pillars and, finally, by the towering skeletons of harbour cranes, ever-further away from the moor, and out towards the sea.

FOUR

Summer

From out here you can no longer see the island. Wherever the water pushes onto the land or the land back against the water, a hard line limits your sight, resembles an end. It only begins to blur within the endless movement of the waves. The empty image fills, forms edges and trembling crests there where the breakers rear. In between, fleeting valleys open onto a strip of sand and bright grass.

The ground flattened, traces begin to stand out. Rocky reefs and the craters left by the coastguard's dredgers which drain the sand then flush it back out onto the beach. The remains of broken wooden groynes whose smooth black heads stare out of the water in falling rows and, at low tide, when they begin to dry out in the wind, resemble the half-destroyed backbone of a long-ago stranded whale with their gnawed-away vertebrae. Piles of star-shaped concrete tetrapods that have been spread out by earthmovers like food for a stone-eating giant; only the tips of the lowest lying blocks still peeking out of the sand. Above that, visible for only a few seconds, the tracks of the crabs, a seam of dead sea grass and the soft clinking of mussel shells which, with every new wave, are washed into bands and bows, random patterns at the water's chewed edge where for one short moment this incessant migration comes to a rest.

No need to be afraid, I will not cause you any pain. With the pills in your blood, you have almost overcome the feeling of being yourself, the old pain only the fading memory of a bad dream. Now I am going to slam your forehead against a rock, so that you will lose consciousness. Your body will glide across the ground along the ragged beards of algae, be ripped apart by the barnacles. In their black serried rows, the mussels lidlessly watch you sink. A crab escapes this strange creature by darting into a crevice, then looks back out, extends its claws. Barely visible within the underwater light, a school of young herring form a cloud about your head, but quickly scatter, tiny mouths kissing you coldly. The sea grass at the foot of the reef billows out and would pillow you, but I tear you away from the soft coffin and steer you, in the undertow of low tide, ever-further away from the island.

Your body, which on land had always seemed a little ungraceful and, as of late, thanks to the appetite of a persistent pain, even more awkward, now dances weightlessly in the lazy thrusts of the water, arc or tentlike, your hind end at the top, your face turned inwards and the casually downward hanging limbs, your fingers swishing here and there with the tide across the at-times craggy, at times sandy ground, as if seeking something to hold amid the stones and waving branches of seaweed, and even when your incidental and almost playful caresses with the ground begin to wane and both your fingers and arms and your in the rhythmic movement of the water seemingly breathing torso harden at the onset of rigor mortis, your aimless wandering through the depths seems to be the most easy-going of your now fading life.

The violence begins a few hours later. I drag you over the stones, lug your body through the sand. You can hardly see the blood in the gloomy light, but the fish have already scented you. Crabs gnaw at your skin, the fish take advantage of the rare treat, the first algae spores settle on the nutritious host. A thornback ray shoots out of the silt of a trench which had camouflaged it. Frightened by your shadow, it swings upward; on the flat, clear underside the shadowy outline of its viscera. It circles you, takes a nibble of your shoulder, floats a little while longer above you, the back and forth of its white waving fins like a slow flapping of birds' wings, the flight silent, dreamlike, unearthly, an angel from out of the depths. Then it turns away, takes the last glimmer from your eyes or whatever was once your soul and departs.

Your face darkens and swells. Your fingertips shrivel and split, at some point the current strips away the washerwoman's skin from your bones like a glove. The boundaries between you and I become indistinct, I enter you without any trouble at all, through your anus, your pores and your open mouth. Your veins are now cold and large, the blood within them almost gone, your features hardly human, broken open and crusty, plaque-studded lips, what you most resemble now is the moray eel, the ugliest of all my inhabitants. You have now become one of my own.

One comes and bites a fist-sized hole in your chest while another much smaller one eats out an eye, then crawls inside. A new paradise is born within your head, inhabited by creatures you never saw even in your most fantastic dreams. At some point your bloated body floats up into the middle layer of water. With your already-almost disbanded limbs, from which your skin now hangs in shreds, you appear to be a bright, translucent sheet I propel, loop-like, back to land with the rising tide. There, in the breakers, I perform the ecstatic dance of drowning with you one final time, but in reverse. Soon I will have had enough of the game and will toss you back onto the sand. Before anyone finds you, the beaks of the seagulls will have definitively obliterated your face.

Da birst das Moor, ein Seufzer geht
Hervor aus der klaffenden Höhle;
Weh, weh, da ruft die verdammte Margret:
'Ho, ho, meine arme Seele!'

The turf splits open, and from the hole
Bursts forth an unhappy sighing,
'Alas, alas, for my wretched soul!'
'Tis poor damned Margaret crying!

From the 1842 poem 'Der Knabe im Moor' (The Boy on the Moor) by Annette von Droste-Hülshoff (1797–1848). Translated into English by Anonymous. Available at: https://goo.gl/-qYAC5V (last accessed on 12 December 2016).

TRANSLATOR'S ACKNOWLEDGEMENTS

Grateful acknowledgement and thanks to Isabel Fargo Cole and Katy Derbyshire for selecting an excerpt of this translation to appear in the journal *No Man's Land* (Issue 10, November 2015).